APPALACHIAN MEMORY

A Survivor's Tale

MARY JANE SALYERS

This book is a work of fiction. All incidents and dialogue, and all characters with the exception of some well-known historical and public figures, are products of the author's imagination. Where real-life historical or public figures appear, the situations, incidents and dialogues concerning those persons are not intended to change the fictional nature of the work. Any resemblance to persons living or dead is entirely coincidental. All scripture quotations are from the King James Version.

ISBN-10:1977530338
ISBN-13:978-1977530332

ACKNOWLEDGEMENTS

I owe a deep debt of gratitude to the many readers of my first novel *Appalachian Daughter* who begged for more. Without their encouragement I might never have set out to write another novel. I must give heartfelt thanks to the many friends and family members who have read various drafts of *Appalachian Memory* as it developed, especially Sallie Abba. Their encouragement and feedback was immensely valuable.

I am grateful for access to many historical and cultural reference materials, including books, documents, diaries, and memoirs—many found on the internet. One especially helpful book was *Civil War Curiosities: Strange Stories, Oddities, Events, and Coincidences* by Webb Garrison. Many thanks to Anita Jackson for that book as well as for other historical works she provided. Also thanks to Blanche Williams, who allowed me to read a Civil War soldier's diary.

Thanks to my husband, Bill Salyers, for buying books and searching online for other resources as well as giving his loving encouragement and computer savvy. I'd never have gotten it done without the tech magic performed by Bill and our daughter Joy Salyers.

Cover photo by Cindy Salyers

CHARACTER LIST

CAMPBELL FAMILY
Jedadiah Campbell (Jed)
Frances Dodson Campbell - his wife
James - oldest son
Camellia Taylor - his bride
William - son #2
Elliott - son #3
Harvey Michael - youngest son
Stuart Campbell - Jed's brother
Cousin Maybelle - Frances' cousin

PITTSBURGH CHARACTERS
Grandma Campbell
Uncle Phillip
Cousin Chester
Cousin Jasper
Hilda Worthington - William's girlfriend
Bradford Perkins - Partner in Campbell and Perkins Company

EMPLOYEES
Caleb - A freedman
Jake - Hired hand
Luke - Hired hand
Larry - Hired hand
Thomas - Hired hand
Scott - Hired hand
Pete O'Malley - Cook
Jim Morgan - Farm manager
Mina Morgan - His wife and laundress
Dan Simpson - Oxen driver
Martha Simpson - His wife and assistant cook
Sylvia Simpson - Their daughter

NEIGHBORS
Marvin Jackson - Blacksmith shop and trading post owner
Evan Jackson - His son and Harvey's best friend
Old Bob and Sara - His slaves
Elijah Baker - Minister and school teacher
Josephine Baker - His wife-also a midwife
Mary Louise Baker - Their daughter
Jasper Gray - Moonshiner

CIVIL WAR MARAUDERS
Bart Woodson - Home Guard member (Union)
Captain Hatfield - State Guard member (Confederate)

VIRGINIANS
The Sheep Lady
Carl Henley - Disabled Confederate veteran
Granny Henley - His grandmother
Sadie Carter - Girl at a party
Lucy - A prostitute

CONFEDERATE SOLDIERS
Corporal Jack Smith
Private Jones
Private Miller
Private Davidson

PRISON INMATES
Charles Summers - From Atlanta
Sam - A Morgan Raider
Jess - A Morgan Raider
George - A Morgan Raider
Preacher - Friend
Simon - A pervert
Malcolm - Smallpox victim

OAKMONT CHARACTERS
Nate - Butler
Nellie - His wife, the cook
Philip Granger - Farm boss

1863

Laureltown, Kentucky

Suddenly six armed men on horses surrounded us. Two wore Home Guard uniforms. When I saw Bart Woodson, I was sure we was in big danger. My heart pounded so loud I could hear it in my head, and I wanted to run, but they wasn't no way to get past them.

"How old are you?" The man on the gray horse pointed his gun at me.

"Fifteen," I managed to croak.

"Ain't you Jed Campbell's boy?" I nodded but didn't say nothing.

"Jed's a Union man," Bart looked at the man on the gray horse, "so this boy ain't fair game." Then he pointed his gun at Evan. "How about you, boy? How old are you?"

Evan looked straight at him and announced in a loud voice. "Fifteen, sir."

"What's your name?"

"Evan Jackson, sir." His loud, confident response made me ashamed of my scared mumble.

"Your pa runs the trading post and the blacksmith shop?"

"Yes, sir"

"Ain't you got brothers?" I could feel my legs beginning to shake. I had heard how these bushwhackers forced men to fight for the Union even if they didn't want to join, and they also had stole horses and burned the homes of some Southern sympathizers. I wanted Evan to deny it, but I knowed he was proud of his brothers and would never say "No."

"I got two brothers." He stood straight and tall like a good soldier would.

"Where are they?"

"They've joined the Confederate forces, sir.

Bart turned to his buddies. "Well, how do you like that? He's too young to conscript, but his brothers are our enemies. So what do you think we should do with him?"

"Appears to me he's a enemy too." The man on the gray horse grinned and raised his gun.

"No! No! Stop!" Screaming at the top of my lungs, I lunged toward the man's horse, hoping I could grab his gun, and then everything went black.

PART

ONE

PART

ONE

CHAPTER 1

November 1874

Campbell Holler, Tennessee

It's a beautiful fall day here in Campbell Holler, almost like summer. Miz Simpson used to call it Indian summer. She worked for my family back in Kentucky. She told me all about nature. I learnt more from her than I ever did from any books.

I bought fifty acres at the head of this holler three years ago, and I worked hard to get a homestead set up. It's finally looking like a place where a family could prosper. The closest neighbor lives about a mile away where the holler opens into the valley. About halfway between my humble abode and the valley a rock pile marks the site of the first home built in this holler. The tale the neighbors tell is Indians killed the settlers and burnt their cabin, and old timers in the valley claim when the moon's full, you can hear a baby crying near those old ruins.

Now that I've built a house, a barn, and a hen house and cleared land for a corn field and garden, I think I made a good choice. In my 27 years on this earth, I've had many disappointments and hardships. Most all my life I've felt like a loser. Even when I's aiming to do my best, it turned out wrong. Finally, I have hope my luck will turn here. Me and my beloved have set a date for our wedding next spring. With her by my side, we can make this holler a place of good fortune and bliss.

As I look back on my life, one disappointment is how my oldest brother hated me. James is 13 years older'n me, he's the favorite son, and he was trained to take over the family business someday. From my earliest memory, he called me rude, insulting names, and physically attacked me ever chance he got. I never understood why he disliked me so much, and I never understood why my parents allowed it. His cruel treatment finally drove me to leave my Kentucky home and come to this lonesome holler in these Tennessee mountains far away from his dirty, cheating ways.

I remember like it was yesterday one time when I's about ten, me and my friend Evan Jackson played along the creek at the edge of my father's property in Rock County in the mountains of southeastern Kentucky.

All afternoon me and Evan had played in Mossy Creek, even though at that point, it was more big boulders than water. We made small rafts by tying sticks together with long blades of dried grass that growed along the creek bank. But our boats kept getting wrecked by the big rocks. We decided to dig a canal to bypass the worst of the boulders. But we couldn't dig more than a few inches even with the mattock Evan brought because of all the roots and rocks. I now realize it was more than younguns like us could do, but at the time it seemed like a good idea. We both was frustrated when we couldn't make our grand plan work. Tired, wet, and cold from wading in the creek, I throwed up my hands. "Let's take a rest."

We stretched out on a big flat rock at the creek's edge. We'd played in the cold mountain stream till our teeth chattered and our lips turned blue. The rock, hot from the late summer sun, warmed us up. I started thinking how come me and Evan become such good buddies.

Evan's family had moved to the valley a couple of years earlier. His father run the local trading post and the blacksmith shop. After I got to know him, I slipped off to play with Evan ever chance I got. We ran through the woods pretending to chase wild Indians and made bows and arrows to shoot rabbits and squirrels—not that we could hurt anything with our flimsy weapons.

I flipped some water at Evan. "Remember that time we snuck into the spring house to steal some milk?"

"Oh, I'll never forget the look on your face when you knocked that bowl of custard off, and it crashed to pieces."

"I was scared to death I'd get a lickin."

"Did you get in trouble?"

"No. When our cook brought in a apple pie for our dessert that night, he looked right at me and said he'd made some custard for the pie, but somehow it got dumped in the water in the spring house."

"Did you ever fess up?"

"Nah, I think Pete O'Malley thought I's guilty, but he'd never snitch on me."

After me and Evan laid on that hot rock awhile, I was feeling like a roasted chicken. I set up and punched Evan on the arm. "Where did you live before you moved to this lonesome Kentucky valley?"

"We lived in North Carolina till I's about five. Then we moved to Tennessee for a while."

"Why'd you move here?"

"After my mother died, Pa got restless I reckon. He heard about this valley and thought it'd be a good place for his business."

"Well, I'm glad you come here. You're the only boy my age in the whole valley. I hope you're gonna stay."

"Pa says we struggled at first, but since more people's moved here, business has picked up. Customers come to the forge most ever day, and lots of folks come to the store. My brothers have started planting tobacco and hemp. Pa says we're doing better all the time." He frowned. "Pa says I have to start helping in the fields now, so we may not have as much time to play."

"But your pa also got a slave, don't he?"

"Yeah, Old Bob and Sara's been with us since before I's born. Sara's been like a mother to me since my mother died. Old Bob's always done the blacksmithing. He helps my brothers if he don't have any work in the forge." Evan sat up and looked at me. "Ain't your pa got a slave too?"

"No, Pa don't believe in owning slaves. Caleb's a freedman. He's worked for Pa as long as I can remember, even in Pennsylvania before we come here. Pa pays him just the same as all the other hired hands." We was quiet for a while, staring at the water lapping against the rocks.

Evan stood up and reached for a stick about three foot long laying on the creek bank. "Have you always lived here?"

"No. I's born in Pennsylvania, and I really liked it there." I picked up some small rocks and watched the splashes as I tossed them into the water. "Pa's a partner in a big lumber company there. For some reason him and his brother decided to come here and claim this land before other businesses gobbled up all of it. They own all the land from this creek all the way to the top of the mountain."

"What'd he want with all this land? Nothing grows on mountains except trees."

"That's why he bought it. He's gonna start cutting the trees before long."

"How come he ain't started cutting before now?"

I stood up and felt to see if my trousers had dried. "He and his brother is building a sawmill down towards Beattyville—supposed to be ready soon. No sense cutting trees if they's no place to saw them into boards. The roads ain't good enough to haul logs in wagons, so they'll have to float them down the river. When the sawmill's finished, he'll be ready to do a big business."

I jumped off the big rock and walked over to the bridge my father and Uncle Stuart built by laying a couple of logs across the creek and nailing planks crosswise. Since it had no rails, I could set on the edge of the bridge and dangle my bare feet over the water. The creek was about ten foot wide at the bridge but seldom measured more than two or three foot deep in mid-summer. Howsomever, in late winter or early spring, heavy rains caused the creek to rise over its banks, flooding much of the valley and sometimes washing away the bridge.

Farther downstream the creek was wider and deeper. My brothers and the hired hands often went there to clean up and cool off after a day's work. But Ma insisted I couldn't go there unless one of my brothers took me till I learnt how to swim. She allowed as how I wasn't in no danger playing in this rocky part of the creek.

Evan come and set beside me on the bridge and was splashing the water with the stick. "Hey, don't be making the creek so muddy." I punched him lightly on the shoulder with my fist. "You're chasing away all the minnows."

"Aw, we ain't needing no minnows today. We can't go fishing now cause I gotta be home soon. I'm prob'ly late now. Today's my birthday and Sara's making me a cake." Evan stood and stretched hisself as tall as he could and wrenched up his ragged pants. "I'm ten years old—pert near to being a man."

"That ain't nothing. I been ten since April and I ain't about to be no man. To hear James tell it, I'm just a good for nothing baby."

"That's cause William babies you so much."

"William don't baby me," I argued with a mite of anger. "He just treats me like a good brother oughten to. That's more'n I can say for James. He thinks cause he went to Western University of Pennsylvania he knows everthing. He thinks he's my boss and orders me around like I's his slave."

Evan broke the stick into pieces and threw them into the water and watched as they floated downstream. "Wonder how far they'll go. Reckon all the way to the river?"

"Well, if they don't now, they will when they's a tide in the Fork."

"You see," I explained to Evan, "My family moved from Pennsylvania to this valley in the Kentucky mountains ten years ago. The men found a level area in a nice cove and built a large house, a barn, and various other buildings, including a bunk house for their hired hands. They cleared enough ground to plant a acre of tobacco and a large garden. They raised enough corn to feed theirselves and the livestock, made hay, and cleared a pasture for their cows and horses.

"My mother stayed in Pennsylvania with me and my next brother Elliott for several years until the men finished the buildings. I was six years old and Elliott was nine when she brought us to live in Kentucky."

4

"I hear a horse coming," Evan said and looked toward the road into town.

I jumped up hoping to see some excitement, but lost heart when James showed up. He slowed Blaze to a trot as he reached the bridge and pulled him to a stop right beside me. "What are you doing here, you little slacker? Did you take the drinking water to the men in the hay field like I told you?"

I shook my head. "No, I plum forgot all about it."

"Like always, you little dummy. Can't remember anything. You better get home and take them some water. I guess you'll be in big trouble, and you won't get out of it by batting your big brown eyes this time."

James turned to look at Evan. "I just come from the forge. Your pa said if I saw you to tell you to come home and stack the wood for the fire. So you better hit the road."

"Gotta go, Harvey. I'll see you tomorrow if I don't have too many chores." He picked up his mattock and trotted off.

"Bye Evan. Hope you have a good birthday cake."

James bent down from the saddle and grabbed me by the nape of the neck. "When are you going to grow up, Harvey Baby? You're always finding ways to shirk your chores; now get home before I knock your head off."

"Ow, you're hurting me." I twisted away. "My name ain't Harvey Baby and you ain't my pa. I don't have to do what you say." I slapped Blaze on the hip making him jump sideways.

"You little devil." James took his foot out the stirrup and kicked me off the bridge into the creek. I put out my hands to break my fall, and landed on a sharp rock. I stood up in the knee-deep water, soaking wet, my hands balled into fists. Blood dripped off my fingers. I screamed, "Look what you done to my hand. I'm telling Ma." Tears streamed down my cheeks.

James laughed, "Go ahead and cry, you little crybaby. Tell Ma if you dare. You know what will happen if you do....Harvey Baby." He gave Blaze a little nudge and trotted toward home. I picked up a rock and hurled it as hard as I could, hoping it would hit him in the head, but it fell short. I promised myself right then I'd get even with him somehow, someday. I climbed out of the creek and begun slogging down the road dripping a trail of water and blood behind me.

***

After James kicked me into the creek, I started looking forward to our annual trip to Pennsylvania. I wouldn't have to worry about James' meanness then. I tried to steer clear of him as best I could. Even so, he managed to catch me alone a couple of times—dumped me in the horse trough once and tripped me so I fell in a cow pie another time.

Ever fall since coming to Kentucky, my mother made a several-week-long trip back to Pennsylvania. She always took me and Elliott with her. My father still owned the house in Pennsylvania where my Grandma Campbell lived. I loved visiting with all our kin folks there. My mother also did her shopping for our clothes, shoes, and any household goods we couldn't get in Kentucky.

Finally the day arrived early in September for us to start our trip. Uncle Stuart went with us—not only to make sure we was safe, but also to visit Grandma since he's her favorite son. Pa and Uncle Stuart put the canvas top over the wagon to protect us and our baggage from the sun and rain. We started out with Ma and Uncle Stuart in the wagon, and for the first time I got to ride my horse alongside Elliott. It was the first long ride I had made since I got a horse of my own. He was a beautiful roan with white stockings and a white star on his forehead. I named him Scout because my favorite story was about a Indian scout. It seemed like a good name for a horse that liked to roam through the woods and along the roads.

When Pa and Uncle Stuart first started making the trip ten years earlier, the steep roads through the mountains made it hard to travel with a wagon. They carried axes in case a downed tree blocked the road. Back then, they made only about ten miles a day till they got closer to areas where more people had settled and the roads was improved. But by the fall of 1858, more people had moved into the valley, and better roads made our trip a little easier and faster.

We rode through our small village of Laureltown, named after all the mountain laurel on the hillsides. I waved to Evan as we passed the store and forge. Three horses tied to the hitching post stomped their feet and switched their tails to shoo away the flies.

We rode on past a few houses and the grist mill. I noticed a group of men working on a new building.

"What are they building there?"

Elliott raised his head from the book he was reading and looked to see where I pointed. "That's going to be a church and school."

"Will we go to that school?"

"Maybe."

We took the road running along the river as it flowed downstream with mountains rising on either side. I looked at the mountains covered with thick forests. It was like going through a huge green canyon. "I don't know why we had to move here to this backward country anyway."

Elliott looked at me and nodded. "I know you wish we still lived in Pennsylvania. I liked it there too, but you know why we came here."

"Yeah, yeah—so Pa could cut down the trees and make a lot of money, but I still don't like it."

We stopped for a quick lunch beside the river and let the horses rest and drink. The afternoon seemed very long, and my rear end burned like it was on fire. I thought I couldn't ride another minute. Finally when the sun dipped low in the sky, Uncle Stuart turned into a wide grassy spot beside the road. "This looks like a good place for our first camp."

I got off my horse and dropped onto my stomach in the grass, so glad for a chance to rest my weary bones, but the next thing I knowed Ma stood over me. "Harvey, get up and take care of your horse. You can rest later when it's dark." I didn't have the energy to move and thought I'd rest a few more minutes, but immediately fell asleep. I woke when Ma turned me over. "Harvey Michael Campbell, get up this minute and take care of Scout."

"But Ma, I'm so tired and my behind hurts so bad." But I knowed when she called me by my full name she meant business, so I managed to get on my feet.

She put her arm around my shoulders as I walked over to Scout, munching grass nearby. "I know you're tired. We all are, but we need to take care of the horses before it gets dark and before they wander off. Put Scout's saddle and bridle under the wagon, and get him some water."

I led Scout to the nearby river where we both waded into the knee-deep water to cool off. By the time I got him curried and tethered with a rope tied to a picket and unloaded some hay from the wagon, Ma had supper ready for us. As it grew dark, we made our beds. Me and Ma slept in the wagon. Uncle Stuart and Elliott spread their blankets in the roadbed where they wouldn't be as exposed to chiggers and bugs. I laid in the dark and listened to the frogs and locusts. A owl hooted and a whippoorwill answered. Often when the sun goes down as I set here in Campbell Holler by myself, I hear the evening calls of the owls and frogs, and I remember camping on our way to Pittsburgh.

We continued this way following the river till it joined the other Forks becoming the Kentucky River. When we reached Beattyville, we stayed in a boarding place. From here on, we had much better roads and not as many mountains so we could travel farther in a day's time. We come to villages and small towns where we could find food and a place to stay. When we got to Harrodsburg, we boarded our horses and stored our wagon with some friends of Uncle Stuart's. We would need them for our return trip. Ma bought us passage on a small steamboat called the *Frontier Belle* that would take us down the Kentucky River to the Ohio River, where we would take a different steamboat on to Pittsburgh.

The *Frontier Belle*, a shabby-looking sidewinder in bad need of some paint, had paddle wheels on both sides. We stood on the wharf and watched a family load horses and a wagon filled with household goods onto the first level. They told Uncle Stuart they was moving to Missouri. The family had two children—one a boy about my age. I smiled at him and waved, but he just looked at me.

I saw Negro men carrying big crates and bales onto the boat. I pulled on Uncle Stuart's sleeve. "Are they freedmen like Caleb?"

He shook his head. "No, Harvey, they're slaves whose master has rented them out to the freight company."

"Do they get paid?"

"They probably do, but I expect they must turn over their earnings to their master."

When we walked up the gangplank, the captain, dressed in a dark blue coat with big brass buttons and a fancy hat, greeted us and escorted us to the second level. He had funny looking chin whiskers that reminded me of a goat, and he waddled like a duck as he showed Ma to a dormitory room at the front with bunk beds and explained that women slept in the front room and men slept in the other dormitory room at the back of the boat. He pointed out the dining room located in the middle between the two sleeping rooms. A walkway circled the outer wall with big open windows and benches where passengers could set and watch the scenery.

"Passengers have free reign anywhere on this level," the captain said and looked at me with raised eyebrows. "Passengers may visit the top ONLY by invitation of the captain."

"What's up there?" I wanted to know.

"The pilot house is up there, and we don't want passengers interfering with the pilot's work."

"What does the pilot do?"

"The pilot guides the boat. He makes sure it doesn't hit something like a tree or a sunken boat or get grounded on a sand bar."

That sounded very interesting, and I wanted to see how the pilot did all that, but Ma put her hand on my shoulder. "Harvey, remember what the captain said. Stay on this level. Now go with Uncle Stuart and Elliott to the men's bedroom. After you stow your baggage, come back to the benches outside the dining room. I'll meet you there."

When I returned, Ma held my school books. "Oh, Ma, do I have to do lessons? I thought we wouldn't have to do lessons till we got back home."

"It'll help pass the time, and besides, you haven't finished these books. We'll get books for your next level when we get to Pennsylvania, and you need to get these finished before we start new ones." Ma opened the reader and showed me where I needed to start. I didn't like school, especially since Ma was the teacher. When we lived in Pennsylvania, me and Elliott went to the town school. Elliott loved school, but I didn't like it much except for playing with my friends. I struggled with reading and writing. It took me the longest time to see the difference in "saw" and "was." After we moved to Kentucky, we had no school, so Ma said she would be our teacher.

When the Jacksons moved to our valley, Mr. Jackson ask Ma to teach Evan, so then at least I had a friend to do lessons with. I wondered what it'd be like to go to the school the men was building in our village and who'd be the teacher. I decided then if I ever had children I wouldn't make them go to school. If they could read and write and cipher enough to do their business, that's all that's needed. I hold that opinion to this day. I've met too many educated fools in this world. Education don't make you smarter. It just makes a body think he's smarter.

After the slaves finished loading the freight, we heard the whistle blow. I looked out the window and saw the gangplank was up, and the boat shuddered as the paddle wheels started turning. I could feel the vibrations through my feet as we moved into the middle of the river and headed downstream, stopping mid-afternoon to load firewood and pick up more passengers and freight.

"Ma, I haven't seen that family going to Missouri. I wanted to make friends with the boy."

Ma pursed her lips. "They probably couldn't afford to pay for this level, so they have to stay below."

"You mean they have to stay down there with the animals and stuff?" Ma nodded. After thinking about it I wondered, "Where do they sleep? Are they bunk rooms down there?"

Ma shook her head. "They'll try to find a place to sit and sleep on top of some of the freight." That didn't seem right to me.

Our lessons done for the day, I decided to explore the boat. Ma cautioned me to remember the captain's rules. I watched the paddles turn and waved to passengers on a steamboat going up the river. The sun shining through the trees along the river banks made interesting patterns on the water. We passed a flatboat going down river that looked like a log raft with a room on top. Two men held long poles they used to push the boat along and to guide it around logs or fallen trees. It looked to me like they was moving their household furnishings. A couple of cows was tied up at the back and a dog, standing on the back, barked at the *Frontier Belle* as we passed. I thought they must be more people moving west.

As I walked toward the front of the boat, I saw the stairs to the top. I climbed up far enough to see what looked like a little house. I remembered the Captain said passengers was not allowed on top, so I made sure to stay on the steps. I eased up a few more steps to get a better look. Next thing I knowed the captain grabbed the back of my shirt nearly choking me.

"I told you not to come up here." He drug me back down the stairs, still holding my shirt and pushed me along to where Ma sat outside the women's bunk room.

9

"If I catch this here boy on the top again, you'll be getting off at the next stop." He gave me a push, and I landed on my knees in front of Ma. He stalked away brushing his coat sleeves like I had dirtied his clothes.

"Harvey Michael Campbell, stand up." I stood up and rubbed my knees where I'd hit the floor. Ma's mouth, all scrunched up in a straight line, told me I'd made a bad mistake. Her voice trembled, "Why did you go up there? You know the captain warned you not to."

"I just wanted to look. He said passengers was not allowed on top, so I stayed on the steps where I could see. But I didn't go all the way up to the top, and I wasn't interfering with nobody." I thought his treatment of me wasn't fair.

Ma put her hands over her face. I thought she's about to cry. "What am I going to do with you? You can't remember anything for five minutes, and you just do whatever comes to your mind without thinking. Now, sit down here and don't move until the supper bell rings."

She looked at me with her sad blue eyes. I felt terrible. "I'm sorry, Ma. I'll try to be good, but he didn't have to treat me so rough. He pert near choked me to death; I couldn't even breathe." I pulled my britches above my knee. "Look how red my knee is where he throwed me down on the floor." It seemed no matter what I did, everbody was always yelling at me. I couldn't even walk across the parlor at home without somebody screaming at me: "You're tracking mud in the house," "Don't bring the dog in here," "Pick up the paper you dropped." "Hang up your coat." Seemed like I couldn't never do nothing right.

Ma patted me on my back. "I guess you'll have to stay where I can keep my eye on you for the rest of the trip. I do wish you could learn to follow directions."

I set there and watched Ma sewing on a quilt she was making for Grandma Campbell—the Rose of Sharon pattern she said. I couldn't stand the thought of setting here ever day with nothing to do. "How long will it take us to get to the Ohio River?" I commenced rocking forward and back.

Ma put her hand on my shoulder. "Harvey, sit still. It'll probably take another day or two."

"It's already been five days since we left home. I'll be glad when we get to Pittsburgh—ain't much to do on this sorry boat." We had made this trip for years, but I forgot from year to year what the boat trip was like. I just remembered how much I liked to be in the city with all my kinfolks, especially my cousins.

About that time the bell rung for the evening meal. I helped Ma take her quilting materials back to her bed, and we headed for the dining room. "I hope we ain't having beans and cornbread again like we had for dinner."

Ma laughed, "We very well might. But when we get the bigger steamboat on the Ohio, we'll have better accommodations and food." Sure enough, as we approached the dining room, I smelled beans and cornbread.

"Not again. Will we have beans ever meal on this boat?"

Ma raised her eyebrows and laughed again. "If we do I guess we'll just have to be grateful for something to fill our bellies, even if it's not our favorite."

Frankfort, where we stopped to let off some passengers and take on others, was the last town of any size we passed. While there the cook managed to buy some cabbage and turnips to add to the beans and cornbread, which wasn't much improvement to my way of thinking. After that we mostly passed farms, but we did stop once or twice to load wood to keep the boilers steaming. I looked forward to getting on the bigger boat. Meanwhile I had to stay where either Ma or Uncle Stuart could see me. I felt like a prisoner. I chewed my fingernails to the quick.

I stood at the bow and watched as we steamed into Madison, Indiana, on the Ohio River. I could see on the hill above us a steamboat ready to be launched. I had never saw such a big boat—beautiful too—painted red and white. The two big black smokestacks seemed to reach to the sky. I wished we had time to explore the shipbuilding factory, but Ma said the *Merry Lee*, docked nearby, would be leaving within the hour, and we had to hurry to get all our bags and boxes loaded.

***

Ma was right; the *Merry Lee* outranked the *Frontier Belle* by far. It had one very large paddle wheel at the stern and was four stories high. We had two cabins on the third level; me and Ma shared one and Uncle Stuart and Elliott the other. We hadn't hardly reached our rooms when suddenly the loudest music I ever heard shook the boat and made me jump with fright. Ma explained it was a calliope, an organ powered by the steam. The calliope announced our arrival and departure at ever stop. I soon become hardened to it.

We went to the fourth floor to the dining room where we never had any beans, but delicious meals of good meat and vegetables and even cakes and custards. Ma forbade me to go into the saloons, but as I passed by I could see men setting at card tables, where Ma said they gambled away their money playing poker. Men and ladies in fancy dresses set at a bar holding glasses of whiskey and laughing.

Ever day we did lessons for an hour after breakfast and again after lunch. Elliott mostly stayed in his cabin and read the books Ma had brought for him. Between study times, I roamed the boat, made friends with a boy from Louisville traveling to Cincinnati, and listened in on some of the arguments and discussions some of the men seemed to enjoy. I heard lots of talk about slavery— most agin it, but some people for it. One man said, "White supremacy and black slavery are the unchanging will of God."

Later I ask Ma what white supremacy meant. She said "It's the idea that white people are smarter and better than black folks."

"Do you think that's true?"

"Of course not."

"So you think white supremacy is God's will?"

"No, I think the Bible teaches that all people are the same in God's sight."

I've puzzled over this for years. I'm still not totally won over to the idea. I didn't know then what I thought about slavery. I considered Caleb no different from the other hired hands, but then he wasn't a slave. He was more like my friend.

I listened as a couple of men argued about secession. I asked Ma what that meant. She frowned and gave a long sigh. "Some of the states where slavery is legal have threatened to withdraw from the United States and start their own separate country."

"Why would they do that?"

"Many Southerners believe the United States Congress will try to force the Southern states to give up slavery. The plantation owners have invested a lot of money in buying slaves to work on their farms. Without their slaves, they couldn't raise the big crops that have made them rich. They think if they made a separate country, no one would make them free their slaves."

I understood the big plantations had to have workers, and in a way it made sense to have slaves to do that work, but I didn't know if I thought slavery was good or bad.

A couple of preachers had a discussion about predestination, another word I never heard of. One preacher dressed in a black suit with a tan checked vest declared in a loud voice, "God has everything planned and everything goes according to God's plan." I didn't know what I thought about that neither.

Another man, dressed like a mountain man wearing a rough brown shirt, pants held up by red galluses, and a dirty hat, raired back with his thumbs stuck in his pants pockets. "Well now, us Baptists don't hold to that kinda thinking. We believe the good Lord gave man free will." It seemed that their discussion might turn in to a big disagreement, but Ma took me by the arm and led me down the hallway to the library for more lessons.

As a young boy I hadn't realized how good us Campbells had it. On our trips, we traveled with the best means available, stayed in the best rooms in hotels, and ate expensive meals in fancy restaurants. Back then, I had took all that for granted and hadn't realized only a few people could travel in such a style.

The *Merry Lee* stopped overnight in Cincinnati. Uncle Stuart spent the night in town taking care of some business. Me, Ma, and Elliot stayed aboard where the stewards served us a special dinner, and a local group of entertainers come aboard for a special show. When one of the dancers begun to take off her clothes, Ma grabbed my hand and got me out of there. The crew laid on wood, water, and food for the next part of the trip, and the next morning bright and early the calliope sounded our departure— even before breakfast.

We arrived in Pittsburgh early on the tenth day of traveling. Uncle Stuart's younger brother Phillip met us at the dock with a horse and carriage to transport us and our baggage to our house on the outskirts of town. I enjoyed the next few weeks more than anything else that happened all year. Cousins near my age lived next door, and we was never apart; they was at our house or I was at their house. Best of all, I didn't have to worry about James.

My Grandma Campbell cooked all my favorite foods. Grandma made cookies most ever day, and ever time I come in the house she ask if I wanted a snack. Ma scolded her for spoiling me, but Grandma smiled and said, "I only see him once a year. That can't be spoiling."

Meanwhile Ma and her younger sister Elizabeth, who lived in the next block, spent many days in town shopping. By time to start home, we had to hire a extra carriage to get it all to the wharf. I found out Ma had two large pieces of furniture delivered directly to a freight company for storage till departure time. Uncle Stuart had done some buying as well.

"How'll we get all this to our house once we get back to Harrodsburg?"

Uncle Stuart smiled. "I guess we'll have to hire another wagon and some horses to pull it." He patted me on the back. "I made some arrangements with my friend who lives in Harrodsburg. He'll have them ready for us when we get there."

Saying goodbye made me sad, especially because Ma and Pa had planned that Elliott would stay in Pittsburgh where he would enroll in a academy. Me and my cousins promised we would write, and I thought Grandma Campbell would not turn me loose when I gave her a goodbye hug. As we stood on the deck to watch Pittsburgh disappearing, colorful trees dotted the hillsides and red and yellow leaves floated in the river. It'd be mid-November by the time we got home.

I still didn't understand why we lived in the mountains of Kentucky. I thought Pittsburgh was a much better place. I watched Ma continue to look back after she couldn't see the city, and I could tell she hated to leave her sister and her friends. I didn't realize then what a special mother I had. She was educated, she was comfortable in polite society, and she could hold her own in political discussions. At the same time, she could make garden, preserve fruits and vegetables, cook fabulous meals, and run her household. I later realized she was more fortunate than most to have the financial resources to live as she did. But as a ten-year-old, I wondered how she could ever agree to move to the backwoods when we had such a good life in Pittsburgh.

CHAPTER 2

December 1874

Campbell Holler, Tennessee

When I woke this morning and looked out the window, I saw the early morning sun shining on the fresh snow had turned Campbell Holler into a world of sparkling diamonds. As I walked to the barn to feed the horses and milk the cow, my breath froze in front of my face, and the grass under the snow crunched as I walked. A few days earlier I cut a couple of trees, and I had planned to have my horse drag the logs down the ridge today, but I think it ain't a good idea to try that with snow on the ground.

I begun to learn about cutting timber when I was ten, shortly after my family returned from our annual trip to Pittsburgh. First thing I noticed when we got back was lots of changes had took place. The men had cleared the trees from several acres along the creek. Two partially built houses stood on high ground above the creek, and new stables had been added to the barn. Three new hired hands worked alongside the three men who'd been with us for years. Always before the hired hands took their meals with our family, but now the dining room wouldn't hold all of us at once. I didn't understand what all the changes meant, but I soon would see what Pa was aiming to do with those acres of trees.

One morning a few days after we got back from Pittsburgh, I stood just outside my parents' bedroom where I heard them in the midst of a disagreement. "Can't you wait until after Christmas to make this trip? I've

MARY JANE SALYERS

been home only a few days, and I hate to be separated again so soon," Ma's voice was almost a whine.

"I'll try to be back by Christmas. It's important to prepare for felling the logs so we can take advantage of the spring rains to float them down river. The sawmill will be working by then. I need to buy equipment and make other arrangements to make that possible."

"You mean you might miss Christmas?" I thought I heard a sniffle, but Ma was not the crying kind. "Oh Jed, I don't like you to be gone so long this time of year."

"I understand, Frances, but I think it's very important that I go now. You'll be fine. Stuart and the boys can take care of everything. Stuart will oversee the work on the two new cabins. I hope to engage two couples to move here to be part of our team, so the cabins need to be finished as soon as possible. I want to begin taking down trees by the first of the year."

I heard a deep sigh and then Ma said, "All right if that's the way it's got to be. What do I need to do to help you get ready?"

"I'd like a couple of blankets for my bedroll and some food I can eat from the saddle. I'll need my warmest coat and gloves."

I heard footsteps coming towards the door and turned to go down the stairs, but not quick enough, and Ma caught me. "So, you were listening to a private conversation? Is that the kind of manners you've been taught?"

"No ma'am. I'm sorry, but when I heard you say something about a trip, I couldn't help listening. Where's Pa got to go and why's it so important?"

"We'll talk about it later. Now I want you to go to the attic and get two blankets from the big chest beside the stairs. They're right on top. Bring them down and put them on the bed in my bedroom."

"What color are they?"

"I don't remember. Just bring the two on top. You understand?"

"Yes, ma'am."

"Well, don't just stand there; get going."

When I opened the door to the attic stairs, I shivered as the cold air rushed past me. I closed the door behind me and slowly climbed the steep stairs, feeling my way in the dim eerie light from the small window in the gable end of the attic. But the space under the eaves where the chest stood was almost completely dark. A shudder run up my spine as I noticed strange shadows reflected on the sloped ceiling. As I moved towards the big chest, my foot dislodged a pile of boxes and packages. I squatted down to replace the boxes and saw a leather vest like the one I saw in Pittsburgh in one box that had fell open.

I decided these must be Christmas presents Ma bought on our trip. I eagerly opened other boxes and found a chess set like William had wanted and some books prob'ly for Elliott. I started to open another box when I heard my father calling to Uncle Stuart from the front porch. I needed to talk with him before he left, so I jumped up and raced for the stairs. I grabbed my coat from the peg at the back door and run to the front yard where Pa and Uncle Stuart stood talking with my two brothers.

I stood beside Pa and tried to wait till he finished talking. I had got in trouble for interrupting adult conversations before. Finally, Pa turned to me and put his hand on my shoulder. "Who will be the boss of me while you're gone?" I ask.

But before he could answer, Ma called from the front porch, "Harvey, where are the blankets I sent you to get?"

Pa swatted me on the behind. "Go do what your ma told you to do."

"But who is the boss of me?" I was near tears. If Pa said James, I thought I'd not be able to stand it. I hoped he'd say Uncle Stuart or William.

Pa had a hot temper and was quick to take off his belt. I had learnt the hard way not to push him too far, so when he pointed to the house and said "Go," I drew a deep breath and slowly slunk back to the house. Ma waited for me just inside the front door, and I could tell from her steely-eyed glare and the way her mouth was set in a straight line I was in big trouble.

"I sent you to get blankets, but you were snooping in things that weren't your business, and then you ran off and didn't even finish what I sent you to do. Now go to your room and stay there until I come to get you. I don't know when you will learn to do as you're told and not get sidetracked. I honestly don't know what to do with you. You try my patience beyond my control."

I tried to explain, but she wouldn't listen. "Go to your room right now!"

"But I need to talk with Pa before he leaves."

"GO TO YOUR ROOM NOW!"

"But Ma," I wailed.

"NOW." Bawling loud enough to scare the chickens in the hen house, I slowly turned down the hall towards the stairs.

Just then James rushed into the house to get Pa's gun. "What's the crybaby bellowing about now? What's the matter Harvey Baby? Did you stump your toe?"

In spite of my tears, I smiled when I heard Ma tell James to stop badgering me. I crept up the stairs wiping my nose on my sleeve. I watched out the window of my room as Pa loaded up his horse. Ma carried out his bedroll. James brought his saddle bags and gun. When all was loaded, Pa hugged Ma for a long time and then mounted up, waved a goodbye, and trotted towards the road. I turned from the window and collapsed on my bed in sobs. I didn't understand why nobody would listen to me. I meant to go back and get the blankets as soon as I talked to Pa. It wasn't like I was trying to be bad. I felt like everbody was treating me mean.

***

Much to my relief after I finished my lessons each day, Uncle Stuart sent me to help William, Caleb, and Larry clean out the brush left from clearing the land along the creek. We sawed all the larger limbs into logs for the fireplaces, and cut smaller limbs into kindling, just like I do when I cut down a tree on my property here in Campbell Holler. The job Uncle Stuart gave me was to stack the cut limbs onto a sled pulled by Milly, a wonderful grey mule I loved.

"Harvey, be careful as you pull the sled through the new ground. It'll be easy to get it hung up on a stump, so be on constant lookout," William warned me. "You understand?"

"Yes, I understand," I bragged and climbed atop the load of logs and yelled, "Giddy up." Milly leaned against her harness and moved forward. We went along just fine till we started down a little slope and Milly begun to trot. I was a victorious general carrying my captured loot to present it to my king. Next thing I knowed, I was flying through the air and landed hard on a big rock. Stunned for a few minutes, I gradually become aware my head hurt very bad, and blood streamed into my eyes. I saw Milly calmly grazing on some grass a few yards away, the sled turned on its side, the logs scattered onto the ground.

The sled had banged against a stump and turned over. The single-tree had broke, allowing Milly to walk away. I yelled for help, but William and the other men worked too far away to hear. I didn't know what to do. My head hurt so bad, and blood now dripped down the front of my coat. I unhooked Milly from the broken single-tree, climbed on her back and rode back to tell William. I thought he'd be mad at me, but when he saw me, he seemed to care only about my bleeding head. He took out his handkerchief and wiped away the blood. "It's only a small cut," he assured me as he tied the bandana around my head. "Head injuries tend to bleed a lot, but this should stop it."

He put me back on Milly's back and walked her to the house where Ma cleaned and bandaged the cut. He suggested I stay at the house for the rest of the day. "Since he hit his head, he might have a concussion," he explained to Ma. He never scolded me at all, and even apologized for not showing me how I should lead Milly so I could watch out for rocks and stumps. Later when I returned to work, I remembered to be more careful. That job lasted for two weeks, but at its end, we had more wood than we could stack in the woodshed—enough to feed all our fires for the winter. Best of all, I avoided James the whole time.

While we worked with the wood, James and Uncle Stuart supervised the building of the two new houses. Each house had a dogtrot in the middle with a room on either side of it. A large fireplace, designed for cooking, stood at the end of one room. Ma explained Pa planned to find two married couples to live in the houses. The men would help with running the lumber business and the farm while the women would help with the cooking, the laundry, and the gardening.

***

One afternoon near the middle of December, I saw a covered wagon pulled by two teams of oxen coming towards our house. The driver walked beside the oxen with a stout stick he used to direct the huge animals. Pa had hired Mr. Simpson to handle the oxen in the woods as they pulled the cut logs down the mountain. He'd brought his wife and little girl and all their belongings with him, and they would live in one of the new cabins.

Miz Simpson helped Ma and Cousin Maybelle make curtains for the windows of the new houses. It would be her job to help Pete O'Malley prepare meals, make garden, preserve garden products and care for the milk cows and chickens. Pa returned three days before Christmas with Elliott and the other new couple, Mr. and Miz Morgan. Mr. Morgan would oversee the farming activities including care of the livestock. Miz Morgan would do the laundry for the family and hired hands and help with the housework.

So the cooking would not heat up the house in the summer time, Pa had built a kitchen-house about fifty feet to the south with a covered walkway connecting it to the main house. He added an extension to the kitchen house for a dining room for the hired hands. Counting our family and all our employees we now had twenty people living on our property.

It pleased me to have Elliott at home for the holidays. He learnt me to play chess, and I got purty good at it. By the time he went back to Pennsylvania for school, I'd beat him twice. William promised to play with me after Elliott went back to school. The first winter I stayed here in Campbell Holler, I whittled me a chess set when the weather kept me indoors. I set it up sometimes and play against myself. I hope my bride will play chess when she comes here to live.

On Christmas Eve, Ma sent me and Elliott to find a nice spruce tree to decorate for Christmas. We took Milly and the sled and headed up the mountain looking for the perfect tree. We found one we liked and sawed it down. When we got home, Ma and William come out onto the front porch and commenced to laugh. The tree was so big it wouldn't even go through the door. It hadn't seemed so big out in the woods. William helped us cut off enough to get it into the house.

Hearing the commotion, Miz Simpson come into the parlor. "Why are you bringing a tree into the house?" She looked at us like we was all crazy as betsy bugs.

Ma explained it was a Christmas tree. "We learned this custom from our German friends in Pennsylvania. We'll decorate it with streamers of popped corn and fruits and place candles on the branches. Later tonight, we'll light the candles and sing Christmas Carols."

"But what's it got to do with Christmas? I never heard such."

"The evergreen tree represents God's everlasting love that sent Jesus to be born in Bethlehem. And the burning candles represent the light that the Christ Child brought into the world."

Miz Simpson looked confused and wandered back to her chores mumbling and shaking her head. Little Sylvia, the Simpson's four-year-old daughter, danced around the tree and begged to help decorate it.

Ma invited all the families and hired hands on the place to Christmas dinner. Larry, Thomas, and Scott, our newest hired hands, went to visit their own families, promising to be back by January first. Caleb, Luke, and Jake, who had been our employees for more than ten years, tracked down a flock of wild turkeys and killed a couple for the dinner. Uncle Stuart had supervised the butchering of a couple of hogs earlier, so we had fresh pork. We had a grand dinner table loaded down with vegetables from the garden, freshly baked breads, meats and gravies, and a sideboard loaded with cakes, pies, and puddings.

After dinner, the men moved to the parlor to smoke their pipes and talk while the women helped Pete and Miz Simpson clear the table and wash the dishes. I found a place to set in the corner beside the Christmas tree where I could listen to the men talk. Uncle Stuart asked Pa what he had heard about the political situation of the state as he traveled around.

Pa took a puff on his pipe and cleared his throat. "I met Governor Morehead at a meeting in Frankfort. He thinks the state may decide to join the Southern states if they carry out their threat to secede."

Uncle Stuart leaned forward with his elbows on his knees. "What impression did you get from the people you met?"

Pa took another puff from his pipe. "The people are divided. The western part of the state has bigger farms using slaves to grow tobacco and hemp as cash crops, so that area is strongly pro-slavery. The northern and northeastern parts of the state have more manufacturing and merchants and fewer slave owners. The businessmen there talk more about ending slavery." Pa noticed his pipe had gone out and stopped to relight it.

"Well, the talk around here is pretty strongly pro-slavery." James had moved his chair closer to the conversation. "That seems a little strange since not many slave owners live in the mountains, but what the neighbors around here are saying is that while they don't own slaves, they think no government should tell them they can't." That made sense to me. I agreed with the neighbors. I never did like people telling me what to do.

I was surprised when Elliott spoke up. "In Pennsylvania I heard a lot about the Underground Railroad and the work the Quakers do to help runaway slaves escape to Canada. I saw advertisements in the paper most every day for runaway slaves and rewards for their capture."

"Jed," Uncle Stuart spoke to Pa, "I'm worried about Caleb. You know those fugitive slave hunters sometimes capture a free Black and sell him down the river. I'd hate to see that happen to Caleb."

Pa nodded. "You're right, Stuart. We must be sure Caleb's never alone, and we should start carrying a gun when we're out in the woods." Everbody sat quiet for a few seconds; then Pa added, "If the threat gets too strong, we may need to let him go back to Pennsylvania to work in the company there."

Uncle Stuart agreed. "I hope it doesn't come to that because he's such a good worker, and he's been on our team for such a long time. He's more than just a hired hand; he's more like part of our family."

Ma worked in the dining room putting away the china from the dinner, and I hadn't realized she could hear the conversation. But she come into the parlor and stood near Pa's chair. "Speaking of the Campbell and Perkins Company, how're we doing in Pittsburgh? Is the business holding up well?"

Pa looked up and smiled. He made room for Ma to set on the arm of his chair. "Yes, the need for lumber for building ships, wagons, furniture, houses, and barns is greater than ever. Our woodsmen are working farther away as the timber has been cut on most of the easier to reach locations. But our output hasn't suffered much yet. That may change as we harvest more of the available trees. That's why I want to get started cutting our timber here. I think we'll be ready to start by the first of the year."

William, setting quietly in the opposite corner, stood and motioned to me. "Harvey, let's go saddle up our horses and ride over to the forge. We can wish the Jacksons a Merry Christmas."

As I passed James on the way to get my coat, he put his foot out to trip me, but William grabbed my arm to keep me from falling. William stared at James till he gave a smirk and withdrew his foot. I turned to see if Ma or Pa had seen, but they continued talking about the Pennsylvania business.

Ma followed us to the room near the back door where we kept our outdoor gear. "Be sure to wear warm clothes and don't stay too long. Looks like a snow storm might be coming." Ma was always looking out for us. "And take some of the Christmas pudding to share with the Jacksons."

"Wait a minute," Pa got up from his chair and headed to his office, "I have something I need you to take to the forge." He returned and handed William a paper. "It's an order for a branding iron. I got our brand registered at the courthouse on my way home the other day so this is our official brand."

"Why do we need a branding iron?" I hoped we wasn't gonna start branding our stock. I always thought that was so cruel, even though I understood the need to do it.

"We'll brand all our logs so when they reach the mill, we get credit for them. Otherwise someone else could claim them. That's one thing we have to deal with in our Pennsylvania business—people trying to steal our logs."

"But Pa, how can they steal them if they got your brand on them?"

"Good question, Harvey. They saw off our brand and put on one of their own in its place." He handed William a paper. "I drew a picture of it for Old Bob to use as a pattern."

I peeped over William's arm as he held the paper and saw a circle with C&P inside.

"What's the C&P stand for?"

William looked surprised. "It's for Campbell and Perkins, the name of our company.

***

Ma was right. We had a big snow storm that night. Morning dawned with bright sunshine, but extremely cold temperatures. We didn't get as much preparation for the beginning of our logging operation as Pa had hoped because of the cold and snow, but by New Year's Day, the snow had mostly melted and the men was ready to go to work.

Some years later, I made a good friend from Atlanta named Charles Summers. He grew up in the city and didn't know nothing about country life. I was telling him about how we done the logging. He couldn't get his head around the idea that our forests had such big trees.

He frowned like as how I's exaggerating. "How big did you say they were?"

"We cut some poplars that was as much as six foot across. We had white and red oaks, beech, ash, sycamore, linden, cedar, and pine."

"Six foot wide? Lord almighty! I can't believe a tree was that big."

"Well, as Pa explained it, those forests had never been cut before, so some of the trees was hundreds of years old."

"How'd you manage to cut down trees that big?"

"Caleb, he was one of our hired hands, and Uncle Stuart stood on the downhill side of the tree, one on each side. They had a rhythm going; first Caleb and then Uncle Stuart would take a chip out of the tree with their double bitted axes. They kept this up till they had a big notch about one-third the depth of the tree. After that the men used huge crosscut saws to saw through the tree starting on the uphill side opposite the notch." Charles asked a few more questions, and shook his head at my descriptions.

On the first day of cutting, Ma allowed Evan and me to skip lessons and go to the woods with the men. As we put on our wraps, Miz Simpson come into the house carrying little Sylvia. "I never saw such a thick fog. You can't even see the creek. You know what they say: fog in January, frost in May." That was news to me, but I's glad by the time we collected all the equipment and gathered at the site Pa had chosen to start, the sun had chased the fog away.

Pa told me and Evan our job was to stay out of the way. "This is a dangerous business. It's easy to get injured, even killed, so I want you to be careful and don't get in the way." He told me we could start by carrying drinking water for the men. We soon figured out we could bring a bucket of water and a dipper and set it on a stump where the men could help theirselves, while we spent the time watching the men work.

We watched with wonder as the process proceeded. They started with a medium sized oak. When the saw men had cut nearly through the tree, Pa ask everbody to move back cause the tree was ready to fall. I made sure to stand uphill from the tree, but where I had a good view. When the tree started falling, all the men yelled as loud as they could, "Timmmberrrrr!" And it fell with a crash that shook the ground.

All the men grabbed a axe and begun chopping off the limbs. Then they sawed the log into 12-foot lengths. Dan Simpson brought up his two teams of oxen which he hitched to a log with a long chain and slowly snaked it down the mountain, pulling it along the ground. I ask Pa why we didn't use the horses, and he said oxen was more sure footed on the steep slopes. Earlier the men had prepared a deck along the creek beyond the swimming hole where they would place the logs to wait till the spring floods come.

After the men had cut down half a dozen trees, me and Evan got moved up from water boys to lap boys. They called the branches and tree limbs left after the oxen took the logs away "the lap." Lap boys had to clean up the left over limbs. Ma allowed us to work in the afternoons after we spent the morning on our lessons, and Evan's pa agreed. The two of us cut the branches into lengths for firewood and hauled it to the woodshed. When the woodshed got full, we took it to town and stacked it beside the forge, where people could buy wood for heating their homes. By the time the rains come in March, me and Evan had earned $50 from the sale of our firewood.

By mid-March, Pa's team had 100 logs ready to float to the mill. Next come the most dangerous part: following the logs downstream when the floods come. The men filled the wagon with food, dry clothes, blankets and some medical supplies. Uncle Stuart explained what each person's duties would be. They divided into two teams: The first team would go several miles ahead and set up camp while the second team followed the logs to that point. Then the first team would drive the logs while the second team traveled ahead and rested.

Pa called me into his office one day. "Harvey, when the men start driving the logs downstream, you are to go nowhere near them. Do you understand?"

"Why can't I go? I really want to watch them."

"As the logs float along, they sometimes get tangled and make a log jam. The drivers have to climb over the logs and use cant hooks to untangle them. The logs can roll sometimes causing the logger to fall into the water where he might drown. Or his leg might get crushed between two logs. It's very dangerous and I don't want you close to the creek when the time comes."

I wasn't happy, but I knew not to argue. "All right Pa, but if it's so dangerous what if some of our men get hurt?"

"It's always possible, but our men are experienced loggers and they'll be careful. We hope no one gets hurt."

I walked slow down the hall and out to the front porch where I sat on the steps looking out towards the creek and wondered if the rains would come soon.

***

Towards the end of March it rained buckets for three days. The mountains sent down walls of water and the creek spread over its banks. When the flood peaked, Pa announced, "There's a big tide in the Fork! Let's get started." I watched from the front porch as Mr. Simpson drove the horses pulling the wagon and the advance team set out for the first camp. Ma come out to join me.

"Ma, why is Pa taking a gun?"

"You know, he told you that sometimes pirates try to steal the logs. He's just taking precautions. Besides, some of the time they will be in deep woods and wild animals could be a problem."

I put on my oiled slicker and went towards the creek making sure to stay at a distance. Uncle Stuart and his crew cut the logs loose a few at a time and let them roll into the swollen waters rushing towards the river. I gave a big whoop when the logs splashed into the water and begun floating away.

Life at home become very dull with most of the men gone. The women gathered in our house and begun quilting on a colorful quilt that Cousin Maybelle had been working on for months. They said they was having a hen party. When the waters begun to go down, I was allowed to go outside, but I complained of nothing to do. I pestered Ma with all sorts of questions: "When will the men be coming back?" "Do you think anyone got hurt?" How long will it take?"

Her response was not what I had expected. "I think you need a job. I have informed Mr. Morgan you'll be working with him each afternoon." So I spent the next two weeks cleaning out stalls, helping fix fences, and even learnt to milk a cow.

Finally the men come back a few at a time. James and William come first and shared the news of their adventure. Most everone got dumped into the river at some point, but they all managed to get to the shore safe. Scott, one of our newer hired hands, had got caught between a couple of logs and his leg was broke. They found a doctor who splinted his leg, and he was traveling back in Mr. Simpson's wagon. A few of the other men had got minor injuries, but was able to travel and would be home soon. Pa was staying at the mill to make sure the logs was properly processed. All in all, it was a successful project.

Spring finally come, trees begun to turn green, Miz Simpson and Pete made plans for the garden, and once everone had returned from delivering the logs, life settled into a pattern. The men took a break from cutting timber and worked at improving the road into the woods, clearing stumps from the new ground, building new fences, and getting ready to put in the crops. I had hoped I would no longer have to be Mr. Morgan's helper, but it was not to be. I even begun to wish lessons lasted all afternoon.

After the rains stopped, the village men completed the church building that would also be the school. A new family moved into the community— Mr. and Mistress Baker and their four-year-old daughter, Mary Louise. Mr. Baker was the new minister and schoolmaster. He would commence teaching in the fall. Mistress Baker was trained as a midwife. This family contributed much to our little settlement. I didn't know it then, but they would make a big difference in my own life.

CHAPTER 3

January 1875

Campbell Holler, Tennessee

I had the nightmare again last night. It's usually the same and comes when I've had a frustrating day. Yesterday I worked all day long cutting locust trees for fence rails and didn't realize till almost dark my cow had broke through the rail fence and wandered into the woods. I hadn't ate nothing since breakfast, I was plumb wore out, and now I had to light a lantern and go roaming around the ridge to round up my wandering cow. By the time I found her, got her into the barn and milked, I's so exhausted and vexed I fell into the bed without undressing or even eating.

Then just before daylight I woke myself shouting and struggling, my heart pounding, angry tears streaming down my face. It always leaves me tore up and feeling weak. I didn't stop shaking till I lit a fire, made coffee, and ate some fatback and eggs.

It's really strange that my worst nightmare is about my best friend who otherwise brought me so much happiness. Now it seems strange to me that we become such good friends in the first place. We was as different as rattlesnakes and fishing worms. I was the one with a bad temper; Evan was always calm and never seemed to get upset. I took after my pa with dark curly hair and dark eyes. I was tall for my age and had a muscular build, while Evan was short and skinny. He had straight blond hair that hung down in his greenish-gray eyes. Even though he was smaller, he was very strong. We never had a fight, but I always thought he'd prob'ly whip me if we did.

Evan had a great sense of humor, loved to laugh and make others laugh, and always looked on the bright side. When we started going to the village school, Mr. Baker made us memorize all sorts of things: poems, Bible verses, the Preamble to the Constitution. Each student would have to stand in front of the class and recite the required passage from memory.

One of the first things we had to learn was the names of the twelve disciples. When it was Evan's turn, he come to the front, stood there looking bewildered for a long moment, and then spouted out all in one long breath: "Addie, Tabbie, Jackie, Thadie, Eddie, Marvie, Sarie, Bobbie, Ralphie, Marley, Bonnie and Luckie."

I don't know how he thought of those names so fast. Later he told me they was based on the names for his family and his pets. Jackie was his mule Jack. Addie was his mother Addeline. Thadie was for his brother Thadeus, and so on. You can see he had spent time thinking up all those names and then memorizing them just so he could get us laughing.

All of us students and even Mr. Baker was so surprised we just stared with our mouths hanging open for several seconds, and then we busted out laughing. I saw Mr. Baker put his hand over his mouth till he could get a stern look. He rapped his ruler on the desk for attention and glared at Evan. "Young man, enough of your foolishness. You will stay after school today until you can say the names correctly—if it takes all night."

On my way home from school, I had to walk past Evan's house, so we always walked together when school was over for the day. That day as I walked along by myself, I was wondering how long it might take Evan to learn those names. I hadn't gone far when I heard him calling my name, and he run to catch up grinning ear to ear. "I already knowed the disciples, so I just rattled them off for Mr. Baker and here I am."

He was always pulling something like that. When we had to learn the books of the Bible, he said all of them backwards starting with Revelation. I just wish I would dream about some of the good times we had instead of that awful day. After I lost Evan, I never had another friend I felt that close to. Now in this here lonesome holler I sometimes go for weeks without talking with another soul. I dream of the day when my beloved will come here to be my companion. If the good Lord lets me tarry to see that day, I'll finally be a happy man.

I often think of my mother and how she lived so long in that isolated valley in Kentucky with Cousin Maybelle as the only other woman on the place. Poor Maybelle. Ma took her in when her mother died and there wasn't no one else to look after her. She did simple tasks like helping in the kitchen and some housekeeping, but wasn't someone Ma could talk serious with.

Once the Simpsons and Morgans come to work for us, Ma had two women she could share household concerns with as employees, but they wasn't what you'd call good friends. Now I realize why Ma become such good friends with Mistress Baker, the wife of the minister. Mistress Baker and Ma developed a friendship that has lasted till this day.

They gathered the women of the community together for quilting bees; they sponsored pie suppers to raise money to buy hymnals for the church; and since Mistress Baker knowed a lot about using plants for medicine like Miz Simpson, they helped treat illnesses and injuries. At that time Rock County had no doctors. Soon the word got out that Mistress Baker was a midwife, and folks begun calling for her to help with births. And as Miz Simpson also had some midwife experience, Mistress Baker sometimes sent for Miz Simpson to assist her if she had a difficult case. As the summer of 1859 progressed, Ma spent more and more time in Laureltown with her new friend.

The Bakers' daughter, Mary Louise, was the same age as little Sylvia Simpson, and often when Ma went to visit Mistress Baker, she'd take Sylvia along so the little girls could play together. Once in a while Ma would let me go with her so I could spend some time with Evan, but us eleven-year-old boys paid no attention to five-year-old girls.

When we lived in Pittsburgh, Ma saw to it that we attended church ever Sunday. But in Kentucky because the nearest church was 25 miles away, we didn't go to meeting for years. When we had a local church house and a minister, Ma commenced attending church each week. She insisted all of us should go, but usually only me, Miz Simpson, Sylvia, and Cousin Maybelle went along. She was concerned that the church had no hymn books, which is why she and the ladies decided to raise money.

As I look back now, it seems strange because most of the villagers couldn't read. But Ma was determined. Finally a dozen copies of *The Sweet Songster* arrived. A small book, slightly larger than the palm of my hand, it contained only the words—no music. And since not everbody could read, the minister would line it out by singing each line, and then the congregation would repeat the words and tune. Since I thought I's a poor singer, I barely mumbled along, but years later, I found comfort in remembering those old songs. Even now when I'm plodding along behind the plow, I find myself singing some of those hymns.

After the men returned from taking the logs to the mill in the spring of 1859, all the hired hands helped get the crops planted. Then Uncle Stuart took his team back to the woods to cut more trees. Mr. Morgan took two of the hired hands, Larry and Scott, to work on the farm. Ma assigned me to work on the farm team, so I didn't often get a chance to visit with Evan.

I struggled to keep up with the farm men. I helped care for the horses and cows, and sweated along with the rest as we cut hay, and hauled it to the barn when it had dried. I remember one particular day when we worked in the hot sun turning the hay over with pitchforks so it would dry faster. I worked as hard as I could to keep up with Mr. Morgan and Larry, but after a while, I got a bad headache and felt like I's gonna throw up. Mr. Morgan took one look at me, threw down his pitchfork, and helped me stagger over to a tree on the edge of the field.

"This boy's about to have a heat stroke," he said to Larry. "Go fetch some water for him." When Larry come back with a bucket of water, he had me drink a few sips from the dipper and then splashed water over my face and neck. "Now, Sonny, you just set there and rest a bit." Then he and Larry returned to tossing the hay.

Dreckly James come riding up on Blaze and saw me setting under the tree while the men worked in the hay field. "I see you're still a little slacker, Harvey Baby, lazing here in the shade. Get yourself on your feet and get out there where you're supposed to be working." I stood up and felt the world start spinning around and slowly fell back down.

James jumped off his horse, grabbed my arm, and pulled me to my feet. "I said to get back out there." He started shaking me so hard I thought my head might fall off.

"What you think you're doing?" Mr. Morgan yelled as he come running across the field. "He's doing exactly what I told him to do." He helped me set back down. "He got over heated and he's about to get heat stroke." He looked down at me and saw I couldn't hardly hold up my head. He turned to James. "I think it would help if you took him back to the house where his mother can tend to him."

Mr. Morgan lifted me up on Blaze and handed the bridle to James. "Take him home." As bad as I felt, I couldn't help smiling because for once someone had turned the tables on James. It come clear to me then as long as Mr. Morgan was nearby, I had nothing to fear from James. The rest of the summer I made sure to stick close, and James never got a chance to torment me.

The only thing I liked about hoeing corn and tobacco alongside the men was listening to their talk. Mr. Morgan, a Southern sympathizer, and Larry, a strong Unionist, argued constantly about almost everthing. Several times I thought they was gonna hit each other over the head with their hoes. They got even more quarrelsome as time for the local election got close.

I didn't know very much about elections, but I listened as they pointed out the advantages of electing their favorite candidates. In the local election to be held in August, our county would elect a new sheriff and a new county recorder.

Mr. Morgan wanted the Democrat candidate to be sheriff. "He's got backbone and he won't take nothing off nobody. He'll keep order for us."

Larry laughed. "No he won't. He's gonna do whatever the big men in

Frankfort tell him. The Republican guy's the one who'll be fair."

"But you ain't old enough to vote. What do you care?"

"I'm aiming to go on Election Day anyway, and I bet you money I can get someone to let me vote."

"Nah, you just want to go get some of that free whiskey and do some gambling."

"Yeah, I'll do that too, but I bet you a dollar I get to vote."

As the time for the election come closer, I started scheming for a way I might could go along to the voting place. The men said crowds of people come together on Election Day for debates, swapping, bragging, and brawling. Larry talked about tug-of-war contests, cock fights, and other interesting goings on I'd like to see. James even planned to enter Blaze in a horse race. The voting would take place at the Rock County seat, about 25 miles away. The men planned to take the covered wagon with blankets and supplies and make it a three-day trip. I knowed Pa'd never agree for me to go. I finally decided it would only annoy him for me to ask, so I watched with a heavy heart as they loaded up the wagon and set off without me.

Mr. Morgan didn't go to vote after all—said he actually wasn't eligible to vote since he hadn't lived in the county long enough. Of course, Caleb wouldn't be allowed to vote, even though he was a freedman, and William wasn't old enough. The rest of the men, except the new hired hands Thomas and Scott, all went along to the election. That left a small crew to hold down things at home, especially since Scott's broken leg hadn't completely healed.

Miz Simpson ask me to be her helper in the garden and the kitchen. Since Pete O'Malley had gone with the men to vote, she also had to do the cooking. One of the first jobs she gave me was to pick beans and string them up to dry for leather breeches. I didn't like to pick beans and tried to get out of it, but Ma said I had to. She also had me plunking the dasher up and down to churn butter.

In the cool of the evening, I worked with Miz Simpson in the yerb garden. Earlier in the summer she had gone to visit her mother, who lived in Madison County, and had brought back all sorts of plants and seeds. I couldn't tell the difference between the yerbs and the weeds, and she scolded me good when I dug up one of her precious plants.

"What is it anyway?"

"It's called Indian tobacco." She sounded purty put out with me like as how I shoulda knowed what it was.

"What good is it? We don't eat it, do we?"

"No, actually it can poison you if you get too much." She called it "pizen."

"If it's poison, why do we want to grow it?"

She gave a long sigh, stood up from where she'd been replanting the dug up plant, removed her bonnet, and wiped her brow with the back of her hand. "It's used for medicine. It's good for croup and coughs and bronchitis. Some people smoke the dried leaves to help their breathing when they have a cold."

"Well, I sure don't want any of it. I think we ought not be raising poison stuff."

"If you get bad sick with whooping cough, you'll prob'ly be glad to take anything that might help you get well."

I pointed at the plant bed. "Are all these plants in this here bed for medicine?"

"Either medicine or to use in cooking."

I pointed to a plant by my right foot. "Is this one poison too?"

"No, that's called peppermint." She reached down and pulled off a leaf, tore it in half and handed a piece to me. "Taste it, you'll like it." I just watched as she put the leaf in her mouth and smiled. "Don't be afraid. It's perfectly good for you, and it tastes good too. It makes a great tea, especially when your tummy feels a bit uneasy."

I pointed to another plant. "What's that?"

"That's called plantain. It's good for treating any kind of infection. It's one of the most important yerbs. I always use it on bad cuts and wounds." She pointed with her hoe. "And that over there is comfrey. It's used to treat broken bones."

"How'd you learn about using healing plants?"

"My granny. She learnt most of it from a old Indian woman who lived down by the creek on the edge of the settlement." She stooped and gave the soil around the plant a couple of pats. "Now go get some water for this plant you dug up, and let's see if we can save it."

During the next two years, Miz Simpson showed me about all sorts of plants and how to use them for medicine and for cooking. She even took me into the woods where we gathered leaves from plants that didn't like to be transplanted. We dug up roots, gathered leaves to dry, and collected seeds. As soon as I cleared a place for a garden here in Campbell Holler, I made a bed for the plants that's useful in cooking and treating medical problems. There ain't no doctor around here, so if I get sick or hurt, I have to doctor myself.

When the men come back from voting, they had wild stories to tell, and slowly I pieced together some of what had happened. In Rock County, Kentucky, the Democrats, who was for slavery, outnumbered the Republicans about three to one. Democrats posted armed men around the courthouse and tried to keep Republicans from voting. The Democrat sheriff stood by and did nothing to stop them from demanding men vote for the Democrats or else. Others openly gave bribes to voters. Pa said he saw a man with jugs of whiskey in his wagon offering free drinks to anyone who promised to vote for the Democrats. And not far away a Republican did the same. I guess lots of fist fights and arguments broke out, especially between those who visited the whiskey wagons over and over.

Finally, a group of Republicans decided to take back the courthouse. They gathered at the edge of town and come galloping through town on their horses shooting their guns in the air. Everbody run to take cover. The Democrats guarding the courthouse rushed inside. The Republicans took up positions behind wagons and anything else that would provide cover; some even climbed atop buildings across the street. In the shootout that followed, three Republicans got shot, but lucky for them they wasn't serious. Two horses was killed, but the Democrats holed up in the courthouse hadn't suffered no injuries. Then somebody snuck behind the courthouse and set it afire.

Everbody from both parties formed a bucket brigade to carry water to put out the fire, and that seemed to calm down the riot. The fire damaged the back wall of the building, but didn't damage any records.

Blaze didn't win the horse race, but a couple of drunks tried to steal him, and James had to fight them off with a pitchfork. Later, James almost lost Blaze in a gambling game. I must admit I wish he hadda lost his horse. It woulda served him right for all the mean things he done to me over the years.

I wondered what part Pa had took in the fight. I figgered with his hot temper he prob'ly got mixed up in it somehow. The next day as I worked with the farm crew, I ask Larry if he got to vote like he planned.

"Yeah, I did. You see, your pa marched right up to the courthouse and told the Democrats guarding the door he intended to go inside and vote. When they asked him who he was aiming to vote for, he said, 'None of your business.' The guard tried to block his way, but he brushed him aside and walked right in." Larry grinned. "And I followed right behind him."

That impressed me right much. "So nobody tried to stop you?"

"Nope. Your pa woulda made three of that little runt of a guy guarding the door. Even though he had a gun, the poor feller just stumbled aside when Mr. Campbell pushed him, and we walked right in. Good thing we did our voting first thing before things got so rowdy." He turned to Mr. Morgan. "Well, Jim, I spect you owe me a dollar."

"How you figger that?"

"I bet you a dollar I would get to vote. Don't you recollect?"

"Course I do. I remember I didn't take up your bet. I don't owe you a damn cent."

And then they started bickering back and forth again. But I still didn't know what Pa done during the shootout.

***

Along about the end of August that same year, a strange man come and ask if he could find work with the logging team. Pa had gone to the county seat to make some purchases and pick up our mail. I watched from the front porch as Uncle Stuart talked with him for several minutes. Then he ask me to show the man where he would sleep in the bunk house.

"What's your name, boy?"

"Harvey."

"You Mr. Campbell's son?"

"Yes, sir."

"I heard Mr. Campbell was rich. Is that so?"

I thought that wasn't none of his business. I just shrugged my shoulders and ask, "What's your name?"

"Bart Woodson. Ever heard of me?"

"No, sir."

"Well you should have, cause I'm famous in these parts as a fist fighter."

I didn't much like him, but I showed him his bunk and where he could stow his belongings.

He looked around the large dormitory-like room. "Lots of bunks in here. How many hired hands stay here?"

I thought for a minute and counted on my fingers in my pocket. "You'll make eight I guess."

"Huh. Ary one a them like to fist fight?"

"Uncle Stuart would not hire people if they got into fights."

He shoved his bag of stuff into a cabinet. "Oh, is that so? We'll see about that."

"I guess you better report to Uncle Stuart now. You can just follow this road up the ridge, and you'll find where they's working today."

"So Harvey, is that what you said your name was?" I nodded. "I guess I'll be seeing you around." He walked in the direction I had pointed him. I watched him go up the hill and wondered if Uncle Stuart had made a bad decision about this man.

A short time later, Pa come home. After he greeted Ma and unloaded his purchases, he ask for something to eat. While he ate, I told him about the new man and said I didn't really like him.

"What didn't you like?"

"He ask me if you was a rich man, and he wanted to know if the hired hands ever got into fights."

"I guess I'll go meet him and see what I think."

"Can I go with you? I ain't seen the loggers work for a long time."

We walked up the ridge about half a mile and met Mr. Simpson's oxen dragging a really big log towards the creek. He didn't stop the oxen, but took off his hat and said, "Good afternoon, sir."

Pa returned his greeting and asked how the work was going.

"They've got three trees bout ready to come down. Made lots of progress today."

"Glad to hear it." By this time, the oxen had snaked the log past us, and we continued on our way up the hill. When we come in sight of the workers, I noticed Bart Woodson and Caleb pulled each end of a cross cut saw on a large tree. They had sawed almost to the notch and soon the tree would fall.

Caleb stopped to see how far they had to go and saw Bart had sawed almost all the way through on his side. "Don't cut all the way through on your side till I get my side closer."

When they started sawing again, Bart kept pulling the saw towards the notch. Suddenly, the tree begun to fall, but because one side had not cut through, it twisted and fell sideways instead of downhill.

Caleb jumped back out of the way and yelled to Jake and Luke who worked right in the path of the falling tree. They tried to run, but a limb knocked them both to the ground.

"I told you not to cut all the way through!" Caleb yelled over his shoulder as he ran toward the downed men.

Fortunately, Thomas, Uncle Stuart, Pa, and Caleb was able to lift the limbs enough for the men to climb out. Luke's face was cut and blood was squirting out his broke nose. Caleb brought the water bucket and washed the blood off Luke's face. Uncle Stuart and Pa examined Jake's leg and decided it wasn't broke. But it was bruised so bad he limped for over two weeks.

Once he saw they'd be all right, Pa turned to Bart. His squinted eyes and red face told me his anger was pert near out of control. "What did you do that for? Why didn't you follow Caleb's instructions?" He yelled.

Bart held out his hand. "You must be Mr. Campbell. Pleased to meet you, sir."

Pa ignored his hand. "I asked you a question."

"Oh, I don't take orders from no nigger."

Before that man knowed what was happening, Pa's fist smashed into his belly—doubling him over—and then Pa shoved him backwards knocking him to the ground.

Uncle Stuart rushed over, grabbed Pa's arm and pulled him aside. "Let me handle this, Jed. I'm the one hired him." He took the man's hand and pulled him to his feet and looked him straight in the eye. "Caleb is a trusted employee who has worked for us for twenty years. He knows the lumber business inside out, and if you had listened to him, our men would not be injured. They coulda been killed, and...."

Bart interrupted. "But I didn't know the tree would fall in the wrong direction. That nigger didn't tell me that."

Pa lunged at him again, but Uncle Stuart pushed him away and stepped closer until his face was only inches from Bart's nose and said in a slow, loud voice, "His...name...is...Caleb. We will not have him disrespected. In fact, we will not have you as an employee. Go get your belongings and get off the property. Don't ever come back."

"But I worked for two hours. Don't I get paid for that?"

"I just deducted from your wages the cost of medical attention for the two men your behavior injured. The balance is zero. Now get out of here." He turned to Thomas, "Go with him and see he leaves without any problems."

I never seen Uncle Stuart so close to losing his temper before. He's usually the calm one. Him and Pa is as different as me and Evan was. Uncle Stuart is tall and lean. He likes to wear a flannel shirt and a ten gallon hat. Pa is shorter and stocky, and he wears nice suits when he's not working in the woods. Uncle Stuart ain't never married, but claims us as his family. As long as I can remember he has lived with us. I stood beside him as he watched that man slouch off down the mountain. He took several deep breaths and then turned to look at the tree.

Pa had finally calmed down a bit and put his hand on Uncle Stuart's shoulder. "Thanks. I was ready to kick his guts out. Actually, I'm a bit disappointed I didn't. But you handled it well. I hope we never see him again."

I hoped never to see him again myself.

***

When we made our trip to Pennsylvania that fall, Uncle Stuart stayed behind to supervise the logging operation. Instead, Pa and William accompanied us, and William rode in the wagon with Ma while me and Pa rode our horses. I couldn't remember when I had spent so much time with him. As we rode along, he told me stories of his boyhood growing up in western Pennsylvania.

At one point the road turned away from the river and run along a small creek for a few hundred yards to a bridge crossing the creek. Pa stopped on the bridge. "Look, son," he pointed to the west. "Beavers have built a dam in the creek over there."

I could see what looked like a thatch of tree branches and sticks across the creek that had backed up the water into a pond. I didn't know much about beavers, so I ask, "How come them to do that?"

"They made a pond deep enough to keep predatory animals from coming into their den."

"Where do they get all those sticks?"

"Beavers have very strong sharp teeth. They can cut down good sized trees just by using their teeth." Pa nudged his horse and we moved on to catch up with the wagon. "When your Uncle Stuart and I were boys, we used to trap beavers and sell their pelts."

"Did you make a lotta money?"

"Sometimes. One year we made enough money to pay for two horses, one for each of us. They were both yearlings we bought cheap because their owner had died and his elderly wife wasn't able to care for them."

"Was that your first horses?"

"Yes. My horse was a mare, and she later had a little colt we raised to be a race horse. We named him Jack; he was very smart, and he loved to run. We entered him in races every chance we got and made enough money to buy a parcel of land covered in trees. That's how we got started in the lumber business."

This was family history I'd never heard before. "How long did you race him?"

"Not long after we bought the land, your Grandma Campbell found out we were making money gambling on races, and she made us sell Jack."

"Aw, that ain't fair. Why'd she do that?"

Pa laughed. "We knew she didn't approve of gambling, and we respected her opinion. But the money we got from selling Jack helped us get started in the logging business, so it worked out for the best after all."

"How did you and Uncle Stuart get to be partners with Mr. Perkins?"

We had to go single file around a big mud puddle. When we got back side by side, he explained how his lumber business got started. "Bradford Perkins was a boyhood friend of mine. Actually he had the idea first for forming a lumber company together. He had some money to invest in a sawmill, and Stuart and I had some timber-covered land. That's how we got started. Soon as we had lumber to sell, people started buying, and the demand grew very fast. When we cut all the timber on our land, we had enough money to buy more land with trees to cut. It just kept growing each year."

We come to a good place to let the horses get a drink and rest for a little while. I was happy to have some time out of the saddle. William fed the horses some oats and Ma opened up the picnic basket for our lunch. Pete O'Malley made the best fried chicken I ever ate. I helped myself to a couple a chicken legs and some cornbread, ate a couple of boiled eggs, and finished up with a handful of sugar cookies.

When I started to dip my hand into the cookie container again, William grabbed my hand. "Hey Greedy, not so fast; leave some for the rest of us."

That embarrassed me, and I felt real bad it was William who scolded me. He always talked nice to me. I walked over to a tree that had fallen and set with my back turned to everbody.

Ma come and set beside me, put her arm around me and said, "Don't be upset. Just keep reminding yourself to think of other people, too." She rubbed my back and shoulders. "What have you and your pa been talking about?"

I told her and ask, "Was you and Pa married when they started Campbell and Perkins Company?"

"No, not then."

"So how did you meet Pa?"

Ma stood up. "It's time to get back on the road. Ask Jed to tell you about how we met as you ride along this afternoon."

Pa explained they first met when he was a student at Western University of Pennsylvania. Her father was a professor there, and he had gone to Professor Dodson's office to get his advice about a assignment. As he was leaving the office, Ma come to bring her father his lunch, and they started talking.

"Did you just fall in love like that?"

Pa laughed, "No, not immediately. Your mother's a very wise and intelligent lady. She had to be wooed with lots of courting. She did agree that I could call on her at her home on the following Saturday."

"What did you do on Saturday?"

"We sat in the swing on the front porch. She lived in the house where Grandma and Grandpa Dodson still live. We talked for hours trying to get acquainted with each other."

"Did you kiss her?"

"Heavens no. I'm sure Grandma Dodson was watching and listening from the open window in the parlor. We didn't even sit close to each other." Pa chuckled. "But we did find out some interesting facts about each other. Women didn't usually go to college, but since Grandpa Dodson was a professor, she was permitted to enroll. When I met her, she was in her second year and was studying mathematics, literature, Latin, and astronomy."

"That's how she knows so much, I guess. So how long did you court before you got married?"

"Not as long as Grandpa Dodson thought we should. I was in the middle of my last year at the university when I asked for her hand. Frances had already become a silent partner in the company."

"What's a silent partner?"

"She had inherited quite a bit of money from her Grandfather Dodson when she was 18 and she bought into the company with her inheritance. She didn't want to be involved in the day-to-day operation, but would meet with Bradford and me and Stuart each week to go over the financial records. She had an equal vote on any major decision we considered, and she still does. As I said, she is a very bright and sensible person."

All that information about Ma was news to me, and I had to let all that settle in my brain for a little while. I couldn't help thinking if she's that smart, how come she agreed to move to that lonesome valley in Kentucky. I finally had to ask, "Did she vote to buy the land in Kentucky?"

Pa smiled and nodded. "She thought buying up the timber in Kentucky was a good idea. However, I had to do some strong persuasion to get her willing to actually move. We agreed that she would wait to come until we had the buildings up and had the place functioning enough to sustain the family and hired hands." He smiled again and looked at me, "You were just a few months old and she wanted to wait until you got older."

I shook my head in bewilderment. I couldn't understand why anyone would want to move away from the good life in Pittsburgh. After riding along quiet for a while, I got to remembering that Grandpa Dodson thought they should do more courting. "Pa, what did Grandpa say when you ask permission to get married?"

"Grandpa Dodson really wanted her to finish her studies and become a teacher. I promised I would see that she finished at the university after we were married, and he finally agreed we could get married after I finished my last year of university." Later when we made camp that night, I told Pa thanks for telling me the family stories.

We made much better time this trip cause the roads was much better. Even the steamboats seemed to go faster. I was surprised by the strong feelings among the passengers. Seemed like if you started up a conversation with someone, it turned into an argument about politics sooner or later.

Most of the talk was about who should be the nominee for the Presidential election the next year. One day Pa met a group of businessmen in the saloon of the steamboat. They was seated around a table and most of them had drinks. I snuck in and hid behind a big chair where I could listen. Most seemed to be Republicans like Pa, but one or two argued strongly in favor of slavery, so I thought they was Democrats.

Pa said, "I favor William Seward of New York for president. He seems to have the strongest support, and he favors prohibiting slavery in the territories but leaving slavery alone in the states where it's currently legal."

A large fellow in a black suit pointed his finger in Pa's direction. "That's exactly why I ain't in favor of him. Slavery should be legal everywhere. Stephen Douglas is my choice."

"Who's Stephen Douglas? Never heard of him." This from a little man with spectacles balanced on his nose.

The man in the black suit slapped the table so hard the glasses wobbled. "Haven't you heard of the Lincoln Douglas Debates? Abe Lincoln and

Stephen Douglas run for Senator from Illinois last year and had these famous debates all around the state, and Douglas won the election. That's the man the whole country could vote for—North and South."

Some other names was mentioned I can't recollect now, and purty soon Pa drained his glass and stood up. "Excuse me, Gentlemen. I have enjoyed your company, but now I must leave you." He strode out the door, and I waited a few minutes and followed him.

Elliott come to the wharf to meet the boat when we got to Pittsburgh. He throwed his arms around me and lifted me up like I's a little kid. I couldn't believe how much he'd growed since last Christmas. He even had a moustache. While we was there, he spent as much time with me as his studies allowed. We spent many evenings playing chess, and I even beat him three times. I was closer to Elliott than any of my brothers, but unfortunately, that fall was the last time I got to spend so much time with him.

While I was surprised with how much my brother had grown, my Grandma Campbell bragged about how tall I had got in the year since she'd seen me. She sat on her big porch rocking away with her crocheting in her lap and watched me and my cousin Chester wrestling in the yard where I pinned him down several times.

Later she said, "Your shoulders have gotten so much broader and you're so strong. What have you been doing to get all those muscles?"

"Ma assigned me to work on the farm team, and I been working like a dog all summer." Her praise made me feel good, and for the first time I realized that maybe hard work might have some benefits—a lesson that kept me going through some very difficult times in later years.

William and Pa spent much time ever day at the company office. Pa wanted William to keep his financial records, so he worked each day at the Campbell and Perkins office learning their system. But in the evenings, William went out with his cousin Jasper to drink a pint or two at a pub. While I didn't know it at the time, Jasper had introduced him to a young lady, and William fell in love. We only stayed in Pittsburgh two weeks this time, but that was time enough for William to find the girl of his dreams.

On the last Saturday in Pennsylvania, the family had a picnic in a park near the edge of town. All of Pa's family, the Campbells, and all of Ma's family, the Dodsons, come. I saw more of my kinfolks that afternoon than I had ever saw before or since: cousins, grandparents, aunts and uncles. We couldn't have chose a more beautiful, warm, late September day, or a better spot for such a big family gathering.

The older folks spread blankets and quilts under a huge shade tree where they visited and drunk lemonade. Some of the men organized a horseshoe tournament. I'd seen Pa throw a rock and knock a squirrel out of a tree, but I didn't know he could pitch ringers like he did that day. He won four or five games before he retired to the shade with the old folks.

My cousins took turns flying kites. I won a couple of foot races. Some of the younger girls made daisy chains. Finally, my uncles organized a tug-of-war. We divided into two groups—one the Campbell family team, the other the Dodson family. The teams took places on either side of a little stream about three-foot wide that run through the park. The men stretched a long rope over the stream and we lined up along the rope. The team that pulled the opponents into the stream would win.

The Campbell team would pull the Dodsons forwards a few feet, and then the Dodsons would get a good foothold and pull the rope back t'other way. Family bystanders yelled encouragement. The Campbells reached the edge several times, but we always pulled back at the last moment. After about a quarter hour of this struggle, the Campbells had the Dodsons almost in the stream when someone on our team yelled, "On the count of three pull them in!"

But on the count of three when we pulled with all our might, the Dodsons suddenly turned the rope loose and the Campbells fell back into a big pile. Uncle Philip yelled, "That was a dirty trick!" But everybody laughed and clapped each other on the back.

As the sun moved farther to the west, the women started unpacking their picnic baskets. They spread quilts into a long line and set out fried chicken, biscuits, green beans, potatoes, cakes, cookies, pies and much more. I had never saw so much food, which we washed down with fresh apple cider. William and Jasper and their girlfriends arrived as we begun to fill our plates.

I felt sorry for Hilda Worthington, William's new friend. Meeting so many people for the first time musta give her a terrible fright, but she handled it with grace. William, being the caring, sensitive person he was, stayed close by her and helped her to meet all his family.

The following Monday we took all our baggage to the wharf and boarded the boat for home. Hilda come with Jasper and Uncle Phillip to see us off. I could see William's sadness as he bade Hilda farewell. They had no idea when they would see each other again, but it appeared to me they had made each other some promises.

CHAPTER 4

February 1875

Campbell Holler, Tennessee

Yesterday I done the morning chores early, shut my beagles, Sam and Saro, in the barn, hitched up the buggy, and drove the four miles into town for court day. People come from all over the county to hear the cases and visit with neighbors. Traveling drummers always show up on court day ready to sell whatever you might need. I bought a pair of gloves, a box of matches, a 1863 Springfield rifle, and a skillet. I done some peddling of my own; I sold ten jugs of moonshine and a cane-bottom chair.

I started making moonshine back in Kentucky before I moved here. I made my living for years peddling shine around southern Kentucky. When I moved to Tennessee, I brought my still with me and set it up behind some clumps of mountain ivy on the ridge above my house.

I also started making cane-bottomed chairs, which gives me something to do on winter evenings when it gets dark so early. I got seasoned lumber stored in the barn loft, and I order the cane from a import company in Pittsburgh. It takes me most of a winter to get one or two chairs made. But I take great pride in my work, and the chairs turn out quite nice even if I say so. I've made four extra nice ones for our house. I hope my bride will be pleased.

When the court recessed for the day I made ready to head home, but first, stopped at the trading post to stock up on sugar, salt, flour, candles, and jugs to replace the ones I sold. I also picked up my mail—two letters—one from my mother and another from my betrothed. Getting the mail reminded me as how in Kentucky, we had to go to the county seat to pick up mail, about a day-long trip on horseback. I'm lucky; here in Tennessee I can get to town and back in half a day. After William and Hilda begun writing, William kept inventing reasons to go pick up the mail. James made fun of him and called him a love-sick puppy, but now I understand how he felt.

As a boy, I had scary nightmares, and William let me crawl into bed with him when I woke up scared. Often in the middle of the night when I snuck into his room, I'd find him setting at his desk writing another letter to Hilda. He kept all her letters in a small trunk under his bed. It was a leather box about a foot and a half long and eight to ten inches high. The cover had pictures of wild animals from Africa carved into the leather. Many times I found him on the floor beside the box reading Hilda's letters. I don't know I woulda called him a love sick puppy, but he sure was a man in love. Him and Hilda did most of their courting by writing letters, just like me and my woman is doing.

When I got home from court day, I did the evening chores, fed the dogs and made a quick supper of cornbread and buttermilk, saving the letters to pore over when I had nothing else demanding my attention. I put a extra log on the fire, lit the lamp, and settled into my favorite chair to the right of the fireplace. I read Ma's letter first cause I knowed purty much what she'd say. She moved back to Pennsylvania after Pa died and has stayed there ever since. She shared news of the relatives there, especially to say that my Grandma Campbell wasn't doing well. She also said Elliott was now a partner in a lawyer's office. William and Hilda are expecting their third child. She always says she's grateful William and Hilda live close by so she can enjoy the grandchildren. She ended by saying she missed me and hoped I was well and happy.

Howsomever, she added a note at the end to say James had to lay off all but one of his hired hands. So many building companies had gone bankrupt, there wasn't much demand for lumber. The Pennsylvania part of the company also had reduced its work force as the entire country has suffered a economic crisis. The big banks in New York and other cities had invested so much in construction projects, especially the railroads, they begun to go under a couple years ago. She said the bank failures have created a economic depression affecting all the country as well as countries in other parts of the world.

I have to admit I don't feel sorry for James. Since he'd become a partner in the company, he was even more stuck up and mean. It's time he got his due. I found myself smiling with satisfaction as I read about his financial troubles. At the same time I'm sorry loyal employees lost their jobs when they hadn't done nothing wrong.

Here in this Tennessee county where I live, the effects of the financial situation ain't so visible. Most of the mountaineers around here has always been living off the land, making their living by the sweat of their brows. What's happening to big banks in New York don't make much difference here, at least not as far as I can see.

I opened my sweetheart's letter and my heart skipped a beat just to see her lovely handwriting. I guess James would call me a love sick puppy, too. It's for sure I'm a man in love.

Harlan, Kentucky
January 15th 1875

My dear Harvey,

Received your letter of Dec. 30th with thanks to God. Pleased to know you are well. Winter in Tennessee seems much like winter here in Harlan. Snow is ankle deep today and Papa has been knocking icicles from the edges of the roof. He said if one fell off and hit someone, it could stab like a knife.

On these winter days, I've stayed busy sewing for my hope chest. Did I tell you that Papa made me a cedar chest to hold my linens and needlework? It is beautiful. I can't wait to show it to you. I have 4 quilt tops ready for quilting. Mama plans a quilting party when the weather gets nicer. Also I have made kitchen towels and pillow cases. Miz Hutchinson down the street is giving me enough goose feathers to make 2 pillows. So you see I am working to make our little home down in that holler as cozy as can be. Please send me the window measurements so I can *make curtains.*

I am counting the days until I will be your wife—the good Lord willing.

Your bride (soon I hope)

I read her letter several times and tried to imagine what I would write in reply. She's a much better speller than me, and that makes me shy about writing her. I turned in my Bible to the Song of Solomon, Chapter 4 and read:

> *Behold, thou art fair, my love; behold thou art fair*
> *thou hast doves' eyes within thy locks:*
> *Thy hair is as a flock of goats that appear from mount Gilead.*
> *Thy teeth are like a flock of sheep that are even shorn,*
> *which came up from the washing;*
> *Whereof every one bear twins and none is barren among them.*
> *Thy lips are like a thread of scarlet, and thy speech is comely:*
> *Thy temples are like a piece of a pomegranate within thy locks.*
> *Thy neck is like a tower of David builded for an armoury,*
> *whereon there hang a thousand bucklers, all shields of mighty men.*
> *Thy two breasts are like two young roes that are twins, which feed among the lilies.*

I closed my eyes and tried to imagine saying such words to my beautiful bride. But I don't have the nerve. Maybe after we're wed, I'll at least read the words to her. How I long for the time to come. As I do ever night, I said my evening prayers asking the good Lord to look after her.

I had a good night's sleep with no nightmares. After I finished the chores this morning, I decided to try out my new gun. I called Sam and Saro and we wandered along the creek. Soon the beagles picked up a scent and took off baying with excitement. I love to hear them barking when they're on a trail. I just hoped it was a rabbit and not a polecat. I had loaded the rifle before we left the house, and I shouldered the gun, ready if they brought their prey back in my direction.

We was lucky. We got two rabbits and the gun performed to perfection much better than the first gun I ever owned: a Enfield musket 1853. My father gave it to me for my twelfth birthday in the spring of 1860. He took me to the woods hisself and taught me how to load the gun and how to shoot. I had trouble at first and missed my target, but eventually got the hang of it. When Pa was satisfied with my shooting, he made me clean my gun while he watched and coached me. He stressed the importance of taking good care of my weapon. I never forgot his lessons.

My friend, Evan had got his own gun the last Christmas. When I got mine, we decided to go on a hunting trip. Our parents gave us permission to make a overnight trip into the mountains. We packed some food, some blankets, and our ammunition and left about mid-morning after the sun chased all the fog out of the hills. We each had a hunting knife so we could dress any game we was lucky enough to kill. As we went out the door, Miz Simpson said, "If you-uns think you smell cucumbers, be careful."

"Why's that?"

"It prob'ly means they's a nest of copperheads close by."

We climbed farther up the mountain than we'd ever been before. Sometimes we had to backtrack cause we come to a cliff or ledge we couldn't climb or clumps of mountain laurel so thick we couldn't get through. By the time the sun was overhead, we hadn't seen any animals except birds. When we come to a bald with no trees, Evan looked around. "I'm hungry. Let's find a good spot to eat our dinner."

"What about that big rock over there?" I walked closer. "It's almost as big as our dining room table. This should work." It stuck out of the ground about three foot high. We climbed on the rock and put down our packs and opened up the food Pete O'Malley had prepared for us: cold biscuits, ham, hard boiled eggs, some dried apples, and some of his special blackberry jam cake.

"This is so good," Evan spoke with a mouthful, "I could eat it all right now. But we should save some in case we don't shoot a rabbit or squirrel by suppertime."

"That sun feels good." I stretched out and lay back on the warm rock. Even though it was mid-May, the air up on the mountain was quite cool—especially as we'd been in the shady woods most of the morning. I loved feeling the sun warming me up. I felt I could go to sleep right there on that rock.

I caught some movement out the corner of my eye and turned to see a huge snake slithering towards us. I yelled, "Snake!" and we both jumped off the rock and took off running like scalded dogs.

"Stupid us." Evan put his hands on his hips and shook his head. "We left all our gear up there with the snake."

"Well, we have to go get it, I reckon."

"Do you think that snake'll eat our food?"

"Nah, snakes like to catch live creatures. Wonder what kind of snake it is? Did you smell cucumbers?"

"No."

"I didn't neither, so it must not be no copperhead."

We slowly edged uphill to the right till we could see the top of the rock.

The snake had crawled right past all our stuff and curled up in the sun. Evan leaned forward to get a better look. "I think it's just a black snake. It won't bother us. He's just taking a warm nap." He started to climb on to the rock.

I couldn't let him outdo me, so I followed him. We eased up, picked up our gear, and jumped back down. The snake gave no sign it even saw us.

"You know what else we did that was stupid?"

"What's that?"

"We forgot to bring some water. I'm really thirsty."

Evan scratched his head. "They must be a spring or stream somewheres. We just have to find it." We veered off to the left and followed a ridge that branched off the main mountain and worked our way down t'other side. About halfway down, we discovered a cave that extended about a dozen feet back under a large rock. It was dry inside and the floor of the cave was covered with leaves the wind had blowed in.

"You know what, Evan? This would be a good place to camp for the night."

"You're right, but that ham made me so thirsty. Let's go on to see if we can't find some water."

We made our way around a huge clump of laurel and found ourselves standing on a cliff that extended about ten yards in each direction. The drop off was at least 20 foot, but the most surprising thing was the view. We could see below us a small valley covered in grass. I pointed to the left. "Look! There's a waterfall."

"Wonderful! How do we get down there? Looks like there's a little stream that runs away from the falls and all along that ridge on the other side of the valley. Maybe we can get to it quicker if we can figger how to get down this cliff."

We decided to go to the right and found that the cliff sorta tapered off, and we could move down the hillside by going at an angle rather than straight down. It took us quite a while, and by the time we come to the little brook we thought we'd die of thirst. "That's the sweetest water I ever tasted," Evan said, wiping water from his chin.

After we had drunk our fill, we stretched out in the shade and rested our bones. After a bit, I stood up and looked around. The little valley was about twice as long as it was wide. "How far do you think it is to the bottom of the ridge over there?" I asked.

"I don't know; it's not all that far." Evan picked up a small rock about half as large as his fist and hurled it toward the ridge. It landed little more than half way. "If we had a bow and arrow, we could easily shoot all the way across this valley."

We still hadn't found anything to shoot. I suggested we set up some sorta target and at least test our aim, but Evan wanted to check out the falls first. We walked along the little stream. At one point I stopped and looked around. "Hey, Evan," I called. "Come over here. This looks like a path animals made coming to get a drink."

Evan walked closer to the stream. "Yeah, and I see some deer tracks in the mud."

I got excited. "Maybe we can shoot a deer."

"I don't think so. Even if we killed a deer, how would we get it back home?"

"Well, at least we know this'd be a good place to hunt, and next time we could bring Milly to carry our deer back home."

Of course at that time, we had no idea how often in the future we would come to our little hidden valley to get all kinds of game: deer, wild turkeys, foxes, raccoons. We even killed a wild boar once. Some of my favorite memories of Evan are our hunting and trapping trips in that little valley. We learnt how to save the hides of the animals and sell the pelts, and we made a number of kills that provided meat for our two families.

Steep ridges on all sides almost completely surrounded the valley. At one end the falls tumbled down about 40 foot and at the other end the ridges narrowed so tight together, there wasn't hardly room for the little creek to flow out. We continued our walk toward the falls and stood there wondering if we could climb to the top when we saw something move up there.

"It's a bear!" Evan cried. I grabbed for my gun, but Evan warned me not to kill it.

"We could at least shoot our guns to scare it away."

"But that's a waste of our ammunition. Let's set up a target and practice. That way we will make good use of our mini balls and gunpowder." Evan was always more practical than me. We found a piece of a tree limb and stood it up against a fallen log at the edge of the woods. We practiced shooting from three different distances, and when we inspected our target, at least some of the bullets had hit the bull's eye. We also noticed we could no longer see the bear.

We spent several hours exploring the valley. We found lots of wild flowers, some I recognized from all Miz Simpson learnt me. In the edge of the woods I saw some wild ginger and some May apples. I pointed out some bloodroot and told Evan Miz Simpson said it was a good medicine for cleaning scrapes and cuts. Out in the grassy area we saw dandelions, some purple flowers I didn't recognize, and some wild onions. We continued to the opposite end of the valley and agreed anyone would find it difficult to enter the valley from that point, making us feel safe.

In such a narrow valley, the sun don't get above the ridge till mid to late morning and goes behind the ridge by mid-afternoon. When the shadows started moving across the valley, I yelled to Evan who stood near the creek,

"Hey, looks like it's going to get dark soon. We better make plans for our camp."

"I don't want to go back to the cave. It might belong to that bear we saw. I durther stay here in the valley."

"Let's find a place not too far from the water, maybe over there by those cottonwood trees."

On our way, we spooked a rabbit. Evan got his gun first and knocked that rabbit head over heels. We skinned him and planned to have rabbit for our supper. After we found a place we liked, we carried rocks from the creek and made our fire pit. Luckily, we had not failed to bring matches. We found sticks and pieces of dead limbs to feed our fire and drove forked sticks into the ground on either side of the fire to hold our rabbit on a spit. By the time it got really dark, we had arranged our bedding, had our fill of rabbit and leavings from our lunch, and sat by our fire enjoying the peaceful feeling of the valley. The stars started coming out and in the distance we could hear a owl hoot.

One reason this holler where I live here in Tennessee appeals to me is the peace and quiet and safe feeling I have here. No one is giving me orders or badgering me. I'm my own boss and do as I please. I really don't feel lonely much, but when I feel the need for human company, I can always hitch the buggy and go to town. Otherwise I'm happy here with my horses, a cow, chickens, and dogs.

When me and Evan got back to our house, the news of our little valley created quite a stir. Even my father hadn't realized such a valley existed. Over the next decade, this hidden valley, which we named the Back Valley, played a big part in my life.

For the next two years, Evan and I spent ever free moment roaming the mountain ridges and our Back Valley with our guns. I had convinced my father that I had learnt all I needed, and he permitted me to drop out of school, though my mother wasn't happy. Since I's now required to work full time on the farm, me and Evan didn't have as much free time as we woulda liked, but we took advantage of ever chance we had. We both bragged to our older brothers of our hunting successes. We had both become good shots. Even James had to admit that we'd made some impressive kills, but we never did get a bear. Those months was the best of my life, I think. Me and Evan become close as brothers.

In the weeks after we found the cave, we explored it thoroughly. After we raked the leaves out, we found arrow heads and bones and spent hours spinning tales of the Indians who had used this cave. Many nights we sat by our fire at the mouth of the cave sharing our hopes and dreams. We got to know ever ridge and mountain peak on the property. We learnt where to find hazelnuts, hickory nuts, walnuts, and chestnuts. We found where the best blackberries and huckleberries growed. We even found a small grove of chinquapins. Miz Simpson and Pete O'Malley made good use of the nuts and fruit we brought home as they prepared foods for holidays and special occasions.

Miz Simpson also helped us find a large bed of what she called "sang," but many years later I learnt its real name was ginseng. She showed us when and how to dig the roots without killing the plants so they would keep growing. She dried some of the roots to keep in her store of yerbs for medicines. She often made a tea from the roots when she assisted a woman in labor. She said it helped to keep the energy level up when the labor seemed to last too long. Me and Evan dug and dried some roots in the fall and sold them to a traveling medicine man when he come by each winter.

***

I didn't realize during that spring of 1860 events in my state and country would lead to an explosion that would change my whole life. All through that year, it seemed like the arguments between the people who was for slavery and the people who was agin it just got bigger'n bigger. People called abolitionists wanted to end slavery and that made the other side mad. One side described the evils of buying and selling human beings while slavery supporters argued slavery was a economic necessity. The slave owners claimed most masters was not really so cruel, and besides, even the Bible approved slavery.

Much of this great argument took place without my knowledge. In our backwards area, we went about our business and purty much ignored the craziness that had ahold of the rest of the country—at least I did. But as time for the national election drew nearer, I heard more about the political stands of the various candidates. While Kentucky was considered a slave state, the number of slaves was much smaller than in most of the Southern states, but the stubborn Kentucky citizens stuck to their different opinions like two dogs fighting over a bone. Any time a group of people gathered, an argument would break out and often turned into fist fights or even gun fights. Neighbors quit speaking to each other. Even family members took different sides in the dispute, and some feuds got started that lasted long after the war was over.

One night when me and Evan was camping in the Back Valley I ask him what he thought about slavery. "We love our slaves," Evan said. "Old Bob and Sara sleep in a room behind the forge, but the rest of the time they're in our house just like family. Sara took care of me as a baby, and when my mother died, she become like a mother to me. To tell the truth, I can't even remember much about my mother. Sara and Old Bob have always ate at our table with us, and they set beside our fire each evening. We need them, and we take good care of them. They help us and we help them. I don't know what we'd do if someone took them away from us."

"But remember? Mr. Baker told us at school that some plantation owners have hundreds of slaves. He said they live in little shacks with dirt floors and are made to labor in the fields in the hot sun from dawn to dark. If they run away and get caught, sometimes the master whips them to a inch of their lives or brands them with a hot iron or might even cut off part of their foot, so they can't run or walk very fast."

"I know that, but I don't think it's fair to make us give up our slaves because some other masters is so cruel. I get scared sometimes. Last week Mr. Wilkins, who runs the grist mill, come into the store and started a argument with my brother. He said him and his family would never come to trade with us again because we have two slaves. He even hinted that he might help them run away."

I sympathized with Evan. I had ate delicious meals at his house that Sara fixed. I could see she loved Evan and treated him like her own child. Old Bob was always nice to me. He showed me how to make horseshoes and nails in the forge. He let me use the bellows to blow the fire into hot flames. I could see how having Sara and Old Bob was a help to all of them. I agreed that it wouldn't be fair to make the Jacksons give up their slaves.

The slavery debates worried my mother. She didn't say much, but when she would hear Pa and Uncle Stuart discussing the political situation in the country, I saw the frown and the worry lines in her face. I overheard her tell Pa she would feel much safer in Pennsylvania.

When she found out the Bakers was moving over the mountain to Harlan to be closer to Mistress Baker's parents, she couldn't hide her disappointment. She and Mistress Baker had become good friends—the only close friend Ma had in Kentucky—and with the loss of that important friendship, she had even fewer reasons to stay in Kentucky. Pa didn't exactly forbid her to go, but he urged her to stay saying he really needed her to help keep things going, and she agreed to stay, at least for the time being. She and Mistress Baker have wrote each other regular all the years since.

I remember one of the first letters Ma got from Mistress Baker after they moved. She told how the folks in their new community didn't seem to know what the name of their settlement was. Older settlers called it Mount Pleasant. But when the village got a post office, they found out there was already a place called that, so the post office was called Harlan Court House. Mistress Baker allowed as how she was just gonna call it Harlan. She also said almost everbody she talked to there was in favor of slavery, but almost nobody had any slaves.

***

If tomorrow's a purty day, I need to do some worsh. I always put off worshing clothes as long as possible cause it's such a hard job. I carry many buckets of water from the spring about fifty yards away to fill a very large iron kettle that sets on some stones back of the house. I build a fire under the kettle and when the water gets hot, I dip out several gallons into a worsh tub. Then I scrub the clothes with lye soap on a worsh board. After I rinch the clothes in a large zinc tub, I hang them to dry over a rope line stretched between two trees. On the coldest winter days, the clothes freeze stiff as a board hanging right on the line.

The whole process takes all day, the very strong lye soap leaves my hands red and raw, and my back hurts from stooping over the worsh tub. I must have no clean clothes at all to finally get myself to take a day for worshing. In fact, I sometimes wear the same clothes till they smell and are shiny with dirt. I'm at that point now, so tomorrow I must get to it.

As a boy, I never paid much attention to how my clothes got clean till the summer I was twelve. Miz Morgan done our laundry. Clean clothes appeared in my chifforobe like magic, but that summer Miz Morgan was expecting, and as she neared her time, she was not able to do the heavy lifting and back breaking scrubbing. My mother assigned me to help Cousin Maybelle do the worshing. Sometimes Caleb also helped us.

I hadn't give much thought to how clever my father and uncle had chose the site for the house till I got involved in helping with the worshing. I realized they had built the house near a spring located on the hill back of the house. They'd built a wood trough that carried the spring water to a large cistern located under the outdoor kitchen. Miz Simpson and Pete O'Maley could use the hand pump to draw up water for their cooking.

A second wood trough carried water to the worsh house. On worsh day, we just had to open the trough to the worsh house, and water come pouring into our big iron pot which set atop a brick fire box. We also had two huge zinc tubs for rinching. We built a fire under the kettle and heated the water for scrubbing the bed linens from our house and the bunk house. It took half a day just to do that. If the weather was fit, we hung them on a outdoor line to dry. In bad winter weather, we had lines strung in the worsh house where they could dry. On another day we'd worsh the family's clothing, and still another day we devoted to worshing the clothing for the hired hands. Their clothes got so dirty we had to use a battlin stick to beat out the dirt.

Then there was ironing. We heated the irons over the fire in the worsh house. After I scorched a few things, Ma said, "Go work in the garden and leave the ironing to me and Cousin Maybelle. I begun to feel sorry for Miz

Morgan who had been doing our worshing for two years, especially because it was so hot in the worsh house. I couldn't hardly stand it. After her baby boy was born, Pa hired a lady from town to come in three days each week to do the heavy work and Miz Morgan did the ironing. I still don't do no ironing. I just wear my clothes the way they come off the line.

CHAPTER 5

February 1875

Campbell Holler, Tennessee

As I fixed a fence yesterday, I saw trillium growing beside a fallen log in the edge of the woods. It reminded me of all the time I spent helping our gardener in the yerb garden when I's eleven or twelve. She took me to the woods and pointed out all the spring plants. She'd say, "You see that? When you see the trillium coming up, it's time to start getting the garden ready." I don't remember all the plants she showed me, but I do look for a few of my favorites, and when I see trillium, I always think of Miz Simpson.

Now that the weather's got better, I aim to work on the new ground I cleared of trees last fall, so I can turn it into pasture for my animals. When I chose this place to settle, I knowed the trees was valuable. I've used trees from my land to build all the buildings. The limbs too small to use for lumber, I made into fire wood and kindling. I learnt from my father's lumber business how to clear the land and use the trees.

Yesterday was my father's birthday; if he had lived, he would be 67. He was a strict father, often impatient, quick to lose his temper, sometimes hard headed and stubborn, but I knowed he cared for me. He was a man of many interests and skills—built his lumber company from nothing into a successful business that made him rich. He was smart and interested in the business and political issues of the day. He traveled all over the state of Kentucky making business deals and involving hisself in state affairs. I know he musta been disappointed I didn't take to school like the other boys. Book learning always seemed too hard for me to catch on to. My mother quit trying to teach me correct English when I quit school. The truth is I didn't want to sound like a educated man. If education made people act like James, I didn't want nothing to do with it. But I did admire my Pa; I thought he didn't let his education make him uppity.

In May 1860, Pa traveled to Chicago as a delegate to the Republican presidential nominating convention. He was gone nearly a month cause he come home by way of Pittsburgh to visit Elliott and Grandma Campbell and to look into the business there. On the Sunday afternoon after he returned, Uncle Stuart, Pa, James, and Ma gathered on the shady veranda on the east side of the house as we often did after Sunday dinner. I claimed a seat near Pa as I wanted to hear about Elliott, my cousins, and other relatives in Pittsburgh. William stayed in his room to write a letter to Holly.

At first the conversation turned to catching up on our relatives. But when Uncle Stuart got his pipe lit, he ask, "Well, did the convention turn out like you thought it would?" We all knowed Pa's pick for president was William Seward of New York. That's what he'd been saying for over a year.

Pa frowned. "Unfortunately, Seward didn't win the nomination. Abraham Lincoln from Illinois hoodwinked him." He paused and smoked his pipe a bit. "Actually it was Lincoln's campaign team that did the trickery since the candidates themselves didn't attend the convention."

"What sort of tricks did Lincoln's men do?"

Pa looked at me and smiled. "For one thing they had the advantage of being from the host state. Lincoln's team managed to arrange where the delegates from each state would sit, and they made sure the New York delegation was surrounded by states that didn't have many delegates for Seward. That made it more difficult for Seward's supporters to persuade delegates to change their votes for the second ballot."

"That doesn't seem so down and dirty to me. Sounds like they were just playing it smart." Uncle Stuart chuckled. "Everybody knows politicians are great tricksters."

"But that wasn't all they did. They printed up a bunch of fake tickets and passed them out to Lincoln supporters. They told them to come early and fill the seats so Seward's delegates would have no place to sit."

Uncle Stuart made a face. "Now that's getting dirty."

Pa nodded. "New York had 70 delegates and all had pledged to vote for Seward. I guess Seward thought his team backed up with all those delegates and supporters would go to Chicago and win the nomination for him." Pa stopped to relight his pipe. "But they made one bad mistake."

"What was that?" For some reason the dirty work and bad mistakes fascinated me.

"Instead of working to win over delegates from other states for the second ballot as Lincoln's team was doing, Seward's team threw a big champagne party the night before the first ballot. So the next day Lincoln's team was prepared to get lots of votes on the second ballot, but Seward's delegates had failed to secure enough second ballot votes."

Ma seemed puzzled. "But didn't Seward have more support than Lincoln? I thought he was expected to win."

"He was expected to win, and he had more votes on the first ballot than any other candidate, but not enough to win the nomination. Even after the second ballot, no candidate had enough votes to get the nomination."

Ma looked disappointed. "So Lincoln finally won on the third ballot?"

Pa puffed on his pipe and nodded.

"Then I guess Lincoln is the Republican candidate," James said, "but can he win the election?"

Pa held up his hands in a frustrated gesture. "I talked with several members of the party about that. They think since the platform does not outlaw slavery in the southern states, maybe they can win over some Southern voters. They also are hoping that the split in the Democratic Party will prevent either of the Democratic candidates getting enough votes. But we shall see."

"Pa," I asked, "Will you vote for Mr. Lincoln?"

James stood up. "I don't know anyone in Kentucky who'll vote for him even though Lincoln was actually born in this state. Most people I've talked to are in favor of John Bell." He turned toward Ma. "Thanks for a good dinner, Ma. I'm going to see if any of the fellows want to go fishing." He pointed his finger at me as if to say, "I'm going to get you." Fortunately, I had grown to nearly his height in the last year, so it wasn't as easy for him to push me around. And I took care to stay out of his way, so I ignored his evil look.

No one said nothing for a few moments after James left. I watched a butterfly flitting around the climbing rose bush that covered the lattice work at the end of the patio. Then Ma asked, "What do you think will happen if Lincoln is elected? Will the South carry out their threat to secede? And if they do, what will Kentucky do?"

Pa stood and walked to the edge of the veranda where he knocked the ashes out of his pipe. "I met with Governor Magoffin in Frankfort on my way home. I don't have much faith in him. His sympathy is with the South, but he has no control over the legislature, so what the state does will depend on the legislature, not Magoffin. I don't know what to expect, but if the Southern states do secede, I think the country will go to war. The Republican platform is strongly for preserving the Union, and I believe they'll fight to keep the country together."

As I sat there and listened to this discussion, I had no idea what would be happening in the coming months. If I ever thought about war, it was to think of glorious heroes carrying the flag to victory. I certainly had a lot to learn, and I learnt it in a very hard way.

Uncle Stuart stood, thanked Ma for the dinner, and picked up his hat. "I'm gonna go flag the trees we'll be taking down tomorrow. We have a good start on having a large batch of logs to float down river when the floods come."

***

Earlier today, I went to town to collect my mail. I'm pleased to say I had another letter from my sweet bride.

Harlan, Kentucky
February 7th 1875

My dearly Beloved,

Your letter arrived today and thrilled my heart. I really wish it weren't so long until we will be together forever. Each day seems longer than the day before. Your letter made me long for that day to come more than ever, so I sat right down and counted the days till May 20. Can you believe it is 101 days? I immediately wished I hadn't counted because 101 seems like so long. But I will mark them off one day at a time and watch the days dwindle down to zero!

I have chosen blue calico material for our curtains. Mama has helped me cut the material to the sizes you sent for our windows. I should have them finished in a few days. My next project is to use some worn out clothes to tear into strips which I will crochet into rugs for our floors. Soon my hope chest will be full to overflowing. I'm so excited about making our little cottage beautiful and comfortable for us.

You won't believe what my Aunt Sue gave me last Sunday. You remember that she taught me to play her mandolin. Sunday afternoon she came to our house and gave me her precious instrument. She said I had learned to play it so well I deserved to have it. She said rheumatism had crippled her hands until she couldn't play it anymore. I am so excited.

Mama is helping me write down all her favorite recipes in a book, and I am practicing making all of them. I look forward to cooking all your favorite meals. I can imagine you and me finishing our evening meal and sitting on the porch together in the twilight listening to the birds. By the way, does our house have a porch? I hope so because I love a porch.

I hope I get another letter from you soon. I love your letters and I love you.

May our God watch over you. Genesis 31: 49

Your Doodlebug

It tickles me how she uses my pet name for her. Ever time I see "Doodlebug" I can't help but grin. That letter really perked me up. Calling me "dearly beloved" almost brought tears to my eyes. I can honestly say no other person has ever called me that. I can't think of anyone else who ever said I was loved except my mother. I know my father loved me in his way and William also treated me with great care, but neither ever said those precious words.

When I finally got up my nerve to ask her to marry me, I was scared she would say "No." But she simply said, "When you get a nice house built, I would love to marry you." I was even more amazed when she let me kiss her.

I do find that mandolin troublesome. I believe fiddles and mandolins is instruments of the devil, but I won't say nothing about it now. I don't want to upset my bride. That can wait.

I turned back to her letter once more and realized I needed to get busy adding a porch to the house.

***

After Pa come back from the Republican Convention back in the summer of 1860, the talk of politics grew even more intense. I got tired of Mr. Morgan and Larry arguing about who should be president. Mr. Morgan favored the Southern Democrat candidate, John C. Breckenridge, a Kentuckian.

"But he supports slavery, so nobody in the North will vote for him. He can't get enough votes to win. The country'll be better off choosing John Bell from Tennessee," Larry argued. "He's the candidate for the Constitutional Union party, and if he's elected he'll keep the Southern states in the union."

"But Bell's got a huge plantation with a whole lotta slaves. What makes him better'n Breckenridge?"

I couldn't stand to hear any more. "Will you two quit jawing about the election? I'm so sick of hearing it. I'll be so happy when the election is over, and I won't have to listen to this talk no more."

Mr. Morgan stopped hoeing and looked at me. "You're old enough to understand politics. Who's elected will make a big difference in the future of this country. You should care about that."

"It ain't got nothing to do with me. Who's president won't change nothing."

Mr. Morgan chuckled. "Wait and see. If the country gets divided and war breaks out, you'll see how much things'll change."

"What makes you think you know what's gonna happen? You're just a farmer. You can't tell the future." I was angry. I didn't like to be lectured. Looking back, I know now I shoulda listened to him.

Meanwhile life went on. While the loggers continued bringing down trees, the farm team kept the weeds chopped out of the corn, made hay, tended to the tobacco, cared for the animals, mended fences, and on rainy days oiled harness and saddles. I really hated it when I had to pick the tobacco worms off the leaves. I also hated to clean out the stables and spread the manure on the fields. Picking up the rocks in the fields didn't give me a thrill neither. Some days I would get so hot and smelly I couldn't stand myself, and I'd run to the swimming hole and dive in clothes and all.

I continued to help Miz Simpson in the garden. Sometimes I got so tired of working daylight to dark, I even wished I hadn't quit school. But now I can see how that hard work helped me. I'd grown much stronger, I'd learnt how to do all the work of farming, and I's learning that I needed to do my share as a member of the team. When I messed up, Mr. Morgan was patient with me, and he bragged on me when I done good.

***

Since the Bakers had moved away, more women called on Miz Simpson to help them in giving birth as there wasn't no other midwife in the community. Sometimes if it seemed a difficult case, Ma would go along to help her, and sometimes they would ask me to drive the buggy. Of course, I wasn't allowed into the birth room, but I carried wood to keep the fire going and made sure to have plenty of hot water.

Miz Simpson always took her bag with various yerbs and some clean towels and rags. If she knew the family was dirt poor, she brought a small quilt as a gift. The bag also held a clean cup for making tea, and she always took a axe to put under the bed to cut the pain. Sometimes, especially if Ma didn't go, she would ask me to get certain yerbs from the bag and make a cup of tea—raspberry leaf tea would slow bleeding, catnip tea for pain and to relax the body, shepherds purse tincture to stop bleeding. She also made massage oil perfumed with lavender, which she carried along.

I had helped her gather and dry leaves and roots from our yerb garden and from various places in the forest. It made me feel important to be trusted to help with the medicines. I knew I had to be careful to follow instructions exactly, and as far as I know I never made a mistake.

I recollect one time me and her was coming home on a hot summer night. It'd been a difficult birth, and we was past midnight getting started for home. But Miz Simpson wouldn't leave till she was sure Miz Gilbert's bleeding was normal and the baby was nursing good. As we approached the cemetery beside the church, she ask me if I believed in ghosts.

I wasn't sure what I believed, but Ma always said they's no such things, so I said, "No, I don't."

"That shows what you know. I used to live in a haunted house. We had a friendly ghost who liked to play tricks. He was the ghost of a little boy who'd lived in the house many years earlier and died of smallpox."

"What sort of tricks did he play?"

"Mr. Simpson lost his spectacles once and hunted for them for days. Finally he found them hanging from a peg behind the door by a piece of red yarn."

"That's strange. How do you know someone else didn't put them there?"

"Me and Mr. Simpson was the only ones living there, and we hadn't had no visitors. Another time Johnny—that's what we called him—took my bonnet and put it on the lamp beside the kitchen table. When I first saw it, I thought it was a person setting there. So yes, I believe in ghosts."

We was quiet for a few minutes. Then she asked, "Do you know who Miz Donaldson is?"

"Never heard of her. Who's she?"

"She's the mother of a woman, whose baby I helped deliver one night last winter. They live in the holler after you pass the bridge on Dexter Creek. While we waited for her daughter's labor to progress, she told me so many stories she liked to talked my arm off. I's relieved when her daughter's labor picked up and she had other things to do than talk, talk, talk.

One story she claimed really happened to her son. She said her son and a friend was coming home on a cold winter day from taking corn to the grist mill. They saw a boy standing in the edge of the woods without a coat. He looked half froze, so they stopped and ask him if he wanted a ride into town. He said he did, and he climbed into the back of the wagon. Miz Donaldson said her son took off his coat and handed it to the boy because he looked so cold. They ask him where he lived and he said two houses past the forge."

She stopped talking for a bit as she took off her bonnet and fanned her face. "When they got to his house, they turned to look and he wasn't in the wagon. They thought he musta jumped off before they stopped, but they couldn't see him nowhere. They went up on the porch and saw a rocking chair beside the door gently rocking and her son's coat hanging on the back of the chair. They knocked on the door and after a few minutes a pale young woman opened the door. They explained what had happened and ask if the boy had come inside."

I begun to think Miz Simpson was talking as much as Miz Donaldson. It seemed like her story would go on forever, but she'd made me curious so I ask, "What did the woman say?"

"She said the boy was her son, but he'd fell through the ice in the creek two years ago and drowned. His grave is right over there in the cemetery. She said on cold winter days he wants to come home to get warm." I shivered in spite of the heat.

Miz Simpson looked at me and nodded. "The next time I was at the church I went out to the cemetery and found his grave. So I guess that's a true story."

I wasn't convinced, so the next day I told my mother the story and she laughed. "I heard that story as a girl back in Pennsylvania except it was a little girl that had drowned. That's the sort of tall tale those old men who hang around the stove at the trading post like to tell."

"But Ma, Miz Simpson said she had saw the grave."

"The fact a child is buried in the cemetery doesn't mean the rest of the story's true."

But I still had my doubts, and I'm not totally convinced there ain't no ghosts, even today.

***

My father liked to brag his tobacco was as good or even better than what the big tobacco farmers up around Lexington raised. He took a big interest in ever part of the growing process. He had made a bed for growing tobacco plants with sideboards about a foot high and fixed a cover for the bed from glass window sashes. In late winter, we piled dead limbs from trees in the tobacco bed and set it afire to kill the weeds and bugs. After the ashes was raked away, he planted the seeds. The glass cover helped keep the earth warm and protected the tender plants from frost.

When the cold weather was over and the tobacco plants was big enough to plant in the field, we prepared the tobacco patch real good—plowed and then smoothed it level. We laid off rows about two foot apart. We planted the tobacco seedlings from the bed in the rows, one bout ever two foot. It was my job to carry water for the plants. All summer, if we'd had no rain for a week, I had to water ever one of those plants. And if no rain come within four more days, I had to water them again. It was backbreaking work.

If Pa checked the tobacco patch and found weeds or wilted plants, he called Mr. Morgan into his office and really laid him out. Then Mr. Morgan gave me, Larry, and Scott the devil. It didn't take many times of that till we kept the tobacco looking good. We had to go through the patch and inspect each leaf for budworms and hornworms. I hated that about the worst thing. Then near the middle of July the plants would start to bloom. Before more than one or two buds opened up, we had to cut the bloom stem off. We called it topping.

"Why do we have to do this?" I complained.

Mr. Morgan explained, "If the plant blooms, it puts its energy into making seeds instead of giving nourishment to the leaves."

We also had to pull off the suckers that would grow out where the leaves joined the stalk. Like the blooms, the suckers took the nourishment from the leaves. As soon as a sucker was long enough to get ahold of, we'd pull it off. Not a week went by all summer that we wasn't out there tending to the tobacco plants.

Really, growing tobacco took most of the year—from planting the seeds in the plant bed in late winter till taking the tobacco to sell late in the year. Three or four weeks after we done the topping, the leaves started turning yellow. When almost all the leaves was yellow, we cut the stalks down and hung them in the barn. We let them hang for several weeks till the stalks dried out and turned brown. We had doors in the barn that we opened and closed to regulate the heat and moisture. Each day Mr. Morgan watched the weather and often sent me to open or close the doors.

Before it could go to market, we had to strip the leaves from the stalk by hand, and then sort them by quality, and pack them for shipment. Pa always supervised the stripping hisself. He made sure the leaves was separated into the proper grades. My job was to carry the empty stalks and scatter them over the tobacco patch. The next spring we would plow them under. Most years we had the tobacco stripped and packed up by the first of December. If Pa got a good price, he gave all the hired hands who had worked the tobacco a bonus—even me.

***

The Presidential election was held Tuesday, November 6, 1860. This time the men all rode horses instead of taking the wagon and they took their guns. They started early and got back a little after dark. Prob'ly cause they was armed, they had no trouble getting to vote, but later we heard a man was killed when a big argument broke out. I was glad it was finally over. Now maybe people would settle down and quit making such a big fuss.

We didn't learn the results for several weeks. Even though Pa had supported Lincoln and was glad he won, he was disappointed when John Bell carried Kentucky. Pa come home from going for the mail with a copy of *The Louisville Courier Journal* which told of fights and protests in several towns when they heard the election results. Many people was predicting the South would secede and we would have a war.

I didn't care about the election, but I was disappointed when Ma told me Elliott wouldn't be coming home for Christmas. Pa wasn't able to go get him, and they thought it wasn't safe for him to travel alone. On

Christmas Eve we learnt that South Carolina had seceded a few days earlier. We saw the New Year in without much encouragement life would get better, but we had no idea how bad it would be.

CHAPTER 6

March 1875

Campbell Holler, Tennessee

Been busy lately. Repaired old fences. Built new fences for the new pasture I cleared last fall. Most important, the porch is half done. Two neighbors was helping me, and we was planning to work today, but it's pouring rain. I promised to work for them one day for each day they work for me. I'm grateful I could find men willing to help me.

When I come here three years ago and begun building, my cousin Chester come and lived with me for two years. The first summer, we lived in a tent while we built the house. We cut down trees and snaked the logs down the side of the ridge. We rubbed the logs with sand till they was smooth as ice on the creek. After we got the logs prepared, we had a house raising where neighbors helped put up the walls. We made the logs air tight with mortar. We built a typical log house with two rooms and put in glass windows. We carried rocks from the nearby creek to build the fireplace and chimbley. I'm really grateful to Chester for helping me for those two years.

I know this house ain't as good as the houses I lived in in Pennsylvania and Kentucky. But it's the best I can offer my betrothed under the circumstances. I hope she'll like the bed stead I made. I worked on it for weeks last winter. I used beautiful cedar wood that has such a purty finish.

I even carved dogwood blossoms in the headboard. I pray the good Lord she'll be happy here. We'll be better off here than many people who suffered so many losses in the terrible war.

The war changed my life in ways I could never imagine. I remember clearly the day in mid-April 1861 when my father come home from a trip to Pennsylvania and brought several newspapers. I come into the house after feeding my new beagle pups and found my mother, Uncle Stuart, James and William gathered in the parlor reading the papers.

Before I got to the parlor door, I heard Ma's voice. "Why would they fight each other? Aren't they all Americans? It's like fighting your own family."

I looked around the room. "Who's fighting?"

James lowered his paper and looked at me with his usual scorn. "The country's at war. Don't you know anything?"

I stood beside Ma. "What's he talking about?"

Ma made room for me to set beside her on the love seat. "The Confederacy has attacked Fort Sumter in South Carolina and forced the United States to surrender the fort. It looks like there'll be a war between the United States and the Confederate States."

"Why don't our new President stop it?"

William come and knelt beside me. "President Lincoln and his advisors have tried, but the Southern states have withdrawn from the United States and formed a country of their own called the Confederate States of America. President Lincoln believes their country is not legal, and he wants the North and South to stay one country."

"Not only that, the Rebels have taken over forts, arsenals, ships, post offices and other property of the United States all over the South." Uncle Stuart frowned and pointed to his paper. "This article says President Lincoln has ordered 75,000 militiamen from the states to report to his command. His advisors think they can put down the rebellion in 90 days."

It all seemed far away. I didn't understand why they was sounding so upset. How could what was happening hundreds of miles away matter to us. But in the coming weeks, I watched my family become more upset. My pa announced one evening that Kentucky Governor Magoffin had declared the state was neutral and wouldn't send troops to either the Union or the Confederacy. The Governor also said neither the Union nor the Confederacy could move troops through the state.

Pa gave half a chuckle. "That's what he thinks. Kentucky is right in the middle between these two armies. You can bet that we'll be invaded from both sides."

That sounded more serious to me. Did that mean armies would be marching right through our village? Soon I discovered Pa was right. Federal troops come from Ohio and Confederate troops come from

Tennessee. I overheard conversations between my family and hired hands and begun to put the pieces together. Ma said it wasn't safe for us to travel to Pittsburgh because Union troops occupied several cities along the Ohio River, and they was battles on the river between Confederate and Union ships.

Mr. Morgan and Larry argued constantly. As I look back on it now, I guess they sorta enjoyed the jawing at one another, but at the time it upset me. Howsomever, I did learn some of what was going on from them. I recollect one particular day when we was hoeing corn. Larry started it when he said, "I guess you ain't too happy the election last month put a majority of Union men in the state legislature, and now they voted to support the Union."

Mr. Morgan stopped hoeing and looked up at Larry. He took off his hat and rubbed his forehead. "Well I guess you know that's because the Yankee troops kept Southern sympathizers from voting. But that don't bother me none. In case you ain't heard, a Confederate general name of Zollicoffer done brought in his troops from Tennessee and made a camp over at Cumberland Ford. What the state legislature does ain't gonna stop them."

That scared the willies outta me. "You mean they's going to fight right here in our state?"

"Course. They's already fighting in this state." Mr. Morgan looked at me. I guess he saw I was getting upset. "Oh, don't worry Harvey, they ain't likely to come close to here."

Later I learnt it wasn't just Confederate invaders who was fighting in Kentucky—even some Kentucky citizens was joining in. Larry started taunting Mr. Morgan again.

"I heard some of your Southern sympathizers is organizing to secede from Kentucky and join the Confederacy."

Mr. Morgan smiled. "Why, I guess you're right. They's a whole bunch of people a ways east of here that don't agree with Mr. Lincoln and his gang. They aim to elect their own governor and apply to join the Confederacy."

"You mean they're taking part of our state and giving it to another country?" I didn't understand how that was possible.

By the end of the summer1861, several of the hired hands told Pa they was leaving to join the army, some to join the Union forces and some to join the Confederates. Pa offered them a bonus to stay till the tobacco was in the barn, but most decided to go. Fortunately, Mr. Morgan and Mr. Simpson stayed. I heard Ma say she thought their wives prob'bly persuaded them not to go. Caleb, Jake, and Pete O'Malley stayed, but all the other hired hands left. That meant both the logging crew and the farm crew was cut way back. Pa and Uncle Stuart decided to have everbody work on the farm till the crops was harvested and the tobacco was ready for market.

That fall me and Evan planned a camping trip to the Back Valley. We was gone two days. We spent one night near the falls and the other night in the cave. We took our dogs with us and they treed some coons and rabbits. We was quite proud of the three coon hides and five rabbit hides we saved to stretch and cure so we could sell them when the trader come to town. On the second night we made camp early and built a fire in the mouth of the cave. We sat there staring at the fire and talking for hours. At one point, Evan leaned towards me. "If I tell you something, will you promise not to tell nobody."

I raised my right hand. "I swear I won't tell."

Evan looked a little shy, like he didn't know whether to tell me, but finally he looked up. "My brothers joined the Confederate Army. They left two weeks ago, but I wasn't supposed to tell nobody. I guess everbody knows Pa has slaves, but he tries not to offend nobody on either side. He made me promise not to tell."

"I promise. I'll not tell a soul." And I didn't ever tell nobody, but the word got around somehow. Later Evan told me strangers come around asking questions. It was a scary time. You didn't know who you could trust. And then, a few days later when the men was in the barnyard getting ready to go to the tobacco field, six or seven men in uniform rode into the yard with their rifles raised. The man with the fanciest uniform asked, "Who's in charge here?"

Uncle Stuart told me to go get Pa. When me and Pa got back, there was a dispute going on. Uncle Stuart yelled, "Who are you to demand we give you our horses?"

"I'm Captain Hatfield of the State Guard. We've been commissioned to procure horses, cows, and hogs to support the troops."

"Commissioned by whom?" Pa was upset.

The Captain pointed his gun at Pa. "The State of Kentucky established the State Guard last year. It's our job to protect the citizens and round up support for the troops."

"But which troops are you supporting?"

"The Confederate troops. Now we want one horse, one cow, and one hog." All the armed men raised their guns.

"Now wait a minute," Pa said, "The State Legislature earlier this year voted for Kentucky to support the Union and declared war on the Confederacy. How can you say you are representing the state?"

"Enough of this chatter!" The captain motioned to his men. "You take that roan horse over there," He pointed to another. "Go get a cow from the pasture by the creek." He pointed his gun at me. "You show Corporal MacDugle where you keep the hogs."

I was horrified. I couldn't move. I watched as a man dismounted and walked toward Scout. "Don't take my horse!" I run screaming my head off and grabbed Scout's halter.

The captain pointed his gun at Pa. "Control your son or we'll take two horses." Pa come to me and prised my hands loose and drug me away. He told William to show the man to the hog lot. I fell to the ground shaking with sobs.

We watched as they led Scout and the cow away. A couple of the men herded the hog along towards the road. Then just before he turned to leave, the captain seemed to see Caleb for the first time. "Maybe we should take your slave, or maybe we should conscript some of these fine fellers for the Confederate Army."

He laughed at the horror on our faces, "We'll save that for the next time," and he turned his horse and rode towards the road.

Pa told me later they's actually three groups of them bushwhackers. Besides the State Guard, they's a group called Home Guard that claims to be for the Union and a third group was just ruffians and thugs who like to torment people. These gangs made life miserable for people all over the state—stealing property, burning houses and business, and forcing young men to join an army. If they forced you with a gun in your back to take the oath to join the army, you was stuck. The penalty for desertion was execution. If you did manage to desert, the bushwhackers would hunt you down. Later I learnt most Southern states was also plagued with such gangs.

Pa wasn't gonna risk another raid. The next day he told Uncle Stuart to get ready to build a cabin in the Back Valley. For the next several weeks we worked ever day building a one-room cabin far enough away from the creek it wouldn't get flooded when the big rains come. We also built corrals for the horses and cows. While us men worked in the Back Valley, Ma, Miz Simpson, and Cousin Maybelle begun cutting the tobacco. They loaded it on the sled and Milly pulled it to the barn where they unloaded it, but they wasn't able to hang it. So ever day Mr. Morgan, Mr. Simpson, and Jake come home in time to hang the cut stalks. I can still see those three women out there in the hot sun, bonnets shading their faces, whacking away at those stalks.

By the time of the first frost we had moved most of the horses, cows and hogs to the valley. Ma rounded up bedding, cook pots, dishes and spare pieces of furniture. Caleb would live in the cabin to keep an eye on things and to stay out of sight of any other raiders that might come. And they did come. The State Guard come again and took Milly and one of Mr. Morgan's horses we had kept in the barn. They wanted to know what we had done with all our livestock. Pa said, "I guess somebody musta beat you to them."

When the Home Guard come, I recognized Bart Woodson, the feller who wanted to work as a logger and almost got Jake and Luke killed. He pointed his gun at me and grinned. "Remember me?" He had his men look in the barn and fields but they could find only one cow. "Where's all your horses and cows? I know you got more'n one cow."

Pa shrugged his shoulders. "Take the cow and get off my land."

At other times thieves stole chickens and bushels of corn right out of the field. One night we heard the dogs barking and Pa saw some fellers trying to raid the smokehouse. He shot his gun in the air and they run off yelling, "Don't shoot!" But we didn't suffer as many losses as some others in the state. And none of the raiders discovered the Back Valley.

***

I got another letter from my bride. Her and her mother's making a lotta wedding plans. The wedding will be at their home. They plan to invite all their neighbors and friends, and there'll be a party after the ceremony. I ain't too excited about a big crowd and a hifalutin party. I ain't seen her since last fall when I visited her, and we set the date for our wedding. I just want to be with her. Get the ceremony done and get back here to start our life together. But I guess I'll just force myself to grin and try to look like a happy bridegroom. I ain't wanting to upset her or her family on our wedding day. But I do wish we could skip all that tomfoolery. I don't know how to act around people like that, and I get real anxious, especially when they's strangers.

In her letter she ask me what color I wanted her wedding dress to be. What do I know about wedding dresses? I think she's beautiful in any color, but I'll tell her to make it blue, the color of the sky. And I guess I need to start thinking about how to get myself a wedding suit. I ain't had any dress up clothes since I went to James' wedding nine years ago. I'll ask that preacher down at the Baptist church where he gets his Sunday-go-to-meeting clothes next time I see him.

I also had a letter from my mother. She had planned to come to our wedding, but now Grandma Campbell's very sick, and she can't leave her. I wish she could come. I ain't seen her since I moved here. I been looking forward to seeing her, so I'm disappointed. I'm also sorry my Grandma Campbell's not well. She must be getting pretty old by now. Ma said she was sending me something special to be my wedding gift to my bride. I'm very curious about what that could be, but I guess I'll have to wait till it gets here.

I just looked out the window and seen the sun shining, but it's still raining. Miz Simpson used to say "If it rains when the sun is shining, it'll rain again the next day." If it does rain again tomorrow, I guess working on the porch will be put off again. I hope we can get the porch finished soon because I want to have time before the wedding to dig a root cellar in the hill behind the house. It will be big enough to hold our root vegetables, cabbages, and apples for most of the winter. I noticed yesterday that the buds was starting to swell on the apple trees I planted three years ago. Maybe they'll bear some fruit this year. If they bloom, I hope the frost don't kill them. I remember one spring in Kentucky we had a freeze so late we had no apples at all, and we had to replant most of our garden because everthing froze.

That was after most of the workers had left to join the war, so it was hard to get all those crops replanted. Fortunately, the glass cover for the tobacco plant bed kept the plants from freezing. Pa didn't say much, just started planning what to do. I know he was disappointed everbody had left, and we was so short-handed, but he seemed to accept the situation and worked around it as good as he could. He said, "Getting upset doesn't get anything done."

We was really short-handed when right after Christmas in 1861 both James and William decided to join the Union forces. Pa used his connections to get James into one of the Pennsylvania Calvary regiments since he planned to take Blaze. Because of his age and education, he soon become a Lieutenant. His regiment saw action in northern Virginia and Maryland. Of course with his luck, he served two years without so much as a scratch, although he did lose Blaze in one battle. William joined one of the infantry units from Ohio that saw action along the Mississippi River. He suffered a broken leg from a rifle ball and was reassigned to desk work at the Camp Chase Prison in Ohio until he was mustered out in late 1863.

Ma was beside herself with worry the whole time they was gone. She made them promise they would write ever week, but we didn't often get letters from them. One reason was the State Guard or other ruffians kept robbing the U. S. Mail. We never knowed when we sent a letter if it would get delivered, and my brothers claimed they wrote more letters than we got. We was sorta off the main routes through the state, so we didn't get battles in our valley or troops traveling through, but the various marauders brought enough destruction to our valley without a battle.

We had Union troops somewhere in the state from the beginning of the war to the end. While the Confederate Army never moved into the state with large forces, the state did suffer from raids of Rebel troops that come through trying to recruit soldiers and spreading destruction and terror. Besides Zollicoffer's troops that tried to set up a camp east of us, the other big Confederate raid was led by General John Morgan. He led his troops into the state from Tennessee some miles west of Laureltown. I was glad they didn't come through our valley.

***

My memory of the years after James and William left for the army gets all muddled up. I can't remember exactly when things happened. We was able to get the corn, hay, and tobacco taken care of each year, but not much logging got done, partly because somebody destroyed the sawmill at Beattyville. Pa said he wouldn't try to get it going again till the war was over. We hadn't drove no logs down the river since the hired hands left to join the army.

Miz Simpson and Pete O'Malley made a garden each year, and preserved as much food as they could. It was hard to get some foods like sugar, salt, and flour. We had our own corn ground into meal at the grist mill, and we had lots of cornbread instead of Pete's wonderful, fluffy biscuits. Because we couldn't get sugar, Pete started looking for someone that made molasses. He finally heard of some farmer over in Breathitt County that made molasses, and he let me go with him to watch the process and to buy several gallons of the brown syrup. Pa let us take the buggy and we was gone about three days.

When we finally found the place, they was in the middle of a big molasses cook off. I was fascinated by the whole process. It seemed like lots of folks come to watch. They was dozens of people just standing around. A very sweet smell filled the air and a slight breeze carried the heat from the fire towards the watchers.

First, the stalks had to be stripped of leaves and cut down. They had this mill set up where a little donkey walked around and around in a circle pulling a long pole that made the mill turn as it mashed the juice out of the stalks.

A big long pan about nine foot long was divided into three sections with a fire burning all along under the pan. They poured the juice into the first section of the pan where it begun to boil. As it boiled, foam formed on the top and the man would rake the foam off with a big paddle and put it in a bucket. They explained they would feed it to the hogs, but a bunch of little boys who come to watch got a stick and would dip it in the foaming mess and then lick the stick.

After the juice cooked in the first pan, the man would slowly move it around the partition into the next pan with his paddle. Then it cooked some more and as it cooked, the juice got thicker and darker. I don't know how the feller could tell when it was time to move the juice on to the third pan, but dreckly he moved it. At the same time he was watching the new batch of juice that had been poured into the first pan. It looked like a really hot job, hovering over those boiling pans, keeping the juice moving from one pan to the next, but he knew what he was doing. I heard one woman say he'd been making molasses for five years and hadn't let a batch burn yet.

When the man dipped his paddle into the juice in the last pan and it dripped off thick, he pulled the stopper out of a drain hole and the syrup slowly filled a small bucket. I couldn't believe how much of the syrup had cooked away, but I guess that's why it got thicker and darker as it moved through the three pans.

Pete bought four gallons from the farmer's wife, and we set out for home. Pete got very good at using the syrup in his cooking. It added a interesting flavor to so many things he made. But it didn't help the flavor of tea or coffee. I ask Pete if he thought we could make our own molasses, but he said "I don't want to go to all that work. It's too hot, takes too long to get even one gallon, and makes a big mess. I'd rather buy it from someone who will do all that hard work." I ain't sure when it was we went to see the molasses making, but it musta been in the fall sometime.

***

One thing I do remember for sure was the terrible winter of 1863. Folks said they hadn't never remembered it getting so cold. A big snow come about the first of January, and then the temperature dropped lower'n anybody could remember. All the creeks and rivers froze over. We had to go out each day and chop holes in the ice so the stock could drink. Pa was worried about Caleb and the animals down in Back Valley. They wasn't no barn down there to give shelter to the animals. Him and Mr. Simpson put on their boots and tramped over the mountain to check on things. They helped Caleb make a wind break in the edge of the woods to give some shelter for the animals and they made sure they was plenty of hay and grain feed.

Caleb assured them he had plenty of fire wood and the cabin was warm. Pa ask him if he wanted to come up to the bunk house. "No one's gonna come looking for you in this cold." But Caleb said he'd rather stay in Back Valley.

Ma was worried about William and James out in such cold on the battlefield. She prayed they was able to be somewhere warm and safe. It was later that terrible winter of 1863 when Evan come riding up on his horse. I was surprised to see him because after our brothers left for the army, we both worked daylight to dark to help our families with the work. We hadn't spent time together since late in the fall after all the crops was harvested. I thought he seemed upset about something; he was quieter'n usual, and he looked sad.

Ma asked him if they'd got a letter from his brothers yet, and he just shook his head. I ask him if they got all their tobacco sold. He finally smiled. "Yes, actually we got the best price ever from this year's crop."

It was getting close to dinner time and Ma ask him if he'd eat a bowl of soup with us. Pete could make the best bean soup in the world. Pa was not at home, so just Ma, Cousin Maybelle, Uncle Stuart, me and Evan come to the table. I know I complained when we had beans and cornbread on the steamboat. But that was pig slop compared to Pete's soup, and the cornbread was still steaming when Pete served it up with fresh churned butter.

When we finished Pete's soup, Evan thanked Ma for the dinner and said he had to be getting back. I walked out with him to get his horse. When we got into the barn, he turned to me, "I have some bad news."

I thought maybe he'd heard something about his brothers. He looked down at the dirt floor for several moments and then looked up with tears in his eyes. "Sara and Old Bob have run away."

I put my hand on his shoulder. "What happened?"

"Well, you know President Lincoln signed that Emancipation Proclamation?"

"No, what's Emancipation Proclamation?

"It set all slaves in the Confederate states free."

That's the first I'd heard about it, but I said, "Kentucky ain't a Confederate state."

"I know, but we had heard that lots of slaves in Kentucky had decided it meant they was free too, and so they was running away. But I never thought Sara would ever leave me." He shut his eyes as the tears slowly run down his face. He sniffed and wiped his arm across his cheek. "She was like my mother." He turned to me and put his head on my shoulder and sobbed.

I didn't know what to say, so I just put my arms around him and held him till he stopped sobbing. He finally looked at me. "I don't know what we'll do. It's just me and Pa to run the forge and the store and do the farming." He managed a crooked smile. "Besides, me and Pa can't cook worth a darn." He gave me another hug. "Thanks for letting me blubber. I knowed you'd understand how bad this hurts me. I just needed somebody to hold on to."

"Do you know where they went?"

"No. I was surprised the fire hadn't been made and breakfast started when I come downstairs this morning. I went around to their room and the door was standing open. They was nobody there and their clothes was all gone."

"I'm so sorry, my friend." I thought for a moment. "Is it all right for me to tell my folks?"

"Yes. And tell your mother thanks for the soup." He swung himself up on his horse and waved goodbye.

CHAPTER 7

March 1875

Campbell Holler, Tennessee

The porch is finished and it's a dandy. I made a porch swing for us to set in after supper like my little Doodlebug said and built a lattice around that end of the porch to keep it in the shade. When the weather gets a little warmer, I'll plant some morning glories to climb up the grate. I also got the root cellar dug and put doors on it.

Next Sunday is Easter Sunday. Miz Simpson always said to plant radishes, cabbage and onions before Easter Sunday, but the ground's still purty cool, and we had some rain a couple of days ago, so I'll prob'ly wait a few more days to plant. But I have the garden plowed and ready. Miz Simpson used to go by the moon for when to plant crops. I can't remember what she said to plant in the full moon and what to plant in the dark of the moon. I just plant when the dirt gets warm and it seems like the frost is over. Sometimes I get it right and sometimes I have to replant what gets froze.

Slowly I'm getting everthing ready for my beautiful bride. I've started making a pie safe, and I plan to put some shelves beside the fireplace for her cooking pots and such. I talked with that preacher, and he told me that Mr. Fritz at the trading post in town could order me a suit. It's supposed to get here sometime next month. I'm feeling encouraged that my life is about to turn around. It's about time. The Good Lord knows I had about as much bad luck as a man can take.

But I did have some more bad luck yesterday. I was in the hog pen trying to get Betsy to go in the barn because she was about to have her pigs. The pen was muddy cause we had some rain a few days ago and before I knowed it, I slipped and fell into that squishy, nasty mud. I hope the Lord will forgive me for I took his name in vain. I said "Godamighty, shit, damn and hell." The words just slipped out before I could think. I's covered in stinking mud from head to toe, and had the devil of a time getting myself back on my feet.

When I finally got Betsy in the barn, I took off my stinking muddy clothes and threw them in the creek. I'd have jumped in the creek myself, but it was too cold. I took a stick and stirred the clothes around to rinch the mud off and hung them on the fence. I'll have to put them in the worsh tub in a day or two.

I never heard much cussing when I was a boy. Ma forbid it and Pa and my brothers was careful not to cuss around her. Uncle Stuart discouraged the hired hands from cussing, so it wasn't till I was older and on my own that I heard it much, and then I heard lots. I sorta took up the habit. Sometimes it seems like a feller can't help hisself. The words just pop out.

After I got religion I remembered the Ten Commandments that Mr. Baker made us memorize, and tried to break myself of cussing. I didn't think much about religion till I met Preacher. I don't know what his real name was; we all called him Preacher. He kept telling me I needed to give my life to Jesus. He had a Bible and he let me read in it sometimes. At first I just read it cause I didn't have nothing else to do, and it helped pass the time. After a while I begun to look forward to getting a chance to read his Bible. Sometimes, when it was hard for me to understand, we talked about what it meant.

I really liked the story about Joseph. I guess it was because the same things happened to me. His brothers hated him like James hated me. At least James didn't sell me as a slave like Joseph's brothers did, but I think he prob'ly woulda if it was possible. It seemed like Joseph just kept having bad luck like me, but finally his life turned around. He got to be a rich governor and when his brothers come to him, he forgave them. I don't think I'll ever forgive James. But I hope that my life is turning around.

I went to town this morning to buy some supplies and check my mail. I got a letter from my sweetheart and a package from my Mother. Ma often sends me a package with things she thinks I can't, or won't, buy here. This package included two sets of underwear, four pairs of socks, a pocket watch that had been Pa's, and a small box covered with blue silk. I opened the box and saw a beautiful heart-shaped necklace with a gold filigree center surrounded by stones of red, white, and crystal. Ma's letter explained that this necklace had been in our family for several generations. My Grandmother Campbell wanted me to give it to my bride.

When I took it out of the box, sunlight coming through the window struck it, and suddenly rainbows radiated around the cabin. I felt tears leaking down my face. To think my Grandma Campbell wanted me to have it. What a honor to get to pass these beautiful jewels on to my beautiful bride. I put it back into the box and picked up the watch. I always admired this watch when Pa wore it in his vest pocket with the gold chain looped through the button hole and into the pocket on the other side. I wondered why she gave the watch to me instead of one of my brothers. Looking at it suddenly brought back his memory, and I begun sobbing. I had let the dogs in the house to feed them earlier, and they stood beside me looking up with those big brown eyes full of worry. I dried my tears, scratched the dogs behind their ears, and then put them outside.

I had saved my beloved's letter to read last. I sat in my favorite chair and opened it.

Harlan, Kentucky
March 15th 1875

My dearest Harvey,

It's just 66 days. When I think about it I get so excited. Last night my mother and I were trying to remember what flowers will be in bloom by our wedding day. We want to fill the house with all kinds of flowers. We thought we'd have the ceremony on the front porch with the guests seated in the front yard. Do you think that's a good idea? It would be hard to get all those people inside. We can have the party outdoors too. I don't know what we'll do if it rains. But worrying about that now won't solve anything.

The material for my dress came yesterday, and Miz

Lynch has agreed to make the dress for me. It's a beautiful color of blue and the fabric is so soft. It made me want to wrap it around me as soon as I saw it. I know you'll love it. I was glad you have ordered your suit. It pleases me that you want to look good for the wedding. I hope you haven't shaved off your beard. I love it. It makes you look so handsome. You know I've always thought you were such a good looking fellow—even when I was a little girl. I'll be so proud to be the wife of such a dashing man.

Last night I went with Mama to assist with a birth. She gets called on quite often since there's no other midwife on our side of town. The birth went well and the baby girl was so sweet. It made me wonder how many children you and I will have. How many children do you want? Since I have always been an only child, I think I want to have more than one. I've always thought I was cheated by not having any brothers or sisters. So what do you think about four? Would that be a good number?

We are having the quilting party next Saturday. We have invited all the women, and we plan to set up four quilting frames in the church. We should get all four of the quilts finished that day. Then I'll feel like I have most of the linens we will need for our new home.

This is so exciting I can hardly stand it. And I love

you to pieces!

Your Doodlebug (soon to be Miz Harvey Campbell in 66 days.)

Now that letter makes me feel like one lucky feller. It always makes me smile when she says I'm handsome. I guess when she gets here, I'll have to take more care in my dress. I plan to keep my beard, so I'm glad she likes it. But I guess I'll have to do a better job of keeping it trimmed and neat. I ordered some new shirts and shoes along with the suit, so I hope I will please her when I show up for the wedding.

I never thought about how many children I would like. I hope the good Lord will see fit to give us children, but I will leave how many up to the Lord. I know I'm marrying a godly woman. She makes me want to be a godly man. After she started writing me, she encouraged me to listen to Preacher and believe on the Lord. I tried to do that, but I wasn't sure I really wanted to. After I started going to the camp meetings where I really could feel the spirit, I finally felt like I'd found God. I hope to find a meeting to go to somewhere around here. I tried to go to the church down in the valley, but I can't feel it there like at the camp meetings, so I don't go no more.

Evan and I once had a conversation about God. It was on one of our camping trips to the Back Valley. It was the summer after Sara and Old Bob run away. Caleb was still living in the cabin, so we made our camp at the opposite end of the valley. We had cooked our supper and was lazing beside our fire as the evening twilight lingered. We listened to the night calls of the frogs, owls, jar flies, and even a fox barked at the top of the falls.

I punched up the fire and put on another piece of wood. I said to Evan, "This peaceful valley makes me think that God made it special for us."

Evan picked up a rock and hurled it towards the creek. "I don't believe in God."

I was shocked to hear him say such a thing. "Why do you say that?"

"If they was a God, he wouldn't let Sara leave me."

I didn't know what to say. It never had come to my mind that someone would think God didn't exist. I really got to thinking after that about how do we know God is real. That was one thing I talked to Preacher about. I guess what finally convinced me was the wonderful feeling I always get at the meetings. It's got to be God that does that to me.

***

It was not too long after that camping trip with Evan when we was stopped on the road about a mile from my house by Bart Woodson and his gang of Union Home Guards. I don't remember what happened after the gun went off. I guess I fainted. I don't remember seeing Evan in the road bleeding, but somehow I knowed he was dead.

Ma said she heard me before she could see me running up the road toward the house. She said I was screaming, "They killed him" over and over. I don't remember getting to the house, but somehow I musta made them understand what had happened, and Pa and Uncle Stuart jumped on horses and went to find Evan. They told me they took him home and told Mr. Jackson what had happened. Pa went to see the sheriff, but he said there wasn't nothing he could do about it. They buried him in the church yard.

I didn't go to the funeral. When Ma finally got me to stop screaming and sobbing, I took to my bed. I didn't want to eat. I didn't want to talk to nobody. I didn't even want to open my eyes. I didn't get out of bed for three days. Then I wandered around the house like I was a stranger and didn't know where I was. If someone made a loud noise like slamming a door, I started screaming all over again. I'll never forget the first time I heard a gunshot after Evan's death. I hit the ground and covered my head with my arms, and even now sometimes sudden noises give me a jolt.

I never knowed what sadness really was till I lost Evan. It wasn't just the shock of the shooting. He was my best friend. I guess I really loved him. I sat on the front porch staring into the distance for hours. I didn't go help the men in the fields. I went to the table for meals when Ma took me by the hand and led me there, but ate only a few bites. My anguish lasted for weeks. I lost weight and begun to stumble when I walked. Pa wanted to force me to eat and come back to work, but Ma insisted he leave me to my grief.

Finally, sometime in the fall, I heard Uncle Stuart telling Pa Mr. Jackson had sold his store and moved away. That made me see I had been thinking about my own loss, and I hadn't thought of what this had cost Mr. Jackson. Now he was gone and I hadn't even told him goodbye or how sorry I was. That night I come to the supper table and ate the first full meal since the shooting. The next day I followed the men to the hay field and worked all day. But the sadness didn't go away. One thing I was sure of then: there ain't no God.

***

Remembering that sad time makes me wish my sweetheart was here with me. I know she could cheer me up. I went to the bedroom and got the little chest I made to hold her letters, just like William did with Hilda's letters, except mine was made out of cedar wood. I made it fancy with little leather hinges and carved dogwoods on the cover. Reading some of her letters got me over my sad spell, and I was able to go to sleep almost as soon as my head hit the pillow. I didn't even have a dream.

I first started having those terrible dreams not long after I quit moping around the house and went back to work with the men after Evan was killed. I would be screaming, "Stop, don't shoot" over and over till Ma would shake me to wake me up. Then I would start crying and shaking. She would get in bed with me and hold me and try to comfort me till I could go back to sleep. I think Pa thought I was some sort of weakling, and I should talk myself out of those bad memories that haunted me. But I couldn't help myself that way. And I still have those terrible frightful dreams to this day. I hope when I bring my wife here life will be smooth, and I won't have those dreams no more.

That fall after Evan died, I helped get the tobacco cut and into the barn, and helped dig potatoes. We cut the grass in Back Valley, and when it dried made it into hay stacks for the animals during the winter. We still had three horses, one cow, two hogs, and the four oxen in the valley. We kept one or two horses and one cow in the barn so we could milk the cow and have the horses nearby when we needed them. Ever day Caleb would ride one of the horses over the mountain and work with the men in fields away from the house where he wouldn't be seen by unexpected visitors. Especially after Evan was shot, we was afraid someone might try to harm him or make him join the Yankee troops that had started signing up black men.

I ask him one day if he got lonesome staying in Back Valley and he grinned and said he really enjoyed it. "I love to set on the door step in the evening and hear the sounds of the animals. Sometimes a deer will come to get a drink from the creek. Once I saw a beautiful big bird with long legs and a long bill swoop down and wade in the creek for several minutes before flying away."

About the time we got the tobacco stripped and ready for market, we got word that Pa's partner in Pittsburgh, Mr. Perkins, had died suddenly. Mr. Perkins never married and had no family so he had willed all his assets to the company. Pa left about the middle of November to travel to Pittsburgh to take care of things there. He ask Caleb if he wanted to go with him and work in Pittsburgh, and Caleb agreed.

When they got ready to leave, Caleb gave me a hug and said, "Take care of yourself." That hug meant a lot to me. He always treated me like a little brother. Then he went to Ma and bowed from the waist. "Thank you Mistress Campbell. You always made me feel like one of your boys. I'll miss you." Then he put his saddle bags on his horse and mounted up. I understood that he would be safer in Pennsylvania, but it made me sad to see him go.

Pa said he'd try to be back by Christmas. Fortunately, there was not a whole lot to do that time of year except take care of the animals and make needed repairs to fences and buildings. It was my job to ride over the mountain every two or three days to make sure the animals in the Back Valley had feed and see that the cabin and everything was all right. I rather enjoyed doing that, but I would be glad when the war was over and life returned to normal.

Two days before Christmas, Pa come back and brought William and Elliott with him. I was so happy to see them. We hadn't heard William was out of the army, so we had a big surprise. He looked bigger than when he left for the army almost two years before. His wounded leg seemed to have healed well; he didn't even limp. Ma said when I saw William I smiled for the first time since Evan died. William had been mustered out of the army in late November and had gone straight to Pittsburgh to see Grandma and, of course, Hilda.

We was surprised again the next day when James come riding up on a strange horse. He was dressed in his officer's uniform and even had his sword strapped to his side. He paced around like he was lecturing troops and told us how he had lost Blaze in a battle, but looked at William and said, "At least I didn't get wounded," like he was mocking William cause he had got a broke leg in battle. He totally ignored me till Christmas Day when I walked into the room and he said, "Oh, hello...Harvey Baby." I was glad he had to leave the day after Christmas to go back to his regiment. I didn't know it then, but that turned out to be the last time our whole family was together.

For three days after Christmas, Ma, Pa, and Uncle Stuart spent most of the day in Pa's office with the door closed. Then one night after supper, they called me, William, and Elliott into the parlor and explained that Uncle Stuart would head up the company in Pittsburgh now that Mr. Perkins had died, and William would head up the accounting office there. The day after New Year's William, Elliott and Uncle Stuart left for Pennsylvania.

Now we was really short-handed, but Pa announced he had hired four new men to be part of the work crew. Two would help Mr. Morgan with the farming and two would help Mr. Simpson and Jake with the logging. I was surprised he planned to start cutting trees again, since he had first said he wouldn't cut any more till the war was over. But he said the demand for lumber had picked up, and the sawmill was being repaired. He hoped to have enough logs to do a log drive when the river flooded.

By mid-January the four new hired hands arrived and moved into the bunk house with Jake and Pete. Since there was nothing much to do on the farm till the worst of winter was over, all the men went to the woods and soon the logs was piling up beside the creek. Since Evan got shot, we hadn't heard of any guards or marauders roaming about, so Pa decided to move all the animals back over the mountain. My job was to take care of the barn animals. Ma insisted that I couldn't be around the tree cutting work. I had to see that the one milk cow got milked twice each day and keep the stables cleaned out. We had plenty of hay, but I had to climb into the barn loft and fork it down for the horses, the oxen, and the red cow. I wasn't really happy with my work assignment, but complaining got me no relief.

For some reason Pa decided to buy another milk cow. Now I had two cows to milk. Our red cow was easy to milk. When I called her to the barn from the pasture, she come trotting along with her full bag swinging and squirting milk in all directions. I didn't hardly have to do much more than put the milk pail under her. But the brown cow Pa bought was mean. She wouldn't stand still while I tried to milk her, and more than once she kicked my bucket over. I had to pull and squeeze so hard on her teats that my hands would be in a bad cramp, and I couldn't open my fingers. I would wake up in the night with my hands aching.

When I complained to Pa, he just laughed and said I shouldn't be such a complainer. After about a week, I told Ma someone else would have to go milk that cow. It hurt my hands too much. She mentioned to Pa that she thought there really was some problem with that brown cow. When he tried to brush it off, she said, "Why don't you go milk her and then you'll know whether or not there's a problem?"

He took the milk pail and went to the barn. He was gone a long time, and when he come back, he didn't say nothing. But the next day he told Mr. Morgan to take the cow and sell her.

***

Since Uncle Stuart had gone to Pennsylvania, Pa spent much more time in the woods working with the men than he had done before. He made no trips to Pennsylvania during that winter and spring. He did go visit with the governor a couple of times and also checked on the progress of restoring the sawmill, but most days he was working with the men in the woods from near daylight to near dark. They did take most Sundays off. Pa wasn't a church going man, but he thought it was only fair to give the men a day to rest up.

Life settled into a pattern: one day was pretty much like the one before. The pile of logs by the creek got bigger. The seeds got planted in the tobacco bed, and by the end of March, Mr. Morgan and his crew begun the spring plowing. Pa was working hard to get more logs ready before the rains come.

Pa always rode his horse to the work site, so it would be available if some emergency happened. One day I was working in the barn when Mr. Simpson galloped up on Pa's horse. He yelled for me to help him hook two horses to the wagon. Then he told me to go get Ma and have her bring her medicine bag. I tried to ask him what had happened, but he didn't answer. He helped Ma into the seat at the front of the wagon, and I climbed into the back and we took off up the mountain.

Mr. Simpson was talking to Ma, so I scooted up close, and I heard him say Pa was hit by a falling tree. I saw Ma's jaw tighten. I had imagined he come for Ma because someone was hurt, and she was the closest thing to a doctor for miles around, but I hadn't expected Pa to be hurt. He was always so careful and made everbody else take care. We made the trip up the mountain in only a few minutes. The horses went faster than I could walk. Now I understood why Pa had insisted they must always have a cleared path wide enough for a team and wagon all the way to the work site.

By the time we got to the downed tree, the men had sawed the tree trunk in pieces so they could lift it off Pa. Ma jumped off the wagon and ran to Pa just as the men lifted up the log. He was laying face down, but he had a big gash on the back of his head. Ma felt his neck for a pulse and said he was still alive. She took some bandages from her bag and held them to his head to stop the bleeding. His coat was torn on the right shoulder, but he didn't seem to be bleeding there. He didn't respond when she spoke to him.

The men worked together to do what Ma advised and got him into the wagon and then into the house after they got down the mountain. Ma set beside him and held his hand. He struggled to breathe for a couple of hours, but as the sun went behind the mountain he died without ever opening his eyes. She hadn't tried to treat his injuries. She told me later she knew his brain had been damaged so bad he couldn't live.

I was falling apart, but Ma was calm. She gave me a cup of tea with some laudanum and put me to bed. Meanwhile she told Mr. Morgan to make a coffin from the cured lumber in the barn loft. First thing the next morning she sent Mr. Simpson and three hired hands to dig a grave in the bald place at the top of the ridge where me and Evan ate that time we saw the snake. She said Pa didn't want to be buried in the church yard, but had showed her the very spot he wanted for his final resting place.

Shortly before sundown the next day the whole household followed the wagon up the mountain as it carried Pa to his final resting place. Ma and

Miz Simpson had washed the body and dressed him in his best suit and laid him out on the dining room table. Ma had me come and say my goodbye. Me and her stood hand in hand beside him. His arms was folded over his chest and his eyes was closed. I couldn't convince myself that this dead man was my father. I kept looking around for him—resting in his favorite chair, coming from his office, walking through the door with his hat in his hand.

I stood nearby when the men carried in the coffin and placed him inside. I left the room when I saw Mr. Morgan get his hammer and nails to fasten the lid. I couldn't stand to watch, but I can hear the thuds of that hammer to this day. There was no preacher, no Bible reading, no prayers. We walked up the mountain, watched as the coffin was lowered, and then when the men begun to shovel in the dirt, we walked back down. Ma explained that we would have a proper service later when all the family could come. Since travel was difficult and since they was no way to keep a body from beginning to smell, especially in warmer weather, it was common to bury the body as soon as possible and hold the funeral later.

***

I fell into the depths of grief again. Ma insisted I eat, but otherwise left me to stare into nothing. If she was grieving I couldn't tell it. She kept herself busy because now she was the person in charge. She and Mr. Simpson discussed the logging and decided not to take the logs down the river because it was too dangerous for men who wasn't experienced with driving logs. That turned out to be a good decision because the rains was so light, the river didn't rise enough to float the logs anyway.

After four days Ma insisted I come out of my gloomy paralysis and drive the buggy to take her to Beattyville where she could send a telegraph message to the family in Pittsburgh and to James. She had decided the funeral would be on Saturday, May 7, and wanted as many of the family to come as possible. She knew it might be difficult since the war was still going on. Ma also wrote the Bakers and asked if Mr. Baker could conduct the funeral. She didn't much like the new pastor at the church in Laureltown. His theology didn't agree with her Presbyterian beliefs

She met with Mr. Simpson and Mr. Morgan each Monday morning to discuss what work needed to be scheduled for the week. They decided to let three of the new hired hands go and just work mostly on the farming. I thought she didn't seem that sad and wondered how she could go about her work as usual till one night I happened to see a lamp was on in Pa's office and the door wasn't completely closed. I peeked through the crack and saw

85

her at Pa's desk with her head resting on her arms and her shoulders shaking as she sobbed. I pushed the door open a little more and started to go to her, but Cousin Maybelle took my arm and pulled me out and closed the door.

I finally realized everbody has to grieve their own way. Because someone doesn't fall apart like me doesn't mean they ain't feeling sad. I started to wonder whose fault it was the tree fell crooked. I finally got up enough nerve to ask Mr. Simpson. He told me it wasn't nobody's fault. They had pulled the crosscut saw out and the tree started to fall, but the top limbs caught on a nearby tree, and that caused it to twist in the wrong direction. They yelled and Pa was trying to get out of the way, but he tripped and fell right where the tree landed.

***

I'm not too clear on what happened between the time we buried Pa and when everone come for the funeral. I found myself spending most of my time in my room because everwhere I looked I saw memories of Pa. If I passed his office door, I saw his empty desk with his pipe stand right on the left corner where he always kept it, and it would hit me like a rock. When I went to the barn, I saw his empty saddle in the tack room. If I went out the door I saw his hat hanging there. At mealtime his place was empty. I couldn't come out of my room without being struck by his death all over again. It seemed like Ma understood and sometimes she would just bring food to my room instead of asking me to come to the table. Somehow the days went by and eventually people begun arriving for the funeral.

Uncle Stuart, William, and Elliott come first. William and Elliott took Ma into a big hug, and they had a good cry. First thing I knowed, I was hugging them and crying too. They said Grandma Campbell wanted to come, but didn't think she was up to making that trip. Later in the afternoon I took William and Elliott up the mountain to Pa's grave. It was the first time I had been there since the burial.

William looked around. "I see why Pa wanted this to be his final resting place. It's near the highest point of the property. It's like he's watching over everything."

"Yes," Elliott agreed, "I think we should build a picket fence around the grave to make it special. And we could plant some flowers, maybe some roses to climb over the fence. Pa was really proud of the roses that grew up the lattice on the veranda."

I listened and watched as my brothers begun to plan where the service would take place. "We'll need to bring up chairs and make some benches where people can sit." William looked for the most level place.

"You mean we'll have the funeral right by his grave?" I thought that was strange.

"Yes, that's what folks do when the funeral is delayed until sometime after the burial." William turned towards Elliott. "I guess Mr. Simpson could get his oxen to snake up some logs that we could level to make some seating."

"Yes, but the first thing we should do is to talk to Ma and see what she wants."

"You're right. Well, tomorrow we'll get things organized."

We got back to the house just as Pete announced supper was ready. It was hard; everbody was there except Pa. But I got interested in hearing Uncle Stuart and the boys talk about their journey. They barely missed a skirmish between some Union troops and the State Guard.

"We were warned we should not go through a little town near Lexington and took another road, but we could hear the guns." Elliott looked at Ma. "I admit I was not very comfortable until we got away from that."

William took a drink of water and set his glass on the table. "Ma, Caleb wanted to come. He said to tell you how sad he was, and he wished he could tell you how much he respected Pa. But we persuaded him it was too dangerous, and it's probably a good thing because we met some wicked characters on the trip down. If Caleb had been with us, I would have been frightened for him."

Ma stopped chewing, put her fork in her plate and stared out the window. Finally she started eating again. "Thank you, son, for telling me. I'm glad you persuaded him to be safe. I know he and Jed were more than boss and hired hand. They respected each other and shared a long unusual friendship—even before Jed and I married."

"We stopped at the sawmill." Uncle Stuart put down his fork and wiped his chin with his napkin. "They're staying busy with the logs people have brought in. It's good to be getting that income since we've been shut down for so many months."

Ma nodded. "I'm glad to know that. Jed was trying very hard to get that part of the business working again."

After some minutes Elliott looked at Ma and ask, "Is James going to come home?"

I hadn't heard Ma say anything about that, so I looked up quick. "Yes," Ma nodded. "He has resigned his commission and will come home permanently. I expect him any day now, certainly before the funeral."

I felt like a rock had fallen on my head. James was coming home? To stay? It had been such a relief he wasn't around to torture me for the last two years. Now with Pa gone, would James take over? If he was in charge, would he try to boss me around? I excused myself and went to my room. After a while, William knocked and come into my room.

"Are you all right? You left the table rather suddenly."

I sighed. "Yes, I guess. It's just…I didn't expect James to come home to stay. He's always so mean to me."

"I see. Well, you're getting to be a pretty big fellow. Aren't you 16 now?" When I nodded he said, "I think you can take care of yourself, don't you?"

I stood up and walked to the window. "I think I can defend myself if he tries to hurt me. But if he's the boss, he can make my life miserable in other ways. I don't know why he hates me so."

William come and stood behind me and put his hands on my shoulders. "I know he can be hard to get along with sometimes, but I don't believe he really hates you. Maybe being in the army has taught him a lesson or two." He turned me around to face him. "How about a game of chess?"

***

Ma was right. On the day before the funeral, James come riding in on a beautiful black stallion he called Storm. He was dressed in his uniform, even wearing his sword. I hoped that meant he wasn't out of the army after all, but it was soon clear he just wanted to show off. He saw me standing on the front porch. "Harvey Baby, come take care of my horse." He marched into the house, dumped his bags in the hall by the stairs, and walked into Pa's office like he owned the place.

Ma had been in the outdoor kitchen where Pete and Mrs. Simpson was preparing all sorts of food to serve the guests who'd come to the funeral the next day. I started to lead his horse toward the barn when she saw me and ask, "Whose horse is that?"

When she heard that James had come, she rushed into the house. I didn't really want to take care of his horse, but I could tell by the way the stallion hung his head he was tired from the long trip and at least needed a drink. I thought I would take care of his horse this once, mostly because I felt sorry for the horse. Next time, I told myself, I'd tell him to do it hisself. Any hope James was changed flew clear out of my head.

Even though my brothers and the hired men had made seating places from logs and chairs they'd taken up the mountain, the places were all taken and many guests stood during the service. All morning people had arrived riding horses, driving buggies, and even walking. Some were neighbors I recognized, but many were perfect strangers to me. Ma told me later the governor had come as well as the foreman of the sawmill and businessmen from as far away as Louisville.

Mr. Baker had arrived the day before, and Ma invited him to use her bedroom while she shared Cousin Maybelle's room. He and Ma sat on the front porch after supper and made the plans for the service. Ma was very pleased he had come, and she wanted to hear all about Mistress Baker and the town where they lived.

I can't tell what happened at the service. I sat on the front row with Ma and my brothers, but I was so tore up all the words just flew over my head. I remember several people talked, and it seemed to go on for a long time. The sun was hot, and several times Ma put her arm around my shoulders and held me against her to help me stop fidgeting. Finally it was over. People shuffled by shaking hands with all the family and making some comments. Then Ma invited everybody to the house for a meal.

As the crowd begun moving down the mountain, I remember going to stand at the head of the grave. There was no gravestone, although Ma said one had been ordered. William come and stood beside me. "He was a very good man. I will miss him."

Suddenly I was shaking and William put his arms around me. We stood there for a long time with our arms around each other while we sobbed. Finally I raised my head from his shoulder and searched my pockets for a handkerchief. After wiping my nose, I looked off at the mountains in the distance. "Yes, he was a good man. I hope I can be at least half as good."

PART

TWO

PART

TWO

CHAPTER 8

May 1864

Laureltown, Kentucky

I set on the front steps watching the covered wagon carrying William, Ma, and Cousin Maybelle disappear around the bend in the road. In the three weeks since the funeral them two women was the workinest women I ever seen, sorting and packing clothes, favorite linens, dishes, and various other items in huge trunks. And now they was moving back to Pittsburgh. Uncle Stuart and Elliott had returned to Pennsylvania three days after the funeral, but William stayed to help the women make the move. Me and James was the only family left here, and I wasn't too happy about that.

The day after the funeral, Ma and Uncle Stuart spent several hours in the office with the door closed, and then they called all the family together to explain how the company would work according to Pa's will.

Uncle Stuart started the conversation. "Frances and I are the only partners for the immediate future. I will head the operation in Pennsylvania and Frances will continue as a silent partner."

"I own the house in Pittsburgh," Ma added, "and I will move there as soon as possible."

Uncle Stuart looked at his notes and continued, "James will manage the operation in Kentucky, and William will work closely with me in Pennsylvania." He paused and looked at his notes again and addressed

James and William who stood in front of the fireplace. "At the end of five years from today, the partners will vote to make both of you full partners in the company, assuming you have earned it."

Ma turned to Elliott. "You will continue your studies at the academy, and, Harvey, you will continue to work for the company here in Kentucky." I felt like the floor had fell out from under me.

"Elliott and Harvey," Uncle Stuart continued, "your father included in his will a provision that each of you upon reaching age 21 will receive an inheritance of five thousand dollars, which you may spend as you wish. After that you will no longer have any obligation to the company nor the company to you unless you choose to be involved."

Now they was all gone and I was stuck in Kentucky with James. I didn't know how I could work on the farm without Ma to stand up for me against James. I was sure he would take ever chance to make my life miserable. I thought at least I still had Mr. Morgan to protect me from him. I looked about the porch and the lawn for something that would give me some hope. I saw lots of things reminding me of Ma. There was her rocking chair where I often found her in the evening after supper. I saw her favorite yellow rose had three big buds. I was sorry she wouldn't get to see them bloom.

James rode up on Storm, and I wondered why he had that stupid sword strapped to his side. I was glad he'd quit wearing his uniform. "Come here, you little slacker," James commanded.

I walked across the lawn and stood shielding my eyes with my hand as I looked up at James astride the black horse. I wondered if this was what it was like to be under his command in the army.

"What are you doing lolling around like a country gentleman? Why aren't you in the field with the rest of the men?" He put his hand on the hilt of the sword. "Ma made me promise not to call you Harvey Baby, but I have lots of other names for you. Now get your lazy bones out in the field where you belong you spoiled little sissy." He swung Storm around and trotted down the road. He was gone for three days, giving me a little peace.

On Sunday after James returned he called Mr. Morgan into his office. I heard some loud voices but couldn't make out what the problem was. Pete had asked me to help out in the kitchen since Miz Simpson had gone to visit her family in Madison County. I set two places at the table for me and James. Mealtime was so sad since the rest of the family was gone. As I carried a couple of dishes of food from the outdoor kitchen to the house, Mr. Morgan suddenly busted through the door, almost knocking me over.

"That no good damn Yankee brother of yours just fired me!" he yelled as he marched off toward his cabin.

I rushed into the house, placed the dishes of food on the dining table, and barged through the office door.

"Don't you know how to knock on a closed door, moron?"

I ignored him. "Why'd you let Mr. Morgan go?"

"I'm the manager now, and I decide who goes and who stays. It's none of your business."

"But what's he done wrong?"

"I said it's none of your business. He has three days to move out of his house. I've got someone else to be the farm manager. Now get out of here and mind your own business, you nosy little creep. And close the door on your way out."

I was plumb dumbfounded and climbed the stairs to my room. I suspected James had fired Mr. Morgan cause he was a Confederate sympathizer. I stretched out on the bed and sighed. Would it never stop? Evan was gone. Pa was dead and buried. All my family had left. Now the only one on the place who would take up for me was leaving. I thought I couldn't stand to stay here no longer, but I had no place to go. I stayed in my room the rest of the day. A little after dark Pete knocked and brought in a plate of food. I appreciated Pete. I guessed I still had one friend on the place after all.

The next three days I wandered around in a fog trying to stay out of James' sight as I helped the Morgans pack their belongings. Early on the third day, I watched as Mr. Morgan helped his wife and baby climb into the wagon and roll down the road and out of sight.

Before I could get my hoe and go to the corn field, James was yelling. "What are you standing here for? You should have been in the field hours ago. How many times do I have to tell you what to do? I should fire you as well."

I picked up my hoe leaning against the fence and stepped toward James till I stared directly into his eyes. I was now as tall as him. "I dare you to fire me." When James put his hand on his sword, I lifted the hoe and held it in both hands with the blade up. I knowed I could beat James in a fight, and I really hoped he would draw that sword. "I'm sure Ma would love to hear about that." We stared at each other for a full minute, till James broke the stare and turned to walk away.

During the next few days, James was busy reorganizing his work force, and I was able to stay out of his way, except for meal times. I would wolf down my food as quick as I could and leave the table, but James still preached at me about all sorts of things, and called me names like "idiot," "imbecile," "infantile," and almost everything else except "Harvey Baby."

It all blowed up when I forgot to milk the cow one evening. At breakfast the next morning, I suddenly realized I had forgot when there was no cream for the coffee. I jumped up so sudden I turned over my coffee as I made for the door with James hollering, "What a moron. Can't even remember to do your chores."

I felt terrible. I knowed it was painful for a cow if her milk bag got too full. I hated I had caused her to suffer. It was clearly my fault. I hadn't realized how much Mr. Morgan helped keep me on track. He was always reminding me of tasks I needed to take care of. When we worked in the field, Mr. Morgan would dismiss me before the other workers so I could go do the barn chores. With Mr. Morgan gone, there was no one to remind me. I was gonna miss him in more ways than one.

I had worked very hard the day before trying to prove to the new farm manager that I could hold my own with the other farm workers. We worked in the hot sun till close to sun down. I was so sweaty and dirty I went along with the other men to the swimming hole to wash up and cool off. By that time it was dark, and doing chores totally left my mind. I was mad at myself. I don't know why I forgot what I shoulda been doing. I supposed that was why Ma insisted I shouldn't go to the woods to work. She probably thought I'd get myself hurt, or maybe even hurt somebody else.

After doing the morning milking and turning the cow out to pasture, I heard a gunshot and run to see what was going on. James stood near the barn with his gun, and I saw my dog laying a few feet away from him. "What happened?"

James grinned. "You hurt my cow, so I hurt your dog."

I ran to the beagle and saw her head was practically gone. "Why'd you kill my dog?"

"I'm teaching you a lesson. When you fail to carry out your responsibility to the company, there'll be consequences."

"You have no right to kill my dog. Bonnie didn't do nothing. She's mine; she don't belong to the company. " I was near crying, but I was determined not to let James call me a crybaby.

By this time, Pete O'Malley and Miz Simpson come from the garden to see what was happening.

James motioned toward the dog with his gun. "Harvey, take that animal and bury it and then get to work where you belong." He nodded to Miz Simpson and Pete and returned to the house.

Pete went to the barn and got a mattock and shovel. "I know the perfect place," Pete said, "in the corner of the garden where we always plant the sun flowers."

Miz Simpson went with us and helped bury Bonnie. "She'll be happy here," she said when they had smoothed the dirt over the grave. She patted my back.

***

The new farm manager assigned me to work in the tobacco field, pulling off suckers and tobacco worms. I was working alone and had lots of time to think about what was happening since James took over the management of the place. I couldn't understand why he had killed my dog. I hadn't damaged the cow. She had been uncomfortable for a few hours, but no real harm had come to her. All I could figger was he must think he had to prove to all the men he's the boss, and they should take him serious. But I couldn't figger out why he was taking it out on me.

I didn't even go to the house for dinner, but kept working until I had checked all the plants in the entire field. I pulled off and stomped on lots of worms, and the suckers I pulled off made a green path between the rows. By the time I left to go do the barn chores that evening, I had made up my mind. I can't stay here.

At the supper table James started yelling at me again, calling me the usual names. Finally just as I stood up from the table, James said, "What I ought to do with you is enlist you in the army. That would shape you up in a hurry."

I wondered if James really could make me join the army. I figgered if he could, he just might try to do it. When James went into the office and closed the door, I went to find Pete O'Malley. He was setting in the outdoor kitchen doorway smoking his pipe. He ask me if I was all right and made a place for me beside him.

"I've decided to leave. I don't know where I'm going, but I have to get away before I kill James." I asked Pete to make me a stash of food, especially dried foods that would last awhile. "If James asks you, tell him I told you I was leaving, but I didn't say where I was going. I'll go early tomorrow before anyone else is up." Pete said he would leave a packet of food on the table in the outdoor kitchen.

Before she left, Ma had give me a envelope of money. She told me to keep it a secret, but to use it in a emergency. I'm sure she prob'ly knowed James wouldn't give me my allowance like he's supposed to. Once us boys reached age fifteen, we was supposed to get our allowance ever payday.

I put together my backpack like I used to do when me and Evan went camping. I had my canteen, a cook pot, a cup, and hunting knife. I packed several pairs of socks and underwear and my bedroll. I still had no idea where I would go, but I kept thinking about what James said about the army. I wasn't joining no Union forces, that's for sure, but I could join the Confederate Army if I could figure out how to do it. I thought maybe I could kill a Yankee to pay for what they done to Evan.

I remembered when Mr. Baker was here for the funeral, him and James had a long conversation about the war. Mr. Baker said the area to the eastern part of the state was dominated by Southern sympathizers. He also said the State Guard was very active in that area, and he had come by way of Virginia in order to avoid a unpleasant confrontation with them.

James had bragged about how well the Union Army was winning. The Union now controlled all the major rivers in the South and had successful blockades of all the Confederate ports. He said General Lee still had a stronghold in Virginia, but the Feds was slowly taking over the major cities. He predicted the war would be over in a few months. I decided I should go to Virginia and try to find General Lee's army.

I waited in my room till I heard James come upstairs. I blowed out the lamp and cracked the door so I could listen. When I heard the clock in the parlor strike midnight, I slowly crept down the stairs carrying my backpack. I lit a lamp to see how to take my gun from the gun cabinet. I looked around the parlor. I could almost see Pa beside the fireplace in his favorite chair. I wondered if I'd ever see the parlor again. I turned out the lamp and made my way to the kitchen door as quiet as I could.

The moon was barely peeping over the mountain, but made enough light for me to find the way to the outdoor kitchen where I found the food stash Pete O'Malley had made. I carried the food, backpack, and gun to the barn and placed them in the tack room. I had something to do before I left. I took the lantern hanging in the tack room cause I knowed it would be dark in the woods where the trees blocked the moonlight. I lit the lantern and climbed the mountain. When I got near the top, I could see the fence my brothers made around Pa's grave. The moonlight made the whitewashed pickets glow. Suddenly someone stepped from the shadows and liked to scared the daylights out of me.

"Don't be afraid, Harvey, it's me."

I recognized Miz Simpson's voice. "What are you doing up here?"

"I saw Pete packing up your food, and he told me you was planning to leave. I figgered you would come to say goodbye to your pa, so I come here to wait for you." She moved closer and led me through the gate to stand beside the grave. "Take all the time you need; I'll wait to walk back down with you."

I looked at the grave. It was like a ugly gash in the mountain. I wondered if the grass would grow to cover it before winter come. I looked to see Miz Simpson stood at the edge of the trees. I kneeled down at the head of the grave. I looked again to be sure Miz Simpson couldn't hear me. "Pa, I hope you won't be disappointed with me cause I'm running away. If you can see what's going on down here, you understand why I'm doing it. I just want to tell you I love you and miss you so much. I hope someday I can make you proud of me." I glimpsed a glow as the moonlight hit a small rock and picked it up and put it in my pocket. It was something I could take with me to remind me of Pa.

We didn't talk as we walked back down to the barn. I blowed out the lantern and hung it in the tack room, put the food in my backpack and strapped it to my shoulders. I picked up my gun and headed for the road. Miz Simpson walked with me till we reached her cabin.

"Thank you, Miz Simpson for all you learnt me about the yerbs and plants. I'll never forget that, and I'll never forget you."

She put her arms around me in a big hug. "Be careful out there. It's a dangerous world. I plan to see you back here, so take care of yourself."

As I walked down the road, I was puzzled that she knowed me so good. How could she know I was gonna go to Pa's grave? It's almost like she could read my mind. She didn't even try to talk me out of leaving, and she didn't ask me where I was headed. I adjusted the straps on the backpack and hurried along. I had something else to do before getting out of Laureltown.

A half hour later I stood beside Evan's grave. The moonlight shining through the leafy trees cast ghastly shadows across the graves. I found the stone Mr. Jackson had made to place at the head of the grave. "Evan, I'm gonna go find those bad Yankee soldiers and pay them back for what they done to you." I couldn't hardly talk for crying. "I won't never have another friend like you, and I'll never forget you." I stood there for a few minutes just watching the shadows shift as the breeze rustled the leaves. "So I come to say goodbye."

***

I wanted to get plumb out of the community before daylight, so I wouldn't see nobody who knowed me. I left the road when it turned to the west and headed south, glad to have the moonlight. I would need to get across the river, but I knowed where they was a foot bridge that would take me across. By daylight I had walked past all the familiar trails, so I figgered I prob'ly wouldn't see nobody I knowed. I also was feeling tired since I'd not slept, so I looked for a place to rest awhile. I found a good spot and slept for a couple of hours and woke with a stiff neck.

I guessed it was about breakfast time, so I opened the food pack and took out some cornbread and a slice of ham. I took a drink from my canteen before strapping on my backpack and hitting the trail. The sun was on my left side which meant I was facing south. I would have to depend on the sun to guide me in the right direction. I'd been following a small stream that ran along the foot of a mountain for some time, but I knowed I would have to cross that mountain and move more toward the east soon. I thought it would take about three days to reach the Virginia border.

By the time the sun was directly overhead, I left the trail because it turned more toward the west. Now I had to be careful to keep going south. Most of the time I was in the forest, so it was harder to determine if I was still going right. Occasionally I climbed a tree to see where the sun was. I stopped for a quick lunch beside a stream and refilled my canteen, then begun walking again. I hadn't seen a single person and very few animals, but I didn't feel lonely. I did wonder what Ma would think when she found out I had run away. I told myself I would send her a letter when I got to a town with a post office.

When it started getting dark, I found a place to rest for the night. I knowed it would be foolish to try to walk in these woods in the dark. I reminded myself to be careful not to sprain a ankle or fall down. After arranging my blankets for the night, I listened to the night sounds. Most of the birds had gone to roost, but I heard a owl, and I thought I heard a fox. I hung my food pack in a tree where some animal couldn't get at it. Me and Evan learnt that the hard way when we had camped out in the Back Valley. We thought it prob'ly had been raccoons that had drug our food several yards away and devoured every crumb.

Before I dropped off to sleep, I wondered if I was doing the right thing. I reached into my pocket for the rock from Pa's grave. Holding it seemed to make me feel better. I felt sure, Pa would understand if he knowed how James treated me—killing my dog like that. When I woke up the next morning, I was still holding the stone. I thought that was a sign. Miz Simpson was always looking for signs.

I was up by daylight, washed my face in the cold stream, and ate the last of the ham and some dried apples. By the time the sun was overhead, I decided it was time to go over the mountain. I filled my canteen since I didn't know when I would find a stream again, and started climbing. Then I reminded myself to keep the afternoon sun at my back because I wanted to go east, but it was harder to do. Sometimes there was thickets of laurel I couldn't go through and big rocks I couldn't climb over. The trees was thick so it was hard to know where the sun was. I had to stop often to make sure I was still going east. But by dark I had reached the top. I climbed a tree to see what lay ahead and was happy to see a valley below that would continue to lead me south. I felt pleased and fell asleep almost as soon as I put my head on the blanket.

The next day going down the mountain was easier than climbing up. I spotted a big rock formation on the mountain side across the valley and tried to keep it in sight so I didn't get confused and go in circles or lose my way. I remembered how me and Evan had tromped all over the mountains, how more than once we got lost, but we always figgered out how to get back home. Those was valuable lessons. I got careless going down a very steep incline, lost my footing and slid about fifty feet on my back. When I got stopped, I scolded myself for not paying attention, "No wonder James called me a stupid idiot." I stood up careful and moved my arms and legs to see if I had busted anything. My backpack and gun seemed fine. But I started being more careful, and I realized my feet hurt. To tell the truth, they had been hurting most of the day, but I had tried not to pay any attention to it. I guessed I had bad blisters. As the pain got worse, I tried to remember how Miz Simpson had treated blistered feet.

By mid-afternoon I reached the valley and found a trail I could follow. I started looking along the trail for familiar plants Miz Simpson had learnt me to recognize. Finally, I saw some plantain and remembered Miz Simpson used that to treat infections. I gathered several handfuls of the leaves and put them in my pocket. A little later I spotted a soap bush and broke off several small limbs full of leaves.

As the sun moved behind the mountain, I looked for a safe place to spend the night. I come to a small stream and followed it several yards toward a small cove. First, I filled my canteen then scooped up handfuls of water to wash my face. I found a large flat rock at the edge of the water and set on it to take off my boots. I was shocked and a little scared when I saw how bloody my socks was. Another stupid mistake. The water was very cold, but felt good on my feet. After soaking my feet till the cold water got uncomfortable, I used some of the soap bush leaves to make some suds and washed my feet careful. I rubbed the blisters on my heels and toes easy, but made sure to get them good and clean. Then I washed my dirty, bloody socks and spread them out on a rock.

While I let my feet air dry, I found a small smooth rock and used it to crush the plantain leaves in the cook pot. Miz Simpson always mixed the yerbs with some kind of rendered fat to make a poultice. I opened the food pack and found some pork fat left from the ham. I thought I could mash the fat up somehow and mix it with the crushed leaves. I wished I had some way to make a bandage but decided to pull on clean socks after I spread the mixture over the blisters. I sat on the bank watching the water. I wondered what I would do if the blisters got infected. Maybe I should go back home and let Miz Simpson doctor my feet. I felt for my stone but couldn't find it. My heart begun to pound and I felt dizzy. What if I've lost it? That would be a bad sign.

After going through my pockets, I told myself to calm down and think. It musta fell out when I pulled the plantain out of my pocket. The near darkness made it difficult to see, but I kneeled down where I mashed up the leaves and felt the rocks and grass. After a few minutes, I found the little stone and held it tight in my palm. I thought if I hadn't found the stone, it would mean I should go back home, but since I found it, I must be doing the right thing. I decided to keep it in my backpack where it would be safer.

Before I put my food pack in a tree, I ate some dried venison and some biscuit. I figgered I would run out of food by the end of the next day. When I stood to put my food in a safe place, I smelled smoke. Was they a house nearby? Was it a forest fire? Was I in danger? I hurried to repack my bedroll, put my food back in the pack, grab up my wet socks, and with my gun in my hand begun moving farther down the valley. I thought I could smell the smoke stronger in that direction. Soon I spotted a thin wisp of smoke rising from the hillside on the right.

As quiet as I could, I moved up the hillside and decided it wasn't enough smoke for a forest fire and there was no clearing for a house. I stood behind a clump of laurel where I could barely see the glow of the fire. I moved a little farther uphill and saw a man setting by the fire holding a stick with a small fish over the flames. The man had a shaggy beard and wore ragged clothes. I couldn't see no bedroll and no belongings. I looked all around to see if the man had a gun, but I couldn't see one.

After watching for several minutes, I decided to greet him. "Hello there."

The man jumped up and faced me holding the stick with the fish dangling on its end. "Who are you?"

I moved a few steps closer, making sure my gun was in sight. "My name's Harvey Campbell. What's your name?"

The man had a horrified look on his face. "What do you want?"

"I'm just passing through and smelled your smoke. Thought I'd stop to say hello."

"You ain't the Home Guard, are you?"

"No, like I said, just a traveler."

I took off my back pack. "Mind if I set by your fire a little bit?" The man just stared at me. "Go ahead and cook your fish. You look hungry."

After staring at me for several more seconds, the man walked around to the other side of the fire where he could keep me in his sight. "This here's the first I've had to eat in two days."

"That don't look like a very big meal."

"It ain't, but it's all I got." He took the fish off the stick and started eating it. With each bite, he stopped to take the bones out of his mouth. "It ain't got much meat, mostly just bones."

I felt sorry for him. After thinking about my food supply, I finally opened up the pack, took out three pieces of venison jerky and handed them to the man, who stared at them like it couldn't be happening and then reached for them. "Thank you. What did you say your name was?"

"Harvey Campbell, but you didn't tell me your name." When the man didn't answer, I asked, "You live around here?"

"No, I live near Lexington."

"What are you doing here?"

"Trying to get home."

"Where did you come from?"

The man, across the fire from me, stared at the flames. Finally he said, "You shore is nosy." He looked at the food pack. "Got anything else to eat?"

I closed up the food pack and held it in my lap. "I got enough for breakfast which I will gladly share with you in the morning. That is if you let me spend the night here by your fire."

The man shrugged his shoulders, which I took to be agreement. I looked around for a comfortable place to make my bed and spread my blankets. Before climbing into my makeshift bed, I looked for some dead wood to add to the fire. It wasn't cold, but I wanted the light so I could continue to see the man. Then I hung the food pack from a limb directly over my bed. Shortly before I closed my eyes, the man asked, "Where you headed?"

I sat up. "I'm aiming to go to Virginia. You know how to get there?"

"Yep, I come through there on my way here."

"How far is it from here?"

"It's about one day straight on down this valley."

I thought it looked like the man had decided to talk. Maybe he thought he'd stand a better chance to have some food for breakfast if he got more friendly. He told me he was a deserter from Union forces that was fighting in Tennessee, and he was trying to get back to his family without the Home Guard catching him. When I ask why he deserted? He started describing how terrible war is.

"I couldn't stand it no more. We walked in the hot sun till soldiers fainted and fell out by the roadside. Half the time we didn't have enough food to feed a dog. We had to rob the poor people to get food; sometimes we burned their crops and even their houses. The battles are full of confusion: noise, screams, cannon balls flying. There's so much dust and smoke you can't tell who's a Reb and who's a Yankee, so you just shoot at whatever you see. And so many get wounded or killed. Blood was everwhere. I had to carry the wounded to the field hospital where the surgeons made them drink whiskey and then chopped off their legs or arms. The screams was terrible. I couldn't stand it no longer." He studied the fire. "If I can just get home to my wife and sons, I ain't never gonna fight in no man's war again."

I didn't say nothing. I didn't want to tell him I planned to join the Confederate forces. Even though the man had sworn off war, I thought he might still hold some hate for a Southern sympathizer. I stared across the fire and shook my head in sympathy. "I hope you get home soon. Get a good night's sleep so you can be on your way tomorrow." And I stretched out on my blankets.

***

When I opened my eyes the next morning, dawn was breaking over the valley. I sat up and stretched. The fire was out and the man was nowhere in sight. I walked around a bush and relieved myself and returned to pack up my bed and get on the road. I reached for the food pack, but it was gone.

"Hey, you scalawag. Why'd you steal my food?" I yelled as loud as I could, but of course got no answer. I rolled up my bedding and placed it in my backpack. At least he didn't take my gun. I don't know how he got that food without stepping right on me. It was right above my bed. I guess that's what I get for being stupid enough to spend the night beside his fire. He looked like he's half starved. I guessed he needed the food worser than me.

I took off my socks careful like and examined my feet. The blisters looked red and inflamed. I got out the cook pot and smeared the rest of the potion on the blisters. The socks I'd washed was now dry, so I put them on and laced up my boots. I hoped the plantain would do its work like Miz Simpson said.

As I walked along the trail, I watched for familiar plants. I found some wild onions and wild carrots and pulled them up, wiped off the dirt, and ate them. I knowed I'd have to find something more filling before the day was over. I wished I had Bonnie with me so she could track down a rabbit or a squirrel. Damn James for killing my dog!

When the sun was directly overhead, I stopped to rest. Although I'd kept a eye out, I hadn't saw no animals, but I did find some more wild carrots. I wondered what to do if I couldn't find something to shoot for my meal. I guessed I'd go hungry like that man. My feet was burning, but I didn't want to take off my boots cause I had no way to treat the blisters. I thought if I could find a stream later, I'd bathe my feet again.

All afternoon I walked down the valley, watching for some movement that might be a rabbit or some other animal. I wanted to go as far as I could before stopping for the night, and then I hoped to be in Virginia. I found a stream large enough I could actually bathe my whole body. I walked upstream away from the trail till I was out of sight, stripped off all my clothes and dipped myself in the cool water. The sun had been hot all day and I felt filthy. I'd saved some leaves from the soap bush and used them to make some suds to rub over my body. I climbed out of the water and set on a nearby rock to dry off. I washed the cook pot and my socks which wasn't as bloody as last night, so I hoped that meant my blisters was getting better.

I decided I was too tired to travel farther, even though there'd be at least two more hours before dark. I got clean underwear and socks and dressed. Suddenly I thought I heard a clucking sound. I picked up my gun and stood very still. I couldn't believe my eyes. A wild turkey come walking towards the water. I raised my gun and when I got the bird in my sights, pulled the trigger. I knowed I wouldn't be able to use all the meat before it spoiled. I cut off the wings since they didn't have much meat on them, threw them aside, and skinned the bird. I was so hungry I couldn't hardly wait till I got it cooking over a fire. While it cooked I took the skin and entrails far enough upstream that they wouldn't entice a wildcat or some other animal near the campsite. I was very pleased with my good luck.

***

I woke up sudden when a loud clap of thunder echoed through the valley. Quick like I put on my boots, grabbed my blankets, the backpack, the left-over turkey, and my gun, and run to the trail. It was barely light enough to see, but I was looking at the mountain sides for a outcrop that would provide shelter from rain. Just as the rain drops hit my face, I spotted the perfect spot up the hill to the right. The space under the overhang was just large enough to get comfortable with my gear around me. With the dark clouds overhead, I couldn't tell what time it was, but at least it was sometime after daylight. The temperature was dropping, so I unfurled a blanket around my shoulders, made a snug nest, and listened to the rain.

I fell asleep and woke sometime later to find the rain still fell steady. The grey sky looked like it would continue for some time. I took off my boots and socks to give my feet some relief, and closed my eyes again. Later I remembered I hadn't had no breakfast, so I got out the turkey I had packed in the cook pot. The day dragged on and so did the rain. I ended up spending the night in the cozy nook. But before I went to sleep, I took the stone and held it for a few minutes. It did seem to make me feel better.

The next morning the rain stopped and the sun come out. I ate, put on a pair of clean socks and my boots, and started down the trail again. I hated I'd lost a whole day, but at least I wasn't hungry. By mid-morning, I noticed the valley was widening and the mountains seemed not so high. I stopped to eat beside a stream where I filled my canteen before moving onward.

Towards evening the trail led into a wide space where there was few trees. I rested on a rock and ate the last of the turkey. I looked all around wondering where I might set up my bed, but I didn't see no hiding places. Then I heard a tinkling like a small bell that seemed to be coming closer.

Soon I saw a sheep coming up the hill, the bell around its neck jingling with each step. I watched as a dozen sheep come in sight with a woman and a dog following after them.

She saw me and waved, but she didn't seem surprised to see me. When she got closer, she said, "Good day," in a strange voice.

I thought I should reply, so I said, "Hello, ma'am."

"You traveler?"

"Yes."

"Alone?"

"Yes."

"Need bed to sleep?"

"Yes, ma'am"

"Come." She motioned with her hand and led the way.

I thought she must not be from around these parts. She was dressed in bright shades of red, orange, and yellow and had gold bangles on her arms and hanging from her ears. Her hair was covered in a bright cloth, but around the edges I could see stray curls of grey. The dog herded the sheep along and I followed behind the woman till we come to a small log cabin and a larger log structure that was the barn. I helped her put out feed for the sheep and shut them in a large stall.

I offered to milk the cow while she called up the little donkey and fed him. By the time the chores was done, the sun had gone over the mountain hours earlier, and I couldn't hardly see to follow the woman to the house. I figgered she would send me to sleep in the barn. That would certainly be better than where I had slept for the last several nights.

The woman hurried to light a lamp. I noticed a fire had been laid in the fireplace, so I offered to get it started. Then I looked around. The cabin was even smaller than it had seemed from the outside. A long table was near the fireplace with a long bench beside it. A large loom was in front of the only window and took up a large part of the floor. A spinning wheel stood in the corner near a large basket full of sheep's wool. Opposite the window was a very small cot. At the foot of the cot was a stack of cured sheep skins. There wasn't hardly enough room to turn around. I was sure I would sleep in the barn.

She invited me to a seat at the table while she set out some bread and cheese and poured some fresh milk into a mug. We ate in silence. I had loads of questions but thought I should wait for her to lead the way. When the food was cleared away, she sat at the other end of the bench, reached into her pocket and pulled out a drop spindle. I watched as she begun spinning the wool into yarn. Her golden bracelets made a soft tinkle as she moved her hands.

"Keep in pocket. Use when watch sheep."

"What do you do with your yarn?"

She pointed toward the loom. "Weave cloth. Sell trading post Mump's Fort. Dye yarn. Ladies knit. Make moccasins."

"Where is Mump's Fort?"

She pointed to the east. "One day."

"Is this Virginia?"

She nodded and pointed to the north. "Kentucky one day." She pointed south. "Tennessee one day."

That meant I'd been in Virginia a whole day. That was good news.

A sudden noise startled me and I looked towards the mantle over the fireplace and seen a clock with a little bird popping in and out counting the hours. I thought it must be bed time. I was worried about my blistered feet and decided to take a chance by asking for her help.

"Ma'am, I need to ask you something."

She looked at me and nodded.

"I've been walking for five days, and I have blisters on my feet. I wonder if you have any medicine to treat my feet?"

She stood up, put her spindle back in her pocket, and picked up the lamp to move it closer to me. She motioned for me to take off my boots. I was embarrassed because my socks was even bloodier than before. She held the lamp closer and shook her head. She placed the lamp on the table and went out the door. When she returned in a few minutes she carried a wooden tub which she set on the floor. She warmed water, gave me some soap and motioned for me to wash my feet. When they was dry, she looked at them closely and shook her head while she made a "tsk, tsk" noise.

She poured out that water and heated more. She climbed a ladder into the loft and brought down some dried leaves that she crushed and poured into the water, then motioned for me to soak my feet. The warm water felt good at first, but after a bit started to sting. The woman lit a lantern and went out the door. She come back with a jar of salve. She smiled and her dark eyes twinkled. "For sheep."

When she decided I had soaked my feet long enough, she gave me a cloth to dry them and handed me the salve. She motioned for me to cover each blister with a big gob of the salve. After she handed me a new pair of wool socks, she pointed to the loft. "Sleep?

***

The odor of coffee brought me awake. I looked around the little attic. It had been too dark last night to see anything. There wasn't room enough to stand, so I had crawled from the ladder to the pallet. Piles of wool and sheepskins covered most of the floor space. Bunches of dried plants hung from the rafters. I remembered I'd dreamed I was helping Miz Simpson prepare plants to dry. Must have been the yerbs in the attic space that made me have such a dream. When I heard her moving around, I climbed down the ladder.

She put out more bread, butter, and jam for breakfast. When I finished, I laid a dollar on the table and started to thank her for her hospitality. She got a fierce look in her eyes and shook her finger at me.

"You help me. You not pay." She put the money back in my hand. "I go sheep today." She put her hand on my chest. "You stay. Feet get well"

"I need to move on. Maybe if I get to Mump's Fort, I can get a ride with someone going farther east."

"You stay. Feet get better. Go trading post two days." She pointed at me. "Take you."

I thought I had to keep moving, but she had a point. My feet did need to get better. I finally nodded and reached for my boots. If I stayed, at least I could lend a hand. Again she protested and pushed my boots away. "Not good." She rummaged around in the space beside the sheepskins and come back with a pair of moccasins. "Good for feet." She made clear I was to stay at the cabin while she took the sheep to graze.

For the next two days I made myself as useful as I could while she was away. The soft moccasins with the fuzzy wool on the inside didn't irritate my feet. I carried water from the nearby creek and washed all my clothes. As I come through the door, I noticed a strange symbol above it that looked almost like a hand with a bright blue eye shape in the center. I wondered why she would have a eye above her door. I couldn't imagine. I gathered vegetables from her garden and prepared them for supper. I mucked out the stables where the cow and donkey stayed and shelled corn for the chickens.

On the second day she returned early with the sheep because clouds coming from the west looked like a storm. We got the chores done early before the rain started and had extra time in the evening. She climbed the ladder and handed down stacks of woven wool which I stacked on the table. There was also bundles of yarn of different colors. After she come down, I helped her carry the cured sheep skins, and a dozen pairs of moccasins to the table. We would load the little wagon in the morning. She left room at one end of the table for supper. She carried a stool from the loom and sat opposite me.

She appeared to be worried and restless, but I didn't know why. The rain beat hard on the roof and lightning flashed through the window. "Rain not go," she said. I thought she was worried about the rain preventing the trip. She took a wooden box from the mantle and took out what appeared to be cards. After shuffling the cards, she turned them face down on the table and stared at them before picking up one and turning it over. It was a picture of a golden chariot. She smiled. "Good." Then she chose another card which had a picture of scales like the peddlers used. Again she smiled. "Good." She stacked the cards up and put them back in the box, appearing to have found out what she wanted to know.

She took the cards out again and motioned toward me. "You like?" I wasn't sure what it was all about, but she was being so nice to me I thought I should give it a try. She shuffled the cards and spread them face down on the table again. She nodded for me to pick one. From the back they all looked the same, and even if I knowed what the pictures was, I still wouldn't know which one to choose. I picked up the second one in the third row. It was a picture of a foreign looking man dressed in a long robe.

She seemed happy with this choice. She pointed to the man. "Judge. He make right." I wasn't sure what that meant, but it sounded like I was getting some sort of a good deal. I sure hadn't had any good deals lately. Maybe this meant my luck would change.

She motioned for me to take another card. It was a picture of a man and woman embracing. She laughed out loud and clapped her hands. "You got woman?" I shook my head. She turned her mouth down at the corners but then smiled. "You get woman." I scratched my head. At least this was amusing her. I thought the last thing I needed was a woman.

My third choice was a picture of a devil. She seemed disappointed with this choice. "You sick." Was she saying I was going to be sick? I had had very few illnesses in my life, so I didn't think I was like to fall victim to some bad disease. I shrugged my shoulders.

The picture on my last card was a moon peeping through very dark clouds. Again she looked disappointed and shook her head. "Bad man trick." Well, I could believe that. Look how James has treated me. I wasn't discouraged—two good ones was better than three bad ones. Besides, I didn't think cards could tell the future anyway.

Each night she had treated my feet. Now she looked at them again and nodded her approval. She gave me two pairs of wool socks and explained I should change socks ever day and always wear two pairs. That will help cushion my feet and should prevent more blisters.

She made me understand that we would be leaving early the next morning. I climbed the ladder thinking she no longer seemed to be worried about the rain, even though it still pounded the roof.

**

We arrived at Mump's Fort in the late afternoon. I had expected we would find a fortress hopefully occupied by Confederate troops, so I was surprised to see a simple mountain settlement much like many other little mountain towns. And there was no armed guards in sight. I wondered why this was called a fort. The little donkey seemed to know exactly where to go and pulled up in front of the trading post.

She unhooked the harness and made me understand I should take the donkey to the watering trough around the corner for a drink. She went into the store. By the time I had the donkey watered and tied to the hitching post, she come back, looked at me and said, "Good boy. You help." She placed her palms together in front of her chest and bowed.

I realized she was dismissing me. I tried to tell her how much I appreciated all she had done for me, but she waved me away and then opened up the cart to unload. A young man come out to help her. I backed away a few steps and waited to see if she would ask me to help, but she didn't look at me again.

I knew someday she would find the money I left in the little wooden box on the mantle, and then she'd know I was really grateful. My stomach growled, and I remembered I hadn't eaten since the bread and jam before we left. I shouldered my backpack and gun and wandered down the street looking for a place to get something to eat.

As I passed the door of a tavern, the aroma of cooking food lured me inside. I set at a table in the corner enjoying my bean soup and cornbread, thinking about the last three days. The woman hadn't seemed afraid of me even though she could see I was armed. She left me alone in her cabin for two days while she took the sheep to pasture. She didn't even ask my name, actually didn't ask me anything. I don't even know her name. I decided I would always remember her as the Sheep Lady. After finishing my meal, I started walking down the main street wondering where I could sleep for the night.

I was still thinking about this strange experience as I walked along. I had gobs of questions I'd never know the answers to. Why was she living way out there alone? Was she a widow woman? Or was her husband away somewhere? Was she a foreigner of some kind? Why was her speech funny? How did she get the sheepskins? Did she butcher the sheep herself and cure the hides? If she took the sheep to pasture every day, how did she have time to do all that weaving, spinning, sewing moccasins, making garden and all the work it takes to keep the place going? Was she some sort of magician or maybe even a witch?

I finally accepted I'd never get any answers, but I would always remember all the kindness she had shown me. I walked till I was near the edge of town. I didn't know what to do. I needed to find a place to sleep, but I didn't want to spend any more money. I also didn't know what road to take to get to the battle grounds. I'd heard James bragging how West Virginia had split off from Virginia to support the Union. I didn't want to end up in West Virginia by mistake. I needed to find someone who could give me directions.

Ahead, I saw a shelter—a roof held up by some poles. A man set underneath caning the seat of a chair. Ma had cane-bottomed chairs for the dining room table at the Kentucky house, but I'd never seen how they was made, so I stopped to watch.

"Howdy, stranger. Would you like to set a spell?" The man smiled and pointed to a finished chair nearby.

"Thanks. Do you mind if I watch?"

The man held out his hand but didn't stand up. "Name's Carl Henley; what's yours?"

I shook his hand and took a seat. "Harvey Campbell. Pleased to meet you."

"Where you from, Harvey?"

"Kentucky."

"What brings you here?" When I didn't answer right away, he ask, "Am I too nosy? My granny always says I am."

A crutch was laying beside Carl's chair and then I seen he had only one leg, so I ask, "Do you mind if I ask if you was in the war?"

Carl nodded and moved the chair he worked on so I could see his leg was off above his knee. "Yep, lost my leg in the Battle of Gettysburg. I thought we was gonna whup those Yankee sons of bitches good, but in spite of all General Lee could do, they beat us. So many brave soldiers lost their lives. I was lucky to only lose a leg."

"So you was in General Lee's army?"

Carl nodded his head and concentrated on his work.

I had been afraid to say too much to this stranger, but now that I knowed he had been a Confederate soldier, I felt free to tell my plans. "I'm hoping to go fight for General Lee."

Carl looked up in surprise. "You ain't old enough, are you?"

"Sixteen."

"Are you sure you want to go fight in this crazy war? It ain't much fun."

"I ain't doing it for fun." Carl just stared at me. "I want to know how I can get to where Lee's fighting."

"Well, last I heard they was fighting in the Shenandoah Valley."

"How do I get there?"

Carl studied about that for a while. "Best way is to catch a ride with the mail wagon over to Goodson and then take a train. The mail driver takes passengers for a small fee. But he only comes ever three weeks and he come yesterday, so I guess it'll be three weeks till he comes again."

I shook my head. "If I stayed here, what would I do while I waited? I ain't got money to stay at a boarding house."

Carl worked awhile without talking, then looked up. "You know

111

anything about farm work?"

"I grew up on a farm and worked in the fields since I's big enough to heft a hoe."

Carl gave me another good look. "If you'll give me a hand, I can get you a good meal and a place to sleep tonight." I nodded. "See that pony tied to the tree behind this shed? Bring him around and hitch him to that little cart over there."

Soon me and Carl had loaded the chairs and caning supplies into the cart and was on the way out of town. Carl explained, "I live with my granny out on the side of a ridge. She has a little farm, but she ain't able to do much work, and I ain't no good with only one leg. I don't think she can pay you, but I'll try to talk her into letting you sleep in the barn and work for your meals." He looked over at me. "You interested?"

I nodded and said I would give it a try. I didn't know how long I wanted to hang out here, but it was a solution for at least one night.

***

Granny Henley, a tiny woman with silver hair, wrinkled as a dried up potato, welcomed me like a long lost cousin. She listened as Carl explained I wanted to hitch a ride with the mail wagon and needed a place to stay for a few days till the wagon come again.

She wiped her hands on her apron as she looked me up and down with twinkling blue eyes and nodded her head. "Sure, he can stay here."

Carl quickly told her I was a good farm worker and was willing to work to pay for my meals.

Granny nodded again. "We sure can use some help."

I learnt the daily routine right quick. Up at daylight. Milk the goats and feed the pony. To the house for Granny's breakfast. To the barn to get Sam's pony cart loaded and see him off to his shed in town. To work at whatever task Granny give me. To the house for dinner when Granny rang the dinner bell. Back to work till Carl come home. To barn to do evening chores. To the house for supper. To bed when it got dark.

Granny's meals was plain—fried corn meal mush and gravy, turnip greens, bean soup—but there was always enough and I never felt hungry. Granny was concerned because she was late getting her garden planted, so that was the first task. The ground had been plowed so I followed her directions for planting beans, potatoes, okra, beets, turnips and corn. Once that was done to her satisfaction, she pointed to fences that needed repair. The days went by quickly.

I had been watching Carl hobbling so awkward along with only one crutch and remembered the crutches Caleb had made when Scott broke his leg while driving logs down the river. I thought I could make a pair of crutches that would help Carl get around better. At dinner time I ask Granny if she thought that would be a good idea.

Her eyes sparkled with delight. "Why yes, I think that would be wonderful. What would you make them out of?"

"Well, I saw some wood out in the barn, could we use that?"

"Umm." She scratched her head. "I think that's Carl's lumber for making the chairs. I think we'll have to ask him if you can use it."

As soon as Carl hobbled in that evening she rushed to him. "Harvey's got the idea to make you a pair of crutches. He says he knows how, but can he use some of your lumber to do it?"

Carl was pleased and after asking me some questions, we went to the barn to pick out the lumber. First thing the next morning Granny helped find tools and I got to work. It took me a couple of days to get the wood cut and planed smooth. I was glad I'd paid attention to Caleb when he was making the crutches for Scott. I ask Granny to help me make some padding for the tops of the crutches so they would be more comfortable under Carl's arm pits.

Granny laughed with delight when she saw Carl trying out the crutches. In no time he could go as fast as I could walk, and it didn't look like hobbling at all. She made a special supper to celebrate.

On the Saturday, two days before the mail wagon was to come, I was surprised when Carl's cart showed up in the lane mid-afternoon. I rushed to see if they was some problem.

"No, Harvey, nothing's wrong. One of my friends is having a party at his house, and I thought me and you would clean up and go over there."

Once the evening chores was done, we headed to the creek with a cake of lye soap. I was glad I'd helped Granny do some laundry the day before so we both had clean pants and shirts.

After a quick supper, we set off in the pony cart. I was uneasy about this party. I'd never been to a house party, but I remembered Mr. Baker had preached against them when he was the preacher for the little church in Laureltown. But I thought it would be rude to refuse to go after Carl and his granny had been so good to me.

Carl gently slapped the reins on the pony's back to get him started. "It'll take about an hour to get there because we have to go back through town and over a ridge."

As we passed Carl's shed in town, I ask him why he worked there instead of working at home.

"Most of my work is done for people in town. I'd miss out on their business if it wasn't easy for them to find me."

"That makes sense, I guess."

People on the street greeted Carl as we rode past stores and businesses. One lady yelled for us to stop and Carl pulled up. "Oh, Carl. I'm glad I caught you. I need two more of your chairs."

"Thank you, Miz Hooper. I have one finished and another to be finished by early next week. I could deliver them next Wednesday. Would that be satisfactory with you?"

"That's wonderful. I'm pleased you can have them so soon."

Carl flicked the reins and the pony moved forward. "I guess that answers your question." Carl looked at me and grinned.

By the time we reached the house party, the sun had set and buggies and carts littered the lawn in front of the house. Carl tied the pony to a nearby tree. "Let's go see what we can stir up."

I followed him to the house. I noticed how smooth Carl moved along on his new crutches, even went up the steps like he'd had these crutches forever. A dozen or more people stood around on the big front porch, a couple with fiddles tucked under their arms. Carl introduced me as his new friend, and I shook hands with all the men and bowed to the women. About that time the lady of the house come through the door and invited everybody inside.

The four-room house was larger than most mountain cabins. The front room had been emptied of all the furniture except for straight backed chairs placed around the walls. Opposite the fireplace a table held a large pot with a gourd dipper and a bunch of cups. "Just help yourselfs," the lady yelled. "They's more where that come from."

Carl leaned his crutches against the wall and chose a chair.

I watched as the men gathered around the pot, filled their cups, and gulped down a big swallow. Almost all the men yelled, "Whoooeee!" and stomped their feet. I turned to Carl. "Would you like me to fill a cup for you?"

"Sure Harvey, that'd be great."

I filled a cup for Carl, but put only a small amount in my cup. I figured it was moonshine whiskey, and I worried I would embarrass myself if I tasted it. Me and Evan had tried white lightning only once, and I choked and coughed for five minutes. I didn't want to do that again.

Carl thanked me and took a good sip. He shut his eyes tight and then opened them wide and shook his head, but didn't say nothing. He nodded to me that it was my turn. I took a deep breath, lifted the cup and let a tiny sip into my mouth. I held it there for a few seconds before I swallowed. I shook my head, batted my eyes and let my breath out. It seemed like the burn went all the way to my toes. But no one seemed to pay attention to me, so I guess I done good enough.

A few more people arrived carrying more music instruments and soon the room was filled with music like I hadn't never heard before, and two couples took to dancing. I took another tiny sip from the cup. It didn't burn quite so bad. Carl had already emptied his cup so I ask if he'd like a refill. When I returned, a pretty woman was beside Carl.

Carl motioned to me. "This here's Sarah Jane and this is my new friend Harvey."

I bowed to her. "Could I get the lady a drink?"

"That would be nice, if you would be so kind."

I thought if I could just keep going back and forth to the table, maybe people would think I was drinking all these cups.

I decided to move to let Carl and his lady friend have some privacy, so I edged around the dancers and peeked into the kitchen. The hostess, who I remembered was Miz Carter, and another lady was making popcorn. They invited me to come in and help. A sweet smell like molasses filled the room. "We're making popcorn balls as soon as the molasses syrup gets cooked enough," Miz Carter explained. "If you'd like to help you can shake the popcorn skillet to keep the kernels from burning."

I introduced myself to the younger lady, who said her name was Sadie. I stole glances at her when she wasn't looking and decided she must be near my age. When Miz Carter announced the syrup was ready, she poured it over the fluffy white kernels in a huge wooden bowl and showed us how to rub our hands with butter so the sticky syrup wouldn't stick to our hands as we formed the popcorn into balls. "Watch out, cause this stuff is hot. Don't get burnt."

They laughed when I yelped and dropped a handful of popcorn back into the bowl when it burnt me. When all the corn had been made into balls, we took them into the front room and put them on the table. I saw the pot of moonshine was more than half gone. I got my cup from the kitchen, and Sadie got herself a cup and led me out on the porch.

Sadie told me she was the Carters' only child, that she had finished all the grades in the local school, and now wished she knew what the rest of her life would be like. She looked at me. "You're not from around here, are you?"

"No, I'm from Kentucky, but I'm leaving with the mail wagon on Monday on my way to Goodson."

"Oh, that's too bad. I thought maybe we could be friends." She took a sip of her drink."

"I'm sure it would be nice to be your friend." I took another sip from my cup. It was getting easier to swallow all the time.

When she emptied her cup, she said, "Drink up and I'll go fill our cups and get us one of them popcorn balls."

By the time I had emptied two cups, I no longer felt it going down. My head felt big, sort of like when I was a little boy and turned around and around till I fell down. Sadie grabbed my hand and said, "Let's go dance."

I didn't know how to dance, but I let her lead me into the house. It looked like the dancers was mostly just jumping around anyway, and I figured I could do that much. I looked for Carl and found him holding one crutch, hopping and swaying a little while Sarah Jane held on to him with both arms. Carl caught my eye and winked.

Me and Sadie danced—if you could call it that—till I was out of breath. We went back out on the porch and sat in the swing. Sadie moved close to me, and it seemed natural to put my arm around her shoulders. We talked for what seemed like hours. When she squirmed closer and put her hand on my thigh, it most took my breath away.

Carl and his girl come out of the house. "Well, Harvey, you ready to call it a night?"

"Sure, Carl." I stood up. "Wait here and I'll go get the pony cart."

Sadie grabbed my hand. "I'll go with you." We slipped out into the darkness. Maybe it was because she'd never see me again that Sadie was being what Ma would call "forward," but I hoped it was cause she really liked me. She stood close to me with her hands on my chest. "It's been so nice to have a really handsome feller to dance with."

"I've enjoyed your company tonight." I didn't really know what else to say.

"I'm sorry you're not gonna be around here longer. I'd like to get to know you better." She put her arms around my waist and looked up at me, the moonlight shining in her big brown eyes. I thought maybe this was what the Sheep Lady meant when she said I'd get a woman. She was so beautiful standing there in the moonlight, I couldn't help myself; I kissed her. She pushed her body close against me. I felt things happening in my body I'd never felt before. It was almost scary so I turned her loose and stepped back. The top of my head felt like it was floating. I thought, "Maybe I'm a little drunk."

"I guess we better get this cart up there for Carl now." I untied the pony and led him through all the other carts and buggies to the house where Carl and his girl waited.

"Took you long enough," Carl teased me. He hugged his girl and gave her a kiss, stowed his crutches in the back and climbed aboard. When we was back on the road to town, Carl punched me with his elbow. "Sadie sorta took a shine to you, I reckon."

"She seems like a nice young lady."

"Nice young lady, my foot! She's a real pistol."

"What do you mean?"

"Well, she'd like to get herself married off, and so she makes a pitch to every feller she gets close to. And lots of young bucks around here would like to court her, but they's afeared of her pa. It's a good thing he didn't catch you two out there in the dark. He'd have grabbed his gun and chased you off the place."

I studied about that for a while. Then I ask Carl if he was courting Sarah Jane.

"You might say that. I'd like to ask her to marry me, but I'm afeared I can't support her. It's all I can do to support me and Granny. So If I ain't gonna marry her, I prob'ly should quit being around her. It's just that I like her and can't bring myself to quit her."

As we rode along through the dark night, I thought about how strange life is. A month ago, I never would have imagined kissing a girl or most of what else had happened since I left home. Soon I would be setting out on another unknown journey. I hoped I would find friends along the way to help me as much as the Sheep Lady and Carl.

***

On Monday morning I helped Carl load up the cart and rode into town with him to wait for the mail wagon. Carl told me it usually come about noon. Before we left, Granny give me a big hug and wouldn't listen to any thanks. "You done more than earn your keep. I won't never forget you, young feller. Now you just be careful and don't get yourself hurt, and iffen you ever come through these parts again, you always got a place at our table." She handed me a bundle of food to take along.

When we reached the top of the hill, I turned and seen Granny still standing in the doorway watching us go. I waved and smiled when she waved back.

Donald King, the mail wagon driver, welcomed me aboard and we left town headed east by mid-afternoon. "Glad you got your gun," Donald said. "Is it loaded?" When I told him it was, he added, "Good. Cause they's a bunch of marauders that ride up out of Tennessee and rob the mail sometimes. They's no way they get much by doing it cause nobody's got any money nowadays. I guess they just like to cause trouble."

The wagon wasn't as fancy as a stage coach—no windows—but it had a boxed in compartment where large pieces of freight could be stowed. A bench-like seat in front provided a place for the driver and a passenger or two.

While I was waiting for the mail wagon, I went to the trading post and got some paper and a envelope so I could write Ma. I wasn't sure how much to tell her, so I made it short—just that I had decided to go to Virginia and join General Lee's army. I knowed she would worry, but I thought I owed it to her to let her know. I would write again when I actually become a Confederate soldier.

Soon the wagon traveled along roads that climbed steep mountain sides and looped down into deep valleys. The mountains seemed higher and the valleys more narrow than the mountains in my part of Kentucky. Now I understood why Donald had two teams of horses hitched to his wagon. At first I had thought the extra team was not necessary, but now I saw they strained on some of the worst inclines. As we slipped and slidded down steep grades, he stood on the brake lever to keep the wagon from rolling into the horses. Occasionally we met travelers on horses and one covered wagon going west, but mostly we was the only ones on the road.

After one difficult stretch, we come to a small creek and Donald King stopped to let the horses drink and rest awhile. I opened up the bundle of food and shared it. Donald took off his hat and used it to fan his face. "I can't decide which is better—summertime or wintertime. In the summertime, it's so darn hot it tires out the horses more. But the rain and snow in the wintertime really slows us down." He put his hat back on and clucked to the horses. "It's time to get back on the road."

Just before dark, we pulled into a little settlement Donald called Stickleyville. Donald steered the horses into the barn lot behind the trading post. We unhitched the horses, led them to the horse trough for a drink and put them in stalls. Donald ask me to climb into the loft and pitch down some hay. I helped rub down the horses; then Donald invited me to eat supper with him at his boarding house. "The government pays for my room and board when I stay here. I'll put your meal on my ticket." I accepted the offer, and then Donald said I could also stay there at my own expense.

"If it's all right, I'll just sleep in the hay loft. I have my bedroll and can be comfortable there."

The next morning Donald harnessed the horses, and we set out shortly before daylight. "This will be a long hard day for us and the horses as well. The roads between here and Goodson are the worst roads I've ever traveled. We'll be lucky if we make it by dark, but Goodson is my home. I'll sleep in my own bed tonight." He went on to explain that before the war he had been a full-time employee of the United States Postal Service. Now he just had this one route he made every three weeks for the Confederate government.

Donald's prediction was right. It was indeed a difficult journey. I remember one mountain so steep it took three switchbacks to get across, but, as Donald had said, we arrived in Goodson shortly after dark. I thanked Donald for the ride and asked if I could sleep in his barn.

The snorting and huffing of the horses below woke me just as day was breaking. I went to the horse trough and washed the hay out of my hair and took off my socks and washed my feet with the lye soap Granny had insisted I take. I was determined not to get the bloody blisters again. After finding a place to buy some breakfast, I set out to find the train station.

It was not hard to find, but I was surprised to see it was almost deserted; no passengers stood on the platform. Then I saw three Confederate soldiers standing guard at the door of the station. "Do you know when there'll be a train going north?"

"Where you wanting to go?"

I didn't know what to say. I thought the soldiers seemed friendly enough and maybe they could give me some good information and advice. "I'm wanting to go join General Lee's troops." All three looked at me like they thought I's up to something.

The man closest to me stuck out his hand. "I'm Corporal Smith. My buddies call me Jack. Then he introduced the other two: Privates Jones and Miller.

I shook hands. "I'm Harvey Campbell."

Corporal Smith explained they were waiting for a supply train from Knoxville that was to deliver medical and clothing supplies to Lynchburg. "We don't know when the train will get here because the rails have been sabotaged. Hopefully it will be soon because General Early is on his way from Charlottesville to protect Lynchburg from a Union attack, and he needs these supplies."

I sort of fidgeted. "So, when the train comes can I ride it?"

"I don't know about that. We ain't letting civilians on the train."

Private Jones stepped closer, "Now, young feller, if you really want to be a Reb, I'm sure Sergeant Kelly could swear you in. Our relief should arrive soon and we can take you to our headquarters." He smiled like he thought that idea might shock me out of the notion of being a soldier. "So what do you say?"

"Sounds good to me."

"Are you sure? How old are you, anyway?"

"Sixteen."

Jones scratched his chin. "It ain't easy being a soldier, especially for a feller young as you."

"I understand, but it's what I want to do."

"All right then. Soon as our duty is finished here, you can go with us to our headquarters. It's just down the street in a big house we procured."

Sergeant Kelly didn't even bother to ask me anything, just told me to raise my right hand and swear to defend the Confederate States of America. He then turned to the three who had brought me in. "Since you brought him, you'll be responsible for looking after him. Is that clear?"

***

I wasn't sure what Sergeant Kelly meant when he asked my new friends to look after me, but I soon found out. First, we went to the headquarters building to eat in the mess set up in a room that looked like it was supposed to be the parlor, where we ate fat back, eggs, biscuits and gravy, washed down by scalding hot coffee.

"You better enjoy this, Private Campbell," Private Miller said, "Cause once you get on the march, you don't get much to eat." I was pleased to be addressed by my rank and took seriously Miller's advice to eat up.

Since the three had been on duty since midnight, they wanted to sleep for a few hours. They showed me where their bunks was upstairs and invited me to take a nap, but I wasn't sleepy. "I'll just wander around for a while and see you later."

I found a trading post that had a post office and mailed another letter to Ma. With bandits robbing the mail, I wasn't sure my first letter would get delivered. Of course, this one might not either. But I wanted to tell her I was now a private in the Confederate Army.

The trading post had lots of bare shelves. People on the street talked in quiet voices, almost like a friend had died. Some stray dogs was fighting over a scrap of something someone had throwed out in the street. I wandered down a side street and saw many houses needed paint, fences needed repair, and hedges needed trimming. I guessed the men folks had gone off to war and left their families to cope as best they could.

I returned to the headquarters and sat on the porch to wait till my friends finished their sleep. In the late afternoon, Private Jones come onto the porch, stretched his arms above his head and took a deep breath. "Oh, here you are. We were looking for you. Come in and we'll try to find you a uniform. We don't have many supplies here, but maybe we can find a jacket and hat. Fortunately you have your own rifle cause we're way short on guns and ammunition. We're hoping that supply train will have some arms when it gets here."

They found me a new shirt and a Rebel cap and I joined the three of them for another meal in the mess. When we was finished eating, they asked me to join them for a night on the town. "We just heard the train will come tomorrow, so this is our last night of freedom for a few days."

Corporal Smith led us down a side street to a shabby little house on the edge of town. I thought he seemed to know where he was going, so I guessed he had been here before. Inside, the front room held three tables surrounded by odds and ends of chairs and stools. A candle burned on each table. Three other soldiers sat at one table and greeted us when we come in. An elderly gray-headed woman dressed in a long black dress topped by a dirty apron brought out a tray of cups and set them in the middle of our table.

"You wanting your usual?"

"Sure thing, Molly," Miller said. "Bring it on."

Now I was faced with another moonshine challenge. I thought I had to prove to these fellows I was man enough to be in the army. I was determined to follow their example and drink it down as good as they did.

After we emptied the bottle Molly had brought, each of them put money on the table, so I put down money too. I thought I saw Corporal Smith and Private Jones exchange a nod, then Jones yelled, "Molly, bring us another bottle."

All the time, they was teasing each other, making comments about Sergeant Kelly, and occasionally asking questions. I was feeling that lightness in my head and joined in their fun. It was easy to laugh at their crude jokes and to talk with them. By the time the second bottle was gone, I had told them some of my background.

"I'm still not sure you should join the Rebs," Miller said. "With your brothers having been in the Union Army and your family from Pennsylvania, looks like you'd join the Yankees."

I stared at the flame of the candle on the table and finally looked at Miller. "I have a debt to pay."

"Molly, another bottle," Jones said and pointed at me. "Put your money away. This one's on me." He filled all our cups and took a good swallow. "Now, what's this about a debt?"

I explained how the Union Home Guard had shot down my best friend because his brothers was Confederate soldiers. "Now I owe it to him to go fight them."

The three men quietly sipped their drinks. I had kept up with them cup for cup, but now my head was so dizzy and talking about Evan had made me so sad I felt like crying. I pushed my cup into the middle of the table.

"Those bastards!" Corporal Smith, who sat on my left, clapped me on the back. "I get it. You're gonna knock them out first chance you get." He raised his cup, "To a brave Rebel. May he blow up a whole damn squadron!"

"Hear, hear," the other two said and drained their cups.

"This is getting too serious," Miller complained. "What shall we do now?"

"I'd say let's go to Nancy's. Private Campbell needs cheering up."

"What's Nancy's?"

"Oh, she's a nice lady." Jones reached for my cup and drained it. "Do you know any nice ladies?"

I laughed. "Well, my ma is a nice lady."

The men laughed like that was the funniest thing they'd ever heard. I was glad they thought I was funny. It made me feel good when we joked and laughed together. Jones wiped his mouth with the back of his hand.

"That's not the kind of nice lady I had in mind." He gave me a crooked smile and looked at me out of the corner of his eyes. "You ever had a woman?"

"What do you mean?" The men laughed again.

"You ever loved on a woman?"

"I've kissed a woman." More laughter.

"Let's go." Miller took my arm and helped me stand. The room sort of wobbled. I shut my eyes and stood still till my head stopped going around. I followed the men out staggering a little on the steps, but once in the cool night air, I was starting to feel better. We walked back toward town and turned on to a street of nicer houses. At the end of the street we entered the gate of a brick house with bright lamps in all the windows. Several ladies in fancy dresses rocked in chairs on the porch. They seemed glad to see us and greeted Miller, Jones, and Smith by name.

Smith introduced me to a girl named Lucy. "Sweet Lucy can make you feel better. Go with her and she'll take care of you."

I had heard the hired hands talking about their visits to "houses of ill repute," as Ma would say, so I knowed more about what was going on than my three new "friends" realized. I guessed they was playing a trick on a poor innocent country boy, but I was determined to be a good sport, so I went with Lucy when she took my hand and led me inside. The prettiest red furniture I had ever saw was arranged in groups about the large room, which I guessed was the parlor. A huge portrait of a beautiful lady hung over the fireplace. The oil lamps scattered about the room gave a warm glow to the wood paneled walls. It was so purty I wanted to stand and stare, but Lucy pulled me into the hallway and headed up the stairs. She opened a door and invited me into another fancy room. She led me to a love seat covered in scarlet velvet.

"Would you like something to drink?"

"A glass of water would be nice, ma'am."

I thought I knowed what was about to happen, and if so, it would be a total new experience I wasn't prepared for. I hoped I wouldn't make a fool of myself. As Lucy poured water from a pitcher on a table near the fireplace, the lamp on the table gave her face a bronze-like glow. It made me think she looked like a angel. Then it come to my mind that a angel wouldn't be in this business.

My mouth felt dry and the water tasted good. I emptied the glass and set it on the table at the end of the love seat. I didn't know what one should talk about in this situation, but I thought I should say something. I looked at Lucy who had set snuggled close enough for our shoulders to touch. "Do you live here?" She opened her eyes in surprise, and I thought my soldier buddies would laugh at me for such a question.

"Yes, I have lived here for about a year."

"Where did you live before that?"

"I lived with my mama in a little town in Tennessee near Knoxville, but Mama died and I didn't have no place to go. Nancy, who owns this house, is my mama's cousin, and she invited me to live here with her."

"Does she make you work here?"

"No, she doesn't make me. I'm glad to help cook meals, do laundry, clean—whatever needs doing. She's been very good to me, and I'm thankful I have such a nice place to live."

That wasn't exactly what I had meant to ask.

Lucy noticed I was frowning. "Oh, you mean does Nancy make me entertain men?"

I nodded.

"She lets me do what I want. If I like someone and I think he will be kind to me, I enjoy giving him pleasure. I won't touch a man who looks at me with pure lust in his eyes." She put her hand on my thigh. "As soon as I saw you, I knew you was a lonesome man who needed some good loving." She took my arm and pulled it around her shoulders and looked up at me with a smile. I felt the tingling in my lower belly like when I kissed Sadie and lowered my head to kiss her. I decided this must be what the Sheep Lady had in mind.

CHAPTER 9

June 1864

Goodson, Virginia

Before daylight, someone grabbed my leg and yelled, "On your feet, private!" I rolled off the bunk, hit the floor, and faced my three buddies. Miller ruffled my hair. "How's our little lover boy this morning?"

I felt awful. I couldn't think of anything to say and besides my head hurt so bad I wanted to crawl back in bed. Even in the semi darkness, it hurt to open my eyes. I saw they was dressed and figgered I should get dressed too, but my stubborn legs didn't want to move.

In his gruff officer's voice, Corporal Smith said, "Private, you have fifteen minutes to be at the train station with all your gear. We must be on the train when it leaves." Then he and Private Jones marched out of the room.

Miller helped get my gear together while I dunked my head in the wash basin on the dresser. I shivered, wiped my face and hair on the towel, and reached for my boots. On the way out, we grabbed a cup of coffee from the mess and boarded the passenger car just as it pulled from the platform.

When we found seats, I looked around. Confederate soldiers pretty well filled the car. I recognized several men I'd seen at the Headquarters. I took off my cap and rubbed my forehead. That mad dash for the train hadn't helped my headache. "Where're we headed?"

"Lynchburg."

"Why are we going there?"

"This train carries supplies for the Confederate Army and for the large Confederate hospital located in Lynchburg. Our job is to make certain these supplies get there safely. That's also where you can join up with some Confederate forces. General Jubal Early's troops are on their way there to help defend the city. You won't be fighting with General Lee's troops, but it's the best way to join up from this part of the state."

I thought about that for a bit. "I guess that will be the best plan for me." I leaned my head against the seat back and closed my eyes for a few minutes then turned to Miller. "Why would the Yankees want to capture Lynchburg?"

"Lynchburg is a busy city, important to our cause. Tons of manufactured goods and agriculture products are shipped out of Lynchburg every day."

"How do you know this?"

Miller laughed. "I grew up on a tobacco farm on the James River. I know Lynchburg well. We sold all our tobacco at the big tobacco warehouse there."

"It's a large city then?"

"Yes, it's probably the second largest city in the state next to Richmond. This state produces lots of tobacco and most of it is shipped through Lynchburg. Lots of businesses, factories, schools, churches. Many wealthy people live there."

"If it's such a important city, how come the Yankees ain't captured it?"

Miller raised his eyebrows and nodded. "I'm sure they plan to do just that. Our sergeant told us yesterday that General Lee has sent General Early to help defend the city. His forces should get there about the time we arrive." He sighed and ran his hand over his unshaved chin. "I expect as soon as we get these supplies delivered, we'll be sent to help General Early's forces defend the city."

"Then they expect the city to be attacked?"

Miller nodded again. "For months Union forces have been coming through the Shenandoah Valley and attacking towns. Our forces have been pushing them back into West Virginia, but they continue their raids and appear to be headed for Lynchburg."

"So it looks like we're headed for battle?"

Miller laughed. "Yep. You may get a chance to knock off a Yankee for your friend at last."

I looked out the window. We passed farm fields, some looked terrible. A tobacco field had weeds higher than the tobacco plants. "Look at that tobacco. Looks like they planted it and then run off and left it."

Miller took a long breath. "I guess all their slaves run off and they don't have anybody to help them. We'll probably see lots of neglected fields and shabby farms. Lincoln has no idea how important the slaves are to the agriculture production of this country."

We were quiet for a while. I leaned my head against the back of the seat and rubbed my empty belly. I wished we'd had time to eat some breakfast. The headache didn't seem to be going away. It felt good to close my eyes. The sun, beating down on me through the window made me sleepy.

I was jolted awake when Corporal Smith shook my shoulder. "Oh, I guess our lover boy needs his beauty sleep. Sweet Lucy musta give you a real workout." He then handed both of us a mess kit with some sausage, biscuits, and fried potatoes. "This will have to last you till we get to Roanoke tonight, but you'll get a chance to fill your canteens when we stop to refuel in a few hours."

"Thanks, Jack," Miller grinned. "Where'd you get this?"

"Sergeant had the mess cooks prepare it, but they loaded it in the baggage car instead of in this car. I finally found it, so enjoy."

He started to walk away, but turned back. "Lieutenant Morgan is preparing a duty roster for us. We have to guard the train, especially during the stops. We can't allow anyone to board. We'll be on duty four hours and off four hours. I'll let you know the details when he finishes the roster."

Before he could turn to go, I spoke up. "Thanks for the food, Corporal. I was starving."

Smith grinned. "I'll bet all that loving last night whetted your appetite."

Not knowing nothing to say, I just turned to stare out the window. I wished they'd just forget about Sweet Lucy. I guessed they'd like me to give them a minute by minute account. I'd never tell how Sweet Lucy coached me into making love to her. I leaned my head against the glass and smiled. It was pleasant to remember. I sat up straighter in amazement when I saw a woman in a field holding on to a plow pulled by a cow. A young boy tugged on a rope tied around the cow's neck trying to keep her in the row. I motioned for Miller to look.

"Well, I'd guess all the workers and men folk have gone to war and the army confiscated their horses, so there's nobody left to help them."

"It ain't just the soldiers that gets hurt in a war, is it?" I remembered how the Home Guard and the State Guard had taken our livestock including my own horse. "I guess my family was lucky. We was able to hide most of our livestock from them." I wondered if Ma could have worked the fields with a plow pulled by a cow. I was sure she would give it a try if she had no other choice, but I was grateful she didn't have to.

I managed to get another nap before Corporal Smith ordered us to report to Lieutenant Morgan for duty. "Bring your guns, but leave your baggage here." The train must stop to load fuel and water for the boiler. Morgan assigned me and Miller to stand guard at the loading site to be sure no one interfered and no one tried to board the train. "Watch the engine and coal cars especially. We've had several sabotage attempts on this trip. Don't let anyone come close to the train, no matter what reason they give."

The refueling went without any problems, and Lieutenant Morgan told me and Miller to climb aboard the engine cab where we was to watch for any unusual activity along the track ahead. After about a hour we was traveling through a heavily forested area, where about a hundred yards ahead, the rails curved sharply. Suddenly Miller shouted, "Man beside the tracks!" I saw a man waving a stick with a white rag tied to it.

Immediately the engineer applied the brakes and the train gradually slowed, coming to a stop shortly before the curve. "This could be an ambush," the engineer warned us; "we don't know what's beyond the curve." He ordered me to keep my gun on the man who was yelling something we couldn't quite hear. "We'll wait for the lieutenant to speak to him." I was surprised that the engineer gave orders to soldiers, but later I learnt the engineer was really an officer of the Confederate Army.

The lieutenant come forward along the tracks with half a dozen armed soldiers. The man claimed the tracks had been wrecked a few yards down the line. The officer told the man to set down on the ground and assigned a soldier to guard him while they made sure it wasn't no ambush. Then he ordered all soldiers off the train. Twenty soldiers guarded the train while the remaining twenty or so went around the curve to see what the situation was. Several soldiers returned to the train to get tools and supplies saying a rail had been removed.

By the time the rail was back in place, me and Miller had completed our time on duty and returned to the passenger car. "We lucked out this time," Miller smacked me on the shoulder.

"What do you mean?"

"We got to guard the train and didn't have to get our hands dirty putting the rail back, but I guess we'll have to stand guard duty tonight when we get to Roanoke."

"Will we spend the night in Roanoke?"

"Yes, it's too dangerous to travel the rails at night with so many Union sympathizers around. You can't see far enough ahead in the dark to spot damaged tracks in time to stop."

"I just hope we get something to eat. I'm starving."

"The engineer told me we should be there in a couple of hours if we didn't run into any more delays."

"Then I think I'll take another nap." Each time I woke from a nap, my head hurt a little less.

***

We arrived in Lynchburg about noon the next day after spending the night in Roanoke where the soldiers was lodged in a old hotel. Me and my three friends had served guard duty until midnight, but got three good meals out of the deal. When we arrived at the Lynchburg station, a number of army wagons waited to deliver the munitions and supplies. All the soldiers worked hard to unload heavy crates of military equipment and medical supplies.

As soon as the men had loaded all the freight onto the army wagons, Corporal Smith rounded up his squad. "All of us are to report to the encampment on the west side of the city where General Early's troops are preparing for battle against Yankee forces led by Yankee General Hunter. Our squad is to guard the rear to make sure the Yankees don't try to slip around and attack from behind."

I didn't know nothing about how to fight. Nobody gave me training as a soldier. I stayed close to Miller and followed his lead.

"Why are we just standing here? I thought we'd be rushing forward."

Miller grinned. "General Early's famous for his battle strategy. He thinks it's best if we stay here behind the breastworks the city had erected and wait for Hunter to attack us."

Even though we didn't get involved in the fierce fighting, I saw enough to make me step behind a bush and vomit. The noise of guns and cannon made my ears hurt and my headache worse. They was so much dust churned up by thousands of soldiers' marching feet and horses' hooves mixed with the smoke from the big guns I couldn't hardly see more than a few yards ahead. They was so much noise: cannons boomed, riflemen screamed their battle yells as they charged forward, and wounded horses screamed as they fell to the ground.

Then I saw soldiers coming out of the dust and smoke carrying wounded men covered in blood, some screaming in pain, others who might not even be alive. Some wounded, able to hobble on their own, moved to the back of the battlefield. I started helping the wounded to the field hospital set up at the edge of the encampment.

And then after just a few hours of battle, Hunter's troops unexpectedly retreated, and the battle was over for the day. Me and my friends spent the rest of the day helping to clean up the battlefield.

"We have work to do," Corporal Smith explained. "We must take the wounded to the hospital and bury the dead. Private Miller, show Private Campbell how to search in the pockets of the dead for some identity so the families can be notified." He turned to Private Jones. "Shoot the wounded horses and get them away from the battlefield."

I appreciated the citizens of the town who come out to help search for family members among the dead and wounded and helped with the work.

Once our work was done, me and Miller stood in the chow line for an hour waiting for a plate of beef stew. We found a place to squat down to eat, and soon, Corporal Smith and Private Jones joined us.

"This is good stew," Jones said. "I hope they'll allow seconds. I just realized I had no lunch."

"One thing's for certain:" Corporal Smith said as he pierced a chunk of beef with his fork, "the citizens of Lynchburg always make sure we're well fed." Then he turned to me. "Well, Lover Boy, how did you like your first battle? Did you get to shoot a Yankee?"

I pretended I didn't hear him and scraped my plate, all the time thinking I was still hungry.

Jones stood, waving his empty plate like a flag. "I'm glad we're all still alive. We lost quite a few men today. The hospital's going to be busy for weeks." He turned to me. "You ready to go for more stew?"

As we walked back to the chow line, Jones put his hand on my shoulder. "Don't let Smith's teasing bother you. He likes to have his fun, but he's damn good at keeping his men in line. He really looks out for us."

"I guess I'm lucky to meet up with you guys, even if you did play a dirty trick on me."

"Oh, we wouldn't have done that if we hadn't thought it would do you good." He slapped me on the back. "Admit it. You'd never have gone to Nancy's if you hadn't been drunk." I grinned and nodded. "And you have to admit what you and Sweet Lucy did was quite pleasant."

I have to say I was more than a little embarrassed, but I nodded again. "But I wish you all would quit pestering me about it."

"Well, you won't have to put up with us after tonight."

"What do you mean by that?"

"We'll be on the train back to Goodson first thing in the morning."

"Are you saying I won't be going with you?"

"That's right. Our duty assignment is to guard the trains coming from Knoxville to Lynchburg. That's what we've been doing for the last year, going back and forth from Goodson to Lynchburg. But you're a member of General Jubal Early's army now."

I shuddered. "How'll I know what to do if you fellers ain't around to tell me?" I felt a shiver of fear move up my spine.

We got our plates filled with more stew and walked back to join the others. "Don't worry. We'll turn you over to a sergeant who'll give you directions."

When we reached the others, Jones explained he had broken the news to me. Miller watched as I put my head down and stared at my plate. "Hey

Campbell, it's been a load of fun spending these few days with you. We're gonna miss you, but you're gonna make a fine soldier." He reached out and clasped my hand. "Wish we could keep you around. You're good company."

I nodded and continued to stare at my plate. "I'll miss you fellers too. Then I dumped my plate in the nearby bushes. "I guess I'm not that hungry after all."

Miller smiled. "If you're finished, get your gear and I'll go with you to your new outfit."

I shook hands with Jones and Smith. "Thanks for looking out for such a greenhorn."

Smith grinned. "You look out for yourself. I'd like to think that someday when this terrible war is over, we'll meet again, and I want to see you in one piece."

As me and Miller walked toward the officers' tents, Miller said, "You know, I understand how you felt when we got you drunk and took you to Nancy's. That's what they did to me when I was a new recruit. Sweet Lucy was my first time too, but now I'm glad they did it. I think you will be glad too someday."

When a private walked in our direction, Miller stopped him. "Private, this is Private Campbell. He's a new recruit and hasn't been assigned to a company. Can you take him to your sergeant?" Miller shook my hand. "Be safe, my friend." Then he turned and hurried away.

"I'm Private Davidson. Glad to welcome you to our company. Come with me and we'll get you situated."

The sergeant welcomed me and told Private Davidson to find me a place to bed down. "We're expecting another attack tomorrow. So be ready."

I went with Davidson who showed me where his own bed roll was. It'd been an exhausting day, and I was ready for some peace and quiet, but before I could lie down, the town, over a mile away, suddenly come to life. People shouted, bands played, so many buildings was lighted up, the sky over the city glowed with a yellow light. Drums beat like troops was marching. Train whistles blowed, and trains begun coming in and out of the city.

"What's going on?" I couldn't understand why the celebration. We hadn't exactly won the battle, even though the Yankees had pulled back, but we expected they would attack again the next day.

Davidson shook his head. "I don't know, but I'll go hang around the officers' tents to see if I can find out anything."

I settled in my bed, but couldn't go to sleep, partly because of the noise from the city; but also because when I shut my eyes, I saw bloody wounded men with arms or feet blown away being assisted to the hospital and dead bodies being thrown into wagons like sacks of potatoes. I felt anxious now that my friends would no longer be around to guide me. I felt like they had abandoned me. I took the stone from my backpack and held it in my palm. Maybe I'd made a bad mistake. In the moonlight the crystals in the stone glittered. I hoped it was telling me everthing would work out. I held it in the moonlight for several minutes just to see it sparkle before putting it back in my pack.

After some time Davidson returned with an interesting story. "I hear the people of Lynchburg are trying to make so much noise that those stupid Yankees will think large numbers of soldiers are arriving to boost Early's troops." He laughed. "Don't that beat it all?"

I sat up. "Let's hope it works. For a while there today I wondered if we was getting beat. I was real surprised when they retreated."

"You never know. Maybe Hunter ran out of ammunition. If that's the case, unless he gets some supplies during the night, he won't be attacking tomorrow."

I sighed and laid back down.

***

Reveille sounded shortly after daylight. It scared me so bad I jumped up to see what was happening. Davidson laughed. "Yep, that's what wakes you up in the army. Get used to it. Get your boots on and let's go find some breakfast." As we walked through the encampment, I got my first look at the large and jumbled up crowd of support required for all of Early's troops. But it looked like they was packing up to move. Cooks dismantled and packed their kitchens. Some wagons carried loads of huge crates, and others filled with ammunition and guns was forming a caravan. The medics loaded tents and cots from the field hospital into ambulance wagons.

Davidson spoke to a corporal near the kitchen tent. "What's going on? Why are we packing up?"

"Why, haven't you heard? Hunter turned tail and ran off during the night. Looks like he's headed for West Virginia, but Old Jube plans to chase after them."

After grabbing some biscuits and ham and a cup of coffee, we returned to our squadron where the sergeant put us to work. By noon everything was packed and we begun to move out. I stayed close to Davidson as we took our places in the ranks of our company. No one had taught me how to march, but I soon figured it out by watching those around me. We marched at a fast pace all afternoon. I was glad I still had several pairs of socks, and I'd remembered the Sheep Lady's instructions to wear two pairs.

I didn't want to get blisters like I did during the first days after I left home.

Along towards evening, the squadron leader called a halt, and soon a lieutenant on horseback come to report we had caught up with the tail end of Hunter's troops and had captured several wagons, but most of the Yankee soldiers was too far ahead. "We're stopping here for the night, but we'll head out again at daylight."

I looked around. We was in a dirt roadway. To the right a field of grass looked like a hay field. Me and Davidson along with most of the men climbed the rail fence and found a place to spread our blankets. It was now nearly dark, but the squadron cooks handed each of us two hardtack biscuits, a apple and three pieces of beef jerky. It was my first experience trying to eat hard tack. I tried to bite one, but it was so hard my teeth wouldn't go through it. I held it up and ask Davidson, "What is this anyway?"

"It's what the army calls biscuits, but they make them with just water and flour. They'll keep for weeks without spoiling. They taste a little better if you soak them in coffee, but since we don't have any coffee, I just pour some water on them from my canteen and let them soak a little while."

I tried that, but they tasted so awful I finally just threw them at a couple of dogs that had come sniffing around. They couldn't chew them either, but chawed on them like they was gnawing on a bone. They made me wish for some of Pete O'Malley's fluffy biscuits.

We marched again the next day, and I couldn't hardly believe how fast and far we had gone. When we stopped for the night, Davidson did his usual snooping and come back to say the sergeant guessed we had marched at least 25 miles.

I slumped down on the ground. "I can believe it. My feet hurt, my head hurts, and it's hot enough to cook a egg on a rock." I took off my cap and rubbed my forehead with my shirt sleeve. "I ain't got enough strength to go stand in the chow line. Besides I ain't hungry. I'm just going to lay here and sleep."

Davidson took me by the arm and pulled me up. "Oh, no you don't. The rumor is we'll march again tomorrow like today. If you don't eat, you'll pass out like those two fellers did today." I managed to put one foot in front of the other to reach the line where we was handed a couple of real biscuits with a chunk of fat back pork. Davidson looked at his meager ration. "Maybe we'll have a better breakfast."

As Davidson said, we marched fast and far again the next day. After we stopped for the night, Davidson wandered off to see what rumors he could pick up and returned with the news that we was giving up on catching Hunter's forces. They seemed to have disappeared into West Virginia. "But that's the good news. The bad news is we're going to start marching again tomorrow on our way to Washington, right up the Shenandoah

Valley."

"Why are we gonna do that?"

"What I heard was General Lee has ordered General Early to attack Washington so the Yankees will have to pull back their troops from Virginia to defend the capital."

"So how far will we have to march?"

"I heard it would take us 15 to 18 days."

"You mean we're gonna be walking all that time?" I felt like somebody had knocked the breath outta me.

"Looks like it."

"But it's so hot and my boot soles is so thin I can feel the sharp rocks."

I slumped down and ate the rations of beef jerky without saying nothing. I felt the worst since I'd decided to run away from home. I reached into my pack for the rock, but holding it didn't make me feel no better. I expected I would be a disappointment to Pa. I wondered if Ma had got my letter. I finally slept, but the dream of Evan's murder woke me with my heart pounding, and I couldn't go back to sleep.

We finally crossed the river into Maryland. I had lost track of time, but Davidson told me it was July 5th and it had took us fifteen days to get there. I was glad when I found out we would take a day or two to rest before marching on toward Washington.

"I ain't never been so tired," I complained to a nearby soldier. I looked around at the men sprawled in the shade of nearby trees. Many of the soldiers had no hats or caps, and their sunburned, blistered faces was streaked with dirt from the ever present dust. I understood their discomfort.

"I ain't never seen it this hot," One soldier said as he poured water from his canteen over his head.

"If it had just rained on us a little it wouldn't been so bad, but they's been no rain for weeks, and my God, that sun beat us like a furnace ever single day."

"I couldn't stand all that dust. With eight thousand men and wagons and horses tramping along, it was like marching in a cloud. I about choked to death on it."

"Is my eyes as bloodshot as yourn?"

"I'm scared to take off my boots cause I know I got blisters as big as silver dollars."

After listening to this for a while, I stood up and pulled up my trousers. I'd lost so much weight my pants was about to fall off, even though I had put my belt buckle through the last hole. I sighed and turned to Davidson. "Where are we now?"

"We're about 40 or 50 miles northwest of Washington."

"So we're going to do more marching, I guess."

"Seems like we can take it easy for a day or two before we start out again."

"That's a relief. Maybe we can find a way to get a bath and worsh some of this dirt off our bodies."

Two days later we took up our march. We traveled along a dirt road making good time in spite of the hot sun that continued to bake us. Suddenly as we neared Frederick, the sergeant ordered a halt and instructed us to prepare for battle. Out of nowhere, Union troops attacked us, but almost before we could get ready to return fire, the battle was over and the enemy retreated. I hadn't fired my rifle even once.

When it was clear that the short battle was over, I looked for Davidson. He was sure to know what had just happened. I found him helping a wounded soldier to the hospital tent. Davidson was happy to explain. "We were attacked by a small group of Yankee soldiers led by General Wallace. We have way more troops, so they just sort of attacked and then ran."

"If they didn't have many troops, why would they attack us?"

"Maybe to delay us since they can't defeat us. Sergeant says we will take a short break to regroup before we start marching again."

I think if I had rested for a week, I'd still be tired, so I took advantage of the time to rest. I found a place in the shade, made a pillow of my pack and took a nap. I woke with a start when Davidson shook me. "Wake up. Wait till you hear what General Early's done now."

I thought Davidson's latest tale was funny. "Since we were near Frederick, Early took some officers and went to see the town fathers and demanded that the city pay a ransom of $200,000 or the Rebels would attack the city. And you know what? Those cowardly city folks immediately paid up. What a card Old Jube is," Davidson crowed.

Soon we was marching on down the road toward Washington. But unfortunately General Wallace wasn't through with us. As we approached Monocacy Junction, Wallace attacked again, and I had my first experience of a real battle, my first time to fire my gun in battle, and my first time to kill a man. My squadron led the attack on the second push forward. Men rushed toward the enemy on all sides of me, and I shouldered my gun and ran forward with them and stumbled over a dead body. Suddenly I saw a Yankee soldier standing a few yards away reloading his rifle. I took aim, shouted the Rebel yell, and pulled the trigger.

I saw the man's body jolt backwards, falling on the ground. I watched to see if he moved, but all I saw was the big red stain covering his chest. I was so shocked I couldn't move. What have I done? He looked right at me. He knowed I was gonna kill him. Oh, Evan, I did it for you, but I wish I had never done it.

Early's troops made three more attacks against Wallace's forces, but I never fired another shot that day. Finally, Wallace ordered a retreat and led his men back to Baltimore. It was clearly a Confederate victory, but I felt no joy about it. I stumbled along, barely able to keep up with the squadron when we continued our march toward Washington.

*****

By noon the next day as we neared Washington, we was barely able to march in formation; some soldiers was collapsing from exhaustion and the terrible heat. "I guess we aren't going to attack today," Davidson explained. "Early says his men must get some rest."

Some of the men rested, but several details were set to work. I joined a crew that commandeered several houses near Fort Stevens on the northwest side of the city. We allowed the people to remove their belongings, but the army took over the houses as officers' quarters and a hospital. Several of the houses was situated so that sharp shooters could stand on the roof and look right into the fort. From there, the snipers could shoot any people who come in sight within the fort.

Later that night when I tried to sleep, I kept seeing the look of horror on the face of the man I shot. After tossing and turning for a long time without sleep, I took the stone from my pack. Somehow it seemed to have lost its sparkle. I held it for a long time thinking about my home in Kentucky. If Ma hadn't got my letter, nobody knowed where I was. I could die and nobody would ever know it. I was very lonely and felt like crying. I finally put the stone away and closed my eyes.

In the afternoon of the next day, Davidson brought the news that our squadron was to lead an attack on Fort Stevens. I loaded my gun and took my place alongside my squadron mates. Union forces come out to meet us. When the sergeant gave the order to fire, I pointed my gun in the direction of the fort and pulled the trigger without aiming at anything. I reloaded and fired again, praying the bullets was not hitting nobody. The image of the man's face I shot at Monocacy the day before swam in front of my eyes. Sweat ran down my face, sweat soaked my clothes, and dust and smoke from the guns clogged my throat.

Finally Early ordered a retreat, and that was when the rifle ball hit my foot. I fell to the ground, and I think I mighta passed out. Finally I set up and looked at my blasted boot. The top of my right boot had blown away and blood gushed out. The pain made my head swim, and I thought I's gonna faint. I managed to get my boot off and saw my toes barely hung by little strips of skin. I understood the bleeding had to be stopped, so I took off my shirt and tore a strip from the bottom to make a tourniquet like Miz Simpson had showed me. Then I bundled my foot in the shirt wrapping it as tight as I could.

I looked around and saw all the Rebel soldiers had left. The only ones I could see was laying on the ground. They wasn't moving, but I didn't know if they was alive. I knowed I couldn't walk on my blowed up foot. I needed crutches like Caleb had made for Scott. That seemed so long ago. I wondered where Caleb and Scott was now. Then I thought of Ma. She would know what to do if she could be here. I laid back on the ground. I needed to rest a minute and then I'd figure out what to do.

CHAPTER 10

July 1864

Washington, D.C.

I opened my eyes and looked around. I was laying on a pallet in a large space that looked like some sort of public room. Ornamental moldings in a vine-like design circled the room where the walls and ceiling come together. The windows was covered by dark colored drapes so no light could come in, but little lamps was hanging on the wall, and they made enough dim light for me to study the place from my make-shift bed in one corner. I could see men laying on cots and lots of others like me on pallets on the floor. I wondered how I got to this place.

I could hear groans of pain, cries for help, and even one voice begging for mama, and that made me anxious. I noticed here and there some women rushed from one bed to another trying to give some sort of help. I sat up and a sharp pain shot from my right foot to my knee. It was so bad it took my breath away. I had a bandage on my foot, but it was very bloody. Any little move I made with my leg hurt like the devil—even if I just tightened my thigh muscle. I had no shirt and somebody had cut off the right leg of my dirty, bloody pants above my knee. I felt embarrassed to be laying there without my clothes. I took a deep breath and right away wished I hadn't cause it smelled like infected wounds, soiled bedding, and vomit.

In a little while one of the women come to my corner. "Hello. My name is Lily; what's your name?"

She was young, just a little older'n me and purty too. She smiled at me, and I managed to smile back. "Harvey Campbell, ma'am."

"Glad to meet you, Harvey. Would you like a bowl of soup?"

I was in so much pain, I hadn't thought about being hungry, but I couldn't remember when I ate last. "Yes, ma'am, I would."

"Good. I'll bring you some right away." She turned to ask three other men if they wanted soup and then left the room to return in a few minutes with a tray filed with hunks of bread and bowls of watery soup. After the first bite, I felt really hungry, but the thin soup with no meat and only a few pieces of potato wasn't very satisfying.

When Lily come back to collect the bowls, I ask, "Lily, what's the name of this place?"

"Oh, it's called Harrison House Hospital. It used to be the Harrison House Hotel, but they converted it to a hospital a couple of years ago. Right now we have over 400 patients."

"Are you a nurse?"

Lily laughed. "No, I live down the street, and I come here every day to do what I can for the patients."

"Well, I thank you. That's very kind." Lily turned to go, but I had another question. "Where's this hospital located?"

"It's in Washington."

That scart me so bad I jerked, making a pain shoot through my leg so bad I couldn't hardly speak. "So it's a Union hospital?"

"Yes, but we treat any soldier they bring us."

That news shook me to pieces. I wondered what would happen to me. Was I at the mercy of the Yankees? I thanked Lily for the information, and she promised to return later to help us write letters to family. I wondered how Ma would react to this news. I looked around to see if my backpack had come with me to this place, but I didn't see it.

Eventually, a man come through the ward checking on wounds and giving instructions to nurses about changing bandages. I guessed he must be a doctor. He looked at my bloody bandage. "Did a surgeon operate on your foot?"

"Yes, sir."

"When?"

"I think it was yesterday, but I'm a little confused. They made me pretty drunk and then gave me some medicine to make me sleep. I don't even remember coming to this place."

"What surgery did they do?"

"A musket ball took off most of my toes. The surgeon wanted to take off the rest of my foot, but I wouldn't stand for that, so he sawed off about half my foot behind my toes."

"It would perhaps have been a better idea to take your whole foot off. You see, above your ankle he'd only have two bones to sever. As it turns out he cut through half a dozen or more bones. I think your risk of infection is greater this way."

"Yes, sir. He explained that to me, but I wanted to take that chance and keep as much of my foot as possible."

The doctor spoke to a nurse. "Change that bandage. If it keeps bleeding let the surgeon on duty know." He turned toward me, "Good luck, son. How old are you anyway?"

"Sixteen, sir."

As he moved away, I heard him mutter, "My God! When's this hellish war going to end? We're killing whole generations. God forgive us!"

***

I hadn't lied when I told the doctor I was confused. I really didn't know how long I laid on the battlefield after my foot was blowed to bits. I might even have fainted. But I finally roused myself and looked around. All my company had disappeared, so there was nobody to help me. I didn't want to lay there and bleed to death. Then I remembered how, the day before the battle, I had helped the soldiers take over a house to be a Confederate hospital. I needed to find that house.

I looked around and saw a tree limb on the ground about ten yards away. I crawled toward it, making my way around dead bodies, guns, even a dead horse. It took me a long time cause I's trying to protect my foot, but couldn't keep it from scraping the ground. It hurt so bad I had to stop and lay back down ever little bit, but I finally got to the limb. Using it as some sort of crutch, I started hopping on one foot towards the northwest where I thought the hospital house would be.

I was so weak and tired, I had to stop to rest after a few hops. Near dark, a ambulance come along and soldiers lifted me into the wagon, which held several other wounded. They took me to a field hospital and laid me on the ground beside the tent where I spent the night using my backpack as a pillow.

When morning come, I saw the ground around the hospital tent was covered with wounded. One by one, soldiers carried them into the tent where surgeons tended their wounds. I heard their screams and wondered what they was doing in there. Finally by mid-morning they come for me.

When the surgeon finally agreed not to take my whole foot, they gave me several big gulps of whiskey, and four soldiers held me down while the surgeon used a common handsaw to cut through the bones in my foot taking off what little was left of my toes and starting the bleeding all over again. I can't remember, but I'm sure I screamed as loud as the others did.

The next thing I knowed, I was waking up on the floor of this here Harrison House Hospital. I had thought the ambulance workers who picked me up was Confederate soldiers. Now I understood I was not in the care of my own army, but I was in a enemy hospital. What would happen to me?

A man, from a bed three rows over, come and set on the floor beside me. I thought he looked about James' age. His left arm was off above his elbow, but his bandage looked clean.

"I'm Sergeant Dooley, one of Early's soldiers. I overheard you talking with the doctor. Do you mind if I ask you some questions?"

I nodded and perked up. Here was someone who might help me. "Yes, sir."

"So you were wounded in the battle against Fort Stevens?"

"Yes, sir."

"Did I hear you say you're only sixteen?"

"Yes, sir."

"How long were you with Early's army?"

"Just from Lynchburg."

The sergeant frowned and studied me for several seconds. "Does your foot hurt a lot?"

"It doesn't hurt so much till I move my leg. Then it's awful bad."

"Be sure to ask the nurse who changes your bandage to have the surgeon do something about the bleeding. This fresh blood means it's still seeping and that's not good. I suspect you have already lost a lot of blood, and that's why you seem so weak."

"Yes, sir, I'll tell the nurse."

When the sergeant started getting to his feet, I ask, "Sir, what do you think will happen to me?"

"I'm sorry to tell you, but we're prisoners of the Yankees. I expect they'll ship us out to one of their prisons as soon as we're able to travel."

"But you can walk fine; can't you just walk out of here?"

"I'd not try that if I were you. Yankee soldiers guard every door. No way they're going to let us walk out on our own." The sergeant stood there studying the floor. "Tell you what. I'll try to send a message to the hospital superintendent asking that you be paroled since you are so young. Maybe they'll let you go." Dooley paused and looked away for a few seconds. "But don't get your hopes up. It might not work."

"Oh, thank you, sir." As the sergeant turned to walk away, I called, "Sergeant Dooley, one more question, if you don't mind, sir."

Dooley returned and squatted beside me. "What is it?"

"I had a knapsack with some personal things in it. You think I might get it back?"

Sergeant frowned. "I don't know; did you have something valuable in it?"

"I had some money and some personal items I'd like to get back. I need the clothes I had in my pack. I had to use my shirt for a bandage when I got shot, and they tore off my pant leg when they cut off my toes. I've been lying here half naked all this time."

Dooley nodded. "I see. Well, I'll ask about it, but to be honest I doubt you'll ever see it." At the look of my disappointment, he patted me on the shoulder. "Your biggest concern right now is to get your wound healed. Concentrate on that." He stood. "Good luck, soldier." He shook my hand and walked away.

I felt tears welling up in my eyes. I twisted around so I could lean back against the wall and pulled my good leg up so I could rest my arms and head on my knee. I hoped no one would notice I was crying, but I felt so lost. I wished I could hold the stone. It somehow seemed like a link to Pa, but now it was gone. My money—gone. My bed roll—gone. My clothes—gone. My gun—gone. I didn't know another soul in this place. No one knowed where I was. I didn't know what was going to happen to me. I remembered how Evan had sobbed on my shoulder when Old Bob and Sara had run away. But I didn't have nobody to hold on to.

The nurse finally changed my bandage and agreed that the surgeon needed to take a look at the wound, and after some delay the doctor come. He explained he needed to cauterize the wound to stop the bleeding. He had me drink some more whiskey and gave me a piece of wood to place between my teeth to bite down on. Then he rubbed a red hot poker over the wound while a couple of assistants held my leg still. I fainted.

Later Lily brought another bowl of soup and bread. I couldn't even hardly set up. I was weak and shaky and my wound pained me so much I couldn't eat. Sergeant Dooley offered to help feed me even though he had only one hand. "I sent a message to the superintendent by one of the doctors. I don't know if it will actually get relayed, but I wanted to let you know I tried."

I managed to mummer, "Thank you, sir."

In a short while, a older woman I hadn't seen before come to my pallet with a bottle and spoon. "I want you to take this laudanum so you can sleep. Our supply is almost gone, but when I heard about you, I decided if anyone needed this you did."

***

The next morning I still felt very weak, but my bandage wasn't bloody. Although the burns pained me very much and my bones hurt all the way to my hip, I felt a little encouraged I would get better since the bleeding was stopped. I wished I had a poultice of plantain like Miz Simpson used to make or maybe some of the Sheep Lady's salve. Loud screams called my attention to two soldiers carrying in a wounded man and placing him on Sergeant Dooley's cot.

When Lily served a bowl of thin gruel and bread, I ask her what had happened to Sergeant Dooley.

"Which one is Sergeant Dooley?"

"He was in the bed over there where that man is screaming and moaning."

"Oh, they took him away late last night."

"That's what I's afraid of."

"Was he a friend of yours?"

"Not exactly, but he was very kind to me."

"Well, I'll be kind to you. As soon as I finish serving breakfast, I'll come to help you write some letters. I didn't get to do that yesterday."

The only person I wanted to write was Ma, but I didn't know what I should tell her. I ask Lily to do the writing because she could probably spell better. She made herself comfortable beside me, and I told her what I wanted to say.

Harrison House Hospital
Washington, D.C.
July 16th 1864

Dear Ma,

I hope this finds you well. I wrote 2 letters which I hope you received. In case you didn't, this is my story so far.

I left home in early June and made my way to Virginia where I joined the Confederate Army. Last month I participated in a battle in Lynchburg, Virginia. Then we marched northward to Maryland

and fought another battle at Monocacy, Maryland. Afterwards we marched toward Washington and engaged the Yankees at Fort Stevens, outside the city.

I got a musket ball in my right foot during the Fort Stevens battle. Union soldiers captured me and took me to a field hospital where a surgeon removed my damaged toes. I am recovering in this Union hospital. When I am able to travel, I expect to be taken to a Union prison.

When I find out what prison I will be in, I will write you again. They are treating me good here. My wound is healing. I think they will move me soon.

Tell William and Elliott that I miss them as I also miss you.

Your son, Harvey.

I asked Lily to read it back to me. "Sounds better'n I could write it. Thank you very much."

"Is there something else I could do for you?"

"Yes, if you don't mind. Help me stand up."

By steadying myself on the wall and with Lily's help I slowly raised myself. I felt like my head was rolling in circles, but after standing for a bit, the dizziness went away. As the blood rushed to my foot, the pain made me gasp. "I need to set back down, I think." Lily helped me set with my back against the wall.

"Thanks Lily. You're kind to me."

Over the next few days I stood more often and finally I could stand without help. Then a Yankee soldier brought a crude crutch. "Stand up and let's see if you can walk with this."

I put on my boot, stood, and reached for the crutch. I hopped for a few steps.

"Looks like you can manage. Now follow me."

***

I was took, along with a wagon load of prisoners, to the Old Capitol Prison near the Capitol building in Washington. I had to stand in line for over a hour waiting my turn to be processed. By the time I reached the intake officer, I was trembling with pain, but I was able to answer questions about my rank, where I was from and what squadron I had served with.

"How old are you?"

"Sixteen, sir."

The officer seemed surprised and finally took a good look at me. He saw a skinny boy with no shirt and one pant leg ripped off at the knee leaning on a crude crutch. He asked how I had been wounded and what treatment I'd had. After listening to my story, he turned to a soldier standing nearby. "Help this young man get to the prison hospital." He wrote some instructions on a paper and asked the aide to give it to the officer in charge.

As we made our way down a long hall toward the hospital wing, we passed a dark, dingy room I learnt later was the mess. A foul odor like a garbage dump caused me to hold my breath till we got past the room. I was so glad when we finally reached the hospital and I could have a chair. Hopping along on one foot tired me so much and made my wound throb, but putting weight on my wounded foot was too painful to bear, so I had to hop. I wished I could make my own crutches like I made for Carl Henley.

At least, I got a real cot and some clean clothes. The surgeon in charge examined my wound and gave instructions to a assistant for changing the bandage ever day. He turned to me, "You will stay here only until your wound has healed enough to travel on a train. Then you will go to a larger prison somewhere else."

I saw no purty ladies like Lily tending the men occupying the bunks along the walls. Only a couple of Yankee soldiers assisted the doctor. When the time come for the noon meal, all the patients who could walk marched under guard to the mess. A guard explained if I had money I could buy food from the prison store or even order food from a nearby restaurant, but since I had no money, my meals would be brought to me till I could walk to the mess. My food arrived on a dirty tin plate with food dried around the edges. I looked at the unappetizing mess of boiled beans, a piece of fat pork covered with thin molasses, and a thin slice of stale bread. I had a spoon in my knapsack, but since I no longer had my pack, I scooped up beans with the bread. I knowed then I'd not get meals like Pete

O'Malley used to make.

***

After a couple of days, I could put my heel on the floor and with the help of my crutch could hobble without having to hop on one foot. A guard assisted me to the third floor. The stairs opened into a long hall with six rooms, three on each side with a armed guard stationed outside each door. We stopped at the middle door on the right where the armed guard unlocked the door to admit me.

I hobbled into a large room with bunks around the walls, each with three beds. The bunks had no mattress—only a thin blanket covering rough boards. A block of wood fastened at one end served as a pillow. The open windows looked out on the street, but one prisoner warned me not to look out the windows or try to talk to anyone on the street. "The guards out there will shoot you if they see you at the window."

A man, who introduced himself as Sergeant Emerson and seemed to be in charge of the room, arranged for me to have a lower bunk so I didn't have to climb to a higher bed. A man, who looked about my brother William's age named Charles Summers, agreed to give up his bunk for me; then he helped me find a place to set. "I'm from Atlanta; where're you from?"

We exchanged basic information—battles we'd fought, how we got captured, a little family history—and speculated about how long the war would last. Charles looked sad. "I hope it won't last much longer. I haven't seen my family for over three years." He sighed. "I hear we're losing so many battles lately; I just wish we'd surrender and get it done with."

When the guards took us to mess for dinner, Charles explained. "We have only a half hour to eat. If we eat fast, we can go outside to the exercise yard for the rest of our dinner period.

Getting outdoors, even though the heat wave of the last month still hung over the city, gave me some encouragement. I could take deep breaths without inhaling all the terrible odors that filled every room in the prison. All the men on our floor had meals at the same time, so being in the exercise yard gave opportunity to meet others, and I noticed many seemed to have friends in other rooms. I also noticed the guard tower looked directly down into the exercise yard that was surrounded by a high brick wall.

Charles introduced me to a few other men. I motioned Charles close and ask, "What's that scaffold-like thing in the corner?"

"That's the gallows. They try soldiers accused of treason or desertion here in the prison, and if found guilty they string them up right there. I've been told they tried and executed some famous spies here."

That made me sad. For some reason I remembered the deserter, who stole my food, had said war was so terrible he couldn't take it no more, and even risked his life by deserting. I was beginning to understand why he'd do that. Nothing about this war was like I expected.

After we returned to our room from the exercise yard, we settled in for a long boring afternoon. Charles explained that Sergeant Emerson, as the prisoner with the highest rank, had responsibility for keeping order. I watched as some of the men piled into their bunks for a nap; one soldier got out some paper and a pencil to write; another had a book to read. Earlier someone had drawed a checkerboard on the floor and found little rocks for playing pieces. I hoped I might be invited to play.

Suddenly loud noises from the room above us sounded like a whole army marching; shouts of protest poured through the open windows. Sergeant Emerson knocked on the door to get the guard's attention and asked what was happening.

"Oh, they got a rowdy bunch up there this morning. They gave the registration officer so much difficulty, he ordered they couldn't go to the exercise yard for a week, and that made them mad." About that time we heard a group of armed guards stomping up the stairs, and shortly all was quiet. The guard chuckled. "So now they're gonna be sorry." But those rowdies were not through protesting.

I was so interested in watching the checker game, I jumped in surprise when a gun shot rang out, and shouts of protest and more stomping come from above. Without thinking I started to look out the window, but Charles grabbed my arm and pulled me back.

"Don't go to the window. They'll shoot you! I think someone must have gone to the window up there and the guard shot at him. I hope no one got hurt."

The next day the rumor spread through the exercise yard that no one was hit by the shot. The prisoners up there had put a hat on a stick, and held it up to the window to make the guard think someone was at the window.

That night after most of the men slept, I heard some women on the street serenading us prisoners. When guards run them off, the Rebs upstairs begun to sing "I Wish I Was in the Land of Cotton" while they danced and stomped around. Before the guards could bring them to order they had started on "Oh! Susannah."

"Why did the guards make them stop singing?"

"We're not permitted to sing Confederate songs."

After the noise from above quieted and I could hear snores from the nearby bunks, I couldn't fall asleep. Somehow I found it harder at night to ignore the foul air in the room: the body odors of twenty unwashed sweaty bodies, filthy clothes, and gas from all the beans we ate. I crept out of bed and stood to the side of the open window where I couldn't be seen from the street, especially in the dark, but I could take some breaths of fresher air.

The prisoners in the room above continued their rebellion the next afternoon. We heard crashes and thumps followed by hoots and cheers. "What are they doing?" I ask Charles.

"I don't know, but it sounds like they're tearing down the house." A couple of days later in the exercise yard we learnt the latest. The Rebel prisoners up above had torn bricks out of the fireplace and hefted them out the window at the guards below.

When asked why the guards didn't shoot them, the storyteller explained, "They would throw one brick and jump back quick before the guard could take aim. Then they'd wait awhile to make the guard think they had stopped, and they'd sneak up and launch another brick."

"What's happened to them?"

"They took the whole bunch to the guard house where they spent the night with armed guards standing over them. Then the prison superintendent ordered them to stand in the hot sun until they confessed. Anybody who sat down would be shot on the spot. Some of them stood there for most of the day, but all of them finally gave in."

"Then what happened?"

"Well, I hear they're in the dungeon under the guard house where they'll get only bread and water for a week."

***

I enjoyed talking with some of the men in the room. While a few totally ignored me, several would share their stories. A couple even carried me down the stairs once when we went to mess. But Charles was the only one who treated me like a real friend.

I noticed one older man never talked to nobody. He spent hours on the floor in a corner staring at nothing. "What's his name?" I ask Charles.

Charles motioned for us to move to a far corner so the silent man wouldn't hear. "Frank, I think. That's all I've ever heard him called."

"What's wrong with him? Is he sick?"

"I don't think he's physically sick." Charles spoke in a low voice.

I looked over my shoulder at the vacant look in Frank's eyes. "Are you saying he's crazy?"

"Not exactly. But obviously his war experiences have damaged his mind."

"Is he dangerous?"

"No. I haven't seen anything that would make me think that. I think he's experienced horror and violence so bad his mind went into a deep shock that he can't break out of."

I remembered how I'd been in such a state after those evil men shot Evan down in the middle of the road. I didn't say a word for days or weeks even. "I think I understand how bad experiences can affect your mind."

"Do you think that's why you cry out in your sleep?"

I smiled. "Thanks for waking me last night. Sorry I disturbed you. I guess I disturbed some others too."

"If you want to talk about it, let me know."

I didn't know if I wanted to share my scary dreams. I just nodded. I was impressed with Charles' answers. He seemed like a awful smart feller. "Are you a educated man?"

Charles laughed. "Not yet, but I hope to be someday. I had just enrolled in Emory College when Georgia seceded. I hope I can go back to school after this is over."

"Well you sure don't act like my educated brother!"

Later I made my way over to the silent man's corner and took a seat on the floor a foot or two away from him. I didn't say nothing, just shared the man's silence. I sensed somehow we had something in common. After our evening meal, I returned to Frank's corner again.

Early the next day a guard come into the room and read ten names from a paper and ordered them to line up and follow him. Those remaining grew anxious. "What's that about?" someone asked Sergeant Emerson.

"They're being transferred to another prison for the duration of the war."

"Do you know where they're going?"

"The guard told me they'd go to Camp Chase near Columbus, Ohio."

I looked at Charles. "I'm glad you didn't have to go."

"Well, I think I'll get my orders soon."

Later ten new prisoners arrived to fill the empty bunks. One fellow who looked about twenty, immediately went around asking everyone to tell their rank. Then he turned to me. "Well private, I'm a corporal so I outrank you. I want a lower bunk; I'm taking yours."

Charles rushed to my side. "Wait, why are you doing that?"

"I outrank him so I have a right."

Sergeant Emerson watched but didn't stop it. Charles helped me find another bunk.

The next day I went to Frank's corner again. I watched as the corporal strutted around the room. He finally come to our corner. "Hey, private."

He pointed at me. "Did you sleep good last night?"

"Yes."

"Say sir when you answer me."

This man was making me mad, but I didn't want to make trouble. "Yes, sir."

"That's better." He turned to Frank. "What's your name, soldier?"

Frank continued to stare. He gave no sign he had heard.

"I asked you a question. What's your name?"

Frank's silence seemed like a drum roll calling the attention of everyone in the room. "I order you to answer me." When Frank didn't answer, the corporal slapped him.

Without even thinking, I picked up my crutch and whacked the corporal across his shins. "Leave him alone!"

Several of the men rushed to our corner. Somebody grabbed the crutch. Others dragged away the corporal who screamed in pain. When he finally quit screaming, Sergeant Emerson examined his legs and decided the corporal had no broken bones.

"I demand that he's court marshaled."

"I don't think that's necessary, Corporal."

The corporal screeched, "He attacked me. I have witnesses. I'll appeal to the Prison Commander."

I hung my head. I was sorry I lost my temper, but that bully deserved it.

Sergeant Emerson took my crutch, knocked on the door, and asked the guard to come into the room. After conferring, they decided I should spend the night in the guard house and would no longer be able to use my crutch.

***

The next morning a guard escorted me back to the unit. When I limped into the room I noticed right away the corporal wasn't there. Three of the men come and shook my hand. Charles asked, "Are you all right?"

"Yes, I'm just wobbly without my crutch."

"Did they feed you or did you have only bread and water?"

"The guards over there asked me what happened. When I explained, the sergeant clapped me on the back and said 'Oh, we know that corporal. He just spent a week in the dungeon. I'm sure he deserved a whack on his shins. Good for you.' And they brought me food from their mess. I even had eggs for breakfast."

I still had a bandage on my foot. The wound had mostly closed, but if I happened to bump my foot on something, the pain made me gasp, and at night my bones ached so bad I couldn't hardly sleep. Sometimes my knee buckled, so having the crutch had helped me keep my balance. Now I missed it, but Charles said, "Well, you can hang on to me."

"Thanks. You're a real friend." I smiled.

Later that day shortly after we returned to the room from the exercise area, a guard come with another list. The first name he read was "Harvey Campbell." I held my breath till I heard "Charles Summers." The guard called three other names and ordered us to line up and follow him. As we made our way toward the door, I felt someone touch my shoulder. I turned and saw Frank reaching to shake my hand.

Charles asked the guard, "Where are we going?"

"I hear you're headed for Camp Douglas."

"Where's that?"

"Chicago. You're headed for a place that's cold as a well digger's feet in January."

CHAPTER 11

August 1864

Camp Douglas Prison, Chicago

We set shoulder to shoulder on the floor of the hot box car, as many soldiers as the car could hold. Luckily, the armed guard, who had a seat near the door to prevent any escapes, left the door open to allow some light and fresh air into the crowded box car. Me and Charles was opposite the open door and leaned against the wall. After many hours, my leg ached, but the guard threatened to shoot anybody who stood up. Twice someone bumped my bandage which sent sharp pains up my leg.

I watched through the open door as farm fields, forests, small villages, larger towns, and finally hills passed by. I listened to the talk buzzing around us.

"How long will it take us to get there?"

I was already in misery, and when I heard someone reply that it would probably take a couple of days, I felt like screaming.

"What's the name of this place again?"

"Camp Douglas."

"Know anything about this place?"

"I heard it's big, thousands of prisoners."

Finally I closed my eyes and tried to sleep, but my foot hurt, my back hurt, and I couldn't shut out the voices around us. I perked up hours later when I felt the train beginning to slow, and then it stopped. Through the open door I could see open fields extending quite a distance. The guard ordered us to stay seated, but soon a lieutenant showed up and announced we could get out for a latrine break. Charles laughed when I said, "It's about time. I don't think I could hold it much longer."

Charles gave me a hand getting down from the box car, and we walked away from the tracks. Guards had formed a line creating a limit to how far we could go. Of course, nobody had any privacy, but when you have to go, you have to go. When we joined a line waiting for a drink of water, a man I'd not seen before kept standing close to me. If I moved, he moved too. He shook my hand. "I'm Simon; what's your name?"

I told my name, but I didn't like the way the man kept hanging around close to me and even put his hand on my back. It was near dark when the lieutenant ordered us back on the train. Simon tried to push Charles aside so he could climb up after me, but Charles wouldn't let him push his way in. After we set down, Simon ask Charles to let him squeeze in between us.

I was surprised at the rude way Charles responded: "No. Go somewhere else. We don't want you here."

Simon kept trying to force his way between us but the guard yelled, "Sit down, all you yellow-bellied Rebels or I'll shoot." I breathed a sigh of relief when Simon finally found a seat on the other side of the car.

"Why's he wanting to be with us?"

Charles frowned. "I think he wants to sit with you."

"Why? I don't understand. I never saw him before. He's older'n my brother. Why would he want to be friends with me?"

"I guess some men look for a younger man when they can't get a woman."

I still didn't completely understand, but I wondered if Charles meant when men can't go to a place like where Sweet Lucy worked. The guard interrupted my thoughts by pointing to a large man in a corner. "This is Sergeant Collier. He is charged with keeping order in this car. Any prisoner causing trouble will be tried for treason." Then he jumped to the ground, the door slammed shut and locked. All was quiet as our eyes slowly adjusted to the near darkness. Enough light seeped between the cracks of the wooden walls that I could barely make out a head here and there.

I turned to Charles. "I guess we ain't gonna get anything to eat, are we?"

"Looks that way. Think maybe you can get comfortable enough to sleep a little?"

"I'll try."

What seemed like hours later, I opened my eyes to total darkness—not even moonlight come through the cracks, but the train moved steadily along. Sometimes it seemed the train was moving up or down steep inclines. The man on my right apparently slept because he leaned over, his head resting on my shoulder. I hadn't got the man's name. I'd been so upset by Simon I hadn't even noticed who was beside me. I gently pushed him over, but soon he slumped against me again. This time when I pushed him back, I thought his skin felt hot. I said to Charles, "He must be sick. He's hot as fire." I moved enough that my back was to the man and that kept him more upright.

The next time I opened my eyes, dawn had begun to creep through the cracks. I heard someone say, "My God! It's hot in here." I wiped the sweat off my face with my sleeve. Keeping the door closed all night had captured the heat from all the men until the car was like a oven. Setting beside a feverish man prob'ly didn't help. The man beside me sat up, and I looked at him in the dim light. He said his name was Malcolm. His flushed face, bloodshot eyes, and frequent coughs convinced me he really was sick.

As the daylight grew stronger, all the men was squirming, swearing, complaining, but the sergeant in charge didn't try to stop them. Just when the anger, frustration, discomfort—not to mention hunger—seemed about to explode, the train begun to slow and then stopped. We would have another latrine stop, and maybe get some breakfast. Again, we was in open country where level fields stretched away. Another water line formed and each received a small drink of water and one piece of stale bread—not what I'd hoped for. I took advantage of the chance to hobble around and stretch my cramped muscles, but I kept an eye out for Simon and moved away when he got near me.

The day went much the same as the day before, hot and humid, and tempers flared as the day wore on. Things settled down for a little while after the guard threatened to kick a couple of quarrelsome prisoners out the open door. My empty stomach cramped so bad, I tried to roll up into a ball, but that didn't help. Malcolm seemed in a stupor, except for his frequent coughs.

Somehow we managed to get through another day. I watched through the door as we moved into flatter terrain and finally as the sun moved toward the west, the train slowed and come to a stop. Our car was uncoupled from the rest of the train and the engine shoved it onto a siding. We finally got a latrine break, although since I'd had so little to drink, I wasn't as desperate as before. Then a wagon arrived pulled by a team of horses and accompanied by three Yankee officers on horseback. As we crowded around we could see a huge container which we hoped was food, and soldiers started pushing and shoving to get close to the wagon.

Suddenly one of the officers shot his rifle into the air and brought everyone to a standstill. "All right you bunch of Rebel bastards, back in the boxcar. If you want something to eat, you'll have to act like civilized men. I shoulda guessed you'd be a bunch of wild savages." We slowly climbed back into our prison, and I jumped when the door slammed shut with a bang like a rifle shot.

The sun had gone down by the time the guards opened the door and allowed us out. If the soup had been hot when it arrived, it was cold now. The cook had sent only about a dozen tin cups, so only a dozen got a small cup of soup at a time. Then the cups was refilled for another dozen. The soup supply lasted long enough for every prisoner to get two cups, such as it was—no meat, a few turnips and potatoes, and lots of water—but it helped ease my stomach cramps.

When the soup pot was empty, the officer called for attention. "Tomorrow you stinking yellow bellied traitors will march from here to the prison. So back into your cell." I settled into the dark, sweltering freight car. The reality of my situation finally hit home.

***

It rained during the night and the temperature dropped a little lower. Shortly after daylight the doors opened. "All out!" a sergeant bellowed. "March formation." We climbed down and waded into mud. In just a few steps, mud soaked through my bandage. Then I slipped on the muddy ground and fell.

Charles helped me stand. "I think they have an ambulance wagon. I watched them help your friend Malcolm to it. Maybe they'll let you take the ambulance."

"I'd really like to stay with you."

"We'll get back together later." Charles helped me limp through the mud to the wagon. Malcolm lay in a heap where he'd been dumped on the wagon bed. I tried to speak to him, but he didn't respond. Soldiers helped two other wounded men into the wagon as well as a couple so weak they couldn't walk without help.

Meanwhile, the rest had formed a column of four abreast and begun moving forward, our ambulance wagon bringing up the rear. The overcast sky threatened more rain, but at least it wasn't quite so hot. Shortly, the road run alongside a huge body of water. A man beside me shouted, "Look! Is that a ocean?"

The guard who rode shotgun laughed. "No. It's called Lake Michigan. That's where we get all our water."

"Well it's shore a gollywhopper! Most water I ever seen."

In a short time, the road wound between houses. People stood in their yards and called us nasty names. A couple of little boys pelted the marching men with rocks. I saw the road was alongside the railroad tracks. I wondered why they was making us march through the streets when the railroad went to the prison. As we neared the prison, I heard some of the bystanders shouting encouraging words, so I thought maybe everbody didn't hate us.

We entered the prison through a large gate closely guarded by several soldiers, and then into an area surrounded by a high wooden fence. The size of the place surprised me, like a whole town inside the fence. We traveled along a muddy street lined with large buildings on both sides, and we crossed streets also lined with buildings. It extended for blocks and blocks. Scores of men dressed in tattered clothes and standing in mud watched as we passed by and finally stopped in front of a building with a sign reading "Headquarters."

The admitting officer assigned me to Barracks 50 on Thirty-Second Street. By the time I got there, I had mud above my ankles. The sergeant in charge of my barracks assigned me to a bunk, and I looked around. The large room had rows and rows of bunks, three tiers high with narrow aisles running between them. The door to the street was located in the center with three windows on each side of the door to let in the only light. The room so filled with tiers of bunks had little space for anything else, but men in all sorts of clothing filled bunks or set on the floor in what little open area they could find. I fought back tears. It seemed like things was just getting worser and worser.

Standing beside my bunk like a lost puppy, I watched as a young man come up to me and held out his hand. "Hello young feller. I'm Sam. Who are you?" After exchanging some words of greeting, Sam asked if I had eaten. "It's not time for dinner, but maybe the kitchen has a little something to tide you over." Sam led me through a door at the end of the room into the kitchen where a crew worked to prepare the next meal. "Each barracks has its own kitchen," Sam explained, and then he talked the head cook into a hunk of bread for me.

By mid-afternoon the sky had cleared, but a strong wind blew in from the nearby lake. It whistled around the buildings, blowing trash through the streets and whipping hats off. But it did help dry up the mud. I ask Sam if he knowed how I could get my bandage changed. Sam approached the sergeant and got a pass to escort me to the hospital, which was in a square outside the fenced-in barracks area.

About ten foot from the board fence, Sam stopped. "We have to wait here for the guard to check our pass. See this line? It's called 'the deadline.' If you cross this line without a guard's permission, they can shoot you." Sam pointed to a tower that gave guards a view into the area. I promised myself that I'd never make the mistake of blundering across the deadline.

We made our way to the hospital, a two-story wooden building, located in a square closer to the lake. We waited most of the afternoon until a surgeon finally showed up. While we waited me and Sam got to know each other a little better. Sam was older'n me by five years, and had been a member of the famous Morgan's Raiders. "They's a bunch of us here, but they try to keep us separated. They think we might organize a revolt." He winked at me, looked around, and whispered behind his hand. "I guess we just might try that if we get the chance."

When the doctor saw my muddy clothes and especially the muddy bandage, he swore. But he arranged for me to get a bath and issued me a change of clothes. "We don't allow prisoners to wear boots, so you also get shoes. You must take care of these, because we only provide one change of clothes and one pair of shoes. These have to last you as long as you are here. Hopefully, in a couple more weeks you'll be able to wear a shoe on your damaged foot. It's healing well in spite of all it's been through." He also found a cane and explained the way to use it to lessen the pressure on my foot and to keep my balance when my knee gave away. All in all, it had been a afternoon well spent.

***

In the next few days, I learnt the prison routine. Roll call at 7:00 a.m. Anyone who failed to show up for roll call without a good reason got bread and water for a week. Breakfast was next, usually some bread and a small piece of salt pork. Sometimes we also got a boiled egg. We could roam around the barracks area freely so long as we didn't cross the deadline, but no group of more than five persons was permitted. Each prisoner had to eat at his own barracks, but no one cared if someone missed a meal, just his bad luck. We had to be back in our barracks by dark, else we would be locked out for the night.

Sam introduced me to a couple of his friends, Jess and George, also with Morgan's Raiders. They weren't bunked in the same barracks, but tried to meet up each day, and they welcomed me into their conversation and fun. I also hooked up with Charles who was billeted in Barracks 45. We agreed to meet each morning after breakfast near the post office where we found a couple of rude benches. Charles told me Malcolm had smallpox and was in the special smallpox hospital. "I think he might not make it. I've been volunteering to help out over there. It gives me something to do so I don't spend all my time sitting on my duff."

"What all do you do there?"

"I give patients water, read their mail to them, write letters for them, and

156

sometimes help change beds and carry soiled clothes to the laundry, just whatever needs to be done."

"Ain't you afraid you'll catch it?"

"No. I had smallpox when I was eleven, so I won't get it again."

"Lucky you."

The second day me and Charles got together, I ask him how I could get a letter mailed to my mother. Charles was quick to answer. "I've got some money in my account at the store at the end of the street. They transferred it from my account at the Old Capitol Prison. Let's go there and I'll get some paper and a stamp for you." Charles explained we could send only one letter per month, and it would be censored by a officer before it could be mailed. "So be careful what you write or they might just burn your letter." Then he wrote the prison address at the top of the paper for me.

Camp Douglas Prison, Building 50
Chicago, Illinois

Dear Ma,

i got here a few days ago. my friend charles got me some paper. my foot is better. hope your well. please send me a change of clothes and a blanket. and some money.

your son, Harvey.

I soon found out the prison had lots of rules, some I learnt about by failing to follow them. On my third night several hours after dark, I woke with a full bladder needing some relief. I ask the guard for permission to go to the latrine, a couple of blocks away.

"All right Reb, but you have to take off all your clothes."

"What do you mean?"

"That's a rule. If you have to go after lockup, you take off all your clothes."

"What if it's wintertime?"

"Same rule. It's to keep you from trying to escape."

I decided to wait for daylight.

The next day I got kitchen duty. I learnt that each building had its own rules for the kitchen; officers had separate barracks, and they hired other inmates to do the kitchen duty. But in Barracks 50 prisoners rotated for kitchen duty a week at a time. I was to carry water from the water hydrant on the main street. I took a two-gallon bucket but had to stand in line for a long time because the camp had only two hydrants to serve the entire population. I made three trips and poured the water into the huge 40-gallon cooker, the only cook pot available. A delivery man brought a hunk of smelly meat, which someone chopped into pieces and threw into the cooker. Then the whole crew chopped potatoes and added them to the pot, skin and all. Meat, potatoes and water. That was our noon meal.

When the mud had dried up, I spent more time exploring the camp. The mud had turned into dust that the wind whipped around, getting into our eyes and choking us. But I preferred to struggle with the dust as I roamed around outside than to stay in the hot barracks. I found a barbershop and a couple of stores: one that sold only vegetables, but another sold a big variety of goods, such as clothing, tobacco, candles, soap, paper and stamps. I wished I could find out what happened to my back pack. I needed that money. I found the post office, a bakery, a laundry, and even a jail. I counted 64 barracks buildings all built the same, each one had 174 bunks. Sam told me most barracks had more inmates than beds and some slept on the floor. "I hear they's more'n 12,000 prisoners here now. I been here going on two years and it's more crowded now than ever before."

***

On Tuesday of my second week at the camp, I slumped on the bench in front of the post office, waiting for Charles to show up. "What's the matter?"

I looked up at Charles who was standing in front of me. "What makes you think something's wrong?"

"Well, you're sitting there like a sack of potatoes and you look like sin." Charles took a seat beside me.

"I don't know. I sorta got up tired; I'm weak as a newborn kitten. My head hurts. To tell the truth, everything I got hurts. I guess I'm just no good."

Charles put his hand on my brow. "Hmmm. You're really hot. I would say you have a high fever." He studied me for several moments. "Do you have sores in your mouth? Can I look?"

I raised my head and opened my mouth. Charles stood up and peered into my mouth from several angles. "That's what I feared. I hate to tell you, but looks to me like you've got the pox. You have sores on the roof of your mouth and on the inside of your cheeks. That's the way it starts.

He studied me some more. "Looks like some red spots are showing up on your forehead."

"Are you sure?"

"Well, I'm no doctor, but we should get you checked out to be sure. Let's go get a pass from your sergeant and go over to the smallpox hospital." I drug myself to my feet. Charles patted me on the back. "When I found out Malcolm had smallpox, I worried because you had spent so much time sitting beside him on the train. I'm sure if you do have it, you got it from him."

"How is Malcolm?"

"They buried him yesterday."

Fear struck me like a lightning bolt. I was speechless. We walked in silence towards my barracks. Finally, I ask, "Does everbody die?"

"No, the majority get well."

That encouraged me a little, but I couldn't help being afraid.

The smallpox hospital had no more beds, so after the doctor agreed with Charles' guess, I went to the hospital annex set up in the chapel next door. The pews had been replaced with cots, filling the entire room. I managed to grin when I saw my cot had a mattress filled with prairie grass instead of a bare board like the bunk in the barracks. I even had a pillow. A nurse gave me a large sack that had holes cut out for arms and head and told me to undress and put it on.

Charles assured me he would visit ever day and urged me to sleep if I could. I looked around the room. I saw rows and rows of cots, but not many cots was empty. With the hospital full and so many patients in the chapel, I thought they must be a lot of sick soldiers. I shut my eyes and sighed.

Later I looked back on the days in the hospital and realized I couldn't remember much of what happened. I remembered that Charles seemed to be there ever time I opened my eyes. I remembered I was very afraid when the nurse pulled the sheet over the face of the man in the next bed. I remembered the blistery sores on my arms and chest looked like I was covered with a oozing bumpy snakeskin. And I remembered when Charles told me I was going to get well.

***

On a sunny day in mid-September, I returned to Barracks 50. Sam, Jess, and George sat in the shade of the building outside the kitchen door. Sam stood up and held out his hand. "Hey Harvey. Heard you was sick. Welcome back to this hell hole. We missed you." He motioned for me to join them.

"How you feeling? You look like they was starving you. You're skinny as the rail on Morgan's mule." Jess laughed.

I smiled, glad to see some friends. "What's Morgan's mule?"

"Oh man. Wait till you see it." Jess chuckled. "You won't believe it."

"Well, what is it? Where is it? When can I see it?"

"You feel like taking a walk? It's clear on the other side of the square."

"Ready if you are."

My foot no longer required a bandage and I could wear shoes, though I still limped. Using my cane helped me keep my balance. The four of us set off down the street. George seemed to know everyone and exchanged friendly insults with them. After walking a few blocks along the main street, we turned right and approached a fenced-in area near a guard tower.

"There it is. The famous Morgan's mule." Jess pointed inside the fence. I wasn't sure what I was seeing. It looked like a big saw horse so high it took a ladder to reach the cross bar—a long ladder. "It's fifteen foot off the ground."

After staring at it a few moments I turned to Sam. "What's it for?"

"It's a instrument of torture."

"What do you mean?"

"Well, if we break some of the rules they have here, the punishment is to ride Morgan's Mule. They make the prisoner climb up there and set astride that rail."

Jess added, "If the guards are drunk enough and the prisoner gets cocky, they'll tie buckets of sand to his feet. And setting on that rail is like setting on a knife blade."

"How long do they make a man set there?"

"Usually till he faints and falls off."

Jess winked at me. "Now you know why I said you was skinny as that rail. If you turned sideways, you'd be invisible."

"I'm just glad I'm still alive. I'll prob'ly be back to my normal size soon." I had seen no mirrors, so I had no idea what I looked like. I especially wished I could see if I had scars on my face like those on my chest and arms.

Sam shook his head. "You won't get fat on what they feed us these days."

"That's for sure. Our kitchen got no vegetables at all yesterday. We just had hot water with a few shreds of pork. Not enough to keep a gnat alive."

"What happened? Why have they cut back on the food?"

"My best information is they're punishing us because Yankee prisoners got treated so bad at the Confederate prisons."

"That don't seem fair."

"Not much is fair when it comes to war."

160

***

One day as I wandered around, I saw a man on the other side of the street whose walk looked familiar. I watched him for a couple of minutes. I was sure it was Private Davidson. I called, "Private Davidson?"

The man whipped around looking to see who called and saw me crossing the street towards him. "Hey, it's my buddy Campbell. How did you get here?" He shook my hand.

"Prob'ly the same way you did. They shot my foot off at Fort Stevens and then captured me. I been here since early August."

"I wondered what had happened to you when I couldn't find you after we attacked Fort Stevens. I got captured at Kernstown, and they shipped me here at the end of July. Where you been keeping yourself that I ain't seen you around?"

"I got smallpox and spent several weeks quarantined."

"Oh man. Sorry about that. How's your foot?"

"I'm lucky that it's healed up pretty good without getting infected. Trouble is I have no toes, so it's awkward to bend my foot. My shoe feels like it's about two foot long. I'm always tripping myself on my shoe. But thank God, I'm alive."

"I know what you mean. Where you headed?"

"I'm gonna meet some buddies I've been hanging around with. Want to come?

"Sure."

We walked towards the northwest corner of the barracks square where a large elm tree made some shade. The Morgan's Raiders greeted us and welcomed Davidson after I introduced them. Naturally, they started sharing their war stories.

Sam was the first to ask how Davidson got captured, and Davidson wasn't shy about making his experience a good story. "After we retreated from Fort Stevens, we crossed the Potomac into Virginia and set up a camp. As usual, I wandered among the officers' tents to find out what was going on. I come close to Old Jube's quarters, and I heard him explaining to some of his officers about the Battle of Fort Stevens. 'They got some extra troops at the last minute and we were greatly outnumbered. We had no choice but to retreat. We may have lost the battle, but, by God, we scared the hell out of Lincoln.'"

Jess sat against the tree trunk sifting handfuls of dirt through his fingers. "What'd he mean by that?"

"See. We had taken over some houses right next to Fort Stevens to use as officers' quarters and a hospital. Some of our sharp shooters got on the roofs where they could see right into the fort. And stupid-like, Lincoln and some of his friends come out to watch the battle from inside the fort and was standing right in full view. One of the sharp shooters hit the man standing right next to Old Abe, and his guards rushed him away in a hurry."

George laughed. "Serves him right. Too bad they missed that fool."

"Yep, If the Morgan's Raiders had been there, we'd a got him." Sam raised his arms like he had a rifle. "Kerpow!"

Davidson laughed. "What's Morgan's Raiders?"

Jess made a pouty face. "You mean you ain't never heard of the famous Morgan's Raiders?

I listened with interest as first one and then another kept interrupting each other.

"You see, Morgan was a Kentucky farmer. He knowed lots of folks was really in favor of joining the Confederacy, so he raised a small army of fellers and went to Tennessee to fight some battles against the Yankees. Then he got this idea that if he went on a rampage through Kentucky, he'd get lots more to join his troops."

"His superiors ordered him to join a battle in Tennessee but he went against his orders and come busting back into Kentucky. That's when we joined him. See, me, Sam and George is cousins, and we all run away from home and joined the Raiders."

"We went tearing off through Kentucky leaving all sorts of destruction along the way. We stole horses, burned bridges, and robbed stores. Lincoln's army tried to stop us, but we kept right on going till we got to the Ohio River."

Sam added, "Hey, George, you remember when we captured that garrison at Lebanon, Kentucky?"

"Hell, yes, I remember!" George grinned. "Them poor Yankees didn't know what hit them. We trapped about 400 in the town depot during the battle. By the time it was over, we had captured all of them."

"I was disappointed that Morgan decided to parole those Feds." Jess looked around like a cornered badger getting ready to attack. "I woulda lined them up and done away with the whole lot."

"Well Morgan knowed that would just rile up the people more. We just continued our raid, fighting the Union troops across the state to the Ohio River burning bridges, public buildings, and any facility that might house Yankee troops or be used as a hospital." Sam grinned with pride.

"Some Kentuckians joined us as we went along, but we lost more troops fighting the Union troops than we gained. Morgan decided if he couldn't raise more troops in Kentucky, at least he could cross the river into Indiana and maybe create some distraction to help out the Confederates or at least put the fear of God in some Yankees."

"Remember when we robbed the Masonic Lodge in Versailles, Indiana?"

"Yeah, we didn't know Morgan was a Mason. He made us return all the loot."

"One of the best things I remember was when we robbed the town storehouse and stole 2,000 hams. Course, we didn't realize that those hams would begin to spoil in the hot sun, and first thing we knowed, we was dropping hams all along our trail."

"I guess that's how the Union forces finally caught up with us. They followed the hams." Everyone laughed.

"So," Davidson asked, "When did you get captured?"

"Well, we took our plunder all through Indiana and across Ohio, stealing more horses, raiding towns, burning houses and bridges. We tried to cross back over the Ohio River into West Virginia, but we was stopped by a bunch of Yankees. That's where we got captured, but Morgan and about half his men got away."

"They brought us here about two years ago."

Those three fellers got so excited they couldn't wait to tell something more about their raiding journey. They sometimes disagreed and argued, but they did agree on their opinion of General Morgan: he was the bravest, craftiest, smartest soldier of them all.

***

After roll call each morning, the sergeant handed out mail. The day after I met Davidson, I got two pieces of mail: one a letter from Ma and the other a notice to call at the post office for a package. I couldn't wait to read the letter.

Pittsburgh, Pennsylvania
September 2nd 1864

My Dear Son,
I was delighted to get your letter. I'm glad to know where you are. But I am very worried about your situation there. Has your wound healed? I pray you

are being treated well, fed well, and have comfortable living quarters. I pray for your safety every day.

I have mailed a package to you as you requested. I am also sending some money with this letter. William explained to me how they would put your money into an account and you can draw on it as needed. Please let me know if you need anything else. I pray this war will soon be over and you can come home.

William and Hilda are looking for their first child next spring. It will be our first grandchild and I am so sorry Jed won't get to know it. I am pleased that they live close by in Bradford Perkins' house, so Grandma Campbell and I can spoil the baby.

The business has picked up some lately. We had a couple of very lean years because few builders were doing any construction. It looks like things are getting better each month.

Please stay well and safe. Come home soon.

Your loving mother,
Frances Campbell

I had read the letter for the third time, when I realized I was missing breakfast. I rushed to the kitchen to find the food was gone except for two small pieces of stale bread. The post office opened only a couple of hours each afternoon. I would have to wait to pick up my package. Not a good start to my day.

I got in line for the noon meal early and was glad to see the soup had some carrots as well as turnips. Lately the soup seemed to get more watery each day. I set out for the post office as soon as I thought it would be open. As I started out the door, Sam stopped me.

"Where are you headed?"

"Post office. I got a notice to pick up a package."

"Mind if I tag along?"

I nodded and motioned in the direction of the post office. "Let's go."

We made our way around a group of men arguing over some issue and almost immediately run into Simon.

"Well. Lookie here. It's my good friend Harvey." He reached for my hand, but I pulled back. "Don't you remember me, buddy? I was your friend on the train." He rubbed his hand along my arm.

I backed up a step and when I got Sam's eye, I shook my head. Simon reached for me again and Sam stepped between us. "Leave him alone."

Simon whined, "But I just want to be friends."

"Harvey don't want to be your friend, do you Harvey?"

I looked at the ground and mumbled, "No."

"Oh come on, young feller. I ain't meaning no harm." He snatched at my hand.

Sam grabbed Simon's shoulder and twirled him around to face him. "You dirty piece of slime. I said to leave him alone." He gave Simon a shove. "Now git away from him and don't never let me see your ugly face again."

Simon stood up straight and looked at Sam. He was taller by a couple of inches, and his muscular arms flexed as he doubled his fists. "You can't make me."

Now, I was behind Simon. When he took a step toward Sam, I hit Simon on the back of his knee with my cane, causing him to yelp and fall down. The ruckus caught the attention of the arguing men who rushed in to put a stop to it.

Simon lay on the ground screaming and holding his leg. One of the men looked down at him. "Oh, it's you again. We told you to stay away from this side of the prison. What are you doing here?"

"He hit me with a stick. That's not allowed. I'll file a charge."

Two of the men took Simon's arms and pulled him to a standing position. "You wouldn't dare make a charge or we'll tell the guard what you was really up to. Now get out of here."

Simon limped across the street, turned and shook his fist. That was the last time I ever saw him. Sam turned to the men. "Thanks boys. You saved us."

"Well, we didn't want you taking a ride on the mule, although I'd love to see that piece of trash on the rail."

As we started towards the post office, I complained, "Why'd they stop us? We coulda beat him to a pulp."

"Do you know what the penalty for fighting is?"

I shook my head.

"It's Morgan's mule." I opened my mouth in surprise. "They did us a very big favor by stopping it. Those fellows saved me and you from having to take that ride."

I kicked the dirt. "But he was bothering me. You told him to stop. He had it coming."

"I agree, and if we had to fight, I'd have done my best to beat him, even if it meant taking the punishment. But I don't think you understand how bad that torture really is. You better be careful with that stick. If Simon reported you, you'd be in bad trouble."

"But it wasn't my fault. He started it."

Sam didn't say nothing for several minutes. I was so upset I wouldn't look at him. Finally Sam stopped. "Look Harvey. I was trying to look out for you. If you don't want me to try to help you, just say the word and I'll mind my own business."

I didn't say nothing but shut my mouth in a straight line and walked into the post office.

***

I walked towards my barracks carrying my package. I hoped I didn't see Sam. I guessed I was rude to him when he was trying to help me, but I really wanted to beat up that Simon so he would leave me alone. Then I saw Preacher walking towards me.

"Hey, Harvey. First I've seen you since you were in the hospital. How are you? Are you getting enough to eat? You look even skinnier than when I saw you last." He reached out to shake my hand.

I shifted the package and shook Preacher's hand. "I reckon I'm doing all right. I eat as much as they give me. Seems like our kitchen don't get as much food as when I first got here."

"Well, just be sure to eat all they'll give you. Even if it doesn't seem appetizing, you'll get some nourishment from it." We walked along in silence for a few minutes. "Have you done any more thinking about our talks in the hospital?"

I frowned. "No. I just can't be thinking about God now. I don't think a good God would let us be treated this way, and a bad God don't make no sense."

Preacher pulled his Bible from his shirt. "Would you like to borrow my

Bible for a few days? I know you enjoyed reading some of the stories."

"Sure, Preacher. That'd give me something to do 'sides roaming these streets."

Preacher handed me the Bible. "I'll look you up in a couple of days and we can talk if you have any questions."

I thanked him and turned into my barracks.

It was good to get some warm socks and a heavier shirt. The winds from the lake seemed much cooler now. The leaves from the few trees on the grounds had mostly blown away. I'd be grateful for the blanket and coat Ma had sent since winter weather would arrive soon. After examining my package for contraband, the sergeant warned me that lots of prisoners would be glad to take my blanket and coat. "Be sure to watch them carefully."

I chuckled. I didn't know how he thought I could keep a watch on them. I had no place to keep them 'cept on my bunk. I decided the best way was to always wear my coat.

Later on my way back from the water hydrant, I met Sam and Jess. Their clothes looked like they'd been playing in mud puddles. It was the first time I'd seen Sam since the incident with Simon, and Sam surprised me with his friendly greeting. "Bless my soul, it's our friend Harvey. How you doing young feller?" We shook hands. "That's a fine looking coat."

I nodded. "Thanks." I shook hands with Jess. "Where you been? You look like you been mining the dirt."

"You might say that. Meet the grave diggers."

"Why are you digging a grave?"

"People die here all the time, you know. We just thought we'd get some free tobacco."

"Free tobacco? What are you talking about?"

"They get us to dig graves by paying us with tobacco. We've been digging graves for a week." Jess chuckled. "We sell our tobacco to some of the officers and then go buy some extra food from the store."

Sam added, "They ain't supposed to force us prisoners to work, but they get us to do it by giving us stuff. Last summer they heard some big shot from Washington was coming for a inspection tour, and they had us paint a bunch of the barracks. That time they bribed us with liquor."

"Where are these graves?"

Sam pointed toward the lake. "It's a huge grave yard. Acres and acres where thousands of prisoners are buried. The man in charge told us so many died a couple years ago when they had a bad case of typhoid they put them in huge mass graves."

I remembered when the man on the cot next to me in the smallpox hospital died. How scared I was. I coulda died, and they'd put me somewhere out there among those thousands of unlucky Rebels. I shook my head. "I guess I never thought about what they did with the ones that died."

"It's sad. They just dump the bodies in the grave without a coffin or even a prayer. Few of the graves is marked. No one knows who's buried in most of them."

Sam clapped me on the back. "It's good to see you. We've finished with the graves, so we'll be seeing you around." They turned to leave, then Sam stopped. "Oh, meant to say your friend Davidson has been helping us."

"I guess that's why I ain't seen him lately." Sam nodded and continued down the street.

I was pleased Sam seemed to hold no grudge. I walked slowly back to my barracks. I wondered if I could find Malcolm's grave. Even though I'd caught the smallpox from Malcolm, I felt a sort of kinship with him. The next day when I met Charles for our usual conversation, I ask if he thought he could find Malcolm's grave. "I'd like to visit it and pay my respects."

"No, I don't think so. The cemetery is off limits, and besides, the graves are not marked."

"Do you think his family knows?"

"Yes, before he died, he asked me to write them."

That comforted me a little. I could imagine how hurt Ma would be if she wouldn't know I was dead or where my final resting place was. "Just think about all the families who have no idea. This war is so terrible. And what good has it done?" We set quiet for several minutes. I started feeling cold, even though I wore my new coat. I turned and looked at Charles. "If I had died, would you have wrote my mother?"

"Yes. You gave me her address when you were in the hospital. I would have let her know and told her how brave you were during your illness."

"Thanks."

Charles touched me on the arm. "Say, I've been wondering. Do you still have those disturbing dreams?"

I frowned and slowly nodded. "Yes, sometimes." Then I lifted my head and looked at Charles. "But lots of others have bad dreams too. Almost ever night one or two start screaming and someone has to shake them. So I guess it ain't a big problem."

"Would you like to talk about your dreams?"

I didn't answer right away. I worried Charles would think I was weak or a big baby like James always said. I studied the ground as I thought it over and finally shook my head. "Thanks, but I ain't wanting to talk about it now."

"That's all right with me, but if you change your mind, talking about it might help."

After a bit, I ask, "What do you know about the Bible?

168

"Not a lot, but I've heard a good many sermons about it. Why are you asking?"

"Preacher let me borrow his Bible and I been reading it some. Some of the stories in it don't seem possible. Do you think they's true?"

"I don't know. Give me an example."

"I read yesterday about a war they was fighting and as long as the prophet raised his hands up in the air, they was winning. But if his arms got tired and he let them fall down, they lost. So some fellers held his arms up and they won. Now, could that be true?"

"I agree that it seems hard to believe, but I don't know enough about it to say if it's true or not."

"I guess I won't never find out if they's a God. I can't hardly believe some of them stories, so I don't really believe God is real."

Charles stood up. "We'll have to finish this conversation another day. I need to get over to the hospital. I promised a couple of fellows I'd help them write letters." He gave a salute and walked away.

***

The next morning I got another letter after roll call. I thought it probably was another letter from Ma, but I couldn't believe my eyes when I saw it was from Mary Louise Baker. I couldn't imagine why that little girl would be writing me, but a letter from somebody was always a treat.

Harlan, Kentucky
November 12th 1864

Dear Harvey,

Mama told me you had been captured and was in a Federal prison. Your mother wrote you had got wounded and then captured. I was shocked and worried to death when I heard it. I trust you are healing from your wound and getting enough to eat. It's been getting cold here and you are away up North, so I hope you have a warm place to stay.

It will soon be Thanksgiving Day. Did you know that President Lincoln set aside a special day in November to be a holiday for giving thanks? The people at Papa's church are planning to have a big dinner that day for everyone who wants to come and a special time for prayers of thanks. Will you have a special dinner for Thanksgiving Day? I know one thing I will give thanks for—the fact that you are alive and, I pray, also well.

I know you think I am just a child, but I will be eleven in a couple of weeks, so I'm really almost a grown up lady. I hope you will agree for me to write you letters, and I'd like you to write back to me. Will you do that?

Do you know what is my favorite memory of you? I was five years old. It was one day when you were still going to Papa's school. All the students were playing in the school yard, and I fell down and skinned my knee. Do you remember that? I skinned it pretty bad and blood was running all down my leg. Of course, I was screaming like a rabbit with its foot caught in a trap. Do you remember what you did? You picked me up and gently carried me home so Mama could doctor my knee. You kept saying, "Hush, little Doodlebug. It's going to be all right." You looked at me with your big brown eyes and smiled, *and I believed you and quit yelling. You've been my hero ever since.*

The next day I told Mama I was going to marry you when I grew up. So will you write back to me?

Your friend,
Mary Louise Baker

Reading this letter made me laugh. She was just a child—not that I was such a grown up. I had trouble believing she was eleven as she claimed. To me she was the pesky little girl that used to follow me and Evan around the playground at school. We sure didn't have no Thanksgiving dinner. We didn't even know it was a holiday. I read the letter again. I couldn't believe she had liked me all these years. But I had to smile at the thought of getting more mail, so I set off at once for the store to buy some paper and stamps.

As the winter weather settled in, I lost track of the time. Each day seemed the same: cold wind that chilled to the bones and brought snow, not enough heat in the barracks, watery soup to eat, and short tempers among cold, sick, hungry soldiers thrown together in crowded spaces. I spent much of each day bundled in my coat and huddled under my blanket in my bunk. If I went outdoors, I wrapped my head and shoulders in my blanket, partly for the cold, but also to keep someone from taking my blanket if I left it on my bunk. I felt sorry for the many who had no blanket or coat neither.

I continued to borrow Preacher's Bible. I couldn't believe much of what I read, but it fascinated me just the same. I especially liked some of the rules. I agreed with Proverbs 13:24: *He that spareth his rod hateth his son: but he that loveth him chasteneth him betimes.* I remembered the times Pa had took off his belt. I guessed it was the only way I could learn to obey. I decided if I ever had children, I'd make them obey me even if I had to beat them just like the Bible says.

I loved the story in Genesis 2 where God made woman from the man's rib. I agreed with Preacher, who explained that means the man is above woman and she must obey him. *Eye for eye, tooth for tooth: as he hath caused a blemish in a man, so shall it be done to him again.* That sounded fair to me. But nothing I read and none of Preacher's explanations made me believe they was a God.

One bright spot during these dreary days was receiving letters from little Mary Louise. She always signed them "Doodlebug," and that made me smile. The letters come about every two or three weeks. She wrote newsy letters about her studies, her sewing projects, her neighbors, and her hopes and dreams. More and more she seemed like a adult, but I still pictured her as a little girl. I sometimes wrote a reply, mostly so I wouldn't feel guilty when she complained I hadn't written.

Shortly after Christmas Day, which was just like any other day—no special food or any celebration—the weather turned even worse. By New Year's Day the snow was knee deep and the temperature plunged to extreme lows. I heard one man say, "I been here for three years and I ain't never seen it so cold." The cold lingered for weeks. The pipes carrying water to the prison from the lake froze, and the prisoners had to melt snow to even make coffee. Several prisoners got frostbite on their fingers and ears, and a few even froze to death.

I went outdoors only to go to the latrine. Most of the prisoners stayed as near the stove as possible. One day some fellers started debating about who was the smartest commander. One claimed John Singleton Mosby, head of the 45th Battalion of the 1st Virginia Cavalry, won the prize. He bragged, "Mosby led his men on raids against the Union Army where they would attack quick as lightening and then blend in with the local citizens so the Yankees couldn't find them."

"One time," another feller spoke up, "Mosby heard a Union general was billeted in a big house, and he surrounded the house and woke the general from his sleep. They captured the general, two captains, 30 enlisted men, and 58 horses without firing a shot."

"Then, another time Mosby's wife visited him, and they was sleeping in this house and a bunch of Feds broke into the house to surprise him. But when they rushed into the bedroom, they found his wife but no Mosby. After they left, his wife opened the window and told Mosby it was safe to come back to bed. He had climbed out the window and hid in a tree."

No one said anything for a time till somebody asked, "What kind of weapons did you have?"

Several spoke at once. "Springfield rifles, Model 1861."

Someone nearer the stove said, "I had my own gun that I brought from home."

"I never had no gun—just a big club."

"I just had a sword."

"I had a pistol my pa gave me."

I didn't say nothing, but I remembered how my father had give me a gun for my twelfth birthday and then had learnt me how to use it. I was sorry I had lost it. I turned my head to see who had asked if anyone had heard of a Quaker gun? When no one said nothing, the man explained. "I heard a man who fought at Gettysburg say they had some logs they had planed smooth and painted black so they looked like cannons."

"What good would that do?"

"I guess it made the enemy keep their distance if they thought they had a lot of big guns."

After a minute, a tall man stood up and stretched. "I hear the war will be over soon. I hope that's true. I'd like to get home in time to do the spring plowing."

Suddenly I felt a great wave of sadness sweep over me. I had to blink my eyes and take some deep breaths to keep back the tears. I hated to be in this prison. I hated the war. I wanted to see spring even if I had to go back to Kentucky.

***

After what seemed like months, the thaw finally come. The sun would warm enough to start the snow and ice melting in the day time filling the streets with pools of water, and then during the nights the puddles would freeze creating ice covered streets. After several days, the streets was more like rivers of mud because the level ground had no drainage. But at least the water pipes was thawed and we had water. It wasn't till the March winds blowed in that the mud dried up.

I got a letter from Ma saying she had sent more money to my account. She told me to buy extra food, especially for my birthday. I had give little thought to my birthday. I went to the post office to ask the clerk for the date. I was surprised to hear it was already the sixth day of April. In just four more days I would be 17. I rubbed my chin where a beard was beginning to grow and begun to count the days.

On the morning of my birthday, the blare of bugles roused the men from sleep. We rushed outside to see a wagon draped in red, white, and blue bunting slowly coming down the street. On board four buglers announced the arrival of General Sweet, Commander of the prison. The wagon stopped halfway down the street and General Sweet proclaimed in a loud voice. "General Lee has surrendered!" A few men cheered, but I didn't quite understand what all the fuss was about so I asked Sam, who stood nearby.

"Since Lee was commander of the Confederate Army, if he surrendered, that pretty well ends the war. Even though a few smaller armies may still be fighting, they'll soon give up when they hear Lee has surrendered. You might say it means the war is over."

"Can we go home now?"

"Not today, but I think it'll be soon."

Two days later at roll call, the sergeant read an announcement, "All able bodied enlisted men who are willing to swear an oath of allegiance to the United States of America should come to the headquarters building today." I wondered what that was about. It certainly didn't concern me. I had no intention of swearing an oath to those Yankees. I watched as a number of men from my barracks left including Sam.

Charles explained what was happening when we met for our morning visit. "Those volunteers who take the oath will be formed into a special unit to go fight against the western Indians. I heard enough men have volunteered to make ten companies."

"So the prisoners who go will now be Union Soldiers?"

"Yes. When Lee surrendered, that was the end of the Confederacy, so all men who stay in the army will be United States soldiers."

"What if you don't take the oath?"

"You'll be discharged."

"Are you going to take the oath?"

"I don't want to be a soldier. I want to go back to Georgia and finish my education, but I will take the oath so I can have the privileges of a citizen."

A few days later, I walked down the street and noticed the flag in front of Headquarters flew at half-mast. I ask a guard standing outside why the flag was half way to the ground. "Ain't you heard? President Lincoln was assassinated."

"Thank you, sir." I felt myself smiling. Then I felt bad because I shouldn't be glad for anyone to be killed. I looked back at the guard. "Excuse me, sir, but do they know who done it?"

"Yes, but he got away, and they ain't caught him yet."

All kinds of rumors circulated through the inmates about when we would be released. I didn't know what to believe. A few days after we heard about Lincoln, thousands of prisoners gathered on the parade grounds to watch as the volunteers going to fight in the West paraded by, decked out in their new Federal uniforms. Before riding out the gate, they saluted Commander Sweet, who stood with his officers in the viewing stand. I had already said goodbye to Sam, George, Jess, and Davidson. I was most surprised when Preacher looked me up and gave me his Bible. "I guess I might never see you again, but I want you to know I'll always remember you. Use this book as your guide. It will not lead you astray."

Now all my friends was gone except Charles, and if the war was really over, he'd soon be gone too. I started wondering what would happen to me. I was afraid I'd have to go back to Kentucky til I was 21 since that was how they divided up the company after Pa died. I didn't like the thought of working for James. That would not be much improvement over being in this prison. At least here I had had friends. I found a sunny spot where the ground was pretty dry and set enjoying the warmth. Then I remembered after all the excitement of the last few days I'd plumb forgot about my birthday. When I returned to my bunk later in the day, someone had taken my coat and Preacher's Bible.

***

Life continued. Maybe the war was over, but us prisoners was still behind the walls. As spring arrived, the grass turned green and leaves filled the few trees. The second week in May at roll call, the sergeant announced that all prisoners below the rank of colonel would be released. If they took the oath of allegiance, they would receive transportation to their homes. Those who refused to take the oath would get home the best they could. They would be mustered out one barracks at a time beginning with Barracks 1.

I knowed it would take days to process the thousands of prisoners, maybe even weeks. I spent as much time with Charles as I could till he was mustered out. Finally my own barracks was called up. When I finally reached the desk, the officer told me to raise my right hand and swear the oath. I looked at him for a few seconds and said, "No, sir."

"What's your name?"

"Harvey Michael Campbell, sir."

"If you refuse the oath, you will be processed last, and you will not receive transportation home."

"I understand that, sir, but may I ask if I can still get the money in my account?"

"Yes, but you will have to wait for that too." I nodded.

"We will notify you when to come back. So far 1,700 have refused to take the oath, so it will be a while yet."

When the day finally arrived and I had my discharge from the prison, I still didn't have my money. It took two more days of waiting, standing in line, going from one office to another to sign papers, but at last I was free to go. I hoped I had enough money to get me home. My army days was finally over.

PART

THREE.

PART

THREE

CHAPTER 12

July 1865

Pittsburgh, Pennsylvania

I didn't know what day it was. I had lost all track of time, but finally, one morning I stood outside the wrought iron fence surrounding the brick and stone house in Pittsburgh where I was born. I had spent the happiest years of my life in this house. After all I'd been through in the past year, I couldn't hardly believe I'd finally got here. I looked up at the window of my boyhood bedroom on the third floor and wondered if someone else had claimed it in the almost six years since I had slept there. I loved the house with its wide porch that stretched across the front and wrapped around the right side. I smiled to see Grandma Campbell's rocking chair in its usual place on the porch. I hoped she would be as glad to see me as I was to finally be back here.

I noticed someone had kept the lawn looking good. I wondered who was taking care of it. I walked up the gravel driveway, through the porte-cochere on the left side of the house. I could see the stables and coach house in the rear, but I couldn't see no sign of life. I was scared they might all gone off somewheres. I went on around the back to the kitchen door like I always done when I lived here. I wondered should I just walk in, or should I knock. I was so excited I couldn't wait no longer, so I just opened the door and walked in.

Cousin Maybelle stood at the kitchen table folding laundry. She took one look at me and tore off like a bear was after her, screaming at the top of her lungs, "There's a tramp in the house!"

I hadn't give a thought to what I looked like after being on the road so many days. I musta looked awful bad if she didn't recognize me. I didn't know what to do, so I just stood there and waited. The next person I saw was the last person in the whole world I expected to see in Ma's house: Caleb come running into the kitchen.

"Caleb! It's me, Harvey. What are you doing here?"

Caleb looked at me for several seconds, then took three steps and grabbed me in a big bear hug. Even lifted me off my feet. He set me down and wiped at his eyes. "My God, man! You're nothing but skin and bones." Then he led me through the house to the office and knocked on the door. I heard my mother say, "Come in."

Caleb opened the door. "Mistress Campbell, it's Harvey. He's come home." Those was the sweetest words I ever heard.

"Ma!" I ran towards her. She stood, hugged me so tight I couldn't hardly breathe. I was so happy—I don't know why I was sobbing.

"Oh son, I've been so afraid for you." She pulled back and looked up at me and rubbed her hand over the scraggly beard on my cheek. "You're so tall." She turned to Caleb, "Go tell Pete to fix something for Harvey to eat. He looks half starved."

"Pete? Pete O'Malley? Is he here too?"

Ma put her arms around me again. "Yes, he's here. He's getting older and needed an easier job. Besides, he's always been my favorite cook." She rubbed my back, feeling my shoulder blades that stuck out like I's trying to grow wings. "Oh, Harvey, it's so good to know you're safe. God does answer prayers."

I remember the next few hours as a blur of questions, more tears, hugs, and surprises. Somehow I got fed, soaked in a tub of hot water for a long time, got some clean clothes, and took a nap. That evening Pete cooked up quite a feast and all the family was invited. I told Pete I didn't care what he fixed so long as it ain't soup. Although I used to love his bean soup, I had so much sorry soup in prison I ain't ever gonna eat soup again.

I set beside Grandma Campbell on the front porch as we waited for all the family to arrive. She had hugged me over and over all day, ever time I got close to her. Ever little bit she'd pat me on the shoulder. Finally I ask her what Chester, my favorite cousin, was up to.

"Well, Honey, he's apprenticed to a carpenter who works for one of the construction companies in the city. Right now they're building a court house for a town out west of here."

"Reckon he'll be here for the family supper tonight?"

"I don't think so. He comes home about every three weeks or so and brings his dirty laundry." She laughed. "If he didn't run out of clean underwear, he probably wouldn't ever come home." She must have seen the disappointment on my face. "Oh, don't worry. You'll get to see him before long."

Ma had sent Caleb to the company office to notify Uncle Stuart and William and to Grandma and Grandpa Dodson's house to invite them to supper. He returned sometime later and we watched the buggy as it turned into the driveway and stopped before reaching the porte-cochere. Then Elliott jumped out and raced toward the porch.

Even though it was hot summer time, he looked like a big city lawyer with his coat and tie and shiny boots. I stood to greet him and after exchanging hugs, he stepped back and looked me over. I hoped I didn't still look like the tramp that walked into the kitchen and scared the living daylights out of Cousin Maybelle. Pete had trimmed my beard and cut my hair, and Ma had come up with decent clothes and shoes for me.

"You're thin as a rail. Are you all right?"

"Yep, nothing that a few days of Pete's cooking won't cure."

"My word, it's so good to see you." He gave me another hug and carried over a chair so he could be nearby. He gave Grandma a hug and chatted with her a little, and then he turned back to me.

"Are you really well? Not sick or anything?" He noticed my cane. "Ma told us you had lost some of your foot. Is it all healed up now?"

"Lay off, will you?" I laughed. "I said I's fine."

"So, how did you get here?"

"Walked, hitched rides with postal wagons, found a boat and floated it down a river, but mostly walked. I saved up what little money I had, so when I got to Cincinnati I could catch a steamboat, but by that time I's so dirty and ragged, they thought I was a tramp and a policeman shooed me away."

"How long did it take you?"

"I ain't sure. I lost track of the days. I don't even know what day it is now. Trouble is I don't have much strength. I'd walk a while and then have to rest, so it took me longer than I expected."

We had a wonderful evening—lots to eat, all the family gathered around, and everone looked so happy. I had a sad thought: the last time all the family was together like this, Pa was with us. I didn't know how much I had missed him till then.

Everone had lots of questions. When did you get smallpox? Was the winter real bad there? We know you didn't get enough to eat, but was you treated bad in other ways? I answered as good as I could, but I was getting purty tired. Finally, William asked me what was I gonna do now, and before I could say anything, Ma said, "He's going to be here for a while until he gets his strength back. Then we'll decide." She looked at me and saw I couldn't hardly hold my head up. "I think this boy needs to get to bed."

People begun saying their goodbyes, and I was soon tucked up in my old bedroom fast asleep.

The next day Caleb drove the buggy to take us to a appointment Ma had made with a doctor who checked me over. He told Ma I had scurvy. "Look; see how red his gums are, and his teeth are loose. That's because he has had such poor food, and that's also why he gets tired so easily and has no energy."

"What do we need to do about that?" Ma pursed her lips.

"He needs to eat lots of vegetables and fruits. If you could get oranges or lemons that would be good, but bell peppers, and any dark greens are good too." He thought for a moment and looked at some notes he had written. "They did a terrible job on his foot, but it has healed well. I don't see any lingering effects of the smallpox except for the scars. They won't completely go away, but as time goes by they will get less prominent. He needs lots of rest and lots of good food. Give him a couple of months and he should be good as new."

"Well, I doubt that good food will grow his toes back."

The doctor looked surprised. "You're right. I'm sorry he will always have to cope with that injury. It's not just that he has half a foot. His knee was also injured and that's why his foot turns out sideways. The knee joint is so twisted it makes his leg give away sometimes. He'll always need to use his cane to keep from falling." He scratched his bearded chin and smiled at me. "But I believe he can have a good life even so."

When we got back home, I watched while Caleb put Lady in the stable. I noticed for the first time that he was limping. When he had finished with the horse, we walked back towards the house. "Well, Harvey, did you get a good report from the doctor?"

"I guess you could call it that. He told me to eat lots of good food. That sounds good to me."

"Well, here's the place to do that. Pete really lays out good meals."

"Ma says he's always been her favorite cook, but I was surprised to see you and Pete working here."

"Your mother's a saint. I hope I'm not speaking out of turn, but Pete couldn't take James no more. James was working him to death, making him work on the farm and everthing." He stopped in the shade of a large elm, and I noticed his hair was gray about his temples. It was a shock to see he was getting old. "When Mistress Campbell heard about it, she brought Pete here."

I nodded. That made sense. I had no trouble believing James made Pete's life miserable. "So, Caleb, how come you to be working here?"

"It was actually your Uncle Stuart's idea. I was working with the tree cutting team out on a mountain west of the city and a tree fell on me and broke my leg in three places. I was luckier 'n your pa, but my leg never growed back right, and I can't walk or stand for long, so I couldn't work the timber no more. Mr. Stuart suggested Mistress Campbell should hire me, and she ask me and Pete to live in the coach house. He cooks and I take care of the horse and do anything Mistress Campbell ask me to." He looked at me and smiled. "Like I said, "She's a saint." I couldn't agree more.

***

For the next few weeks I mostly slept and ate. Gradually, I started getting some energy back. During that time William come to visit two or three nights each week and we played chess. He ask me lots of questions about my time in prison. He told me he had worried about me because Camp Douglas had a reputation for being the worst prison run by the Union. When I told him some stories of what went on, he shook his head and said, "I'm so thankful you managed to hang on until the war was over. We're all glad to have you here with us."

One evening in the middle of our game, he looked at me and asked, "By the way, did you get paid while you were in the Confederate Army?"

I was real surprised cause I'd never even give a thought to getting paid. I shook my head. "No, never had a payday."

William moved his queen. "Well, I'm going to talk with Elliot and see if we can do some inquiries about that." Then he took a note pad out of his coat pocket and took down information about the dates I served, the companies I joined, the battles I fought, and the time I spent at Camp Douglas. But I never thought no more about it.

I started spending more time outside watching Pete and Caleb do their chores. Sometimes I even helped a little. I liked hanging laundry on the lines in the back yard and pulling some weeds out of the rose garden. One day I watched as they was repairing a gate to the stables. I picked up a couple of short pieces of wood they had sawed off a board, got one of my pa's pocket knives and thought I'd whittle a little. I'd never tried to carve nothing before, so I was surprised when I seemed to have a knack for it. That become my pastime, and day after day I sat in the shade with a puddle of shavings around my feet as I made animals, boats, little houses, and even some flowers.

I looked forward to the times Chester showed up. He couldn't stop talking about all the building projects he had worked on. He had hopes of someday having his own building company. He noticed my little carvings, and after that ever time he come, he brought me a box of scrap lumber. I had enough carving materials to last me for years.

One day Caleb come by my carving spot and handed me a envelope. "Looks like you got a letter."

Harlan, Kentucky
June 30th 1865

Dear Harvey,

My mother got a letter from your mother saying you was home from the prison. I thank the Lord for bringing you home. My family prayed every day for your safety. Your mother's letter said you were sick and needed lots of rest. I hope you are feeling better now.

When you get stronger, I hope you will come to visit us. My father said he would like that very much and so would I. My mother would like you to bring your mother with you.
Be sure to write me.

Your friend,
Doodlebug

I had never told Ma about Mary Louise's letters and she was curious about a letter from her to me, so I let her read it. Then I dug through the few belongings I had brung from prison and let her read that first letter Mary Louise wrote. As she read, she smiled.

"So she has thought you were special ever since she was a child."

"Aw Ma, she's still a child."

"Well, I don't know about that. Josephine tells me she's learning to sew

184

so she can make linens for her home when she's married. That doesn't seem like a child to me." She handed the letter back to me. "Did you answer her letter?"

"Yes, ma'am, but I didn't write very often. It was so good to get mail, and I figgered one way to get mail was to write her. She wrote me ever two or three weeks till the President was shot. I never got no letters after that."

"Well, I have good paper and envelopes in the office. You must send her a reply right away." She got a thoughtful look. "And maybe we can go visit them next spring."

That comment interested me cause as I got my strength back, I wondered what plans Ma had for me. I expected that I would have to find a job somewheres, but I really hoped I wouldn't have to go back to Kentucky.

The very next day Ma handed me a letter addressed to her. It was from Charles Summers. He wanted to know if I had got home and if I was well. He said he got to Atlanta in mid-May, and his old boss had hired him, so he had a job. He also said much of Atlanta was in ruins, and it was hard to find a place to stay. Many families had fled before Sherman's army burned the city, and now their homes was in ashes, so they couldn't return. It was a sad letter in many ways, but I was glad to know he was home safe.

After I read Charles' letter, Ma said, "He sounds like a good friend."

"Yes, ma'am, he nursed me through the smallpox. He gave me good advice. I prob'ly wouldn't be here if he hadn't been my friend."

"I'm grateful God sent you a good friend for that awful time. I will write him and tell him how grateful I am for his friendship with you." She reached for Charles' letter and said to me, "Now you have two letters you need to write."

***

As the leaves begun to turn and the days got cooler, I was feeling stronger and found myself bored with carving little doodads all the time. I needed something to use up the energy that had come back to me. I ain't never been able to be still for long. First thing I know I'm fidgeting like a leaf in the wind. That's prob'ly why I never took to school—too much setting still.

As it turned out, Chester's company had started a new job in the city, so he was staying at his home next door, and we got together some evenings after he got home. He was a good chess player, and we spent lots of evenings with the chess board we kept set up. We talked about his work. I could tell he liked doing building work.

"You know, now that the war's over, lots of new building projects are beginning. Looks like our company will do pretty well for quite some time now." He studied the board and finally decided on a move. "Uncle Stuart says the lumber company is getting more demands for lumber also."

I set up straighter and stretched my arms over my head. "I wish I could find a good job somewheres. With my bum foot, I ain't likely to be hired as a builder or to cut down trees neither one. I'm shore tired of setting around here feeling good for nothing."

Chester laughed and looked me in the eye for a long time. When I made the move to end the game, he slapped his knee. "It's too bad you can't get hired to play chess. That's the third time you've won. I've got to pay more attention to my game."

A couple of days later, Ma called me into the office for a talk. She first ask about my health.

"I'm feeling purty much back to my normal self. I think I've gained most of my weight back, my appetite's good, and I'm loving Pete's cooking."

"I notice you've been having your bad dreams. I came up to your bedroom last night when I heard you crying out, but by the time I got there you seemed to be settling back to sleep."

I nodded and frowned. "Sorry I disturbed you."

"Did you have the nightmares while you were in prison?"

I chuckled. "Most everbody did. Nobody complained cause we all knowed the next scream might be our own."

"Does talking about your dreams help?"

I shrugged my shoulders. "I don't think so. Mostly I dream about Evan or about the battles." I could never tell anyone how I felt about shooting that young Yankee, but many a night his horrified face hovers over me. In my dream, that face chases after me and no matter how hard I try I can't run away from it.

Ma looked out the window. I shifted in my chair in my restless way. About that time a blast of wind slammed a door shut, and I bolted to my feet, ready to run. I took a deep breath and set back down. Ma raised her eyebrows.

"Sorry. That sounded like a gun shot at first."

Ma nodded. "I see." She pursed her lips and looked down at some notes she had written. "I've noticed you're getting pretty restless now that you're feeling better. I've been thinking what you could be doing to put that new energy to work. I also think you're not ready to take on a regular job. So I wondered if you might like a horse of your own to take care of and ride." She studied me for several moments. "What do you think?"

I smiled. "I'd love to have a horse. I ain't had one of my own since those stinking marauders stole Scout."

She stood and come towards me so I stood up too. She put her arms around me and held me tight. "I feel like having you here getting well is a gift from God. I'm not ready to let you go yet." She looked up at me. "Write Mary Louise and tell her we'll come to visit them when the winter weather's over. Then we'll come to some decision about what you'll do next."

I nodded. She handed me some paper and a pen. Sit here at my desk and write her right now." She started towards the door but turned and looked at me. "I've asked William to look for a young filly that's gentle, but not yet accustomed to a saddle. If he can find such a horse, you can train her and maybe when she's old enough she can have a colt."

Now it was my time to give a hug. I was now several inches taller than Ma. I put my arms around her and lifted her off the floor, then held her close while I placed a kiss on her forehead. "Thanks, Ma. That would please me very much." I think I had a big grin that lasted all day long.

The next time William come to play chess, he told me Uncle Stuart had contacted his friend in Kentucky who raises horses. As soon as he could locate the kind of horse we wanted, he would ship it immediately. I started making a list of the equipment I would need, such as saddle, bridle, lead straps. I talked with Caleb about how he gets oats and hay. I think Caleb was as excited as me. We decided which stall I would keep my horse in, and he showed me how he cleaned out the stalls.

Finally toward the end of November, we got word that the horse was on the way. Caleb took me to a harness shop to look at saddles and other kinds of horse tack we would need, but we decided to wait till we saw how old the horse was before we bought anything. It might not be old enough to use a saddle. One of my favorite memories of all time is the day Ma called me to come to the front porch. It was such a beautiful sight. We had had a snow storm the day before and the ground was sparkling white. And up through that snowy field, William was riding his big roan stallion leading the most beautiful horse I had ever saw.

I yelled and started down the steps, but Ma called me back to get a coat. I started to argue, but thought better of it. I raced through the house, grabbed my coat and got to the stables just as William was getting off his horse. I couldn't believe my eyes. She was a three year old filly, with snow white feet and a white blaze on her forehead. Her coat was a yellowish color that reminded me of the center of a daisy, and I knowed right as soon as I saw her that Daisy was her name.

Her big brown eyes was bright and she seemed interested in looking all around the stables. She wore a halter and seemed used to the lead strap. She smelled my palm when I stood in front of her and held out my hand.

William laughed. "She thinks you've got a treat for her. She's gentle and she'll let you pet her, but she's had a long trip. She's probably tired and hungry. Let's get her a drink and some oats and give her some time to get used to her new home."

For the next month, I spent many hours ever day with Daisy. As soon as breakfast was over, I'd take a apple or a sugar lump and head to the stable. I would hide the treat in my pocket and she would nudge me with her head till I showed her the treat. If I let her out of her stall, she would follow me around like a puppy. I brushed her and used the curry comb to untangle her mane and tail. She and Ma's mare become friends right away, and when Caleb harnessed Lady and left with the buggy, she tried to follow.

Uncle Stuart examined her knees to see if they was fully developed and decided by spring she would be ready to train for a saddle. Ma had him take me shopping for all the harness and various things I would need. He helped me coach her into taking the bit of the bridle. By Christmas, she was willing to be bridled with no problems. When I showed her the bridle, she knowed I was gonna take her for a walk. I'd use the bridle reins for a lead strap and we would go about a mile to a field where she could run free.

I was the happiest I'd been since before Evan died. I wished he could see what a great horse I had. I couldn't hardly wait till I could start training her to the saddle. I could see myself sitting astride her parading down the street. I wished I could show her to Charles, and my other friends from the prison. The only upsetting thing that happened was Ma told me James would be coming for Christmas.

***

James arrived the day before Christmas. Much to my surprise, he shook my hand and showed some interest in knowing about what he called my adventures. He didn't believe some of my stories was true, but William took up for me cause he'd worked at another Union prison while he was in the army, and he knowed what prison life was really like.

At our Christmas dinner, James stood up just before dessert and raised his glass. "Here's to Miss Camellia Taylor of Lexington, Kentucky, soon to be Mistress James Campbell." William and Elliott stood and raised their glasses and congratulated him. He explained the wedding would be in June in Lexington and we was all invited. Then, of course, Ma and Hilda started asking questions about the bride. But I was thinking it would be a blessing if she could take some of that snooty cockiness out of him.

When it finally worked out, I decided the real reason James come for Christmas was so he could get his say about my future. Although he wouldn't be a full partner in the family company for four more years, he claimed he had a right to have his say.

Me, Uncle Stuart, Ma, and James met at the company office on the day after Christmas. Ma asked Uncle Stuart if he saw any way I could work for the company and stay in Pennsylvania. "He's my youngest and I wish he could live here with me at least for a few more years."

Uncle Stuart turned to me. "I don't think it would be wise to send you to the woods, but would you be willing to learn how to do office work?"

I shook my head. I couldn't imagine myself behind a desk all day long. "I'm better at working outside. Maybe I could be a gardener."

James jumped in immediately. "But if you get funds from the company, you must work for the company and we don't need a gardener."

"Funny you should bring that up. I ain't had no funds from the company since Pa died."

Ma took in a sharp breath. "James, is that so? You didn't give Harvey the funds due to him?"

"No, because he ran away."

"But didn't you set aside his allowance for him just like we did for you and William while you were serving in the army?"

"No. I figured he wasn't due any funds since he ran off and joined the enemy."

The discussion went along like that for some time. I could tell James didn't want to give me a dime. I didn't understand why he didn't want me to have the money owed me. At one point he argued that I had got all new clothes and a horse and that should count for my back pay.

Ma got really upset with that. "I used money from my personal funds to buy him clothes and a horse. It hasn't cost the company a penny. After all he's suffered, he deserves some special attention. I don't know why you are so determined to punish him."

"I don't think bad behavior should be rewarded. And besides, the company has lost so much because of this war. Can we really afford this expenditure?"

Ma asked me to leave the room. I guess she had some harsh words for James. But the decision was finally reached that after we went to Harlan to visit the Bakers the next spring, I would come to work on the farm for the Kentucky side of the company. After working for six months I would get all my back pay. I wondered who put that delay into the plan, but I was sure I knew the answer. I wondered how come James had overruled her. At least it was settled: I was going back to Kentucky.

After we got home Ma told me we would delay our visit to the Bakers until June after James and Camellia's wedding. "Meanwhile," she said, "I'm going to spoil you as much as I can because I don't think you'll get any sympathy from James." I didn't protest the delay; the longer I waited to be under James' thumb, the more I liked it.

***

When the winter weather permitted, I started getting Daisy used to having a little weight on her back. I put a saddle blanket on her, and she immediately used her teeth to pull it off. When she did that, I put her back in her stall and ignored her for several hours. After three days of that, she finally decided to leave it on, so I gave her a apple. Caleb said "That shows she's real smart."

On a sunny day in February, I brushed Daisy, put a blanket on her and placed a feed sack with about twenty pounds of feed on her back. She stomped her front hoof and swung her head around to see what was on her back. I talked gentle to her, and she swished her tail a couple of times but let me lead her around the stable yard. For the next month I gradually increased the weight until she was carrying close to one hundred pounds. I also showed her the saddle and let her sniff it. Then when I set the saddle on her back, she didn't protest although she did flinch a bit when I tightened the cinch.

I saddled her for several days, but didn't ride her till Uncle Stuart examined her knees again and said she was ready for a ride. At breakfast on the first day of April, I announced, "I plan to ride Daisy today."

Pete heard me and laughed. "This is April Fools' Day, you know. Wonder who's gonna get fooled—you or Daisy."

Caleb saddled Lady and I saddled Daisy. Before I got into the saddle, I made sure Daisy saw I had a apple. When I swung into the saddle, she turned, to look at me and tossed her head. I gave her the apple, and we were off for a ride to the park. For the next few days Ma insisted that Caleb ride along with me just to make sure Daisy wasn't gonna act up. But Daisy loved getting out of the stable yard, and when I showed up with the bridle and saddle, she was ready. I had to hold her back to keep her from galloping away. Uncle Stuart suggested I let her trot, but not let her go all out for a few weeks to give her knees time to adjust to carrying my weight. By mid-May I was taking her out in the country and letting her go as fast as she wanted. We both loved it.

This was the best springtime of my whole life. Ma kept her promise to spoil me, and Grandma helped her. They were like mother hens clucking to their chicks. Ever day Grandma cooked something especial for me. Pete didn't seem to mind when she sorta took over the kitchen. I think if I had told Ma I wanted a steamboat on the Ohio, she would have tried to get it. We visited relatives, went on picnics in the park, shopped for clothes, had big family dinners, and I rode Daisy ever day. Till Hilda's baby was born,

Ma focused on giving me her full attention. Then she had to give attention to her first grandchild, a beautiful daughter they named Matilda, but called Tilly.

Chester introduced me to some of his buddies and we got up a cricket match. My body had completely healed itself, and I felt the best of my whole life, except for my lame foot. I guess I didn't make a very good player since I couldn't run very fast. But the fellers didn't complain and welcomed me on a team. We also found a source for some moonshine and took up smoking tobacco. If Ma ever suspected what we was doing, she never let on.

In the week or so before we departed for the wedding, Ma went on a shopping spree, buying a passel of clothes for me. I wasn't interested is getting dressed up for the wedding, but she insisted I must have a fancy suit and all the other stuff a gentleman would wear. She even bought a new cane with a golden knob for a handle. She reminded me Laureltown had no stores where I could buy clothes, shoes, hats, coats, and so on, so we must get them while we had the chance. I had a whole trunk full of new clothes when we got packed up for the trip.

Finally the day for leaving arrived. Caleb agreed to take care of Daisy and Uncle Stuart promised to have Daisy delivered to the Kentucky place later in the fall. I got up early and took some treats out to Daisy and told her goodbye. I would miss her. She was about the best friend I had.

***

I don't remember much about the wedding, prob'ly cause I was so uncomfortable in the fancy clothes. With my gold-topped cane, I reminded myself of the fellers I saw in the saloons on the steamboats. Maybe that's what William meant when he called me a dandy. Ma got tears in her eyes when she saw me in my new clothes. "Oh, Harvey, you're such a handsome man. I'm so proud of you." Although her comment made me a little uncomfortable, I was delighted to have her approval.

The wedding was a fancy affair, lots of strange people milling around the lawns and gardens of the Taylors' mansion on a farm outside Lexington. All the servants was black people dressed in white jackets and wearing white gloves. I tried to stay close to William so I would know how to behave and not make any bad blunders. I watched Ma move among the guests as she greeted people, looking so comfortable in this situation that seemed so foreign to me, but this was her kind of world. I wondered for the thousandth time how she could ever have given up her life in the city and moved to the backwoods of Kentucky. I guess people will do strange things to prove their love.

I have to admit James picked a purty, good-looking woman. But any hope I had Camellia would take some of the meanness out of James was out the window. I could see she was a spoiled queen bee used to getting her way. Soon I would be living in the same house with her. I wondered how that would work out. Would she expect me to be at her beck and call? I was relieved when the whoop-de-do was over and we could get on our way to the Bakers. I wasn't wanting to see the Bakers so much as wanting to put off going to work for James.

Uncle Stuart and William had come to Lexington for the wedding, but they planned to return to Pittsburgh right away. Ma hired a coach to take us on through the mountains to Harlan. Because so many troops had traveled throughout the state during the war, new roads appeared where none had been before. And while they was dirt roads, we didn't get slowed down by mud since June had been a dry month. We made one overnight stop and arrived at the Bakers in mid-afternoon.

Mistress Baker rushed out of the house as soon as the driver pulled up to the gate. She embraced Ma with tears of joy running down her cheeks. Mary Louse was not far behind her and joined in the hugs, even gave me a quick squeeze. I couldn't hide my surprise at how grown up she looked and acted. I had to agree with Ma's claim she was no longer a child, certainly not the little pest Evan and I tried to avoid. I decided I prob'ly should quit calling her "Doodlebug."

Ma asked the driver to help us unload our baggage, and then she dismissed him after adding a generous bonus to his charge for the coach. Ma turned to Mistress Baker. "You might think we're moving in to stay forever, given all the luggage we have." She giggled like a little girl. "But Harvey had to bring all his belongings because he's moving back to Laureltown when we leave here."

Later when Mary Louise and I went for a walk, she asked me if I was glad to be moving back to Kentucky. "I saw you frown when your mother mentioned it."

"No, I ain't glad, but I just have to stay there three more years till I'm 21. Then I'll find somewheres else to go."

"Why do you have to stay there?"

"According to Pa's will, me and Elliott will each get five thousand dollars when we're 21. But we have to either go to school or work for the company till then."

"You don't want to work for the company?"

"Not if James is my boss, but I'll try to tough it out for three years."

We walked to the center of town which was about a mile down the hill from the Bakers' house. She showed me the ruins of the courthouse the Confederate marauders from Virginia burned during the war as pay back for the Union troops burning a courthouse in Virginia. Mary Louise thought that was very unfair, especially when almost all the citizens of the county favored the Confederacy. But I had learnt that nothing about war was fair.

We was quiet for a bit, then she stopped and looked up at me. "Can you tell me about what happened to Evan?"

I saw a bench in a little park-like place, so I led her there. I tried to tell her how they killed him. She listened and shook her head.

"I can't imagine how awful it must have been. Poor Evan. He was such a good boy. And funny. Do you remember when we had to recite the names of the disciples?"

I nodded my head. "I don't know how he ever thought of all those names."

"I thought Papa was going to have a stroke. He was trying so hard not to laugh. I'm so sorry about what happened."

We sat staring at the ground for several minutes. Then she looked up. "Oh, do you remember when we had to write a poem, and he made up that nonsense poem?"

"I do remember that. I wish I'd ask him to write it down for me. It was real funny."

"Well, I did have him write it in my notebook. When we get back, I'll look it up." She stood up. "We probably should start back now."

When we returned, she got us glasses of mint tea, and we found seats on the porch where she pointed out all the places of interest we could see from this spot above the town. Harlan, or Mount Pleasant as some people called it, was quite a bit bigger than Laureltown, but still didn't have a doctor or a pharmacy, just like most mountain towns. "But we have a barber shop and our own post office." she bragged.

Sudden like, she jumped up and started toward the door. "I forgot about getting my notebook." She rushed into the house and returned moments later carrying a old raggedy-looking book. She flipped through the pages. "Here it is." She stood in front of me and read it out loud.

The fliverchick perched awkwardly on the castle wall
Waiting to see if the purple duck would call.
The dragon swan twitching his whiskers stood tall
Holding his umbrella, bread basket and all.
I ran through puddles of gooseberries to the hall
Laughing at the big trick he played on us all.

We stared at each other. It was so strange—like we was back in the school. I could almost hear Evan's voice. We both felt it. She stood there for a moment and then started crying. I realized I had tears in my eyes too.

It seemed like he was almost there with us. She took a seat beside me and handed me the book. I had the notion of putting my arm around her shoulder, but I didn't. I wiped my tears with my sleeve, looked at the page, and saw it was Evan's handwriting. We sat quiet looking off into the mountains across the valley. Finally she whispered, "I can't believe they would just shoot him down in the road like that."

Mister Baker returned in the late afternoon from making a visit to a sick church member. I greeted him and helped him take his horse to the barn. He showed me around the place. "I have about two acres on this hill, enough to have a nice garden and some grazing space for our horse and cow. Mistress Baker keeps some hens and Mary Louise has a pet duck."

I told him about my horse. "I hated to go off and leave her. But my uncle plans to send her to Kentucky later. You should see her, a real beauty and as gentle as a lamb. She follows me around like a little puppy." I realized I was blabbering, so I changed the subject. I pointed out a piece of machinery I wasn't used to seeing. "Sir, what do you use this for?"

"Well, son, that's what I call a push plow. See, it's supposed to have a wheel here in front, but the wheel broke and I took it to the forge to get it fixed." He set it upright and held the handles like holding on to a plow to show how it worked. "But you push it along the dirt just like a horse was pulling it."

"But wouldn't that take a lot of power? I wouldn't think many men are strong enough to push a plow through the ground."

"No, you couldn't plow up untilled ground with it. But we use it to refresh the soil around plants in the garden. If we push this through the rows, it gets rid of some of the weeds and grass, and then we don't have to use the hoe as much." I thought that seemed like a good idea.

The Baker's house was modest. It had a large kitchen that was also the dining room, a front room they called the parlor, and two bedrooms. Mistress Baker apologized for not having a guest room, but Ma assured her we would be comfortable with whatever arrangements they had made. "We are here to visit with you, dear friends. Please don't go to trouble on our account."

I offered to sleep in the hay loft. Goodness knows I had done that lots of times. But Mistress Baker seemed horrified at the idea. She shook her finger at me. "You'll do no such thing, young man! We have it all worked out. Frances will share a room with Mary Louise, and we have made a nice bed in the attic for Harvey."

The next day I rummaged through my trunk and found some of my carvings and showed them to Mary Louise. "Oh, they're beautiful! Would you make some for me?"

"If you like these, you can have them. I just made them to have something to do while I was recovering from my prison experience. I

194

brung them to give to you."

"Thank you. I'll always treasure them." She started to give me a hug, but seemed to change her mind at the last minute, and it ended up with a sort of swipe across my back.

Later that evening I drug out my chess board and asked Mary Louise if she knowed how to play. "No, I've never even seen it, but will you teach me?" So we had a project to work on. It took a while for her to learn how to set up the board and how to move the pieces. But she really worked hard at learning, and by the time me and Ma left she could play a decent game. Ever day I was more surprised by how smart she was. I had to keep reminding myself that she was only thirteen years old.

Mistress Baker had planned lots of things for Ma to do. They attended the women's meeting at church, went to a quilting party, and made pies to raise money to replace the burned out courthouse. Of course, on Sunday we went to church with the Bakers. It was a special Sunday when the church celebrated a anniversary and had what they called "dinner on the ground" afterwards. I think ever woman had fried a chicken and baked a pie. It was the first time in my life I had ate as much fried chicken as I wanted. And when it was over, plates of fried chicken was still on the makeshift table. After the meal, they had a singing. Mistress Baker called it "old harp singing." I couldn't make much sense of it, because they was singing the do re me notes instead of words. But the voices blended together so beautiful; I listened for the whole time without getting fidgety.

One afternoon a buggy come up to the gate and the man ask Mistress Baker to come help his wife who had started labor. Mistress Baker grabbed her bag and said, "Come on Frances, you can help me. This woman had a difficult time birthing her first baby. I may need some help." They hurried to gather up some food to take for the family's supper and some fresh vegetables from the garden, gave Mary Louise instructions for preparing supper, and rushed off.

The man brought them home after daylight the next morning. They reported the woman had difficulty, but the baby finally come out squalling and everything seemed fine. Ma said she was too excited to sleep, so they fixed breakfast and started another day. I thought Ma seemed very happy as they worked breaking and stringing up beans for leather breeches talking up a blue streak the whole time.

We intended to stay for a week, but Ma and Mistress Baker hadn't done enough visiting to suit them. Ma said we would stay another week if Mistress Baker would agree for her to help with the cooking and house work. I worked in the garden and mucked out the stables and helped Mr. Baker repair the fences. As I weeded the garden I saw Mistress Baker had a yerb garden just like Miz Simpson except she called it "erbs." Mister Baker got the wheel put back on his push plow and I got to try it out. I was surprised at how good it worked.

It turned out that we was there for the July Fourth celebration. Booths had been set up around the courthouse square where peddlers of all kinds hawked their goods. A string band was set up on the courthouse lawn. A horse race was scheduled for the afternoon on the school playground. There was a lemonade stand, a cookie booth, and a candy store. For a few cents we went into a tent to watch a magician do tricks, and a fortune teller would use her cards to tell your fortune. That reminded me of the Sheep Lady. Later when we got back to the Bakers' home, I told them about staying with the Sheep Lady when I was on my way to join the army.

The next day Ma went to the trading post and made arrangements for us to get a ride with the postal delivery man. Our visit had come to an end. The time had come for me to face the fact that my grace period was over, and I was going to work for James.

CHAPTER 13

July 1866

Oakmont, Kentucky

I opened my eyes and looked around my room at our Kentucky house. My trunk stood at the foot of my bed where Nate had placed it last night after we arrived. I thought it was interesting that Camellia now had a black man as a butler. He had offered to help me unpack, but I was too tired to be bothered. Otherwise the room seemed just like I left it two years ago. Through the open window I could hear a rooster crowing, and when I took a deep breath, I smelled bacon. That was enough to get me on my feet.

We had arrived last evening shortly before dark. Nate come out to assist Ma from the carriage and led us into the parlor where Camellia waited to welcome us.

"Thank you, Nate. Please tell Nellie to serve us some of her special lemonade and then carry the luggage to their rooms." Then she turned and took Ma's hands. "Welcome to Oakmont. Please be seated." She and Ma chatted about our visit to Harlan. A short while later, a black woman come in carrying a tray of drinks.

I was glad for the lemonade, which was served in crystal goblets with a sprig of mint. I had to remind myself not to gulp it down. When Camellia looked away, I saw Ma examine the goblet she had always saved for special occasions. I guess we would both have to get used to things being different. When the glasses was empty, Camellia stood. "I know you must be tired from your journey. I will show you to your rooms so you can freshen up, and we'll have our dinner when you're ready." Something else new, I always thought dinner come at noon and the evening meal was supper.

At first I thought it was strange that Camellia showed Ma to the guest room. Of course I should have expected Camellia and James would use the master bedroom, but it took me a little bit to get used to the idea that Ma was a guest in her own house. Ma come to my room and instructed me to wash up and change my shirt. "It appears Camellia plans to be more formal than we are used to, so put on your best manners."

At dinner Camellia told us James had gone to Lexington on business. "He's setting up a lumber supply business there. My oldest brother will be the manager. James thinks it will help increase the demand for lumber if he establishes outlets in some of the larger cities. He expected to get back today, but seems he was delayed."

I watched Ma to know how to act formal. Dinner was served by Nate who now appeared in a white jacket and white gloves. Camellia explained that Nate and his wife Nellie had worked for her family several years, and she was so pleased when James agreed to hire them. I wondered if they had been slaves. Later I learnt they lived in the Simpson's cabin. I was disappointed the Simpsons was gone. It turned out James had replaced ever single one of the employees with new people. I guess he wanted to make it clear he was now in charge, and everthing was gonna be different.

Camellia also told us she had named the place "Oakmont." "I think every estate needs a special name. Oakmont seemed so appropriate since it's all about the trees." I hadn't realized it was a estate. I had always thought of it as a lumber company.

I finally got myself out of bed and washed my face, but I wondered what sort of clothes I should put on. I wondered if I was expected to work on the farm that day. I tiptoed down to the guest room to ask Ma; she told me we would wait for James' instructions. "Today you can browse around the place and get used to the changes. But first, after breakfast I'll help you unpack your trunk."

When my trunk was unpacked and stowed in the attic, I put on my new boots so I could tramp around. I visited the barn and saw it hadn't been mucked out lately. Two new cows and a mule chomped grass in the pasture. I guessed all the horses was working somewheres. The tobacco patch needed weeding, but the kitchen garden looked well cared for. Nellie was picking beans. I ask her if she'd like some help, but she said she was about finished. Two men was mowing hay with scythes, but as far as I could see they's the only ones working the farm. It looked to me like James didn't have enough men to do all the work, or they was doing a poor job of it.

After what Camellia called lunch, Ma suggested that me and her walk up to Pa's grave. We took along a couple of hoes so we could tidy up the burial site. It was the first time since my injury I had hiked over steep ground, and I was surprised when I had trouble keeping up with Ma. We found weeds knee deep around the grave. The stone Ma had ordered had been installed, but it could hardly be seen for the weeds. We worked till we was both tired and still didn't have all the weeds out. Ma leaned her hoe against the fence. "That's all I can do today. I've already made blisters on my hands. Let's leave this for another day."

By the time we got back down the mountain, James had come home. He gave Ma a hug and shook my hand. "Welcome home." I thought it was generous of him to say that. "You look a sight. What have you been up to?"

Ma explained we had been working on Pa's grave. "I'm surprised no one's given it any attention lately."

James looked sheepish. "I have it on my list of things to do, but it seems we always have more important things taking up our time." He looked at the ground. "I'm sorry, Ma; I'll see it gets taken care of right away."

The next two days Ma and James holed up in the office. Later Ma told me she had gone over the books for the last two years. "James is a good manager, and he has kept good records. He wants to make the business more successful than before." She laughed. "I think he wants to prove he's better at the business than Jed." We had taken a short walk to examine the spring house, the wash house, and the outdoor kitchen. Ma was pleased that all these buildings was clean and looking good.

"You realize that these last few years have been hard on the business. James is doing a good job with getting the logging business going again. I've convinced him to hire another farm hand because the farm work really supports the logging business. The tobacco brings in additional income, and the corn and hay feed the animals. It's important the farm operates at the optimum. Trying to do all the work without adequate employees is not good economy."

She paused in the shade of a big oak. "I also persuaded him to assign you to the farm team and to give you responsibility for raising the tobacco. Do you think you can handle that?"

I thought about it. Even with my bad foot and knee, I believed I could get the weeds out and care for the tobacco plants. I remembered all the ways Pa insisted we do that work. So I nodded my head. "Yes, I would like that."

"Then tomorrow you'll report to the farm boss and get started. James has explained to him what your duties will be."

I took a deep breath. "I'll do my best."

"I'm sure you will. I also want you to care for Jed's grave. Get the tobacco under control first. Then as you have time, get rid of all those weeds around the grave and give the fence another coat of whitewash." She started to walk on, but paused and added, "I've made it clear to James that he is not to harass you about joining the Confederate Army."

***

Ma left early the next day. When she was all packed up and ready, she come to my room and handed me a Bible. "Grandma Campbell gave this Bible to Jed for his eighteenth birthday. Now that you're eighteen, I want you to have it. Jed wasn't much for religion, but he treasured this, and I know he would be pleased for you to have it."

"Thanks Ma. I will treasure it too, 'specially since it come from Grandma." I placed it on the table beside my bed. "I'll keep it handy to remind me to read it sometimes."

"It would please me if you read it often."

I watched her leave with a sad heart. I had spent the last year with her, and I treasured the time we had together. Now I would have to deal with James without her. So far he had treated me fair. I hoped that was a good sign. I went to the barn, grabbed a hoe and a straw hat and headed for the tobacco patch.

I soon had sweated through my shirt as the hot sun beat down on me. It reminded me how hot I got when I was marching with General Early's troops. I remembered how I had suffered heat exhaustion in the hay field a few years back, so I took time to go get a drink and brought a bucket of water and a drinking gourd to the field so I could get a drink and pour a dipper of water over my head now and then.

When I didn't show up for lunch, James come looking for me. "Why didn't you come for lunch?" He looked a little irritated.

"Sorry, I guess I didn't realize the time."

"Well, take a break and go eat. You'll get sick if you don't get enough to eat. Besides, you need to take some time in the shade to rest. Ma gave me strict instructions to watch that you didn't overdo your work until you get used to being out in the sun so long."

We walked back to the house together. Nellie brought me a plate of food, and I set on the shady veranda to eat. I was pleased that James was taking that much interest in me, especially when he said, "Wait till the clock strikes two before you go back to the field."

Things moved along pretty well. As I dug at the weeds with a hoe, I remembered the push plow Mr. Baker had and thought it would take out the weeds better and quicker than using a hoe. I talked with Mr. Granger, the farm boss, and explained how it worked. "We could have the forge in Laureltown make the plow points and the wheel. I think I can put together the rest of it."

Mr. Granger removed his hat and scratched his head. "I think you may be on to something there. But I'll have to get James' permission. He insists on approving every penny we spend."

James wanted me to explain how my plow would work. At first he doubted I could push a plow through the ground, but I finally convinced him, and he let me ride one of the horses to Laureltown and make the arrangements. I hadn't been to the village since I'd come back, so I was curious to see how it had changed in two years. The forge looked much the same, but the trading post had many more products to sell. I saw a few new homes and businesses, even a tavern that offered rooms to travelers.

After I finished my business at the forge, I went to the cemetery to visit Evan's grave. I was pleased to see someone had planted a rosebush beside his gravestone, and the grass had been clipped neatly. I wondered who had took care of it.

It took two weeks for the smith to get the wheel and plow points made. I fashioned the plow to have three small points side by side, thinking that would work better than having one large point. When I got it finished, Mr. Granger come to the tobacco patch to see it in action. He tried it out and liked the idea. I discovered I could cover more ground with the plow than with the hoe. Within a month of my start, I had the tobacco free of weeds, had picked off all the worms and suckers, and had kept the plants watered when there was no rain.

James inspected the field like Pa used to do. "You're doing a good job. The tobacco looks really good." I nodded, glad he was pleased. Now that I had everything under control, I had some free time. I worked on Pa's grave and on a Sunday, instead of accepting Camellia's invitation to go to church, I put on my boots, ask Nellie for a lunch, and headed to the Back Valley.

Caleb's cabin stood in the midst of tall weeds. His garden patch looked even worse. As I got close, I saw something had gnawed a hole in the door. I opened the door easy, thinking some varmints might have made a den there. The room was a mess with straw from the mattress scattered all over the floor. I searched all the nooks and places some varmint might hide, but couldn't see any. I decided raccoons musta invaded the cabin. I planned to come back soon with tools and lumber to make repairs. I spent some time roaming the valley and remembering all the good times me and Evan had there. I wondered if James would agree for me to make some hunting trips in the fall.

Topping the tobacco kept me busy for some time, so I didn't have a chance to get back to the cabin. James had no interest in making any repairs. As far as he was concerned, the cabin was no use. I kept thinking I wanted to keep the cabin in good shape. I was sure Caleb would like that.

I tried to stay out of the house except for meals and sleeping. I didn't want to do nothing to upset Camellia. I even made my bed ever morning before I come down for breakfast. She mostly ignored me, almost never spoke to me, and that was fine by me.

Towards the end of August I got a letter from Uncle Stuart saying he would be delivering Daisy soon. I couldn't hardly wait. When they arrived, I was in the tobacco field pulling off suckers. The first I knowed about them, Uncle Stuart come walking toward the tobacco patch and yelled for me. "Daisy's looking for you."

I run as fast as my bum foot could take me towards the barn. When Daisy saw me she nickered and come towards me. I put my arms around her neck and she pressed her head against my face. I was so glad to see her. I took her to the water trough and let her drink and woulda saddled her for a ride, except Uncle Stuart pointed out she needed to rest after her long trip.

Uncle Stuart spent two days in the woods with the loggers. James was using horses to snake the logs down the mountain because Mr. Simpson took his oxen with him when he left. Uncle Stuart urged James to either buy oxen or make a roadway that was not so steep by going sideways down the mountain instead of straight down. He explained it was too risky to use the horses on such steep mountain sides. He pointed out how Pa was always concerned for the safety of the men and animals. But James musta thought he couldn't afford to buy oxen, so he continued to use the horses.

I didn't get a chance to ride Daisy until the next Sunday, but each morning I let her out of the stable to graze in the pasture and fed her and groomed her each evening. The tobacco leaves was turning yellow. Soon we would need to start cutting it and hanging it in the tobacco barn. Me and Mr. Granger planned I would cut the stalks and each evening him and his farm team would help get it hung. He bragged on me and said it looked like a very good crop.

I was pleased with my work and happy James didn't criticize me. Everything seemed to be going good, much better than I'd even hoped.

***

That's when things started to fall apart. Like Uncle Stuart said, James was taking more risks with the safety of his men and animals than Pa ever done.

One day in the early fall, one of the horses fell on a steep slope and broke his leg. James had to shoot him. Then word come that the sawmill had caught fire and would have to be rebuilt. On top of that, two of the loggers decided to quit because they felt the work was too dangerous.

I felt sorry for James until it come time for payday. The amount he paid me was much less than the amount I was supposed to receive as my allowance. Later that evening I knocked on the office door and ask him why I didn't get paid the right amount. He didn't even look up. "I charged you Daisy's stable fee. I've been supplying her a stable and feed and it's time you paid for her. She's not doing any work."

I protested, but he wouldn't give in. "You really don't have any need for the money. I have to cut our expenses way back to cover the loss of a horse and the replacement of the sawmill."

"But that's business expense the company should cover. It shouldn't come out of my allowance."

"Don't push me. At least I'm not charging you for room and board."

"But you don't charge any of the hired hands for room and board. Why would you treat me different?"

He stood up and pointed toward the door. "Discussion is over. Close the door as you leave."

I wasn't satisfied, but didn't know what I could do about it. I slammed the door so hard it shocked me and stomped out the kitchen door. I saddled Daisy and rode her hard. We galloped through Laureltown like greased lightning with me cussing and hitting her with my cane to make her go faster. I kept yelling and hitting her till we was almost half way to the county seat. Then I begun to cool down and felt terrible for taking my anger out on my good horse. I let her slow to a walk and found a creek where she could get a drink. I got off and petted her, telling her how sorry I was. Her coat looked like a wet soapy towel. I sat on a log and let her graze a bit on some grass. By this time it was almost completely dark. We started walking back down the road. I led her for about an hour before I got back in the saddle. I don't know what time it was when we finally got back home. I lit a lantern and gave Daisy a good rub down. I fed her an extra portion of oats and climbed into the loft to sleep.

***

For the next few weeks, I worked very hard to get the tobacco cut and hung. Once that was finished I had some freedom till time to get the tobacco leaves prepared for the market. I finally got Pa's grave cleaned up and the fence whitewashed. I also got the door on Caleb's cabin repaired.

Best of all, I got to ride Daisy, and I started teaching her to pull the buggy.

I hadn't had much to do with the hired hands, but with more free time, I got better acquainted with a couple of them. They invited me to go with them into the village one Saturday night. I'd been curious about the tavern in town, so I readily accepted. We hitched Daisy to the buggy and rode to town in style. When we pulled up to the hitching post in front of the tavern, several of the fellows hanging out on the porch admired my horse. I was feeling purty proud.

I don't know what the loggers expected from me since they seemed surprised when I begun matching them drink for drink. One of them said, "I guess the boss's little brother is more of a man than we thought." I did call a halt after the third round. I didn't want to get James's dander up coming home drunk.

Since most of the other farm work was finished, the farm hands helped stripping the tobacco and sorting the leaves. We had the job finished before the end of November, and Mr. Granger loaded it onto the wagon and took it to the tobacco warehouse. We got a really good price, one of the best years we ever had. But I was very disappointed when James didn't give us the bonus like Pa always done.

The next payday James docked my pay not only for Daisy, but added in a charge for using the buggy. I didn't protest cause I felt guilty about losing my temper and taking it out on Daisy. I didn't want to do that again. I figgered the less said the better. I expected Ma would not be happy that James was not paying me my full allowance, but I decided not to tell her. It seemed the more I protested, the more determined he was to make me pay. I asked Mr. Granger if James kept a close eye on the farm expenses. He laughed. "By God, I have to beg for ever damn penny." At least I wasn't the only one James was watching.

If I could go on a hunting trip and get some pelts, maybe I could make up for the money he wasn't paying me. I decided to go to the Back Valley and spend the night which would give me two days to hunt. I half expected James to forbid me to go, but he said, "Sure, go shoot a deer or two." He even gave me permission to take a gun and ammunition from the gun cabinet.

On the way to the valley, I stopped at the cave Evan and I discovered. I couldn't see any sign that someone had been there since I last visited it. I stood there for a long time remembering some of our talks. I missed my good friend. I promised myself I'd go visit his grave again soon. The weather had turned cold, like it might snow, so soon as I got to the cabin, I made a fire in the fireplace and carried in a bucket of fresh water from the creek. I hadn't seen any animals on my way to the cabin, but I thought some might come out in the evening. It was cold enough that something I killed wouldn't spoil. If I'd had some way to get it over the mountain, it woulda been great to kill a deer. That woulda served James right.

After the sun went behind the mountain, I put on my warm coat and hat, took my gun, and found a spot among some tall weeds where I was purty well hid, but could see the path the animals had made to the creek. No animals would come if they saw me, so I tried not to fidget. Finally when it was almost dark, I saw a deer coming along the path. I watched as it raised its head to look around but I didn't take aim. I wanted to save him for later. It waded into the creek, took a long drink and disappeared in the tall weeds. Soon I saw a raccoon following the same path. I took careful aim and pulled the trigger. It was the first time I'd shot a gun since my last battle. But I could still hit my target.

That was the beginning of my determination to make my own way. During the winter when I had lots of free time, I sometimes spent a whole week at the cabin. I made traps for raccoons, I killed wild turkeys, and I got a couple of deer and a whole bunch of rabbits. I made a small sled so Daisy could pull the deer carcass over the mountain. I made several trips to the trading post to get supplies including a gun of my own. I wasn't surprised when James took money from my allowance for using his gun and ammunition. Since there wasn't a stable in the Back Valley I didn't feel comfortable keeping Daisy overnight when the weather got really cold, but I begun to imagine living in the cabin all the time.

***

Shortly after Christmas I got a letter from William. First, he had to brag about his little daughter. She was starting to babble, and he was sure she was saying "Papa." But the real reason for his letter was to tell me he and Elliott had been sending letters to the War Department trying to get the money I was owed. I had forgot all about it, so I's surprised to know they's doing that. But he said they had searched all the Confederate records and could find no proof I had ever been inducted. So my brother's cheating me, and the army I risked my life for cheated me too. I guess that's just my luck.

I also got letters from Mary Louise right often. I had to really force myself to set down and write to her. I felt guilty when I failed to answer, but I never knowed what to say. After Ma gave me Pa's Bible, I thought Mary Louise would like to know about that. She begun asking me what I had been reading. That gave me something to write about, but if I wrote soon after getting her letter, then she answered sooner and I had to write again. I had used up all the paper Ma had give me, and I sure wasn't gonna ask James for some. So first chance I got I rode over to the trading post.

Ever time I was there I always went to Evan's grave.

When I reached the church yard, I saw someone near his grave, as I got closer, I was so surprised to see it was Miz Simpson. She gave me a hug. "I heard you had come back. I was hoping I'd see you around town sometime." She was full of questions and I had a few of my own. She shivered. "It's too cold to stay out here. Let's go to the tavern."

I found out James hadn't ask them to leave, but she said they was so unhappy with his bossy ways, they quit. "Dan thought James was taking too many risks and pushing his men too hard. After Pete left, I had all the cooking and gardening to do by myself. So Dan found some land—actually it used to belong to Evan's father. We like it better living here closer to town."

"So you're the one been taking care of Evan's grave?"

"Yes, I knowed you'd appreciate that. I also took care of Mr. Campbell's grave as long as we lived on the place. I hope someone's been looking after it."

"Afraid not, till I got home, but I'm taking care of it now." We talked for a long time and Miz Simpson invited me to eat with them after church on Sunday. It pleased me so much that she was still interested in me. I told her about my horse, and we walked down to the trading post where Daisy was tied up. Miz Simpson thought she was beautiful. I was so pleased I almost forgot what I come to town for.

***

The next year the summer was very dry. Even though I carried water till my arms felt like they's coming off my shoulders, the tobacco plants wilted. By the time it started to bloom, the stalks was only a couple of foot high. It was the worst tobacco we'd ever raised and James blamed me. Even though Mr. Granger took up for me and told James I had worked very hard, James was very unhappy. He threatened to cut off my allowance completely.

Next spring when I would turn twenty-one, I was due to receive my five thousand dollars. I was determined to quit the company once that happened. Somehow I just needed to survive till then. I got an idea. Maybe James would rent me the cabin, and I could just live there and have nothing to do with James anymore. All that winter I worked at making the cabin more livable. I repaired the fences that Pa had built to hold the animals during the war. In the spring I spaded up the garden plot Caleb had made. I had saved as much money as I could, so I was able to buy some lumber to make a shed for Daisy.

In April, just two weeks before my twenty-first birthday, I took my plan to James. I had worked hard in the spring to get the tobacco bed planted and the plants was looking good. James had inspected the plants earlier that day and told me he was pleased. It seemed like a good time to tell him my plans.

"Like hell you will!" He almost never swore. I was surprised, but I just laughed.

"What's the problem? I've kept my part of the bargain. I done the work I agreed to do. Now you have to keep your part."

"It was not part of the bargain that you could rent the cabin."

"What have you got to lose? You're getting nothing from the cabin now."

"No. That's final."

I laughed again. I had expected this would be his reaction, so shortly after Christmas I wrote a proposal to Ma and Uncle Stuart. I handed James the signed agreement that had come in the mail two days before. The contract stated I was authorized to rent the cabin for as long as I wanted. It also specified the amount of the rent I was to pay, and I'm sure it wasn't as much as James would have charged if it had been up to him. James hadn't been made a partner in the company yet, so he had no voice in the decision.

The letter with the contract stated five thousand dollars had been deposited in my name at the bank at Beatyville. I could withdraw from the account whenever I wished to. I felt like a bird let out of a cage. I was now free to live my life as I pleased.

I handed James the first month's rent and told him I would pack up all my belongings and move to the Back Valley the next day. He looked stunned, stomped his foot and shut himself up in the office.

On my way up the attic stairs to get my trunk so I could pack, I remembered that time many years ago when James kicked me off the bridge into the creek: how I made myself a promise to get even someday. I was pleased with myself for the first time since I run away from home.

***

That year I had a very good spring and summer. Miz Simpson helped me plant potatoes, carrots, turnips, and onions in my little garden. She gave me a couple of hens so I could have eggs. A couple of times each week, I bought fresh milk from Nellie. Daisy was happy to crop the grass in the fenced in area. I could come and go as I pleased and didn't have to answer to nobody. It was the first time in my life I felt I was in control. I was happy as a buzzard eating kyarn.

Toward the end of the summer, I got a letter from Ma suggesting I come for a visit, and she included money to help pay for the trip. I also had letters from Mary Louise asking me to come visit them before bad weather. The Simpsons offered to take care of Daisy and the hens while I was gone. I closed up the cabin, took Daisy and the hens to the Simpsons, and set out.

As I traveled across Kentucky and along the Ohio border, I could see the state was struggling to recover from the damage the war had brought. I spent one night in a hotel in Lexington where I got involved in a conversation with a couple of business men who had known Pa. I listened as they talked about the condition of the state.

"Before the war, Kentucky was considered a wealthy state, one of the top ten in the country. But now, we're way down about number thirty. So much damage was done to cities, and so many roads and bridges destroyed. It's going to take years to get back where we were."

"Both sides did so much damage not only to the cities, but even to the livestock. They either stole the horses and cows or killed them to keep the other side from getting them. I even had trouble finding a horse to buy when the war was over."

"We used to produce more tobacco than most any other state, but now look at how many farms are in ruins."

"Well, at least we're still one nation and Kentucky isn't under the Reconstruction program forced on the former Confederate states. We get to elect our own governor."

"But we still have so much violence going on. It seems like we're still in the war. Stubborn Unionists and Southern sympathizers can't let it go; they're still fighting each other. We've still got Federal troops in the state, and they can't put down all the uproar and savagery."

After listening to them for a while, I excused myself and went to my room, but I had trouble going to sleep. It made me sad to realize what terror and destruction the years of the war had brought to my state. Was it worth it to keep the nation united and to set the slaves free? I thought of all the ruined plantations I'd seen on my trip. Those farms would still be producing if the war hadn't happened. Now they are grown up in weeds, and the owners is in debt up to their ears. And to think of all the lives lost. There must be a better way.

I spent two weeks in Pittsburgh. Caleb and Pete was interested in all the changes James had made. I told them about how I got around him to rent the cabin, and they got a chuckle out of that. Caleb smiled when I told him all I was doing to fix up the cabin. I knowed it pleased him that it was being taken care of. It was the only house he ever lived in where he could claim it as his own home.

Me and Ma had several long talks. She wanted to know about my plans for my inheritance. I told her I wanted to find some acreage where I could build a house and do some farming. She liked that idea, but she cautioned me to be careful about spending the money for my everday living. I told her I had saved up money from my allowance and earned money during the winter by selling the pelts and selling some of the deer and turkey meat I killed. I hadn't needed to spend any of the money in the bank. She was glad to know I was taking care of my money good.

Of course she insisted I go visit William and Hilda and see their precious little Tilly. I saw how pleased Ma was when Tilly ran to her with her arms reaching up for a hug. She was sweet—blue eyes and hair so white it almost glowed. I was glad Ma was there so she could enjoy being a grandmother. I hope it helped her through the grief of losing Pa so soon.

My cousin Chester and I had some good times while I was there. We hung out at some of the taverns drinking with his friends. When I told him about how the Confederate soldiers got me drunk and took me to see Sweet Lucy, he slapped his knee and laughed. Then he proposed that we see if we could find a Sweet Lucy in Pittsburgh. And we did. She wasn't as good as the first Sweet Lucy, but I did enjoy it.

When I told Chester about wanting to find some land and build a house, he said, "When you do, I'll help you build it." He promised to keep an eye out for a sale of land. He thought for a moment and then said, "It would be better if it was new ground rather than land that was already being farmed."

"I agree, but it would take a lot more work to turn it into a farm."

"True, but look; if the land is wooded, you'll have all the wood to build your buildings."

After thinking it over, I agreed that we should look for wooded property.

I decided to go visit the Bakers before going back to my little cabin. I made the trip to Harlan without too much trouble. The roads was improved a little from when Ma and I visited before, and it was easier to get passage on coaches. The Bakers seemed glad to see me and treated me with kindness. Mr. Baker didn't try to convert me, but we did have some talks about God. I still didn't know if I even believed there was a God. I found the Bible stories about God very confusing. Sometimes God was good to the people, and then something made God mad, and he tried to wipe them out. I thought if God got that mad and did so much destruction, prob'bly I shouldn't feel so guilty about losing my temper.

Mary Louise and I enjoyed some walks around town. I couldn't believe what a young lady she had turned into. She scolded me for not writing her as often as she thought I should. "I want to know what you do every single day. I got your skimpy letters and tried to imagine what your cabin and your valley looked like, but you didn't tell me enough to get the picture."

I promised to do better and tried to answer all her questions. She wanted to know what color my bed quilts was, how I did cooking, where I stored my clothes, and a whole gob of other questions. Then she said, "Looks to me like what you need is someone to take care of you."

That gave me a start, but when I insisted I was doing just fine, she got a twisted smile and rolled her eyes. She also chided me for saying "ain't." I told her it was my choice to be a uneducated man. "Educated people look down on others like they's better'n them. I ain't got no interest in sounding like one of them."

After I'd been there a few days, Mr. Baker told me next week they was going to a camp meeting over the mountain near Jonesville, Virginia, and invited me to go along. This was the first time I'd ever heard of a camp meeting and had no idea what to expect, though in the years since I've attended several. We loaded up the wagon and set out early one morning. Mistress Baker explained we would use the wagon as our home while we was at the campgrounds. I didn't really understand what she meant, but once we got there I saw how it worked.

People travel for miles in their wagons to these meetings and set up camp—some in tents, while others used their wagons as a place to sleep. The site chosen for the meeting was on level ground near a stream where people could get water for drinking and bathing or washing clothes, and where new converts was baptized. Here and there trees provided some shade. Each family brought food to cook and several families would share the same cooking fire. Sometimes a meeting lasted for two or more weeks, and people stayed as long as they could, many for the whole time.

The planners of the meeting usually raised a brush arbor to provide some shelter for the speakers. They'd drag up rough logs with the bark axed off and the top leveled as seating. Some people brought chairs from home, and many people stood around the edges or even watched from their wagons parked in the distance. They hung oil-filled lanterns in trees for the evening services and often someone built fires around the edges and lit torches to give more light when it got dark.

The first service of the day started in the morning soon after breakfast with singing and prayers, often done with great feeling. Then three or more ministers would take turns preaching, which would last past noon. Usually Mary Louise's father preached in the morning session. In the afternoon, people visited with friends, prepared food, bathed or worshed clothes, and got ready for the evening service where the singing was even more fiery, the prayers more heartfelt, and the meeting reached high levels of spirit filled shouting and wild dancing from both the preachers and the audience. Sinners who believed they was so deeply doomed fell down in a swoon. Converts was so happy for their salvation they danced and shouted when the Holy Ghost come over them while onlookers, who come for entertainment, cheered and egged them on.

We arrived in the evening and could see the light of the fires for some distance before we reached the grounds. I could hear music and singing, but couldn't really see what was going on. We searched around till Mr. Baker found some friends who invited us to set up next to them so we could share their cooking fire. Once we got settled and got the horses secured, Mr. Baker led the way through what looked like hundreds of folks to get close enough to hear and see what was going on. I didn't expect to see so many people.

We finally got close enough to hear the preacher. He was yelling as loud as he could and jumping around on a sort of platform. People sat on logs, or stood around the edges. Lots of people was raising their hands and shouting. After the one preacher finished another one took his place. This one talked a little slower and what he said made some sense. But I was getting sort of tired of standing there and was ready to go back to the wagon, when they said for all the sinners to come up and get saved. People come from all directions in streams. Some of them weeping like they lost their best loved one. Suddenly it was like everone went crazy—people clapping and yelling, people dancing, people falling out on the ground. Then I got this strange feeling in my chest. It was like something come over me, and I couldn't help myself. I was clapping, dancing and shouting too.

It was this experience that finally convinced me that God was real. Never before had I felt like I could feel God inside my body. It was like something come over me and I couldn't help what my voice and body did. I determined then that I would read the Bible my ma had give me more often.

Everyone didn't come to these meetings to have a religious experience. First of all, drummers come hawking their wares taking advantage of a crowd of people. Some farmers even brought vegetables and fruits to sell. I guess some people come hoping to meet a lover. I saw couples slipping away into the woods after dark, and once a young lady offered me her services. But on the whole I believe the meetings do reach many people for the Lord even if some use it as a opportunity to make money or to gain a selfish goal.

I stayed for two more days of the meeting, though the Bakers was staying for another week. Mr. Baker explained that it would be easier for me to get transportation back home if we went into the nearby town, so he gave me a ride on his horse. When we started down the main street toward the trading post where I could make arrangements for transportation, I couldn't believe my eyes. This wasn't Jonesville; it was Mump's Fort.

I couldn't get a ride for another day, so I walked down to Carl's shed and spent several hours visiting with him. He explained, "Lots of folks call it Mump's Fort, but really, it's Jonesville. As I watched him work caning a chair, I thought maybe that's something I could do. When he finished for the day, he insisted I go home with him. "Granny would be plumb sick if you don't come to see her."

I spent a pleasant evening with these good people and slept in the barn loft. Of course Granny made up a nice bundle of food for me to eat on my trip home. I wondered if the Sheep Lady still lived in her little cabin on the side of a ridge, but I didn't have time to look for her before my ride come. I was pleased with my trip, but I would be glad to get back to my little cabin and my animals.

***

By the time I got back home, the leaves was beginning to turn. I always loved the wonderful colors of fall, and my valley was beautiful—covered with bright yellow goldenrod and purple iron weed. Bright sunlight turned the sumac next to the woods a bright shade of scarlet, looked almost like they's on fire. And the ridges on all sides was covered with beautiful splotches of color. It filled me with joy just to see it.

I needed to dig my potatoes, carrots and turnips and store them for the winter. But after two or three weeks, I had lots of time and decided to spend more time in Laureltown.

I got to know a older man named Jasper Gray. He lived way out on the west side of the village in a cove beside a creek. He told me he used to make his living by making moonshine, but the Federal troops had found his still and destroyed it. He was afraid to set up his still again because the troops prob'ly informed the tax people. If they caught him again, he'd likely go to jail.

I ask him if he would teach me how to make moonshine. He had a big field of corn almost ready for harvesting. We worked out a deal. He offered to help me build a still and provide the corn if I would make the shine. We would split the profit fifty-fifty. It seemed like a good plan to me.

That's how I come to be a moonshiner. For the next two years, I peddled moonshine all over southern Kentucky. I not only didn't have to spend any of my inheritance, but I added a couple hundred dollars to it. As I worked with Jasper, I found out he also caned chairs like my friend Carl Henley. He agreed to teach me that too. I would go to fairs, elections, court days, and other happenings and sell chairs and moonshine. Those skills would help support me for years.

The only time I saw James was on the first of each month when I took the money for the rent. I steered clear of him the rest of the time. I could use one of their logging roads to come and go without ever getting in sight of the house. If James knowed I was making corn liquor, he never said nothing. I think he's glad to be rid of me, and that was fine with me.

In the fall of the next year, Chester come to visit me and showed me a advertisement he had found for some property down in Tennessee. He proposed we go look at it. We packed up our saddle bags, closed up the cabin, and rode off. We traveled several days before we found the place. It was back in a holler about four miles outside a small village in the Tennessee mountains. The entire tract of land was covered in trees. No one else lived in the holler, but we found the burnt out ruins of a cabin. People told us Indians had done it many years ago. We finally decided to choose fifty acres at the head of the holler, and Chester named it "Campbell Holler." When we got back to Kentucky, I was the owner of my own land. I couldn't hardly wait to get started.

We decided to spend the winter getting tools, and supplies together. We would wait to move there till the worst of the winter was over. Chester pointed out that while Daisy was a wonderful horse to ride, we needed stronger work horses to work in the trees. I hated to let Daisy go, but I understood the need for stronger horses. I contacted Uncle Stuart's friend who raised horses, and we arranged to swap Daisy in on a nice team of work horses.

By the end of February of the next year, we had bought all the equipment we thought we'd need and loaded it in a covered wagon. I said goodbye to my friends and even paid James a extra month's rent, and we set out on a bright sunny, but cold day.

Chester helped me for two years as we built the house and barn. We also cut trees and cleared ground for a garden and a small pasture. After Chester left I got help from neighbors to clear more land and build a chicken house. By the time to leave for the wedding, I felt I had a homestead that Mary Louise would be proud of. It had taken a lot of hard work, but finally it was ready, and I was eager to start this new chapter of my life.

CHAPTER 14

May 1875

Harlan, Kentucky

I left Campbell Holler three days before the wedding. I was very excited for finally I was about to see my dream of a better life come true. I took my cow and chickens down the holler and let a new family that had just built a one-room cabin there borrow them till I got back. They had three small children, and I thought they could use the milk and eggs while I was gone. I had friends who wanted to take care of the dogs, and I sold the hog thinking I could buy another one later.

I tried to really think hard about all I needed to do before I left. It would not be the first time I had forgot what I planned to do, and I almost did just that. I had the wagon all loaded and the horses hitched and ready to go when I remembered I hadn't packed the necklace Ma sent for my wedding present to my bride. I sure didn't want to forget that.

I decided to take the wagon because Mary Louise had written about all the things she planned to bring. I thought we just might end up with a wagon full. I expected to arrive the day before the wedding. I took my time so I didn't tire out the horses cause we had some hard traveling over mountains ahead of us. As I rode along, I had lots of time to cogitate on my life and what I was about to do. When I started working on Pa's farm as a twelve-year-old boy, I never thought I'd decide to be a farmer. I hated the hot sun and long hours, and I thought life was much better at our home in Pittsburgh. But when it come time to decide on my future, I knowed more about farming than anything else. So that seemed like what I was meant to do. It's kinda funny that I ended up in a holler even farther away from neighbors than our home in Kentucky. Everthing had turned out much different from what I expected when I was growing up, but I had lots of hope that from here on things would be better. As I rode along, I found myself feeling proud of my accomplishments so far, in spite of having this bum leg.

I figgered out how to do lots of work in spite of having only half a foot and a twisted knee. I carry a cane or hoe to steady me when I'm walking around on uneven ground. When I'm plowing, I can manage just fine by holding on to the plow handles. It seems like the horses understand and don't mind if I grab on to a mane or a tail to keep my balance. I do fall sometimes and do need help for some tasks, but all in all I manage purty good.

Of course I never coulda done it without Chester's help. One thing I regret is the way I treated him. I knowed he gave up his job with the building company to come and help me, and I did pay him and furnished food and shelter to him and his horse for the two years he lived here. But I'm sorry to say, I didn't appreciate his skill as a builder or his friendship as I should have. We did have some real good times making moonshine, fishing, going to town for Court Day, hunting, and we even spent a week in Knoxville where we went to buy windows for the house.

But we didn't always see eye to eye, and I admit I was quick to get mad when he insisted his way was better. He threatened to leave several times and did go away for a few days a couple of times. One day, one of my horses was being stubborn and managed to get tangled in the harness so bad he tipped over a wagon load of hay. As Chester tried to get him untangled, that crazy horse bit him. That made Chester so mad he started beating the horse. That made me mad, and I hit Chester with a whip I always carried.

I was sorry as soon as I laid the lash on him. I apologized and begged, but he got his bags packed, saddled his horse, and left that same day. I wrote him and ask him to forgive me, but I ain't never heard a word from him since. I wish I'd never hit him. Seems like I won't never learn to control my temper.

Another thing I regret is when I gave up Daisy. I had enough money that I coulda paid for the team and kept her too. I feel like a traitor for letting her go. She was such a gentle beauty. I guess I didn't know how attached I was to her. I missed her real bad, almost like she'd died. I just hope she ended up with someone who is taking good care of her.

I passed some shabby cabins, and they reminded me I was fortunate to have a good house. It wasn't fancy and had only two rooms, but it was made with good materials and was built to last. And I had enough land to support a family. I was grateful for the inheritance. That's what's made it all possible. I've mostly tried to spend the money careful, but I can see that unless I figger out some way to make more money, it'll soon be spent. I'll need to work more on the chairs and make more moonshine, or find some other way to earn money. I want to give my family a good place where they'll have all they need.

I had to interrupt my thinking to guide the horses over a small stream. We soon got going again, and I started thinking how amazed I am that Mary Louise wanted to marry me. I couldn't hardly believe after all this time I was finally on my way to my own wedding. She understood we'd both have to work hard to make a living for ourselves, and I made sure to explain I wasn't rich like the rest of my family. But she insisted she'd always wanted to marry me and didn't mind living a simple life.

I laughed at myself for taking such a long time to have some feelings for her. In the years after the war before I moved to Campbell Holler, I made several trips to visit the Bakers, at first, because she kept begging me to come. Then I started to see she wasn't a little girl no more but a growed up woman. I saw how she loved her family and how much she helped them. She could do all kinds of work in the garden, in the kitchen, or wherever it was needed, and she done it good. Mistress Baker had taught her all about being a midwife and using the healing yerbs. She could milk the cow and muck out the stable as good as me. And best of all, she said she loved me.

As time went on, I found myself going to get the mail more often in case I had another letter from her. Once I admitted that I did care for her, I looked for more times I could be with her. I hadn't seen her much this past year because I was working to get the place ready for her, but the letters we have wrote to each other brung us even closer. I'll never forget how happy I was the first time she wrote that she loved me. That gave me the nerve to say the same to her, and it got better'n better ever since. As I got closer to Harlan, I started to get impatient and wanted to make the horses go faster.

At the same time, I was dreading all the fancy wedding stuff Mary Louise was planning. I'd druther have a short ceremony and get it done and that's it. In her last letters Mary Louise told how many people would be there and all the plans for the wedding cake and then a big party in the evening after the ceremony. I remembered how uncomfortable I felt at James' wedding, and even though this wedding wouldn't be that fancy, I still wished I didn't have to go through all that. But I would do it for my lovely bride.

I amused myself on the journey by thinking how much I liked her bright smile, how it made cute dimples in her cheeks, and how I got a funny feeling in my chest when she turned her big blue eyes on me. For that I would put a smile on my face and go through the torture of all the tomfoolery she had planned.

When my team pulled up at the Bakers' house and I saw her on the porch waiting for me, my heart skipped a beat. She jumped down the steps and rushed to me. She had her arms around me before I could get my balance. If I had had any doubts before, her joyful welcome convinced me I was doing the right thing.

***

Mr. Baker rushed out and shook my hand. "Hello, Harvey. Welcome to our home and to our family. So glad you arrived safe. I'll help you get your wagon in the barn and take care of the horses."

After getting the horses watered and set loose in the pasture, he led me into the parlor. "Please make yourself at home." He pointed to a comfortable chair near the fireplace. Mistress Baker carried in a tray with glasses of a refreshing drink. I remembered the manners my mother learnt me and stood up.

"Please don't get up." She set the tray on a nearby table and gave me a hug. "Welcome to our home. We are so grateful Mary Louise is getting such a good man." I wasn't used to being called a good man, but I's glad my bride's mother thought I was.

After sipping on the mint tea for several minutes, Mr. Baker pointed out a beautiful oak rocking chair with dogwood blossoms carved into the headrest. "This is our wedding gift for Mary Louise. I had a man from over by Pineville make it."

I limped over to examine it up close. It had good balance, so when I gave it a nudge, it moved back and forth several times in a very quiet, smooth rock. The finish was smooth as satin, and the curve of the arms could only have been made by a expert woodworker. I nodded to Mr. Baker, "Thank you, sir. I know Mary Louise will enjoy your generous gift. I think you can count on many generations of Campbells loving this beautiful chair." I stood there for several minutes admiring the beautiful wood and the wonderful workmanship as I touched the carvings and run my hand over the smooth curve of the arm.

Mary Louise took my empty glass, tugged at my arm, and led me to a table by the door and pointed out some boxes and packages. "These are gifts from friends and neighbors. See this big wooden box here? It holds a grandfather clock my uncle made. I'll be so glad to have a clock. Won't

217

that be grand?"

Then she pointed to the kitchen. "I want to introduce you to some people." From that moment till we left the morning after the wedding, it was like a mad house. People I never saw before was coming and going, bringing gifts, food, flowers, and helping in the kitchen. The house was so small, and so many folks was running around, I didn't know what to do with myself. I always seemed to be in somebody's way. I felt like I was playing dodgeball like we did back in school.

That evening about dark, things finally settled down and Mary Louise and I had some private time setting in the porch swing. We held hands while we talked. She was real excited about her wedding dress.

"You can't see it till I walk out on the porch for the ceremony."

"Why not?"

"Well, it's just a custom. The groom doesn't see the bride's dress until she comes to the altar." She reached into her apron pocket and handed me a scrap of blue cloth. "This is what it's made of. Don't you like that color?"

"I do like it. I'm sure you will be beautiful when you finally let me see you wearing it." I squeezed her hand. "So the ceremony will take place here on the porch?"

"Yes. We will set up chairs in the yard where the guests will sit and Papa will do the ceremony up here where they can all see us."

"I see. Where will we get the chairs?"

"Oh, our neighbors are going to bring their dining chairs and set them up for us, and Papa has made a couple of benches." She clapped her hands together. "I'm so excited. It's going to be so beautiful."

"I'm excited too." I lifted her hand and kissed it. "I hope everthing is just the way you want it."

"Oh, did I tell you about the wedding cake?"

"Tell me."

"We had a bunch of friends each make a cake layer. They brought them over yesterday. And Mama made this sauce with sugar and spices and dried apples and stacked the layers up with the sauce between each layer." She held out her hands, one about a foot above the other. "It's about this high."

"I bet it will be delicious."

She took a deep breath. "Oh, and neighbors are bringing in all kinds of food for the party afterwards, and three of my cousins will bring their instruments to play for the dancing."

"I didn't know you was gonna have dancing." I remembered how Carl Henley took me to that party where I danced with Sadie. "I don't think I'm too good at dancing."

"We don't dance like people do at wild house parties. It's more like a reel. Don't worry. Just hold my hand and I'll lead you through the steps."

I was pleased to see her so excited, so I never let on that I was uneasy about all the nonsense. Once she had quieted down, I reached in my pocket for the little blue box and put it in her hand. I was mighty pleased when she opened it, and let out a whoop. She threw her arms around me and ended up setting in my lap kissing me over and over. Then she ran into the house where she could see the necklace better by lamplight and yelled for her mother to come and see.

I followed her into the parlor. She took the necklace out of the box and held it up to the light. "It's so beautiful." She turned when her mother come into the room. "Look Mama. My wonderful bridegroom gave me this for a wedding present. Isn't it beautiful?"

Mistress Baker held the necklace on her palm. "Oh Mary Louise, this is the most beautiful piece of jewelry I've ever seen." She turned to me. "Is there a story behind it?"

"It has been in my family for several generations. It was my Grandmother Campbell who wanted my bride to have it."

Mistress Baker held the necklace out to me. "Would you like to fasten it for Mary Louise?"

I was awkward and the chain and clasp was small, but I finally got it fastened. It nestled against her chest and gleamed against the white blouse she wore.

"It's beautiful. It will be perfect with your dress." Mistress Baker pointed toward the mirror across the room. "Go look at yourself."

Mary Louise stared at herself for a long time. I stood behind her and our eyes met in the glass. "Thank you so much. I feel so honored." She turned and put her arms around me. "I hope I get to meet your grandmother someday so I can thank her."

I couldn't stop grinning. Then Mr. Baker come into the room and announced he would walk with me to the village inn where a room had been arranged for me. He lit a lantern and fetched my grip from the wagon. As we walked along, he explained the room was also reserved for the night of the wedding so me and Mary Louise would spend our first night together there. I was so happy it seemed like my bum foot was almost floating in the air as I limped along.

***

I woke when bright sunshine lit up my room. When I looked out the window, I saw the sky was clear. I ate breakfast at the inn and ambled up the hill to the Bakers', anxious to see my sweet Mary Louise.

She met me before I got to the house and gave me a smile and a hug. "I'm glad you came because you can help me."

She led me down a street and up another hill to a field and explained, "We're going to pick daisies." We spent almost an hour and come back to the house with a big armful of daisies we put into vases and placed on the porch railing. People I didn't know was tacking up large pieces of white material like curtains that was draped and tied to the porch support posts with strips of the blue material used for the bride's dress. Mary Louise explained the bride and groom and the minister would stand on the porch between the support posts. "It's almost like a stage at a theater," she bragged.

Mistress Baker set out cold foods for our noon meal, and afterwards I helped Mr. Baker carry the chairs and benches for the guest seats. Then more people come with their chairs and dishes of food. That's when Mary Louise sent me back to the inn. "The ceremony is set for five o'clock. You should be here shortly before that time wearing your wedding suit." I must have shown I was confused about why she was sending me away. She giggled that delightful laugh I loved to hear. "Don't look so sad. I need to have the rest of the day to get ready, so I'll be looking good for you." She kissed me on the cheek and went into the house.

I was so anxious and working so hard to make no mistakes, I can't remember everthing that happened when I returned to the house as Mary Louise had told me to do. I was surprised to see several horses and buggies pulled up outside the fence, and lots of people had found places in the chairs. Seeing so many people made me even more uneasy. Music started playing, but I couldn't see where it was coming from, and a young lady, who said she was a cousin, led me up on the porch and told me where to stand.

Then Mr. Baker come through the door with Mary Louise on his arm. And she was beautiful, smiling so her dimples showed. Her blue dress lit up her blue eyes. I ain't no good at describing women's dresses, but I thought she was a blue angel. The necklace looked like it had been made special for that dress.

Mr. Baker had me and Mary Louise clasp hands. I leaned my cane against the rail and took both her hands in mine. I don't remember what all he said. I think he read from his Bible and did a sort of sermon about the husband being the head of the house and the wife being subject. I was just looking into her eyes knowing I was a lucky man. I got sort of tired standing there trying to keep my balance, and it seemed like a long time before we had to promise to love till death do us part. But finally it was over.

Mary Louise led us down into the yard where her parents stood with us as all the guests shook our hands and wished us well. Then Mistress Baker invited everone to come into the house and get some food. I was too excited to eat, but Mary Louise led me into the parlor where a large table was filled with all sorts of food. Mistress Baker kept telling folks to come back for more food. It was getting along toward sundown when they brought out the wedding cake.

The cousins set up their instruments and folks danced until dark. Then a bunch of the younger folks gathered around us, and next thing I knowed, they had loaded us into this little handcart and was pulling us down the road. They was singing and yelling and teasing us about what they's gonna do with us. As we passed houses, people come out to see what all the fussing was about, and some of them even joined the parade. I didn't know what to think, but Mary Louise seemed to be enjoying it, so I went along with it.

They took us to the inn and toted us right up to the door. Mary Louise gave all of them a hug and thanked them. I just stood and watched.

***

We were up early the next morning, ate breakfast at the inn and hurried to the Bakers' to pack up our wagon and get on the road. I was glad I had decided to bring the wagon instead of the buggy. Mary Louise had a big trunk holding her clothing, a large wooden chest she said held all the linens she had prepared, her rocking chair, all the wedding gifts, some pots of flowers she wanted to plant at her new home, and even her pet duck. We was lucky to have the help of neighbors as we loaded everthing into the wagon.

As we rode away, I could see Mary Louise was trying to hold back her tears. We left her mother sobbing, and her father's chin trembled as he gave her a final hug. I thought it might be years before we saw them again, so I put my arm around her and we rode along in silence.

I was thinking about last night. When we laid down on the bed, I suspected she was anxious and prob'ly scared, but I remembered how gentle Sweet Lucy had led me through my first time, and I tried to be just as gentle with my new wife. When we had finished, she snuggled close in my arms and sighed. I held her for a long time. I wished I could tell Evan I finally had somebody to hold on to.

We jolted along in the wagon some time before she wiped her tears and set up straighter. She looked at me and smiled. "Can I hold the reins? I love to drive the horses."

I nodded and handed her the reins. She looked quite pleased with herself. We had been traveling a road that run through a wooded area for quite some time. Finally we come out into the bright sun when all of a sudden the sun struck the necklace Mary Louise wore, and tiny rainbows flashed all around.

AUTHOR'S NOTE

While this is a work of fiction, several historical persons, places, and events are included in the story, which I have fictionalized by inventing dialog and imagining action and descriptions. For example, according to one source I consulted, a young boy actually was shot by Unionists when he confessed his brothers had joined the Confederate Army. I fictionalized that event by having Evan come to such a fate.

When I have included historical persons, events, or places I have made efforts to present them in ways that remain consistent with actual history. If I have misrepresented any person, event, or place, I am solely at fault. My apologies. Laureltown and Rock County are fictitious places in Kentucky.

The story that General Early claimed to have "scared the hell" out of President Lincoln is disputed by some historians, but I included it because the fact that Lincoln did indeed put himself in harm's way by coming to Fort Stevens to watch the battle is verifiable.

The timber industry did not develop to any extent in Kentucky until railroads were built into the mountains in the decades following the Civil War. However, it is true that some lumbering was done prior to the war. Floating the logs down the river during floods was a common means of getting the logs to a sawmill. Even before the war, speculators had started buying up timber rights in the Kentucky mountains.

I'm aware that using the vernacular language in novels is often discouraged, but I have chosen to do so because I believe it helps reflect the culture of the place and time. I also think it's consistent with Harvey's rebellious nature and supports his notion that education somehow corrupts a person's morals—an idea that persists to the present day in parts of Appalachia.

Appalachian Daughter is the story of Harvey's great-granddaughter, Maggie Martin, who was born 70 years later and raised in the house Harvey built in Campbell Holler. I am including one chapter here, thinking readers who enjoy *Appalachian Memory* might also like to read about Maggie.

APPALACHIAN DAUGHTER

CHAPTER 1

Harlan, Ky–May 20, 1875   Wedding day. Harvey arrived yesterday. Has wagon and team to haul our goods. Says cabin and barn built. Leave tomorrow for the property in Tenn. So proud to be his wife.

(Diary of Mary Louise Campbell)

May 1949

Kneeling beside her locker in the elementary wing of the school building, Maggie Martin listened with a sinking heart as her eighth grade classmates discussed their summer plans.   Visualizing her own summer as three months of drudgery and tedium cooped up in Campbell Holler like a caged bird, she shook her head as if she could throw off the dread of isolation and loneliness.

Maggie and her best friend, Mary Ann Collins, had emptied their locker, stacking their books on the floor and sorting the various odds and ends they had accumulated. Maggie shot the last piece of scrap into a trash can like a basketball through the hoop. "We better hurry. Time for the last bell, and everyone else has gone back to the classroom."

As Maggie bent to lift the stack of books, someone slammed into her knocking her down, scattering her books in all directions. Lying on the floor, arms and legs flailing wildly, she focused on the face above hers– Walter Spinks, a senior. "Hey, you big ox, get off me!"

"Sorry, Maggie, I tripped." Walter's big ears and wide grin reminded her of a monkey–a monkey who made no attempt to get up, but purposely ran his hand under her blouse.

Maggie shoved at him and screamed, "Get your hands off me, you big ape!" Struggling frantically and kicking the trash can over, scattering papers over the hallway, she grabbed a book and swung as hard as she could from her awkward position, catching his temple with a satisfying thwack.

"Why, you little bitch!" Walter rolled over and sat up holding his head with both hands.

Maggie leaped up, raised the book high, and whammed it down hard on the top of his head. "Don't you ever touch me again or I'll kill you!"

Mary Ann, almost to the classroom door, turned as soon as she heard the commotion and hurried to Maggie. "Are you hurt?"

"I'm not hurt! But I'm mad as a riled up hornet!" She shook her history book menacingly at Walter. "Get up, you big lunkhead, and get out of here, or I'll hit you again!"

Groaning and holding his head, Walter got slowly to his feet just as Mrs. Weldon, the eighth grade teacher, stepped into the hallway. "What's going on here?" she demanded, twisting her head on her long skinny neck like a suspicious vulture.

"I accidently tripped and bumped Maggie," Walter, still holding his head, said innocently while backing toward the door to the parking lot. "I apologized, but she hit me with her book." He pushed the door open and rushed out a second before the bell.

"Maggie, that temper of yours will get you into a peck of trouble if you're not careful. Now get this mess cleaned up." Mrs. Weldon pointed to the trash scattered over the hallway then turned back to the classroom.

Maggie glared daggers at Mrs. Weldon's back. *I hate you, you old hag!* Gathering her books, she joined her classmates exiting the building, leaving the trash on the floor. Fighting tears, she walked toward her bus hardly responding to her friends. "Bye Maggie." "Have a good summer." "See you in ninth grade." She slammed her books onto her favorite seat in the back of the school bus, and opened the window, her face flushed and contorted. *When did it get so hot? Not at all like May weather.* Sweat ran into her eyes. After wiping at the sweat with the back of her hand, she straightened her clothes, tucking her blouse into her skirt, and flopped onto the seat.

She held her honey-brown braids on top of her head while she fanned the back of her neck with her report card. She crossed her legs and jiggled her foot, restless as a mother hen sighting a circling hawk. She brushed her disheveled hair away from her face. *I hate Walter Spinks. I wish he was dead!* She took a deep breath, but the air felt heavy in her lungs like breathing mist. Her side hurt where Walter had crashed into her, and she felt bedraggled like her grandmother's old red hen after a raccoon tried to carry her away.

She smoothed the skirt her mother had made from feed sacks over her knees. Her mother had complained this morning when Maggie had worn it, saying she should save it for her Sunday best. *Seems like Mama and me is always having our differences these days. We didn't used to have so many disagreements, but here lately, she finds fault with everything I do. She probably won't even look at my report card—much less notice I made all A's. She thinks I should forget school.*

Maggie knew her mother agreed with most of their mountain neighbors who said too much education corrupted the young. Maggie's mother, Corie Mae, quit school before she was as old as Maggie. She would like Maggie to stay home and help with the difficult work required to provide for the large family. Thankful her father wanted her to go on to high school and took pride in the good grades she made, she sighed and closed her burning eyes. Now thinking of the long summer ahead of her, she already felt lonesome for her friends. *I feel like the little lost sheep in the Bible.*

"Move your books Maggie Martin."

Snapping out of her reverie, she lifted the books onto her lap to make room for her cousin, JD Campbell, who slouched into the seat, a big grin on his face, his dark, curly hair falling over his forehead. "Wake me when we get to the holler," he murmured, folding his arms over his chest and closing his eyes. She looked at JD's long, dark eyelashes curled up from his closed eyelids. *I see why all the girls go crazy about him.* Although nearer in age to JD's younger brother Kenny, she felt closer to JD, who seemed more like an older brother than a cousin. Having grown up together in Campbell Hollow in houses only one hundred yards apart, they had spent countless hours playing and working side by side since their toddler days.

With disheartened spirit, Maggie stared out the window at the students scurrying for their busses. When the bus driver started the motor, Maggie shook JD's arm. "Quick, JD, check if all the kids got on. Mama'll kill me if one of them misses the bus!"

Slowly getting to his feet, JD counted them off. "One, two three, four, five—yep, everybody's here." He slid down, resting his head against the back of the seat, and closed his big brown eyes again. He had rolled the sleeves of his plaid shirt almost to his shoulders, exposing his bulging biceps. She noticed the lump in the pocket made by a pack of cigarettes. His jeans, though faded, held a sharp crease.

Suddenly Maggie slumped down and hid her face behind a book. "Please don't let Walter Spinks see me."

JD opened his eyes and sat up. "What's he done now?"

"Right before the last bell, while I stooped down cleaning out my locker, he pretended to trip and fell down on top of me. My books went flying like an explosion. Then he put his hand under my blouse. I had to hit him with my history book to get him off. And then old witch Weldon yelled at me for hitting him."

JD stood, slapped his fist into his open palm, and stepped into the aisle. "That no count dog! I'm going to give him what he's got coming."

Maggie jumped up, spilling her books onto the floor, and pulled him back into his seat. "No, JD. Don't do it. Please. He's bigger than you. He'll kill you." Maggie held tightly to his arm. "Besides, I fight my own battles. I hit him so hard he's going to see stars for a week. Please, stay out of this."

JD jerked his arm loose and stood up again glaring at Walter, who had taken a seat behind Johnny Ray, Maggie's little brother. "I don't care. It's time somebody taught him a lesson."

"Please, JD," Maggie begged, dragging him back to his seat again. "Here, help me pick up my books. Mama has a fit if our books get so banged up she can't sell them for the best price. You don't want her taking a switch to me, do you?"

JD sighed and reluctantly stooped to pick up the books, placing them back in Maggie's lap. He slumped into the seat once more. "I'll get him yet, just wait and see."

Maggie punched his arm with her elbow. "Forget about Walter. I don't think he'll have nerve enough to look at me after this, much less touch me. I hope I gave him a concussion that lasts for a week."

"At least you won't have to worry about him after today. I heard he's joining the Marines." JD rubbed his hands together. "Just think. We've got three whole months with no school. I'm going to have one great summer."

"I hate summers. So much work. We plow, we plant, we hoe, we pick, we can, we wash, we iron every day from sunup to dark. I never get to go anywhere or see my friends. I'd rather go to school any day." Maggie slumped under the weight of the dreary prospects for her summer. She understood the necessity of the hard work, and she willingly did her part with a competence beyond her fourteen years. But she chafed under the isolation and loneliness. A blanket of sadness settled over her, and she took deep breaths to keep from suffocating.

JD sat up a little straighter. "I'm aiming to get me a job and buy a car. Then I won't be stuck in that holler working my tail off."

"Where can you get a job at?"

"I don't know, but I'll think of something. I'm sick of Mama treating me like a six-year-old. Getting out the first chance I get." He closed his eyes again.

She sighed. Without JD she looked forward to a totally intolerable summer—like losing an arm or a leg. She wished she could get a job. Then she could buy clothes for high school next year. *I hate wearing feed sack dresses. But Mama'd never let me go to work even if I could get a job.* She swallowed, trying to hold back tears that stung her eyelids.

JD opened one eye and looked sideways at Maggie. "What's the matter, Cuz? You look about as happy as a hound dog with the mange."

Maggie turned toward him. "On top of being attacked by that big ape, I found out today we have to buy uniforms for gym next year. Mama'll never agree for me to wear shorts. She won't even let me wear jeans or pants unless I'm picking berries. She says it's a sin for a woman to dress like a man. But ever'body'll make fun of me if I have to take gym in a dress!" Maggie looked out the window so JD wouldn't see the tears in her eyes.

JD grinned. "Easy. You don't tell her. I do all kinds of stuff Mama would beat me black and blue if she knew. I just don't tell her."

"I can't keep her from knowing. I'll have to buy the gym suit somehow, and I'll have to take it home to wash."

"Maggie, Aunt Corie Mae's too hard on you. She has tied you to her apron strings so tight you'll never get away unless you put your foot down and tell her what you aim to do."

"But you know what a bad temper Mama's got. She don't tolerate backtalk. She'd thrash me like whipping a copperhead if I did that."

JD shook his head and closed his eyes again. The bus had three more stops before reaching the stop for Campbell Holler. Maggie settled back in her seat. *If this is the way the summer will go, I'll never live through it.* She had barely shut her eyes, when Johnny Ray screamed. Both Maggie and JD leaped up, and Maggie's books slid onto the floor.

When they saw Johnny Ray holding his head and crying, they knew immediately what had happened. Walter Spinks liked to turn his class ring upside down and whack people on their heads as he went down the aisle to get off the bus.

"That does it! Going to get that sucker." JD rushed down the aisle after Walter, who had exited the bus.

"You'll get in trouble," Maggie yelled, but JD leaped out the door. The driver, ignoring the ruckus, closed the door and continued down the road. Maggie watched out the back window as JD and Walter slugged each other like mad drunks on a Saturday night.

"Hit him, JD! Beat the stuffing out of him." One of JD's classmates stood beside Maggie in the aisle looking out the rear window until the bus went around a curve.

That's really my fight. I should have got off with JD. But as the oldest, Maggie had the responsibility of seeing all the children home safely. "I hope he beats that bully to a pulp," she said under her breath, as she crawled around on the floor trying to retrieve her books. More likely Walter, a much larger boy, will whip JD, and then Aunt Opal will give him a worse thrashing.

Seated once more, sweat trickled down her back, and her blouse stuck to the back of the seat. The oppressive heat of the unseasonably warm weather added to Maggie's depression. She put her face closer to the open window to get some cooler air and stretched out her long legs. She noticed dark clouds in the west. *Maybe it will rain and cool things off.*

Maggie and Kenny made sure all the children crossed the highway safely after the bus dropped them at the road going up Campbell Hollow. Usually Johnny Ray complained constantly and wanted to stop in the shade, but today he skipped along with the neighbor children, kicking rocks in the dirt road and chanting, "School's out! School's out!"

The six families who lived in the hollow had a total of twelve school-age children. For the Martin and Campbell children, it meant a one-mile walk from the bus stop to their homes at the head of the holler. As they passed the unpainted houses of the neighbors, Maggie marveled at the contrast between those who worked hard to survive on a few hilly acres and those who lazed in careless squalor.

After a quarter mile, the road rose to the top of a hill where a large beech tree made a canopy creating a cool resting spot. They stood in the shade and waited for Johnny Ray, who lagged behind. "Johnny Ray, you better hurry and catch up," Maggie called. "Audie Lee Johnson's house is just ahead." Actually, the Johnsons' house was back a long lane hidden by a grove of pines, so that it was not visible from the road.

"I ain't afraid of Audie Lee Johnson," Johnny Ray called, but he hurried to catch up.

"Is Audie Lee deaf?" Jeannie, the youngest of the three Martin daughters, asked.

"I think he can hear okay, he just can't talk." Kenny kicked a rock from the roadway into the small stream that ran nearby.

"I think he's scary looking. I wouldn't want to meet up with him by myself." Jeannie hugged her stack of books tighter to her chest. "He staggers around like a drunk and always has that tow sack slung over his shoulder. I'd be scared to know what's in it." Jeannie moved to the other side of the road.

"He won't hurt you," Kenny said. "Mama says he's tetched in the head, but he don't hurt nobody."

Johnny Ray, out of breath from hurrying to catch up, argued , "That's not what Charlie Haskins told me. His mother told him if Audie Lee caught him after dark, he'd throw that sack over him and carry him away."

Kenny laughed, "Naw, that ain't so. His mother's just scaring him to make him come inside after dark. In all the years the Johnsons have lived in this holler, I ain't never heard tell of Audie Lee hurting a thing."

In newly planted fields, tiny corn plants made neat green rows stretching away from the road. The ridges forming the holler reached out like two arms hugging the valley between them. By the time they reached land belonging to the Campbells and Martins, the holler had narrowed considerably and the fields rose more steeply toward the sides of the ridges.

As they came over a small rise in the road, Maggie saw the roof of her house. The Martins lived in the old house her great-grandfather Campbell had built when he bought fifty acres at the head of the holler a few years after the Civil War. He originally built a two-room log cabin, but during the years he had added a second story, a lean-to kitchen, and front and back porches. Now the Martins filled it to overflowing with the family of seven children.

Maggie huddled the kids in the middle of the narrow, dirt road. "Don't none of you say a word about JD getting off the bus. Don't want him getting in trouble."

Kenny lifted Johnny Ray's chin, looking directly into his eyes. "That means you, Tattle Tale!" Then he turned toward his own home farther up the hollow.

* * *

An hour later Maggie sat on a low stool with the milk pail between her knees. The crown of her head pressed against Big Red's flank as she bent forward to reach the milk-swollen udders. During her tenth summer, her father had taught her to milk, and it became her job to milk their two cows every evening while her father did the morning milking.

Now that her father did not have to be home in the evening in time to milk, he often got an extra hour or two working as a laborer for other farmers in the area. For the last two years, he also had raised corn and hay on Mrs. Robinson's farm for half the produce. Maggie admired the way her father worked so hard to make things better for the family. He finally had saved enough to hire a well digger. They no longer had to carry water from the spring up the road, but they did have to draw up the water and carry it into the house. If they could get through the summer with no setbacks and have a good harvest, maybe by winter they could have the pump installed and bring the water into the kitchen.

Maggie thought about the many differences between her parents. Her father's calm demeanor, his sense of fairness, his delight in the accomplishments of the children, and his optimistic outlook contrasted sharply with her mother's approach to life. "Like day and night," she said aloud. However, she had to admit her mother was no slacker. Feeding and clothing a large family with their meager resources—a never ending job—Corie Mae managed with great competence, ingenuity, and resourcefulness. In that respect her parents were alike—both working from before daylight until after dark day after day.

Maggie lifted her head to wipe the sweat from her eyes with her sleeve. She extended her lower lip and blew her breath up over her face. Earlier she had pinned her heavy braids on top of her head. Now she repositioned the bobby pins, which had worked loose. *Wonder how JD made out. Hope he didn't get beat up too bad.* Maggie rubbed her face with her other sleeve before she rested her head against Big Red's side and resumed milking. The cow's body had collected all the heat of the day, and now it radiated out stifling her breath and making her feel faint.

When she finished, she stood, carefully lifting the pail of milk brimming with white foam. With her free hand, she pulled her sweat-soaked tee shirt away from her homemade bra, letting in some air, then picked up the three-legged stool and turned toward the door. Maggie carried the pail to the small feed room and carefully covered it with the lid. She took the lead strap from the nail near the door and turned to get Curly, Big Red's calf, from his pen on the east side of the barn.

Back toward the highway, the sky swirled with coal-black clouds, and the air felt cooler *Probably means a hail storm's on the way. Better get Curley and Bossy into the barn right quick before the storm hits.* Once she finished milking Bossy, Maggie grabbed both pails of milk, rushing to get inside before the rain came. About halfway to the house, Maggie felt the first drops. The strong wind flattened her skirt against her legs, and she bent forward as the wind pushed against her. Running as fast as she could without spilling the milk, she reached the kitchen door just as the hail began to rat-a-tat-tat on the tin roof.

In the kitchen, Maggie strained the milk through a muslin cloth into four half-gallon canning jars and tightened the lids. Since the Martins had no refrigerator, Stuart, her nine-year-old brother, would take the milk to Aunt Opal's refrigerator when the rain stopped.

The rain and hail hammered the roof, and the fierce wind howled like a banshee. Maggie could barely hear her mother and her younger brothers and sisters in the front room. Through the kitchen doorway Maggie could see her mother sitting in her rocking chair holding six-month-old Jay hugged tightly to her thin, petite body, her brown eyes full of fear. The children knelt or sat on the floor around her. When a clap of thunder sounded, Corie Mae put her hands over her ears and scrunched down as if dodging an attacker. Jay began to cry.

From all her agitation, Corie Mae's dark braids, which she usually wore wrapped around her head, drooped below her ears. "Sing, you all, and pray," she yelled. "God deliver us from this storm!" Then she began singing "Rock of Ages," rocking in time to the music and motioning for the children to join in. Maggie glanced out the kitchen window and saw the trees bending in the wind, while the hail continued to pelt the roof. *Wow! I hope that wind doesn't blow a tree over on the house. We don't often have a storm this bad. No wonder Mama's so afraid.*

Maggie had heard her mother tell many times about getting struck by lightning as a teenager. Corie Mae had stood beside the stove stirring a pot of soup beans, when the electric current from the lightning had moved down the chimney, knocking Corie Mae back against the kitchen cabinet. *Guess if it had happened to me, I'd panic too.* Maggie frowned, feeling a twinge of guilt for judging her mother.

Maggie had finished washing the milk pails when a sudden flash of lightning crackled, and thunder shook the house. The dogs, huddling under the porch, yipped and whined, and the single light bulb hanging from the ceiling went out. "Margaret Frances, get in here right now!" Corie Mae ordered.

* * *

The wind and fury of the storm passed after a half hour, but the rain continued to fall in torrents. After finishing the supper dishes by the light of a kerosene lamp, Maggie pointed to the milk jars. "Mama. I guess it doesn't make sense to take the milk to Aunt Opal's since the power's off. Should I take it down to the spring?"

"Yes, Maggie, you should. This rain's probably flooded the spring house, so make sure the water ain't over the tops of the jars. You can carry the jars in the bushel basket that's on the back porch." As Maggie went out the back door, Corie Mae called, "Come right back. We got a lot of work to do tomorrow. I want you in bed early."

Fortunately, the rain had slowed to a light drizzle. Once on the dirt road, Maggie saw water swirling in the ditches, overflowing the road in places. A tree had blown across the fence, and in the near dark, Maggie noticed the rain had washed a gully down the middle of the cornfield. A muddy lake stood in the low place opposite the house. Maggie dodged the puddles as best she could in the dim light, but so much mud stuck to her shoes, she could hardly lift her feet.

"Hey, Mag. Wait up."

Maggie turned and saw JD coming down the road, his wet shirt sticking to him like an extra skin. "You okay?"

When JD reached her, he took one handle of the basket. "Yeah, I guess I'll live."

"You look like death warmed over. How'd the fight turn out? Last I saw from the bus, you two really laid into each other."

"I gave old Walter as good as he gave me. He got in a few good licks, but he quit the fight. I bet both his eyes'll be black by morning. I know I knocked a tooth or two loose cause he spit out blood, and my hand hurts like hell."

Until a couple of years earlier when the Rural Electric Co-op finally brought electric lines up the holler, the spring, a few yards off the road between their two houses, had served both families. It not only had kept their milk and other foods cool, it had also provided all their water. JD helped Maggie position the jars of milk on a ledge where the spring water flowed around them.

"Do you think Aunt Opal'll be mad?" Maggie knew Opal had a violent temper and would beat the boys over the smallest infractions.

"She'll probably take a belt to me."

"I'm going with you. I'll tell Aunt Opal Walter Spinks started it."

"Thanks, Cuz, but I don't think you can talk her out of it."

"At least I can try."

They went to the back of JD's house, stepped up onto the porch, and slipped off their muddy shoes before going into the lamp-lit kitchen.

"Oh my God! Where have you been? I been worried sick." Aunt Opal dried her hands and stepped away from the dishpan. "How come you didn't come home on the bus?"

"I got off at Spinks. Had some business with Walter."

"What sort of business?"

JD ignored her question. "I had got almost up to the holler when the storm started. I sat on Wilson's porch until the worst passed."

Aunt Opal grabbed JD's arm. "Answer my question!"

JD shook his arm loose, pulled a chair from the kitchen table, and sat down. He reached for a piece of cornbread which sat on the table. "Something personal. Nothing for you to worry about."

"Don't you talk to me like that!" She jerked JD's face toward the light of the kerosene lamp on the kitchen table. "You've been in a fight, ain't you? Here I been worrying my head off, afraid you was hit by lightning or something and you're picking a fight." She reached for the belt that hung on the kitchen wall. "You know I don't allow no fighting."

"He didn't start it, Aunt Opal." Maggie stepped between them. "Walter Spinks hit Johnny Ray and made him cry."

"Nobody asked you. Now get yourself back home and mind your own business. This don't concern you." Aunt Opal pointed toward the door.

Maggie took a few steps toward the door. "Please, don't whip him, Aunt Opal."

"I said go!" Aunt Opal gave Maggie a push out the back door.

Maggie dallied putting on her muddy shoes, trying to listen. She stepped off the porch and stood in the shadows.

After two or three licks, JD yelled, "That's enough, Mama!"

Whack. "I'll decide when it's enough!" Whack.

With each lash, JD yelled louder. Maggie watched their shadows dancing about the room and heard the crash of a chair turning over. Finally JD dashed out the door with Aunt Opal still thrashing him. As he jumped off the porch, he scooped up his shoes and ran around the corner of the house. Maggie, on the opposite side of the porch, slowly backed deeper into the shadows.

"You come back here or I'll beat the tar out of you." Aunt Opal yelled into the night, but JD didn't answer, and Aunt Opal finally went back into the house. Slipping and sliding in the mud, Maggie ran down the road hoping to catch up with JD, but she couldn't see him. When she reached her home, she gave up. *I can't imagine where he could have gone.* Since she saw no lamplight in her house, Maggie thought everyone had gone to bed. She sat on the back porch taking off her shoes when the screen door suddenly flung open. She jumped up quickly.

Corie Mae grabbed Maggie's arm. "I thought I told you to come straight back. Where you been all this time?"

"JD got caught in the storm. I went to see if he got home." Maggie pulled her arm out of Corie Mae's grip.

"Don't be giving me any sass, young lady."

"I'm not, Mama. I just answered your question." Maggie walked around her mother and opened the screen door.

"Don't you walk away when I'm talking to you."

"Mama, I'm all muddy. I need to light a lamp and wash up so I can go to bed."

"Just because you got all A's on your grade card, don't think you're too smart to do as you're told." Corie Mae followed Maggie into the house and watched as she lit a lamp. "You might have more education than me, but that don't mean you can do as you please. I'll not have you disobeying."

"You don't need to yell at me, Mama. I took the milk to the spring house and went to check on JD." She washed her face and scrubbed the mud off her ankles and legs. "I don't know why you're so mad. I didn't do anything wrong."

"Looks to me like you's getting above your raising." Corie Mae turned her back and went through the front room to her bedroom.

Puzzled by the strength of her mother's animosity, Maggie blew out the lamp and carefully felt her way to the narrow steep stairs leading to her bedroom on the second floor. Surprised to find both her sisters already asleep, she stripped off her clothes and put on her nightgown. Lying in bed in the pitch-black darkness, she felt much too agitated for sleep. *Why does she think I'll disobey her just because I have more education than she does? What's she afraid of? I don't understand.* She fluffed her pillow and turned on her side. *At least she looked at my grades.*

* * *

The next morning Maggie opened her eyes and lay quietly listening to the birds. The sunlight streamed through the little window beside the bed, which she shared with Betty Lou, her twelve-year-old sister. Ten-year-old Jeannie slept across the small room on a makeshift bed her father had built into the wall. Through the open doorway, she could see into the other small bedroom on the second floor where her father had built bunk beds for nine-year-old Stuart and seven-year-old Johnny Ray. All of them slept on mattresses filled with corn husks. Four-year-old Junior and six-month-old Jay shared the downstairs bedroom with her parents.

Being careful so she wouldn't disturb the sleeping children, she dressed and went down the stairs into the front room. The sun made a puddle of light on the braided rug Maggie's mother had made using strips of cloth from worn out sheets and old clothes. Near the front door stood the grandfather clock great-grandma had brought with her from Kentucky when she had married Great-grandpa Campbell. It no longer worked, but her mother valued it as one of the "nice" things in her home. The hand-carved rocking chair, which her mother prized, also had belonged to Great-grandma Campbell.

Through the window, Maggie saw her father sitting in the porch swing smoking his pipe. She walked out, making sure the screen door didn't slam.

"Good morning, Sunshine."

"Hi, Daddy. We worried when you hadn't got home by dark last night." Maggie sat beside him.

"I think that was the worst storm I ever seen. I stayed at Mrs. Robinson's until the worst of it passed over. They's a big ditch washed all the way across the road before you get to Johnsons. It's so deep a car or a wagon can't cross it. Me and the preacher'll have to repair the road soon as it dries up a little."

"Do you want me to do the morning milking now that school's out?"

"Yes, that will help a lot, but I already done the milking this morning. I'm glad you left the cows in the barn last night. Trees have blowed over in a couple places and tore down the fences. We'll have to fix them before we let the cows back in the lower pasture." Ray smoked in silence for a few moments. "I guess the 'lectric's out everywhere cause all the houses was dark when I come home. We're lucky that the crops ain't very high yet, but the hard rain washed some fields out, so I reckon we'll have to replant them."

Maggie watched her father lift his head to blow the smoke toward the porch ceiling. She noticed his clean-shaven face. Grandma Campbell often commented that Ray Martin was the only man she knew who shaved every day before working in the fields. Maggie liked the way his deep blue eyes often twinkled with humor. She felt fortunate to have inherited his tall build and fair complexion. His hard work through the years, mostly outside, had given him a rugged, seasoned look, somewhat older than his thirty-six years.

"Soon as I finish this coffee, I'm fixing to check on your grandma and grandpa. After you eat, I want you to take the cows to the pasture behind the cornfield where none of the fences is down. If the preacher's able, I aim to work with him and the boys to cut up the trees that blowed over."

It always amused her when her daddy called his father-in-law "the preacher." Grandpa Campbell had only a fourth-grade education, and he had never had a church, but he did call himself a preacher. Sometimes a Pentecostal church invited him to preach. His religion, taken mostly from his Kentucky relatives, included snake-handling and speaking-in-tongues. Occasionally he got a ride to a church near Newport where he knew some people would take up the serpents. When Ray had married Corie Mae and come to live in the old home place, he made clear to his father-in-law that his family would not go to a Pentecostal church. He would take his new wife to the Baptist church a couple of miles down the road.

After knocking out the ashes, Ray put his pipe in the pocket of his bib overalls. He handed Maggie his coffee cup, pulled on his muddy boots, and gave her a good-bye salute.

As she made her way to the barn, Maggie detoured from the path in several places to avoid deep mud. Even so, with each step her father's old shoes, which she always wore to the barn, slurped like sucking the last of a Coca-Cola through a straw. When she opened the feed room door to get the lead straps for the cows, she gasped. JD sat behind the big wooden barrel that held the cow feed. "You scared me! What you doing here?"

JD stood up. Now Maggie could see his black eye and a bad bruise on his left jaw. "Wow! Spinks did leave some marks on you."

"Yeah, but that's not half as bad as what Mama done." He turned his back and dropped his jeans. Maggie gasped again when she saw the bruises and welts. Blood had dried in streaks down his legs. He pulled up his pants and turned toward Maggie.

"I'm sorry, JD. I wish you had just let it go and stayed on the bus. Then you wouldn't be in this trouble."

"Heck, it was worth it, Mag. I told old Walter if he ever put a hand on you again, I'd knock the rest of his teeth out."

"Now, that really makes me feel bad."

"It's not your fault. He's had it coming. I should of jumped that bully a long time ago."

Maggie kicked a corncob. "What're you going to do now?"

"I'm leaving. I ain't never going to let her beat me again. I knew she'd be mad, but there wasn't no call to do this to me. When I finally got away from her, I came here and spent the night in your barn."

"Where're you going?"

"Hitchhike to Detroit and stay with Daddy. If I show up, I reckon he'll have to take me in. Maybe I can just live with him till I graduate from high school. I'll wait to leave till after dark tonight so nobody'll see me leaving. Right now I'm starving. I didn't have no supper. Do you think you can help me?"

"You better hide up in the hay loft till dark cause they'll come looking for you. Daddy's gone to check on Grandpa and Grandma. Then he planned to get you and Kenny to help repair fences and stuff. I'll try to get down with some food as soon as I can. First, I have to take the cows to the back pasture."

"You're a good cuz!" JD put his arm around her shoulders and gave her a quick hug. "I hate to ask you this, but have you got any money?"

"Sorry, I don't have one red cent." She looked at him with wide eyes. "I got an idea. Joe Clark's been your best friend for a long time. Why don't you see if he'll loan you some money?"

"Good idea." JD nodded, patted Maggie's arm, and turned toward the ladder to the loft. Maggie took the lead straps and headed for the cows standing near the barnyard gate. *What am I going to do without JD?* The tears ran down her cheeks and fell to the ground in spite of her best efforts to staunch them.

* * *

The week after JD left turned really crazy. Aunt Opal had pretended she didn't know what could have made JD leave. Maggie had no sympathy for her tearful worry about where he might have gone or why he would do such a thing. Finally, Reverend Lewis had come to tell Aunt Opal about the phone call from Uncle Thomas saying JD was in Detroit with him. The Lewises had the only telephone for miles around, and they often delivered messages for people in the community.

The morning after Uncle Thomas' message, Maggie had almost finished milking when her father had appeared at the stable door. He remained silent until she had turned the cows into the pasture. Then he had looked intently at her. "Did you know JD was running away?"

She could not lie to her father, so she had confessed everything. "Daddy, you should of seen how Aunt Opal bruised his legs where she beat him. He made me promise not to tell." She hung her head, no longer able to look at her father. "I'm sorry."

Ray had put his hand under her chin, lifted her face, and looked into her blue eyes for several seconds before finally saying, "I think you probably done the right thing, Sunshine."

Now, she sat on a big rock near the spring. She faced the house, so she could see anyone coming in her direction. At church this morning Reverend Lewis had slipped her an envelope addressed to her in care of the Lewises. On the back of the envelope JD had written, "Don't let no one else see this!"

"I guess you and JD have some secrets," Reverend Lewis had said. Maggie had smiled without saying anything and slipped the letter into her Bible. She had been antsy all through Sunday dinner and until the girls had washed and put away the dishes. Then she had taken the Grace Livingston Hill novel Mrs. Lewis had lent her and told her mother she was going down by the spring to read. After checking carefully to see that the coast was clear, Maggie took out the letter and ripped it open.

> Dear Cuz,
> Thanks so much for helping me make my getaway. I hope you didn't get in no trouble for it. I spent the first night at Joe Clark's house. Like you said, he loaned me some money & helped me get some medicine for my cuts and bruises. You & Joe was the only ones who knowed I was headed for Michigan.
> Daddy was mad as hell when I showed up. But he calmed down a little when he saw how bad Mama had beat me up. He says I can stay here until his vacation in July, but then I have to come back home.
> Here's the part that you can't let nobody else know about.

Maggie scanned the path to the house and the roadway making sure no one approached. She opened her book and placed the letter inside to appear as if she were reading the novel.

> Daddy is living with a woman here. They have been together for nearly three years and they have a little girl. I can't believe I have a little sister! She is really cute & seems to like me. Here's the part you won't never believe. Daddy's woman is colored!

She gasped. Her mouth gaping, she quickly looked around again before rereading the last few sentences. *I don't believe this! Aunt Opal will just die.* Shaking her head from side to side, she returned to the letter.

> Stella's real nice, & she's been good to me. She said she's going to fatten me up before she lets me come back to Tenn. It's hard for me to imagine being fat, but her cooking beats the heck out of Mama's. My black eye is pretty well gone, & my legs don't look too bad neither. I can't say I'm looking forward to coming back home, but I guess I won't have much choice.

Maggie tried to picture Stella, but since she had never actually seen a Negro, her mental image lacked clarity. She took several deep breaths to calm her pounding heart before she started reading again.

Thanks again, Cuz, for your help. I guess I'll see you in about six weeks. I promise after I get home we'll have some good times. Now, take this letter & burn it & keep this news to yourself. DON'T TELL A SOUL! Daddy told me the beating I got from Mama was nothing compared to what he would do if I ever let Mama know about Stella & the baby. I just had to tell someone, & I knowed I could trust you to keep it to yourself.
Your cuz, JD

Maggie hadn't realized she had held her breath until it suddenly escaped with a whoosh, like somebody had stuck a knife in a tire. Still not convinced she had understood, she read the letter once more before tearing it into small pieces and stuffing them into her pocket. She would put them in the stove later.

So... this is our little secret. Uncle Thomas will come home in July pretending to be Aunt Opal's faithful husband, thinking she'll never know the difference. She wondered how long he thought he could get away with this double life. *I guess he's already managed to fool everybody for three years.*

"How could Uncle Thomas do such a thing?" she said aloud. She sucked in a sudden breath when she thought of the trouble ahead if Grandpa found out. Maggie remembered one Sunday last summer, during a dinner at Grandpa's house, she'd heard him brag, "No niggers ever eat or spend the night in this county. We let them buy gas but tell them to keep moving after they pay for the gas." She also remembered later her daddy had made it clear that they were never to say the word "nigger." Instead they should say "colored" or "Negro." But Maggie had had no problem with that since no Negroes lived in her county.

She looked toward the house and sighed. *If this news gets out, it won't be me who tells.* She finally stood to walk to the house. Time to do chores. She thought of all the work they would have to get done before JD and his father came in July. Six more weeks of drudgery, but at least JD was coming back. With that encouraging thought, she quickened her steps and managed a crooked smile. *Maybe my summer won't be so bad after all.*

Appalachian Daughter is available as a paperback book, as an e-book, and as an audio book.

ABOUT THE AUTHOR

Mary Jane Salyers, a native of East Tennessee, earned a BA degree from Carson Newman University with a major in English and a minor in history. After teaching English and social studies in secondary schools for fifteen years, she earned a masters from Indiana University and finished her career as a college instructor.

Following retirement from Robert Morris University in Chicago, she wrote her first novel, **Appalachian Daughter**, published in 2014. *Appalachian Memory: A Survivor's Tale* is her second novel.

Mary Jane now lives with her husband, Bill Salyers, in Hillsborough. North Carolina. They have three daughters, four grandchildren, and two great-grandsons.

Visit **Appalachian Daughter—A Novel** on Facebook which will also feature information about **Appalachian Memory: A Survivor's Tale**

See her blog page   **http://mjsalyers.wordpress.com/**